WATCHING YOU

Also by Arne Dahl

The Blinded Man
Bad Blood
To the Top of the Mountain
Europa Blues

WATCHING YOU

ARNE DAHL

Translated from the Swedish
by Neil Smith

Harvill *Secker*
LONDON

1 3 5 7 9 10 8 6 4 2

Harvill Secker, an imprint of Vintage,
20 Vauxhall Bridge Road,
London SW1V 2SA

Harvill Secker is part of the Penguin Random House group of companies
whose addresses can be found at global.penguinrandomhouse.com

First published by Harvill Secker in 2017
First published with the title *Utmarker* in Sweden by Albert Bonniers förlag in 2016

A CIP catalogue record for this book is available from the British Library

penguin.co.uk/vintage

ISBN 9781911215493 (hardback)
ISBN 9781911215509 (trade paperback)
ISBN 9781473547735 (ebook)

Typeset in 12.25/15.5 pt Dante MT Std
by Jouve (UK), Milton Keynes
Printed and bound in Great Britain by Clays Ltd, St Ives PLC

Penguin Random House is committed to a sustainable future
for our business, our readers and our planet. This book is made from
Forest Stewardship Council® certified paper.

WATCHING YOU

I

1

The aspen leaves are trembling. He can hear them even though he's running, even though he's running like he's never run before, through meadow grass that reaches up to his chest.

Just before the meadow opens out the rustling gets extra loud. He slows down. The trees are suddenly so oppressive that it feels like someone is trying to get through from another time. But then he stumbles, and the rustling sound grows weaker once more. He manages to stop himself falling, but the golden-yellow hair up ahead almost disappears from view between the tall blades of grass, and he has to push himself even harder to avoid losing any more ground.

It's a summer's day, the sort that comes all too rarely. Feather-light clouds cut thin lines across the clear blue sky, every last blade of grass shines with its own particular shade of green.

They've been running a long time, first down the increasingly deserted road from the bus stop, then out across the meadow. Now, in the distance, is the barely perceptible sparkle of water.

He won't be able to see the boathouse while he's running this fast – he's aware of that – but he knows it's there, hidden among the trees by the edge of the shore, greenish-brown and ugly and quite wonderful.

The golden-yellow hair slows down ahead of him. As the head begins to turn he knows he'll be astonished. He has never stopped being astonished, will never stop being astonished. And just as the first hint of the irregular profile becomes visible, he hears it again.

There are no aspen trees nearby. Yet he can't hear anything except the rustle of aspen leaves, which becomes a whisper, which becomes a song.

There's someone, somewhere, who wants something from him.

Then they're standing eye to eye.

He's still gasping for breath.

2

Sunday 25 October, 10.14

The aspen leaves were trembling, and even though the sky was dark with rain in that almost medieval way, a rustling sound, just a little too loud, seemed to be forcing its way out from the fluttering leaves. Berger shook his head, suppressed all superfluous impressions and forced himself to lower his eyes from the treetops. The wooden planks pressing against his back, so rotten they felt soft, instantly reasserted their raw chill.

He glanced towards the other ruined buildings, only just visible through the increasing downpour. Two colleagues were crouched by each one, water dripping from their bulletproof vests, weapons in their hands. All eyes were fixed on Berger. Waiting for the signal. He turned and saw a pair of wide-open eyes. Deer's face was streaming with water, as if she were weeping.

Six cops standing around some ruined buildings in the pouring rain.

Berger peered round the corner. The little house was no longer visible. They could see it as they crept in from the side road and spread out across the terrain. But the rain had swallowed it up.

He took a deep breath. There was nothing for it.

A nod towards the two men by the closest building. They set off at a crouch into the storm. A nod in the other direction: another two men followed the first, disappearing into a murky broth. Then Berger himself set off, Deer's breath almost a whimper behind him.

Still no house in sight.

One by one his colleagues emerged from the rain, four crouching figures radiating concentration.

Plank by plank the house was conjured forth out of the gloom. Dark red with white trim, black roller blinds, no sign of life.

Close now. Close to it all. Possibly even close to the end.

Berger knew he mustn't think like that. Now was all that mattered. Here and now. No other place, no other time.

They gathered at the bottom of the steps leading to the peeling yellow porch. The bottoms of two drainpipes were spewing cascades of water at their feet. Everything was utterly drenched.

Faces looking at him again. He counted them off. Four, plus Deer's breathing behind his back. Berger gestured her forward, looked into ten eyes. Then he nodded. Two men started up the steps, the shorter one with adrenaline shining from his pale green eyes, the taller one with the battering ram in his hand.

Berger stopped them. Whispered a reminder: 'Look out for traps.'

The rain was suddenly their ally. Its drumming on the roof tiles drowned out their footsteps as they went up to the porch.

The ram was raised. Safety catches of various weapons were released in succession. A dull crash of splintering wood forced its way through the rain.

A deep darkness opened up.

The man with the pale green eyes slipped in with his weapon drawn.

Berger heard himself breathing through the sound of the rain, peculiarly slowly. Time stretched.

A noise cut through the roar of the storm. At first it didn't sound human. Then it morphed into a sound more surprised than pained. The clearest tone of mortal dread.

The officer with the pale green eyes emerged from the darkness, his face as white as chalk. His service weapon fell to the porch floor with a thud. Only when he toppled sideways did the noise become a scream. It still didn't sound human. The blood merged with the water on the decking as two colleagues dragged him off to one side. There was a knife sticking out from each arm.

Berger heard his own groan, the pain in it, a pain which mustn't be allowed to take root, mustn't stop him. He glanced quickly into the darkness, then turned round. Deer was crouching below the window, gun ready, torch out, her brown eyes bright and lucid.

'Trap,' she whispered.

'Too late, again,' he heard himself say as he made his way inside.

The mechanism was mounted on the wall of the hall. It had fired blades at a specific height, in a specific direction. Deer shone her torch to the left, towards a half-open door. Probably the living room.

The screaming out on the porch had risen to pain now, no longer pure, astonished dread. There was, paradoxically, something hopeful about it. It was the scream of a man who believed he was going to survive after all.

Berger gestured to two officers behind, pointing them up the staircase to the right.

His colleagues set off upstairs, beams of light playing briefly on the ceiling above the stairs, then everything was dark again. Berger and Deer turned slowly back to the half-open door to their left.

Out with mirrors, to check for traps. All clear. Berger slipped into the darkness first, followed by Deer, as they covered each other. The weak torchlight revealed a bare, spartan living room, a clinical little bedroom, an equally scrubbed kitchen. No smell at all.

The kitchen extinguished the last hope. So clean.

And so empty.

They went back out into the hall as the two officers were coming down the stairs. The first merely shook his head.

It was lighter in the hall now. The wounded man was no longer screaming, just whimpering. Two long, thin knife blades without handles lay on the decking. The rain had washed the blood from them, from the whole porch.

So clean.

Berger looked up. In the distance an ambulance was heading towards the gates of the large, overgrown property. There were already two police vans there, their blue lights flashing next to two rival media vehicles. Curious onlookers had started to gather by the cordon. And the rain had eased to a heavy shower.

Berger's gaze settled on the porch steps – almost two metres high – then he marched back into the hall again.

'There's a cellar.'

'Do we know that?' Deer said. 'There's no cellar door.'

'No,' Berger said. 'Look for a hatch. Gloves on.'

They pulled on plastic gloves, spread out, rolled up the blinds. Light filtered in, refracted through the water. Berger pulled the bed out, dragged the chest of drawers aside. Nothing. He heard noises from the other rooms, then finally Deer's muffled voice from the kitchen.

'Come here!' She was pointing at the wooden floor next to the fridge.

He could make out a slightly paler rectangle. They worked together to push the fridge aside with help from the three uninjured officers.

Between the fridge and the cooker, a rectangle had been cut into the floorboards, but there was no handle.

Berger stared at the rectangle. When it was broken open everything would change. The true descent into darkness would begin.

3

Sunday 25 October, 10.24

They had to prise the hatch open, four men armed with a variety of kitchen utensils. Berger stopped them when it was open just a few centimetres. He shone his torch around the edges of the hatch, and Deer pushed through a mirror that caught the light of the torch. No booby traps. They forced the hatch open. There was a crash. Dust flew up from below. Then silence.

More silence.

Berger switched his torch back on, and could see some steps. He jumped down, his torch and gun raised.

Step by step the darkness grabbed hold of him once again. The torch hid more than it revealed. A fragmented world: no more than claustrophobic cellar walls and low, half-open doors that led to yet more darkness, new, different, yet still essentially the same.

What struck him most was the smell. That it wasn't what he had been fearing. And that it took him such a long time to identify it.

The entire cellar was bigger than expected. There were doors leading off in all possible directions. Cement walls, considerably newer than the house.

The air was thick. It left no room for anything else. And no windows, not a trace of any light but the five beams of lights that daren't linger.

The smell grew stronger. The mixture. Excrement. Urine. Blood, perhaps. But not a dead body.

Not a dead body.

Berger scrutinised his colleagues. They looked pretty shaken as they spread out into the claustrophobic small rooms. Berger was in the one furthest to the left, shining his torch around. There was nothing there, absolutely nothing. He tried to picture the layout.

'Empty,' Deer said, her pale face appearing from behind one of the doors. 'But this smell must be coming from somewhere.'

'This cellar's asymmetrical,' Berger said, putting his hand to the wall. 'There's another room. Where?'

'Spread out,' he said from one of the doorways. 'Search along the left wall. Differences in colour, texture, anything at all.'

He returned to the far left room. The cement looked uniform, nothing that stood out in any way. Berger hit the wall, a short, sharp uppercut. The plastic glove broke, and with it the skin of his knuckles.

'I think we've got it,' he heard Deer say from somewhere.

Berger shook his hand and walked out. Deer was crouched in the corner of a room on the right, as one of the police officers lit it with a shaky beam.

'Something's different here, isn't it?' Deer asked.

Berger inspected the wall. In the far corner there was a square half-metre where there might have been a tiny shift in colour. Footsteps heading down into the cellar. One of the officers appeared with the battering ram in his hand.

Berger stopped him. Asked them all to point their torches at the change in colour. He got his mobile phone out and took a picture. Then he nodded.

The room was too cramped, too low, for a decent swing. Even so, the black cylinder broke through at once. Berger felt the wall. Plasterboard, nothing more. He nodded, and the ram swung back and forth a couple more times, opening a rectangle in the wall. Then it struck thick concrete. That was as big as the hole would get for now.

The hole into the abyss.

The mirror that was poked through revealed nothing but darkness. Berger could see that Deer knew it was up to her. She would be able to get through most easily. She turned to look at him. There was fear in her eyes.

'Just be careful,' he said, as gently as possible.

Deer shuddered. Then she kneeled down, ducked her head and slid in, with surprising ease.

Time passed. More than was necessary.

A flash of terror struck Berger. A feeling that Deer had disappeared, that he had sent her into hell defenceless.

Then a groan emerged from the opening, a restrained whimper.

Berger stared at the officers. They were pale, one of them was trying desperately to stop his left hand shaking.

Berger took a deep breath and crawled through.

Inside the unknown space he could see Deer with both hands over her mouth. He looked towards the other end of the room. Across the floor and some way up the wall were stains, large stains. The smell was now a stench.

No, not one stench. Several.

As he shoved forward, his sensory impressions began to fall into place.

Deer was standing by one wall. An area between two floor

supports made of decaying wood drew their attention. There was a large stain on the concrete floor, next to an overturned bucket. And between the pillars was a larger stain, across the wall, that was a similar colour, but very clearly had a different source.

'Fucking hell,' Deer said.

Berger's eyes followed the pattern of the stain across the wall. And it caught in his nostrils. Even with the toilet bucket spilled on the floor.

Enough blood for it to catch in his nostrils.

On the other hand, the stain on the wall had soaked in completely. They weren't just too late. They were far too late.

He looked at the walls. It was as if they wanted to tell him something. As if they were screaming.

Deer moved towards him. They hugged, just briefly. Any shame could come later.

'We'd better avoid contamination,' he said. 'You go first.'

He watched her feet disappear. Took a couple of steps towards the opening. Then changed his mind. He went back to the two pillars, and ran the beam of the torch down them. There were notches in the left-hand pillar, then similar grooves in the one on the right, at three different heights. He looked down, towards the floor. There was something wedged behind the right pillar. He crouched down and pulled it loose. It was a cog, a very small cog. He inspected it closely.

Then he put it into evidence bag that was almost as small, zipped it shut and put it in his pocket.

He photographed the floor supports from various angles. He turned towards the dried pool on the floor. Photographed that too. He let the torch play over the wall that was partially spattered with blood. Took more pictures, even where there wasn't any blood.

He took care of it all so swiftly that no one even called through to check on him. He was there, sticking his hands through the hole, letting them pull him out.

They made their way up the steps, emerging one by one into a numbing light. They slipped out onto the porch, the rain had stopped. Berger and Deer stood very close together. Breathing freely.

A number of forensics officers, shuffling their feet impatiently, were waiting outside. The overweight head of Forensics, Robin, was on his way up the steps, but thankfully there were no other bosses, no Allan. The wounded officer had disappeared, as had the ambulance. The police vans were still there, blue lights flashing. Media people with cameras and microphones were pressing against the cordon, and the number of onlookers had increased noticeably.

While the forensics team headed into the house from hell, Berger looked out at the crowd. And he was struck by a strange, fleeting feeling. He pulled the plastic glove from his left hand, got his mobile out and took a picture, then a couple more, but the feeling had already gone.

He glanced at his old Rolex. It felt unfamiliar against his wrist, because he changed his watch every Sunday. The hands were slowly ticking onward, and it was as if he saw the ingenious little mechanism tick out each second from nothingness. Then he turned to face Deer. At first she seemed to be looking at his watch, then he realised that her gaze was focused lower, that she was looking at his hands, the right one of which was still at least partially covered by the plastic glove.

'You're bleeding,' she said.

'It's nothing,' he said, pulling the glove off. He pulled a face.

She gave a brief smile and looked up at his face. She studied him carefully. Too carefully.

'What is it now?' he said irritably.

'*Again*?' she said.

He could hear the italics.

'What?' he said anyway.

'When we were about to go into the house you said it was too late. "Again." '

'And?'

'Ellen is our first case, isn't she?'

He smiled. He could feel himself smiling. It felt wrong, there on the porch in front of the realm of the dead.

'I'm pleased to hear you say "is",' he said.

'Ellen isn't dead,' she said.

But her eyes didn't waver.

'*Again*?' he repeated with a sigh.

'Yes?' she prompted.

'I was thinking more existentially,' he said, and shrugged. ' "Too late" is my motto.'

It had stopped raining.

4

Sunday 25 October, 19.23

'Booby trapped?'

Detective Superintendent Allan Gudmundsson had apparently decided to perform a parody of a reprimand. The performance made Berger's stomach turn.

'Yes,' he replied innocently, 'that bastard mechanism probably ought to be called a booby trap.'

'That's not what I was asking, as you're perfectly aware.'

'So what was your question, then?'

'Why the hell did you warn the rapid response unit to look out for booby traps?'

'Fat lot of good it did . . . '

'That's not the point. Why?'

'Because the bastard hasn't left any clues behind him. He's smart, that's all. Smart enough and dangerous enough to booby trap his abandoned hellhole.'

'The address was a clue, wasn't it?' Allan roared. 'The house.'

Berger stopped himself saying any of the things crowding on the tip of his tongue. He looked out of the window. The autumn rain had returned and it was pitch black. Most of the team had already left Police Headquarters. Deer was still there, he could just see her face in the light of her screen through two rain-streaked windows set at a ninety-degree angle to each other. The panes were separated by a slice of downpour.

'No, Sam,' Allan bellowed, unexpectedly combative. 'You're lying to me.'

Berger suddenly realised that could have fallen asleep at that precise moment. He could have closed his eyes and let Allan's squawking lull him to sleep.

It was probably best not to.

'Lying?' he said, mostly to hide his detachment.

'As long as it was nothing worse than little white lies I was prepared to let it go,' Allan said in a considerably gentler tone; it was obvious that he was preparing for a crescendo. 'But the fact that you're telling bare-faced lies to your boss shows that you've elevated your conspiracy theory to a new and dangerous level.'

'You became a bureaucrat far too early, Allan.'

'You've gone off piste, and to cover it up you're lying to your own boss. Do you think that's sustainable in the long run?'

'What should I have done differently?' Berger asked with a shrug. '*Not* gone to the address? *Not* warned the team about potential booby traps?'

'This is more about what you're likely to do in the future.'

'Catch a serial killer?'

Allan's carefully prepared crescendo tailed off into a long exhalation which went way beyond a sigh and suggested an impressive lung capacity for a man of his age. He probably hadn't smoked a single cigarette in his entire life.

With exaggerated slowness, Allan said: 'There isn't even a killer, Sam. At most there's a kidnapper. Every year eight hundred people go missing in Sweden, the vast majority of them entirely voluntarily. That's more than two a day. You can't just pick out a couple of those voluntary missing persons and claim they've been murdered by a serial killer that no one else can see. Christ, we don't even *have* serial killers in this country. They only exist in the minds of corrupt prosecutors and overambitious cops. And overambitious cops are even worse than corrupt prosecutors.'

'There isn't a killer?' Berger said pointedly.

'There isn't a victim, Sam.'

'You weren't in that cellar, Allan. I swear to you, there are victims.'

'I've seen the pictures. And I've spoken to the pathologist. The blood dried in different stages, on different occasions. And it looks as if there's more blood than there actually is. Three decilitres at most. That's not enough to kill anyone.'

Berger stared at the wall behind Allan. It was completely blank. 'Unless perhaps she wasn't dead when she was moved, maybe she isn't even dead yet. But she will be.'

Oxygen freezes at –218°C. Because both nitrogen and argon, the other major components of air, have a slightly higher freezing point, that means the air freezes when the oxygen freezes. So it must have been, if only very briefly, at least 218 degrees below zero in Detective Superintendent Allan Gudmundsson's office in Police Headquarters in Stockholm, because there was no question that the two officers were separated by a block of frozen air.

Eventually Allan said: 'Blood group B negative. The second most uncommon blood group in Sweden. Two per cent of the population. One of them is Ellen Savinger. But that wasn't the only trace of blood we found.'

The frozen chunk of air was still hanging between them.

Berger remained silent.

'There was a fair amount of A positive, which confused Forensics,' Allan went on. 'Is that your blood group, by any chance, Sam? It was found on the walls outside the cell, and on the floor inside it. There were also fragments of skin.'

Allan's gaze moved down Berger's right arm. His hands were hidden by the edge of the desk. Allan shook his head. 'We're awaiting DNA results in both instances, but we don't actually need it. In either case.'

'She's fifteen years old,' Berger said, trying not to raise his voice. 'She's fifteen years old, and she was down there for nearly three weeks. In a dark, stinking fucking cell with a bucket to shit in and only the occasional appearance of a lunatic for company. She lost plenty of blood. Am I really the only person thinking of the devil? And this devil isn't some naive first-timer, he's done this before. Probably plenty of times.'

'But that's not an argument, Sam. *Evidence* is an argument.'

'Evidence doesn't just pop into your head,' Berger said. 'You gather evidence by not ignoring clues, by following up unproven leads. You trust your gut feeling, have faith in experience. In the end the clues turn into evidence. Allan, for God's sake, are we just going to sit and wait for evidence, is that your vision of police work?'

'How come you didn't know the layout?'

'What?'

'You didn't know that there was a cellar. How come?'

'The lead cropped up very suddenly, you know that. I asked you to pull together a rapid response team. Ellen shouldn't have to wait a minute longer than necessary.'

'Imagine if she had been sitting there, then,' Allan said. 'With the correct plans you could have broken into the cellar right away. Then you might have stood a chance of rescuing her. If she and the perpetrator had been there and everything unfolded the way it did, you would probably have killed her. By being so slow and underprepared. By being so fucking amateur.'

Berger looked at Allan. For the first time he was inclined to think he was right. And that bothered him. Allan would definitely have been right – if events had taken that turn. It would have been amateurish.

'He gave us an invitation,' he eventually muttered.

'What are you on about now?' Allan sighed.

'Look at it in hindsight. A new witness all of a sudden, after almost three weeks. An address on the outskirts of Märsta, close to the forest, where someone had caught a glimpse of a young girl at the home of a bachelor no one knew. So those of us on duty had to act fast. And a lot of options weren't available to us because it's Sunday. The local council in Märsta failed, for instance – and in spite of my repeated efforts to encourage them – to find any plan of the building. The first thing we find when we get there is a mechanism – yes, a booby trap – which is far more subtle than anything you could have imagined. That's fair, isn't it, Allan?'

'Knife blades in the bicep. I *have* imagined it.'

'Two points. One: it was aimed at police officers, specifically at police officers wearing protective vests – the mechanism was aimed at the side of the vest. Two: not at head height. It wasn't intended to be fatal, it was intended to mock us. Tough officers rolling around on the floor terrified out of their wits. And everything was set up perfectly. Our man seems to like precision.'

'I don't believe you've asked how Ekman is.'

'Ekman?' Berger exclaimed.

'The officer who ended up with knives in his arms.'

'How is he?'

'Don't know. Go on.'

'The booby trap is the bow on a big parcel. A parcel with several layers, like pass the parcel. After the ribbon we have to get through the first layer, the hidden hatch in the kitchen floor. Then down into that labyrinth of a cellar. Then there's another parcel to unwrap: breaking through the wall. Only when we've untied the bow and opened two parcels does he let us into the inner sanctum.

'I see what you mean,' Allan said. 'But this is all with the benefit of hindsight, as you say. You didn't know any of this then. So you should have had the plans, so you could have struck with maximum efficiency.'

'I had a feeling it was a present,' Berger said.

'Of course you did. Supercop Sam Berger. In that case, why was there such a damn rush?'

'Because there was a microscopic chance that the tipoff was genuine. That we could have rescued Ellen and caught the kidnapper.'

Detective Superintendent Allan Gudmundsson stood up in his sparsely furnished office. 'Thinking things through isn't your strong point, Sam, but I'm going to let you off this time. I can't control what you feel. But I can give you clear orders regarding the line of inquiry which is to be the focus of this investigation. And that line is that Ellen Savinger was kidnapped outside her school in Östermalm, right here in Stockholm, over two weeks ago. That's all. You and your entire team haven't got any further than that. You haven't managed to find a single thing to go on.'

'Which suggests very clearly that he's done this before, Allan.'

'But there's nothing to support that, Sam. Just wild guesses that you are strictly forbidden from sharing with your team. That ban just got even stricter. Thanks to this so-called raid. If you choose to disregard your orders and this ban, you'll be fired.'

'I'm going to assume you're joking.'

'Do I look like I'm joking?'

Their eyes locked. And didn't move. If Allan was joking, he was hiding it very well. In the end he looked away from Berger, sighed deeply and shook his head. 'So what's your next move?'

'I'm going to go through the case with Deer, as soon as I can. We need to get back to basics.'

'You can't go round calling a female colleague "dear", that's just weird, Sam. I've already heard people complaining about sexism around here.'

'Her name is Desiré Rosenkvist,' Berger said. 'And no fucking way can a cop be called Desiré Rosenkvist. Deer is short for Desiré, and is spelled with two e's. Deer as in not an elk. She's got a deer's eyes, after all.'

'Oh well, that makes it much less sexist,' Allan said, and shepherded him out.

5

Sunday 25 October, 19.37

Berger realised he was smiling as he walked down the dimly lit corridor and turned off at the pillar that marked the start of the open-plan office. And sure enough, Deer was the only person left. She looked up at him.

'A bollocking?' she asked.

'Big bollocking,' he confirmed. 'For instance, I have to stop calling you Deer.'

'He could have asked me first.'

'Because, of course, it's all done out of consideration for you.'

Laughter. Weak, though.

'Listen,' she said.

An agitated female voice rang out: '*Look, I'm pretty sure I saw her just now, you know, her, that girl, through the window . . . Well, I'm not sure it was her, but she had that thing, I don't know, that pink leather strap round her neck with that crooked cross, the Greek one, I don't know if it's Orthodox, but she's a genuine blonde, for God's sake, can't have any Greek roots.*'

Deer stopped the torrent. 'What does "pink" mean here?'

Berger shrugged. 'It was vital. That was what got us moving.'

'Yes,' Deer said thoughtfully. 'It was a Russian cross, not a

Greek one, but Orthodox all the same. She could have seen that in the media. But not the fact that the leather strap was pink, that's never been made public. But I'm thinking more about, I don't know, proximity. How close would you have to stand to see that a strap round someone's neck is pink?'

'She wasn't standing anywhere,' Berger said. 'Because she doesn't exist.'

Deer looked at him for a few moments, then restarted the audio file: *'Yes, er, the address. It's the last house up by the edge of the forest, the derelict one. I don't remember the name of the road, but the guy who lives there's a real weirdo, you never see him and if you do he hurries away. He could easily have . . . '*

Deer stopped the playback. 'Then of course she remembers the name of the road and gives us a full address. Forensics estimate that it's been at least two days since the cellar was emptied, probably longer. So this witness can't have seen Ellen through the window *this morning*. The woman claimed to live nearby, and there really is a Lina Vikström at the address she gave. The reason we haven't been able to get hold of Lina Vikström is that she's travelling in south-east Asia. One of those get-in-touch-with-your-real-self holidays without a mobile. Lots of yoga.'

'Really?' Berger said. 'That's new.'

'Claiming to be this unreachable Lina Vikström suggests in-depth knowledge of the area.'

'And rather more than that, actually.'

'Obviously this raises a number of fundamental questions,' Deer said. 'Is there a female accomplice? Is this witness's voice actually the kidnapper's, run through a voice changer? Or is our perpetrator in fact a woman?'

'Nothing from the audio experts?'

'Not yet, no. But if we're dealing with some sort of distortion device, these days there's a chance of recovering the original voice.'

'I'm not holding out much hope of that,' Berger said. 'If Forensics did manage to come up with the original voice, that would be a deception as well. One way or another. He only leaves clues that he wants to leave. If they fulfil a function.'

'No woman involved, then?'

'That's my guess. He's working alone.'

'But he's done it before? You got there "too late again"?'

Berger bit his tongue. He twisted Deer's desk lamp so that it shone on the nearby whiteboard. It contained the entire case. Which wasn't much. Almost three weeks and not a single decent lead; Allan had been right about that. But they did have a jumble of dead ends.

Purely because they refused to see the case from a historical perspective.

Berger moved the beam of light across the confusion of Post-it notes, photographs, receipts, documents, drawings and arrows. It was all manual, old-fashioned, no gadgets. The dull cone of light came to rest on two pencil drawings.

Deer pointed at the photofit on the right. 'We've had this one since day one. A man in a van seen outside Ellen Savinger's school in Östermalm, just before the end of the school day. Two independent witnesses agree on this likeness. And then this more recent picture, produced by a neighbour in Märsta, the only person so far to have seen the "weirdo" on the edge of the forest.'

'And what conclusions do you draw?' Berger asked.

'If it's the same man, his face doesn't have any distinguishing features. This is just a standard picture of a white man of about forty. On the other hand, it does give us an age and ethnicity. Although it has to be said, neither of those comes as much of a surprise.'

'Anything else?'

'Nothing else,' Deer said, shaking her head.

'Does he look like a novice?'

'It's hard to say.'

'If this is the right person, then he's done it before, I know you can see that too, Deer. It's written all over his face.'

'You really are piling up the sort of firm evidence that Allan loves. So tell me, what have you been keeping to yourself while you've been conducting an entirely separate investigation?'

Followed by that Bambi look.

Berger was well aware that rather than a sign of weakness it was actually one of Deer's greatest assets.

'Allan expressly forbade me from discussing that,' he said. 'And our investigation is covering all lines of inquiry supported by the evidence.'

'Since when do you care what Allan says?'

'Since he threatened to fire me.'

They exchanged a glance in the gloom. Deer pulled a face as Berger aimed the lamp so that it was shining on the latest photofit picture.

'Erik Johansson?' he said, putting his finger on the picture. 'The most common name in Sweden.'

'That's the name on the rental agreement for the house in Märsta, yes,' Deer said. 'The estate agent has never met the tenant. The house is owned by some Swedes who live in Argentina.'

'The estate agent . . . ' Berger said. 'How does he explain the fact that he's never met the tenant?'

'Email. The estate agent claims he's already deleted their correspondence. That could be true. The perpetrator has had the house for over two years, and emails that old tend to get ditched. But I've got a feeling the agent consciously deleted a paper trail.

Samir compared the original advert with the tenancy agreement. There's a difference of three thousand kronor per month. Our perpetrator probably added the three thousand to avoid having to show his face. The estate agent has no scruples about pocketing the difference before transferring the rest to Argentina.'

'Can we get anything from the email address?'

'Samir's been working hard on that,' Deer said. 'And has probably exhausted all possibilities.'

Berger stared at the picture of Erik Johansson. 'Play the recording again.'

Deer did as he asked. They listened intently to Lina Vikström's agitated voice.

When it was finished Berger said: 'If that is Erik Johansson himself talking – and I'm completely certain he doesn't have any accomplices – then a simple call would have done the job. He didn't need to act it out with such intensity.'

'What does that suggest?'

'I don't know,' Berger said, flicking the picture. 'Nothing good, anyway.'

'Well being a paedophile isn't a great start.'

Berger was about to speak but stopped himself and looked at Deer.

'I don't think he is a paedophile,' he said.

Deer fell silent and looked at him. Her brown eyes shone sharply through the gloom.

'OK,' she said eventually. 'That was the moment when your secret investigation went off in a different direction from ours.'

Berger met her gaze.

'There is no secret investigation,' he said.

'You don't believe in this investigation,' Deer exclaimed. 'All along we've been assuming the bastard sitting outside a school waiting to kidnap a child is a fucking paedophile.'

'As long as that assumption didn't lead us astray it didn't make any difference. I'm not sure that's the case any more.'

'And what's changed?'

'He's being so damn *precious*.'

Deer was restrained, loyal; that was one of the things he liked about her. But the look on her face as she gazed out at the bad weather was neither restrained nor loyal.

'I'm an ordinary cop,' she said to the rain gods. 'I haven't got any other training except for Police Academy. Thanks to my Social Democratic working-class parents' unshakeable optimism in the future, I've been cursed with the stupidly pretentious name of Desiré Rosenkvist. Even so, I'm the first person in my family to get any education beyond high school, and I've had to sweat blood to become a detective inspector. Can you, Supercop Sam Berger, please explain what you mean by "precious"?'

'He's precious, affected, pretentious, exaggerated. He packages his gift to the police as a beautifully wrapped parcel. He wants praise, he wants us to admire him. I agree, that sort of behaviour also exists within paedophile networks, but there we're talking about hermetically sealed groups. People cross new and increasingly diabolical boundaries and want to boast about it to their peers, get a response, praise, admiration. But I've never heard of a paedophile who wants to boast about his transgressions to a wider audience, least of all the police. Outside that closed circle they get nothing but shame.'

Deer turned slowly back to face him. Her face was no longer streaked. 'And then there's the whole fifteen thing,' she said. 'Ellen was fifteen years and one month old when she disappeared. Which means it wouldn't be sexual assault of a child – not technically paedophilia, in other words, as long as they're not related. Which they're not. We have at least managed to discount the Savinger family. That's something we've achieved, anyway.'

'Perhaps we could try thinking of it as an alternative hypothesis. That there could be other motives besides the two obvious ones, a ransom – which he hasn't demanded – or paedophilia.'

'Maybe,' Deer conceded.

As Berger started to gather his things together from the next desk, Deer's phone rang. She didn't say much, and the conversation was over in twenty seconds.

'Forensics have finished with the house,' she reported. 'No fingerprints, no traces of DNA apart from the blood. Disgustingly clean, according to Robin.'

'Scrubbed clean,' Berger nodded. 'Shouldn't you be home with your family now?'

'Johnny and Lykke are at the cinema with Grandma. I'm out on licence. Beer?'

'Tempting,' Berger said. 'But I actually had a couple of small jobs in mind.'

'For me, presumably,' Deer said with a wry smile. 'While Supercop Sam Berger heads off on yet another dodgy internet date.'

Berger snorted. He wasn't sure if it was a laugh. 'There's been one,' he said. 'Just one. A first stumbling step. And yes, it was a bit dodgy.'

'What was it Madame X wanted to do, again?'

'You just want to make me say it out loud.'

'Oddly enough, it just gets funnier every time you say it.'

Berger tried not to smile and shook his head as he pulled his rucksack closed over the bulky files. Then he looked up at Deer not even a hint of a smile on his face.

'You were the first person into that cell in the basement. How much blood would you say there was?'

Deer's smile faded.

'A lot,' she said. 'Back at the house I said I thought Ellen was alive. But I don't know if I was just trying to console you, console both of us.'

'An educated guess, then?'

'I don't know. Two litres?'

'According to the pathologist's preliminary evaluation, it was no more than three decilitres. First: a bit of homework. What would be the point of pumping Ellen Savinger full of blood thinners?'

Deer nodded, with a frown.

'And my second job?'

'You can do that one right now. Which hospital is Ekman in?'

'Ekman?'

'It would be useful to have a first name as well.'

6

Sunday 25 October, 21.54

Berger walked through the rain, all the way from Södermalm Hospital. It was strangely restorative, as if the walk were rinsing all the crap away. The grim darkness of the autumn night competed with the weakly illuminated softness of Södermalm, and somewhere in the tension between them was where the act of cleansing happened. As he took the last few steps over the brow of the hill on Bondegatan and turned into Ploggatan, it really did feel like he'd been given an opportunity to start again.

It didn't feel anything like the way it usually did when he tumbled into the lift and was carried up four floors. Not the way it had recently. For over two years. Could that really be called recently?

As always, the front door announced that *Lindström & Berger* lived there. The fact that it still said that wasn't because of inertia, but because it would have felt even more hopeless to walk in through a doorway bearing the name Berger alone. So it was still there; he told himself it was an active choice.

He stepped into the valley of the shadow of death. He stopped on the hall mat with his whole body dripping. He could feel water trickling down his face, neck, ears, scurrying downward. It was like his whole body was weeping.

The damp chill had time to eat its way into him before he made his way to the bathroom. He pulled off his wet clothes and dropped them in the bath. Even his underpants were wet, and he was left standing naked in front of the mirror, towelling himself off.

Then he caught sight of himself in the mirror. That stopped him smiling. It made the silence of the flat echo extra loudly, a flat that had once received complaints from neighbours trying to sleep.

After picking up the post and his rucksack from the hall floor and grabbing a pair of underpants, he took another look at himself; it seemed somehow inevitable. This time, in the gloom of the hall, the sight was forgiving enough for him to feel like lingering on it. That was a delusion he always regretted. The full-length mirror in the hall showed a dishevelled, brown-haired character with a bit of stubble and traces of grey in both beard and hair. No baldness yet, though, thankfully. Apart from a slight protuberance than was the beginning of a pot belly, possibly even a beer gut, the tall, hairless, nearly forty-year-old male body looked relatively intact, with one exception. And that was only visible on closer inspection. There was a depression in his upper left arm, and when he ran his fingers over the edges of the five-centimetre-wide crater, the skin was just as insensitive to touch as usual. A dead patch on his body. Untouchable.

He walked closer to the mirror to defeat the gloom. When he got close enough he could see that something was trickling below the crater, like red, glowing lava down the side of a volcano. A brief second of horror was followed by the realisation that the blood was coming from his fingers. He tore the bandage off and wiped the stubbornly bleeding right knuckles with the white parts of the bandage, then looked down his left arm instead. On a leather strap round his left wrist sat his Rolex Oyster Perpetual Datejust from 1957. Eighteen carat gold.

He looked down at it, took it off, failed to read the time. It was the second time that day that he had forgotten to protect it from the wet.

He went into the bedroom, dropped his rucksack beside the bed, put the post down on the desk, switched the desk lamp on and pointed it at his watch. For a moment he thought he could see condensation, possibly even some droplets inside the glass, but after using his underpants to wipe the face he realised it was just an illusion. The water had been on the outside. He breathed out.

In pride of place on the desk – next to a photo frame that was turned away, presenting its bright blue back to the room – stood a rectangular wooden box. He opened it, revealing six velvet-lined compartments. He put the Rolex in one of the empty compartments, briefly ran his fingers over all five watches, then shut the lid and closed the gilded catch. That was when the feeling returned at last, the cleansing feeling, the feeling that he had been given a chance to begin again.

There wasn't really any rational explanation. On the contrary: Allan had blocked his way more effectively than ever, and his encounter with Christoffer Ekman at Södermalm Hospital hadn't inspired much hope.

Berger pulled the underpants on, now annoyingly damp from wiping the watch, and was suddenly back in the dismal hospital room. He wouldn't have recognised Ekman if it hadn't been for the heavily bandaged arms sticking out at an odd angle. His face looked pretty much unfamiliar – just one colleague among many others – but as he got closer and Ekman opened his eyes, he recognised those strangely bright green irises. The two men said hello, communicating in clipped, polite – almost official – tones. Berger noted that Ekman's injuries were lower down his arms than he remembered from the drenched porch, close to his elbows, in fact. From the outline under the sheets he quickly calculated Ekman's height and came up with one metre seventy-five, no more.

The first officer going through a smashed-in doorway would usually have his weapon raised. No torch, not the first officer, that came later. At the moment of entry he'd have both hands on the pistol, arms slightly bent, usually held off to one side of the body. So the knives must have flown past Ekman's raised pistol. Just above it. While Berger went on talking to Ekman on autopilot, he figured out that a reasonable estimation of the average height of an officer would be around one metre eighty-five, possibly slightly more, in which case the knives would definitely have passed below most officers' arms if they were bent.

Somewhere a seed started to germinate and finally took root when Berger left the hospital. It was watered and nourished during his purposefully meandering walk through the rain-soaked backstreets of Södermalm, only to blossom fully now, by the desk in his bedroom in Ploggatan.

Had Berger just noticed the first sign of a possible mistake?

Christoffer Ekman had produced one single memorable remark during their conversation. It was right at the end; Berger was already on his feet.

Ekman fixed him with his bright green eyes and hissed: 'This is pure evil. You've got to catch the bastard.'

A cliché. But true. As clichés all too often are.

He had to start again.

Berger went over to his bed and lay down. He piled the

pillows up against the wall, pulled the covers over him and leaned over to dig about in his rucksack. He pulled out three bulky folders. He put the one marked *Ellen Savinger* to one side and placed the other two on his thighs. The one on his left was marked *Jonna Eriksson*, the right-hand one *Julia Almström*.

Start again. Look with fresh eyes. Find more tiny mistakes. Where the execution didn't quite match up to the ambition.

If a man of Berger's height had been first into the house the knives would have passed below his arms. The scum hadn't actually considered that. Berger detected a sudden crack in his perfect facade.

In his head he always called the perpetrator the Scum.

Start again. He moved 'Jonna Eriksson' to one side and opened 'Julia Almström'. The first one.

Then he fell asleep.

When he woke up an indeterminate amount of time later – because *Julia Almström* had fallen to the floor with a thud – he was still in a swirling world where a fancy school building merged into a load of oily, rattling chains and revolving cogs, where a truck waiting on Kommendörsgatan in Östermalm somehow became a sweaty man's torso above which a pair of twin boys aged about eleven hovered like cherubs, where an artist's drawing verified by two independent witnesses suddenly came to life and slowly opened its mouth until it became unfeasibly large, then, as scarily as every other time over the past few weeks, when it bared its teeth and got closer to his bicep, it merged with another drawing and the two faces became one, their features distorted, skull-like, as the merged teeth started to snap all around them, sinking into raw flesh until the faces faded away and were replaced by a bucket of stinking urine and excrement that bubbled and boiled and overflowed, suddenly leaving just a naked concrete wall, with a brown stain that grew redder and redder as it spread, and when the bright red stain covered the whole wall he woke up as the folder hit the floor.

Crap dream, he had time to think. Then he opened his eyes and stared out at nothingness. Or – even worse – into nothingness.

He felt the same distaste as usual about the cherubs. They shouldn't be there. This was a work dream, a typical procedural dream; he'd had so many of them over the years, always along the same lines. And the twins definitely shouldn't be there.

Yet that wasn't what lingered. Berger leaned over the edge of the bed. The contents of Julia Almström's file lay strewn across the floor – photographs of notebooks, Post-it notes, receipts, newspaper cuttings – but that wasn't what he was after. He reached for his rucksack and managed to dig out a very small plastic bag. The documents from the investigation stuck to his feet as he walked over to the desk.

The box of watches sat there is splendid isolation. He opened the gilded clasp, stared down at his five watches and briefly ran his fingers over the empty compartment. His eyes hadn't regained their focus, everything was still dreamily blurred. He took hold of a couple of the velvet-lined dividing walls and lifted them. The entire row of watches came loose, revealing a cubby-hole underneath. It contained a number of small plastic bags, each one bearing a label. He opened one of the desk drawers, took out a pack of tiny labels, wrote *Ellen Savinger* on it in shaky handwriting, then pulled it off and stuck it to the little plastic bag he had taken from his rucksack. He held it up to the light and examined the tiny cog. It was no more than a centimetre in diameter. He adjusted the order of the other bags – the names Jonna Eriksson and Julia Almström were visible on a couple of them – and then put the new evidence bag in alongside them.

Berger stood there for a while. Half-formed ideas swirled

around him until one of them dived down and grabbed hold of him. He hurried over to the bed, reached for the file labelled *Ellen Savinger* and opened it. Hunched over, he spread out the police photographer's pictures from inside the house in Märsta. The cell in the basement, the overturned bucket, the bloodstain that wasn't quite as big as he remembered it. Plenty of angles, but not much else. He slammed his hand down on the pictures and bowed his head. Then another idea grabbed him. He pulled out his mobile phone and sat down on the edge of the bed. Eventually the photographs appeared.

The twins were the fixed point. The pole star, the still point of the turning world. Everything stemmed from there. Even though he was on his way back into the revolving world he stopped himself there. To get his bearings. Marcus and Oscar. They were about eight years old there, in a ditch full of coltsfoot. He felt the peculiar calm that reigns in the eye of a hurricane. Perhaps their presence was his attempt to stop the passage of time. Stop the constant rotation.

But time did exist. As did chaos. Beyond the pole star was the revolving world. All that we really have.

He scrolled through the photos. At the end were a couple of pictures he had taken from the porch in Märsta, looking towards the ambulance, police vans and cordon. He paused and felt himself frown, then scanned backwards to the cellar again.

He couldn't recall having taken so many photographs. The light was considerably worse than in the police photographer's professional efforts. In fact the pictures were pretty useless. He scrolled back and forth through them. He paused a couple of times at pictures of the wall, with the bloodstain towards the bottom of the frame. He zoomed using his fingers, the way Deer had taught him. Then he returned to the still point. Marcus and Oscar. Paris. He could never just scroll past them, no matter what else he might have on his mind; it was impossible. But in the end he swiped his finger across the screen and brought up the next photograph, the first one from inside the house.

It was an unassuming picture. A patch of wall lit up by the beams of at least three torches. Down in the corner, half a square metre of cement looked slightly lighter. He moved on to the pictures from inside the cell. He selected one in which the patch of blood had almost completely slid beyond the bottom right corner of the frame. He zoomed in on the concrete wall as far as he could.

As usual he tried not to look at the time on the mobile phone. Time was marked by clocks and watches, that was one of the laws of nature. He got his Rolex out of the box. Half past three, the hour of the wolf. It was a bonus that he'd fallen asleep without his usual nightly whisky; he could drive at the risk of nothing more than a lack of sleep. And possibly hydroplaning.

Berger dug out his toolbox from an unbelievably messy cupboard in the hall, tossed a couple of things in his rucksack and set off.

7

Monday 26 October, 03.32

One of the very few advantages of the bizarre rank of 'detective inspector with special responsibilities' was access to a car. One of the many disadvantages was that it didn't come with a place in the garage. When he reached the car down on the offshoot of Bondegatan, at least three yellow parking tickets had dissolved and seeped through the grille on the bonnet.

It was always strange to drive through Stockholm without any traffic, he hadn't reached the northbound motorway that fast since he was in uniform. He allowed himself the luxury of driving fast. He pulled off at Märsta, drove through it to the outskirts. The extensive forests of Uppland got closer and closer.

To be on the safe side he parked outside the last apartment block before the more rural scenery took over. He walked through the rain with the rucksack over his shoulder, no umbrella; police officers didn't use umbrellas, full stop. Without seeing a soul, he finally spotted the derelict buildings in the weak glow of the street lamps. He felt he could see just how porous the rotten wood had become.

Blue and white tape had been stretched across the gate.

Bracing himself, hand on metal, he swung over. It was surprisingly painless.

The porch was barely visible. Berger was there again, behind the backs of the advancing rapid response team, Deer's odd, whimpering breath behind him. The house was gradually conjured up out of the nocturnal curtain of water. He reached the bottom of the porch steps and wove through the web of police tape. While he was picking the lock, the moon suddenly broke through an invisible crack in the dark sky, sweeping the dirty white porch with icy blue-white.

The sudden light made Berger jerk sideways, but when he opened the door, crouching down to one side of it, he was struck by one thing, and one thing alone. Sorrow.

Sorrow at what must have taken place in there for almost three weeks. Which must have felt like three years to a terrified fifteen-year-old girl who had never harmed a fly. And who had then been taken to an unknown location in order to further develop her acquaintance with hell.

Sorrow followed the beam of Berger's torch, past the disarmed knife-throwing mechanism in the hall, grew stronger in the living room, became even more tangible in the bedroom, and, as he approached the thicket of blue and white tape over the hole in the floor between the fridge and the stove, carved its way into his brain.

He removed the tape and could just make out the steps when he shone the light into the hole. He lowered himself down and crept through the labyrinth. The beam of the torch played across the walls.

He crouched down by the roughly hacked entrance to the cell. The hole was larger now; he assumed that was thanks to Robin, who was without question the best forensics officer, but also the fattest. He couldn't help a fleeting, misplaced smile as he slipped, much more nimbly than before, through the opening. Dust from the past powdered him as he snaked his way in.

He had the same feeling as before. But this time Deer wasn't there to hold him.

Once again he got the feeling that the walls were screaming at what they had been forced to witness. He shook his head hard until all that was left was the sorrow that had already invaded it.

Eventually he managed to hold the circle of light more or less steady. He moved it across the bloodstain on the far wall. He moved closer to inspect the wall on either side of the stain, then glanced at the two decaying wooden pillars a couple of metres from the wall.

Ellen Savinger had sat here, as if in a cage with invisible walls. She had sat still. Wetting the same patch, on several occasions. He left the wall and went over to the posts. They framed the invisible cage, and together with the wall formed a block no bigger than two cubic metres. He ran his fingers along the grooves. They were at three different heights, the top ones at eye level, almost invisible. Then he went back to the bloodstained wall, took a chisel from his rucksack and held it against a well lit patch of wall.

Because this looked the same as the entrance they had smashed their way through. There were definitely lighter patches in the cement, weren't there?

After all, that was why he had come out here, in the middle of the night, the hour of the wolf.

Berger reached for the hammer. Then he set to work.

A couple of centimetres into the wall he was on the point of giving up. Practically every other blow resulted in a recoil as brutal as if he'd been hammering away at solid rock. But then something appeared. A piece of metal, a hook, embedded deeper in the wall. Overcoming the resistance of his shoulders, he went on hammering.

It took him almost half an hour to reveal the outline. It was a thick metal loop; was it called a mooring ring? And it was screwed into a deeper part of the wall.

Berger put the hammer and chisel down, grabbed hold of the ring and pulled as hard as he could. For one bizarre moment he had both feet up on the wall, pushing with all his might. The ring didn't shift.

He picked up the hammer and beat all round it. More concrete came loose. It was clear that the composition of the wall changed ten centimetres in, where the ring was screwed in. Was this yet another false wall?

He rolled his shoulders a few times and craned his neck until it creaked. Then he set to work again.

He had no idea how much time passed, but slowly, slowly, dripping with sweat, he managed to cut around the rings, one after the other until there were six of them, three on either side of the stain formed by layer upon layer of blood.

Berger stopped. His muscles ached as if they had suddenly realised the exertion they had been through. He returned to the two pillars and ran his fingers over the grooves in the rotting wood once again. They were at the same height as the mooring rings.

He couldn't make any sense of it. Had the Scum added another ten centimetres to the entire wall just to cover up the rings that were fixed into it? Hard physical graft, while fifteen-year-old Ellen Savinger sat shackled there? However, she had bled onto the wall, day after day, like the rings in a tree. If some sort of chain had been attached to the mooring rings then the whole wall would have had to have been almost ten centimetres further back at the start of her captivity. So how could the blood have seeped into a wall, day after day, if that wall hadn't actually been constructed yet?

Berger's brain was perhaps not at its sharpest – lack of sleep and the brutal physical exertion had each taken their toll – but this looked like a genuine paradox. One of Escher's impossible images, steps curling round for all eternity, a hand drawing the hand that was drawing it.

But perhaps not. The cement had been a different colour where the rings were fixed. Perhaps the Scum had merely drilled deep to fasten his terrible mooring rings. Perhaps he knew there was a more solid wall back there.

Perhaps there was no other meaning to the hidden mooring rings than the fact that they had been wrapped up. Like a present.

Wrapped in a parcel. Inside a parcel.

Whatever the rings had been used for, they were supposed to be found. The Scum was showing off again. Wanted to show how clever he was. Wanted to be admired. But who the hell by?

Berger was feeling tired as he took a couple of pictures. He tried one last time to imagine the scenario. He couldn't, the images kept slipping away from him. He hoped he'd be able to drive home without hydroplaning his way into a hospital bed.

Mind you, how long had he actually been down in the windowless basement? Before he checked the watch on his wrist he had time to worry that dawn had arrived, that the neighbours would have started to stir.

It was ten to seven.

Time wasn't on his side.

He slid out through the opening in the wall, up the stairs, and stepped out onto the porch taking several deep breaths. It was fortunate that the autumn had progressed to the point where the mornings had got darker. And the persistent rain, still falling just as heavily as before, was keeping any early birds indoors.

He stood on the porch and looked down towards the gate. For a brief moment a considerably lighter image flared in his mind – ambulance, police vans, cordon, onlookers – before he took one last deep, damp-laden breath and looked down as the hand resting on the rail of the porch. His eyes settled on the knuckles of his right hand.

The wounds actually seemed to have healed.

8

Monday 26 October, 07.26

The fact that it was Monday wasn't the only reason why the morning felt darker than usual. Autumn had settled in with a vengeance and when Detective Inspector Desiré Rosenkvist tapped in the entry code to Police Headquarters it felt like the middle of the night. But at least it had stopped raining. In fact it hadn't rained since she had left home, waved goodbye to Lykke at nursery and then, feeling weighed down as usual with guilt, got in her environmentally unfriendly old car. When she snuck out onto Nynäsvägen ahead of the morning rush the carriageway seemed almost dry.

Even so, Berger was wet.

She said a quick hello to the rest of the team as she headed towards Berger's corner like a pre-programmed robot. It also happened to be her corner.

He looked like a wet dog, just staring straight ahead. They barely greeted each other, she sat down, as usual with her back to him, and started to tap at her computer. Even though she very obviously angled the screen away from him, she got the feeling that Berger didn't care what she was doing.

He really was staring blankly into space. It was his way of

having a crafty nap. No one really noticed the difference between a power nap and deep concentration; the question was, did he? He was old enough to have done national service, and a lot of that involved trying to look awake even though you were asleep.

Deer turned round and said: 'The movement of rain clouds.'

It was a sufficiently cryptic comment to rouse Berger from his trance. He turned towards her. She went on: '*Micrometeorology*, that's a word suited to your class, Sam.'

'We're from exactly the same class, Deer. What are you driving at?'

'There's been a heavy autumn storm hanging over us for longer than we can bear to remember. But it's capricious, and this morning it eased up, briefly, and slipped away towards Norrland. Check the times on this map.'

Berger looked at the screen. A large thundercloud slid upwards as a clock indicated the time. The cloud moved very fast. As 06.00 approached, a map started to emerge, and he vaguely recognised the geography. Deer paused.

'Skogås,' she said, pointing. 'Where I live.'

Then the storm slid further north, uncovering the familiar outline of Stockholm. Deer paused again when the whole of the inner city was clear, then pointed and said: 'And that's where you live. Ploggatan, the north side of Södermalm. The rain cleared there at about twenty past six.'

The storm moved on towards the north. When the timer reached 06.45 Deer paused it for a third time.

'Are you with me?' she asked.

Berger nodded, reluctantly fascinated.

As the heavy cloud moved on, the name Märsta appeared on the map.

Deer turned to Berger, fixed her eyes on him and said: 'For

you to be that wet, Sam, you must have been pretty far north, very recently.'

'Get back to work.'

As he turned his chair away he couldn't help smiling. His eyes settled on his wrist. For the third time in twenty-four hours he had neglected to protect his old Rolex from the wet, and now it really looked like some water had seeped into the casing. For the first time since 1957. An ominous layer of condensation was obscuring the left half of the glass, where the hands were.

For the time being there was no time.

He pulled a tissue from his drawer and placed the watch on top of it. Then he angled the desk lamp to shine on its face. Maybe the heat from the bulb would be enough.

With great reluctance Berger looked at the time on his mobile phone instead. He glanced over his shoulder at Deer. She was immersed in photographs from the house in Märsta, as if she was on his tail. He shook his head quickly and pulled up the pictures on his mobile. The twins, Marcus and Oscar, it always started there. Marcus and Oscar Babineaux. And the vacuum that swelled inside him every time. Then he scrolled through towards the end, past the pictures from his first visit to Märsta – inside the house, the basement, the porch – until he reached the most recent ones.

He turned and tapped Deer on the shoulder. She spun round at once, at if she'd been waiting for it.

Without a word he passed his mobile to her. She glanced at him and took it. Then effortlessly she zoomed in on the rings set into the wall. Berger watched her, saw the frown spread across her forehead.

After scrolling back and forth she handed the mobile back. 'So what's that?'

'Mooring rings,' Berger said. 'Deeply embedded in the wall.'

'Is it part of some contraption?'

'Don't know. Maybe.'

'We need to tell Robin.'

'He's on his way. We're seeing him at half past eight.'

Deer nodded. Then she said: 'So no morning assembly today?'

'There's hardly anyone here,' Berger said, waving his hand. 'And we haven't got anything new to say anyway.'

'That's new,' Deer said, nodding at the phone.

'Not until it's been past Robin.'

There ought to have been a meeting at eight o'clock, known as morning assembly, but most of the team was out in the field. Three of them were leading the door-to-door inquiries in Märsta, and their collective grumbling could be heard all the way to Police Headquarters. Syl was down in the media room, grumbling almost as much, as she scrutinised the news reports. Two officers were revisiting the handful of witnesses, before going back to Ellen Savinger's poor parents. Only Maja and Samir were at their desks, Maja as coordinator, Samir with his sights on the subcontracting estate agent.

Berger called Märsta. His three sets of boots on the ground had just set in motion their own team of uniformed boots on the ground. The previous day's door-knocking was continuing, further and further from the crime scene, colder and colder.

'No sign of activity in the house?' Berger said, earning him a wry glance from Deer.

Then Samir was standing there, trying to hide his youth with a steadily lengthening hipster beard. He leafed through some papers and said: 'It actually looks like that dodgy estate agent has managed to dig out an email address.'

'Let me guess,' Berger said. 'Hotmail?'

'Does that still exist?' Samir said, running his fingers through his beard. Then he handed over a sheet of paper.

Berger took it and passed it on to Deer, who took it and carried it over to Maja. Like a game of pass the parcel.

'Dig as deep as you can,' Berger said to Samir. 'Even if the chances of finding anything at the other end are pretty slim.'

'I don't know where we'd be without such enthusiastic leadership,' Samir deadpanned, then went back to his desk.

It was hard to tell how much time had passed when a strikingly overweight man in an elegant three-piece suit appeared at the edge of the open-plan area. Because his suit was a nondescript shade of pale violet, his two companions faded into the colourless background behind him. Berger stood up and went to meet him.

'Robin,' he said, holding his hand out. 'Good to see you managed to get the dirt of the cellar out of your clothes.'

Robin shook his hand and pointed at Berger's knees: 'You, on the other hand, still have a surprising amount on you considering that it's been twenty-four hours since you were there.'

'I'm surrounded by wannabe detectives,' Berger complained, and gestured towards the next corridor.

The three visitors followed him, and Deer brought up the rear of the quick march. Berger led them into an utterly sterile meeting room. They settled down around the bare table.

'You know Vira,' Robin said, indicating the woman with him, who didn't look a day over twenty-four.

Vira gave a doctor's nod that instantly added ten years to her age.

'So Medical Officer Höög has sent one of his assistants,' Berger said coolly.

'For the simple reason that there isn't much to say,' Vira said, even more coolly. 'We estimate that the oldest blood has been there eighteen days old, the newest four. In total there wasn't much more than three decilitres. But there are two types of DNA found in the whole house. Most of it Ellen Savinger's. Rather less, Sam Berger's. How's the wound healing?'

Berger looked at his right knuckles. 'Toxicology?'

'What?' Vira said.

'If you've already managed to get hold of the DNA, then presumably you've also conducted toxicology analysis. Checking for drugs in the various layers of blood. You must have figured out a timeline for the introduction of any poison or drug.'

For the first time Vira looked slightly wrong-footed.

'Do it again; do it right,' Berger said. 'So who's your other little friend, Robin?'

'Cary,' Robin said. 'Sound technician. But we'll leave him for a while. Because the more I see of your not-long-since-dried appearance, the more obvious it is that I don't have the whole story. I was thinking of setting out the forensic position, but I can't do that now. Have you spent the whole night in the cellar, Sam? Sleeping your way towards the truth like some shaman? Contacting restless spirits?'

Berger held his mobile phone out to Robin. The impeccably dressed forensics expert took it and wrinkled his nose.

'Bloody hell,' he said.

The man who never swore.

'It's OK,' Berger said, putting a soothing hand on Robin's broad shoulder. 'Even eminent forensics experts can have off days.'

It was clear that Robin had a whole library of sharp replies on the tip of his tongue. The fact that he refrained from using any of them made Berger like him even more.

'What led you to it?' Robin asked simply.

'The same difference in colour as at the concealed entrance.'

'Not good,' Robin said. 'I shall do it again, and do it right.'

'Pleased to hear it,' Berger said joylessly. 'Please, just give me something else.' Robin buried his wide face in his equally wide hands. It wasn't a despairing gesture – that would have been out of character – but rather a reflective one.

'This changes our assumptions about the marks in the wooden pillars,' Robin said eventually. 'We need to rethink things. They must be more recent than our first estimation suggested. They've probably been made to look older on purpose.

'What else?' Berger said.

Robin looked at him for a while, then said: 'There were scratches in the floor.'

'Scratches?'

'A few smaller scratches close to the wall, slightly larger about a metre from the wall.'

Robin looked around, as if he was waiting for a penny to drop.

'No,' Deer said, opening her eyes wide.

'Yes,' Robin said, giving her an appreciative look.

'In a cement floor? Nails?'

'I'm afraid so. Scratches made by fingernails close to the wall, toenails further away. No trace of keratin, however.'

'Keratin?' Berger said.

'A fibrous structural protein,' Vira said, with another doctor's nod. 'High-sulphur protein that makes up hair, nails and horns.'

'Horns?' Berger exclaimed. 'There ought to be a fuck of a lot of evidence of both sulphur and horns in that infernal basement.'

'He used a vacuum cleaner,' Robin said calmly. 'Just like he did on the rest of the house, and a very good vacuum cleaner at that.'

'A *traceable* vacuum cleaner?' Berger said.

'Possibly,' Robin said. 'There are a fair few portable precision vacuum cleaners on the market. I'll get back to you about that.'

'Do,' Berger said. 'Anything else?'

'Then there's the knife-throwing apparatus in the hall,' Robin went on. 'You could describe it as a double hair-triggered crossbow. An intricate mechanism for two separate knife blades. Throwing knives have a particular balancing point. Normally when you throw one it rotates on the way to its target. Even though the target was only a couple of metres away in this instance, the knives still need to be carefully balanced to fly straight. And these were very carefully balanced.'

'Modified by hand?' Berger wondered.

Robin nodded and shook his head at the same time.

'As far as I can tell, yes.'

'Why not use arrows?' Deer said. 'Crossbow bolts or arrows. They're made to fly straight. Instead he modifies a weapon which *isn't* supposed to fly straight. Why do that?'

'Because knives are more frightening,' Berger said. 'Because he wants to show us how clever he is, again.'

'I'm having trouble getting my head around the knife blades,' Robin said. 'I don't know what it is. I'll have to get back to you on that as well.'

'What about the shit bucket?' Berger said.

'A very literal mess of faeces and urine. As with the blood, the National Forensic Centre – as we have been so smartly known since 1 January – is working with the Forensic Medical Unit on the analysis. Vira?'

'Water and bread,' Vira said.

'Is that the technical terminology?' Berger said. 'Like keratin?'

'Margarine too,' Vira said, ignoring him. 'Water, bread and

margarine. Different sorts of bread, white and something more wholemeal. No meat, no vegetables, no cheese, no sign of any liquid except water. The analysis is ongoing.'

'Although the toxicology is higher priority,' Berger stated.

Vira fell silent. Robin didn't say anything.

'And Cary?' Berger prompted.

'Cary is one of Sweden's foremost sound technicians, in spite of his modest appearance,' Robin said. 'He's got news about the voice.'

'We're talking about Lina Vikström's voice here?' Deer said. 'The woman who called to say that Ellen was in Märsta?'

'Correct,' Robin said. 'Cary?'

The barely visible sound technician cleared his throat and said: 'I've analysed the sequence in every imaginable way, sequence by sequence, and I've also applied a few more experimental methods. I'm afraid I have to admit that I'm not quite finished yet, despite working all night. The voice has been run through so many filters that it's actually difficult to tell if it was even a human voice originally.'

'Was it?' Berger asked.

'Everything suggests that it was. But it hasn't been easy to uncover the original sound. I need another day or so to . . . '

'No,' Berger interrupted. 'We need something to go on.'

'Right now I can't actually say for certain . . . '

'Now. Please.'

'OK,' Cary said, and leaned forward. 'I haven't yet been able to identify the speaker. The sound quality is far too poor to be able to find any individual characteristics of the voice. We've got a probable gender, but, once again . . . '

'A man?' Berger interrupted. 'A man calling and pretending to be a woman?'

'No,' Cary said. 'It's a woman's voice.'

Berger froze, spreading a chill through the whole room. Everyone was looking at Berger. In the end he said: 'Should I interpret that as a guess?'

'The probability is 97.4 per cent,' Cary said.

Berger stood up and left the room.

It actually took a little while for a state of bewilderment to spread. Once it had ebbed away Robin stood up and navigated his way out of the meeting room, with Vira and Cary following in his wake.

Deer was left alone. Half a minute later she sighed deeply and stood up.

When she reached the open-plan office Berger was sitting at his desk staring into space again. She approached cautiously, sat down on her chair and turned it towards him. She couldn't catch his eye. This went on for so long that Deer eventually said simply: 'Is our perp a woman?'

Berger looked at her without expression.

'Or has a female accomplice?' Deer pressed.

Extremely reluctantly, Berger emerged from hibernation.

'Could be an actor,' he muttered. 'Or someone he just picked off the street and made an offer she couldn't refuse.'

'In which case she probably saw him.'

Berger frowned and held her gaze just a little too long.

'Saw him,' he said.

Then he pulled out his mobile again and dived in. The photographs. The pole star. Marcus and Oscar. Then the pictures from the house. The hellish cellar. Then, right after that. Up, out on the porch, the strangely fresh air. Berger and Deer close together. It had almost stopped raining. That was when he had been struck by a peculiar, fleeting feeling that left just an echoing void behind it.

What sort of feeling was that?

A vision?

The photographs. The photographs from the porch.

Deer watched him. He scrolled through them and deftly zoomed with his fingers. In the end he lowered his head towards the screen as if he were hopelessly short-sighted. And then he got to his feet. He stood there for a while. Then he grabbed his rucksack. And walked, deeply distracted, towards the exit.

'Where are you going?' Deer called out, in the absence of anything better.

'Dentist,' Berger said, turning round. 'If Allan shows up, tell him I've had to go to the dentist.'

'For God's sake!' Deer exclaimed.

'The dentist,' Berger muttered, and carried on walking. 'That's it. I'm at the dentist.'

'Any chance you might be back this afternoon?' Deer said in a tone that betrayed her utter disbelief in any further communication.

But the disappearing Berger replied: 'If I'm lucky I'll be back this afternoon with considerably sharper teeth.'

9

Monday 26 October, 09.28

The fact that it didn't come with a parking space was by no means the only drawback of the car that went with the job. Another one was the seats. There was no question of leather, not even the most artificial sort, and beneath the flimsy but quick-drying material was some sort of highly absorbent padding. It might look nice and dry while deep down it was soaking. In other words, Berger's clothes – now dry again, at last – returned to what was starting to feel like their natural state.

Not that it mattered in the slightest. Berger tore through the city, all the way to an unexpected parking space right in front of his door on Ploggatan. The lift was waiting on the ground floor, but for the first time in about six months, he hurried up the four flights of stairs two steps at a time, with surprising agility. He even managed to ignore the threefold phantom pain that always followed the sight of *Lindström & Berger* on the front door. Once he was inside he was careful not to glance through the wide-open door towards the bath, strewn with the previous day's wet clothes – which had been faced with a choice between drying and rotting and had evidently picked a side – and made his way into the chaos of the bedroom. The chaos from the hour of the wolf. It was a scene frozen at half past three that morning, with the contents of *Julia Almström* strewn across the floor, and papers from *Jonna Eriksson* and *Ellen Savinger* mixed up on the undisturbed side of the oversized bed. He pulled out one desk drawer and took out a magnifying glass. Then he gathered the files together and lined them up along the edge of the bed. He crouched down in front of them and took out his mobile phone.

He scrolled quickly through the photographs until he got to the porch. Three pictures, largely identical. They had just emerged from the nightmarish basement, every impression was new, untested. The wounded Ekman had been taken away, the ambulance had gone, and the last traces of his blood were being washed from the porch. Deer pushed closer to Berger, the post-rain freshness of the air was remarkable, a mixture of ozone and spores that the dampness had released from the depths of the earth.

And then. That feeling. So fleeting.

Was it as simple as that? So damn banal?

He studied the first photograph. It was shaky. The mobile held in his bleeding right hand, the left one sweaty from the plastic glove. Down by the cordon there were two police vans; the phone's tremor had stretched the blue lights sideways, in irregular waves. Next to the police vehicles was a throng of cameramen, sound technicians and reporters, together with about twenty indistinguishable onlookers. The second picture was a considerable improvement: the blue lights were now points of brightness and at least one reporter was recognisable from television. Berger zoomed in and revealed face after face, first the media, so clearly identifiable, then the curious spectators. As their faces paraded past on the small screen, he paid close attention to his physical responses. Would the feeling manifest itself again?

After five or six faces it was back, toned down but unmistakable. A woman.

She was blonde, mid-thirties, her face half turned away, as if caught glancing over her shoulder. Her profile was reasonably clear; he could even make out a snub nose. Only her head stuck up behind the front row of onlookers, so her clothes were mostly hidden, apart from the collar of a light-coloured raincoat that might have been beige.

He moved on to the third and final picture taken from the porch, and zoomed in once more. Now the woman seemed to be looking straight into Berger's raised mobile phone. The men in front had moved slightly, making it easier to see her. Her coat was more off-white, and she seemed to be standing at an odd angle, her legs apart. Only when he zoomed even closer and the picture started to break up into individual pixels did he see that she was straddling a bicycle.

He scratched his head and pondered his reaction.

A strong gut feeling. Yes, this was the woman he had seen. Yes, she was the cause of that strong but fleeting feeling out on the porch. Yes, she was the reason he had pulled his mobile out and started taking pictures.

Berger put his mobile down on the bed next to the three files, two of which he had managed to persuade Syl to pull without Allan's knowledge. He opened the middle file – *Jonna Eriksson* – and searched frantically for images. Somewhere there were pictures from a winter forest. There, at last. Three of them, one after the other. The press photograph was mediocre, the resolution atrocious, but behind the blue and white tape a crowd was clearly visible.

Berger picked up the magnifying glass and held it in front of the press photograph. His first instinct was correct – the resolution was much too low. That wasn't where he had seen it. But it was there in the second picture. The magnifying glass enhanced the view of the cycle. The rider's head was covered by a heavy fur cap, the lower part of the face wrapped in a thick scarf. But the nose was bare, slightly redder, but with the same upturned angle.

He tossed the file aside and grabbed Julia Almström's. More photographs, all of slightly chaotic scenes. Biker gangs, cordons, curious onlookers. The magnifying glass again. Shit. Yes.

How the hell had he managed to miss that?

His legs had long since gone to sleep. When he stood up they felt like they were on fire. Ignoring the pain he took pictures, photographs of photographs, sent three emails, made two calls, initially while staggering round the bedroom in an attempt to get his circulation going again. The first call went as follows:

'Syl? Are you still in the media room? Good. You've got mail.'

The second, made as he lurched down the stairs with an overstuffed rucksack, went:

'Deer? Bring the afternoon meeting forward to eleven . . . Just under an hour, yes. Try to bring in as many people as you can. But not Allan, whatever you do.'

Just under an hour? He had no idea what the time actually was. Only now, as he was getting into the car and glanced at his wrist, did he realise that he wasn't wearing a watch. Highly unusual.

As he entered the open-plan office, he could see his watch from an improbable distance. It shimmered beneath the glow of his desk lamp. Deer was sorting things out and clearing space around the whiteboard. Samir was setting out chairs as the officers traipsed in from Märsta. Berger shut the whole lot out, closed his mind to all the agitated yet soundless activity and gazed at his Rolex as it lay there on its tissue. If anything, the condensation seemed to have spread behind the glass, and more than half the face was now obscured by moisture. Had he by any chance . . . ? He fumbled in the rucksack and took out the magnifying glass.

Then in his desk drawer he managed to find a case opener, a special tool that he quickly used to remove the back of the watch. He held the magnifying glass up to the opening and inspected the innards of the watch. The perfectly coordinated constellation of tiny cogs and pinions always lowered his heartbeat dramatically. This was as close to a perpetuum mobile that mankind had got so far. The endless fascination of the self-winding mechanism. The daily movements of the wearer managed to provide the watch with all the power it needed. It remained a perfect mechanism, no matter how rapidly electronics developed. Humanity's powers of innovation had never got closer to *life*.

Yet the ticking was utterly empty.

Something found its way into the gentle, perfect ticking. Even before he looked up he'd realised it was someone clearing their throat. And long before he looked into those brown eyes he knew that Deer had everything ready. He carefully turned the watch over. The condensation had both grown and moved, but the top third of the face was still untouched, and there the hands were pointing at eleven o'clock. Precisely.

Deer really had managed to bring almost everyone in for the eleven o'clock 'afternoon' meeting. Berger rolled his shoulders and moved the naked watch, still ticking on beneath the warming glow of the lamp. He put the magnifying glass and case opener into his rucksack, heaved the files out and set off towards the whiteboard.

Without condescending to look at his assembled team he stuck three photographs to the board. Then he began.

'The official view of this investigation is that Ellen Savinger's kidnapping is an isolated event. Allan has chosen to keep the investigation free from speculation, and I can understand that. Even so, one or two of you are aware that I don't agree. This has been too perfectly carried out; it's far too professional for a first attempt.

Digging through the many cases of people who disappear without trace I thought I'd managed to find two possible precursors, but there was no evidence of a connection whatsoever, not even anything circumstantial. Apart from the fact that they concerned fifteen-year-old girls who vanished without any warning. Only later was sufficient evidence found to suggest that both Julia Almström from Västerås and Jonna Eriksson from Kristinehamn had made plans to run away with their respective boyfriends, both of whom wanted to disappear off the radar for a variety of reasons. After investigations lasting a month or so, both were believed to have disappeared voluntarily, possibly changing their identities and leaving the country. Cases closed.'

'But we haven't got anything like that in Ellen's case,' Samir said.

'Something's happened,' Berger said. 'Something that's made him change his method.'

'This sounds like the sort of vague idea that Allan hates,' Deer said. 'So you've found something that means you dare make your secret, unofficial investigation public. Sharpened teeth?'

And then that look.

Berger couldn't help smiling. Bloody Deer. He pointed to one of the photographs on the whiteboard.

'Here, my dear Deer – this was when you and I were standing on the porch outside that bloody house in Märsta, right after the raid. You remember?'

'You took pictures then? Why?'

'Because I got a feeling. Don't ask me to explain. Intuition is nothing but a concentration of experience.'

'Old jungle saying,' Deer said tonelessly.

'Let's start here instead,' Berger said, pointing at a fairly grainy photograph featuring a number of motorbikes and biker jackets. 'One week before this photograph was taken, fifteen-year-old Julia Almström vanished from her home in Malmaberg in the north-east of Västerås. It was March 17, a year and a half ago. Because her disappearance was confirmed in the morning, Julia was assumed to have disappeared from her home during the night. She certainly had the opportunity, and eventually a secret email correspondence with a young man was uncovered, in which he claimed he wanted to flee from a criminal past to "somewhere the sun never stops shining". Which, taken literally, is everywhere on the planet, because otherwise we'd all be dead.'

'Was the boyfriend identified?' someone wondered aloud.

'No,' Berger said. 'There were hints that he'd recently been released from prison, and among men who had been let out within a plausible time frame, there were at least eight who had disappeared without trace. A completely ordinary phenomenon. Fake passports are easy enough to buy these days. In other words, a perfect choice of persona.'

'Persona?' Deer said.

'Exactly,' Berger said, pointing at her. 'That's exactly the sort of prompt a sidekick with perfect timing should be asking.'

'Leave it out,' Deer said calmly, accustomed as she was to that sort of line. 'What do you mean by persona?'

'That this young criminal was a persona, a mask. That he never even existed. That the whole email exchange was fake. That it was all a matter of constructing a narrative which in hindsight looks pretty similar to the phone call which led us to the house in Märsta yesterday, the call from our so-called Lina Vikström. Who is standing right *here*.'

With that he drew a thick circle in red marker pen on the busy photograph featuring a biker gang.

He looked round. Never before had he seen so many furrowed brows in one room.

'But,' Deer eventually said. Her jaw had fallen open.

'A raid on a local biker gang in Västerås,' Berger said. 'One week after Julia Almström's disappearance, before the email exchange was discovered. There were suggestions that the gang offered "fresh meat". In many ways it was a fortuitous raid – a large amount of cocaine seized, two underage Ukrainian girls, and assorted stolen goods worth a total of three million kronor – but no Julia Almström. Among the curious onlookers: this woman. Blonde, snub nose, mid-thirties, on a bicycle.'

The room was still thick with frowns, but at least now there was a certain focus to them. Berger pointed at the next photograph.

'Almost one year later. Now we're in the depths of the Värmland forests. February this year, the forest between Kristinehamn and Karlskoga, so maybe not the deepest depths. Either way: fifteen-year-old Jonna Eriksson from Kristinehamn has been missing for a few days. Because her boyfriend, Simon Lundberg, disappeared at the same time, the investigation has been fairly half-hearted. Jonna and Simon aren't exactly angels, they were both raised in foster homes and had a history of running away and then coming back with their tails between their legs. But then someone raises the alarm about a freshly dug grave in the forest, right on the boundary between Värmland and Örebro, in the new police district of Bergslagen. In the twenty-four hours that follow each of the former police forces succumbs to the temptation of blaming each other, even though they've actually been part of the same district for a month or so. It's basically a disaster from a policing perspective: what ends up being disinterred from the snow-covered grave in the forest is nothing more than an illegally shot elk calf.'

Berger paused and looked round at his subordinates. Then he continued: 'The investigation evidently leaked like a sieve, because local media from at least two cities were there, and in the pictures taken by both police and press you'll notice more curious bystanders than we had during yesterday's rain-soaked Sunday morning on the outskirts of Märsta. Do you see?'

They saw. Although they weren't really sure what they were seeing.

Berger raised the marker pen and drew another heavy red ring.

'One of the police's own photographs. Note the bicycle. OK, the head is covered by a big fur cap, and the bottom of the face is wrapped in a thick scarf. Correct me if I'm wrong, but it's the *same damn woman* in the crowd. One year later, 160 kilometres from Västerås. With a bicycle, in the middle of a wintery forest.'

The frown had actually disappeared from Deer's face as Berger pointed to the third photograph and said: 'So, back to the porch of our house in Märsta, just after yesterday's raid. And here we have a blonde, snub-nosed woman in her mid-thirties with a bicycle.'

And his red pen circled another figure.

Then Berger put the pen down and shook his head.

'I'd discounted women,' he said. 'For my part, I was convinced that this bastard was a man, a lone, dysfunctional man isolated from everyone, especially the opposite sex. I seem to recall a somewhat older colleague in this building saying that it's refreshing to have your prejudices turned upside down.'

'He's not in the building any more,' a forceful male voice said from the direction of the corridor.

Berger looked up and met the gaze, which had a distinct chill to it, even at a distance.

'He's off in Europe,' Allan went on. 'Europol. God knows why.'

'Allan,' Berger said coolly. 'Good to have you here.'

'Go on,' Allan said, adopting an apparently relaxed posture as he leaned back against a pillar. 'We can deal with the rest later.'

Berger took a deep breath and was just about to continue when Deer said: 'Was it that simple? So incredibly fucking banal? Going back to the scene of the crime?'

'Maybe,' Berger said, glancing over towards the pillar. 'But now I get to do a bit of an Allan: "Don't let's draw any hasty conclusions." '

'Such as this woman with the bike being Sweden's first female serial killer?' Samir suggested evenly.

'We don't know what role she plays in it all,' Berger said, with a sharp sideways glance at his most heavily bearded underling. 'But we need to get hold of her. As I implied, I think she was the woman who called us pretending to be Lina Vikström. That would have put her in the right place at the right time. She probably steered the police in the other two cases as well, so that she could be there to watch. But in those cases she led the police astray, to the biker gang in Västerås and the buried elk in Värmland. This time she's started by leading us in the right direction. To the point that it's actually extremely frustrating. Now she can humiliate police officers into the bargain – that knife mechanism is something new, after all. Julia and Jonna are almost certainly already dead, but Ellen is still alive, I'm convinced of that. Something has changed, and I can't help wondering what.'

'How do we proceed?' Deer asked.

'What do you say, boss?' Berger asked impertinently.

Allan made a tolerant and inviting gesture, but his face was saying something completely different.

'I've already started,' Berger said eventually. 'I've emailed the pictures to Robin so that his people can clean them up as much as possible and get a face that we can then run through every facial-recognition software going. There may be more photographs, shots that weren't used by the media. And that's where Syl comes in.'

A stern-looking woman in her forties cleared her throat and said sharply: 'Feel free to call me Sylvia.'

'I'll happily call you Hera or Gaia or the Virgin Mary, as long as you've got something for me.'

'Freja, to keep things Nordic?' Deer suggested mildly.

Berger gave her a dark look. The sort of look a one-eyed god might give.

'I've found out the following,' Syl went on in a neutral voice. 'A number of names of press photographers who were present at the three crime scenes – I'm calling them crime scenes, seeing as unlicensed hunting is also a crime. I've also got all the police photographs. And lastly, I managed to get the two television stations from yesterday to hold off deleting any unused footage. There's also a rumour that there was a TV crew present at the biker gang's headquarters in Västerås, but nothing was ever broadcast. I haven't had time to look into that rumour.'

'Excellent,' Berger said. 'Keep at it, Syl. And those of you who are out in Märsta, get back there and knock on some more doors with photographs in your hands. If I know Robin's team at all, these pictures are likely to get a lot better soon.'

'Surely we ought to release the pictures to the media?' Deer asked.

Berger looked at her. 'That's one of the most delicate questions I've ever been faced with.' He scanned the now largely frown-free gathering and went on. 'Our only real task is to find Ellen Savinger as quickly as possible. While we're talking, somewhere out there she's going through hell. Every word we utter, every step we take needs to be anchored in this innocent girl's pain. Every second counts.'

He pointed to the picture of a smiling Ellen Savinger. That was the smile that the team had been faced with every day for almost three weeks now, a slightly reserved smile which still seemed to hint at a future of unlimited possibilities.

Beside the photograph were pictures of the clothes Ellen had been wearing when she disappeared, including an elegant if slightly too summery floral dress.

Berger went on: 'We could probably find bicycle-woman much quicker if all media outlets published her picture simultaneously. But then we'd also be tipping her off. And I don't want to risk a repeat of Märsta. Right now we have the advantage of knowing something that she doesn't know. And it has to stay that way for as long as possible. As long as we have the slightest advantage, we need to make the most of it.'

He stopped himself, but it was clear that he hadn't finished.

He pointed at the two photofit pictures of Erik Johansson and then stuck an enlarged photograph of bicycle-woman's face next to them.

'This is the best picture we've got of her at the moment,' he said. 'And her relationship to him is unclear. She exists. Whether or not he does remains to be seen.'

Another pause. Then he said: 'There's just one thing that matters. We have to catch her.'

Berger still wasn't quite finished. The team stopped halfway out of their chairs and stared at him.

He looked over towards the pillar by the corridor and said, emphatically: 'OK, people, we're not supposed to say it out loud, but we're chasing a serial killer.'

As the meeting split up a powerful baritone rang out.

'My office,' Allan said with his eyes fixed on Berger.

Not unexpected.

10

Monday 26 October, 11.34

Bosses' offices are almost always impersonal, but Allan seemed to have taken pains to break the record. No books worthy of the name on the bookshelves, just unmarked files and folders with militaristic abbreviations on yellowing labels, not a single photograph on the desk, not a single object that hinted at the slightest decorative instinct, not even any diplomas on the walls. No golf clubs, no fishing rod, no football lapel pin, not even a lawnmower manual.

'So?' Allan said, flashing a glance across the desk.

'I did exactly what you said,' Berger said. 'To the letter. I didn't say a thing until I had evidence. And if that bicycle-woman isn't evidence that these three cases are connected, then we may as well abolish the word *evidence*.'

'And then you said the S-word.'

'To my team, not the media. They're under the same oath of confidentiality as you and me.'

'Even if they've got less to lose.'

'I'm not sure I've got much to lose,' Berger said. 'Detective inspector with special responsibilities?'

'Your life,' Allan said.

'My life? How can you say that, Allan, with this emotionally dead office as the centre of your world?'

'So what does your workplace look like?'

'I don't have any walls to decorate.'

'But you do have a framed photograph, I know, it looks very cosy there in your corner. Is it the Arc de Triomphe?'

'Stop it,' Berger said.

'They're no longer part of your life. They're gone. Your life is here now. Here, and nowhere else. And you don't want to lose that.'

'What are you trying to say, Allan?'

'As everyone knows, I'll be retiring soon. And I'm assuming that you'll be taking over. You *have* got a lot to lose, Sam. You shouldn't have said the S-word. But because you did, we'll be reading about it in the papers within the next few days.'

'Three missing fifteen-year-olds.' Berger said. 'One of them gone for more than a year. This is a serial killer, I promise you, a serial killer who for some reason has decided to specialise in fifteen-year-old girls.'

Allan looked at him intently. Then he turned away and pulled a sheet of paper out of a pile on his desk.

'The knives,' he said with a gesture that was hard to read. 'Homemade, according to Robin. So now there's something as unusual as metallurgical analysis underway at the National Forensic Centre. Forging iron at home is so rare that some part of the process ought to be traceable.'

'Possibly also the skill itself,' Berger said. 'How the hell would anyone know how to forge knives so that they fly straight instead of spinning? You'd have to be an expert.'

'That's under investigation too,' Allan said. 'Robin has been very busy, he's got a whole list, topped with the heading "Do it again, do it right". Does that ring any bells?'

'No,' Berger said serenely.

'The list consists of the following: knives, knife-throwing mechanism, mooring rings, newly built wall, vacuum cleaner, labyrinth.'

'Not toxicology analysis?'

'I haven't got to the Forensic Medical Unit's analysis yet. I'd like to go through Robin's list point by point, if you don't mind.'

'I don't mind,' Berger said. 'Labyrinth?'

'So that caught your interest?' Allan said scornfully. 'Just be patient, we'll go through the list in order. So, the knife-throwing mechanism.'

At that moment Berger's mobile phone had the good sense to ring. And happily it was actually a call requiring his attention. Without any great haste he took his phone from the inside pocket of his jacket, and while it squealed like a stuck pig he said: 'I ought to take this.'

Through the hysterical grunting sound he watched Allan, who eventually made an impatient but consenting gesture.

Berger answered by saying his name, then said nothing more for the duration of the call. He merely stood up, put his mobile back in his inside pocket and said: 'We're going to have to do this later, Allan.'

Looking perfectly calm, Berger walked out. He strolled slowly down the corridor until he was confident he was out of sight of Allan's office. Then he speeded up.

He threw himself down the stairs and ran through the corridors. After several more flights of stairs and corridors he reached an anonymous door and yanked it open. Three men were sitting in a confined area filled with bare desks and framed by bookcases. They all looked up when Berger stormed in, but with a complete lack of interest. He raced on to a set of doors beyond the bookcases and jerked open the one on the left. A stern-looking woman in her forties turned to face him from a veritable phalanx of computers, looking slightly less stern than usual. Her thin, mousy hair was sticking out in all directions.

'Syl,' Berger panted.

'Sambo,' Syl said in a subdued tone.

'Talk to me,' Berger said.

'Västerås,' Syl said, pointing vaguely at the nearest screen. 'The bikers' clubhouse. Local television were there after all, but they dropped the item to make way for sport. Ice hockey, apparently. The edited version no longer exists, but the photographer found a backup disk containing some of the raw footage.'

'You said you had something to show me,' Berger said curtly.

Syl looked at him in a way that didn't feel altogether comfortable. Then she clicked her mouse and a very shaky image appeared.

The first thing that came into view was a winter landscape with a number of moderately overweight men in leather waistcoats pinned to the ground by police officers, at least a couple of officers per biker. Five buildings were just about discernible, and from the middle one a pale, undernourished young girl was being led out with a blanket round her shoulders. As she approached the camera, Syl said: 'Oksana Khavanska, fourteen years old. She was actually given asylum in Sweden afterwards. Said to be living in Falun with a new identity, attending high school. But look at *this*.'

The camera swept past a number of people on the other side of the cordon before coming to rest on a young man with a microphone who tried to stop people and talk to them. After a particularly unsuccessful attempt to communicate with one of the officers in command, who firmly pushed the microphone back into his face, the reporter turned towards the onlookers with his pride visibly dented. Syl speeded the film up while the bystanders got to churn out a few pointless remarks to a saliva-spotted microphone, but the sound had vanished. Then the lens turned and captured a bicycle.

As the camera focused on the wheel of the bicycle Syl slowed the film down to normal speed. The sound returned. The reporter sounded neurotic.

'And how do you come to be here?'' he asked while the cameraman tried to adjust the focus on the bicycle wheel. In the end he succeeded and the camera panned up.

It was her. Bicycle-woman. There was something remarkable about seeing the muscles of her face move. As if she had only now become real.

There was actually an awful lot going on with the muscles of her face. As if they were governed by an incredibly complex process of decision-making. Her body seemed to be on the point of cycling off. But then her body language changed completely and she replied: 'I just happened to be cycling past.'

An unexpectedly deep voice, Berger thought, watching her face.

'What do you think about all this?' the reporter asked desperately.

'What exactly am I supposed to be thinking something about?'

'The police raid on the biker gang.'

Then she pointed briefly over the reporter's shoulder and said: 'Apparently they managed to free someone who was kidnapped. So that's obviously good.'

To his surprise, Berger found himself thinking very clearly: *I want you in an interview room.*

'Thank you,' the reporter said, genuinely, from the sound of it. 'What's your name?'

Berger froze. Watched.

The facial muscles again. A similar pattern of movements. Then she said: 'Nathalie Fredén, but you're not going to broadcast this crap on television, are you?'

'Pause,' Berger said quickly.

From the corner of his eye he saw Syl's face move closer to the screen. Just like his own.

'What do you think?' he asked.

'About what?' Syl asked, without taking her eyes off the screen.

'What was that?'

'I don't get what you mean.'

'Yes, you do. What was that she just did?'

Berger had to admit that Syl wasn't Deer. Brilliant at going through archives, not quite so brilliant at analysis. He admired Syl – they had been at Police Academy together. She was the only person who still dared to call him Sambo; she was a genius when it came to anything digital, looking things up and digging them out – but he suddenly found himself missing Deer's way of seeing things.

Micrometeorology, he thought, and chuckled.

Syl looked at him dubiously.

'She replied: "Nathalie Fredén, but you're not going to broadcast this crap on television, are you?" What was that?' he asked.

Syl blinked hard a couple of times. 'I presume you want to know if I've found a Nathalie Fredén?'

'Definitely. In a minute. But first this point, specifically.'

He could see the tension in Syl's neck.

'She seems to think before saying her name,' she said eventually. 'And she thought very hard before she decided to speak at all.'

'After which she gives a name which might or might not be her own,' Berger said. 'Then what?'

'OK,' Syl said. 'She says her name, then says very quickly that this crap shouldn't be broadcast on television. More or less.'

'Why?'

'I don't know. Why?'

'Because she wants to make sure it won't be broadcast,' Berger said. 'But at the same time she wants to get her name out. Who to?'

'Don't get carried away here,' Syl said. 'Seeing as she gave her name, it could very well end up on television, as a caption. At the bottom of the screen. But there was no broadcast; they showed the hockey instead, even if she couldn't have known that. If she didn't want her name on television she could simply not have given it.'

'You're right,' Berger said thoughtfully. 'It's definitely a risky strategy. Even so, it was a conscious decision to reveal her name. Why?'

'For God's sake, Sambo,' Syl exclaimed. 'It's almost two years ago. She's not talking to *you*.'

Oddly enough, Berger felt himself blush.

'I didn't think she was. It just seems like she was aiming her comments at the police in general somehow. But OK, that can wait till later. So, you've managed to find someone with the fairly unusual name of Nathalie Fredén?'

'There aren't many in Sweden. This is Västerås. Do you want to take that as the starting point and move out from there? Do we assume that's where she's from, and then she expanded her field of operations?'

'Don't know,' Berger said. 'It's not even certain that Julia Almström was the first victim. Is there a Nathalie Fredén in Västerås?'

'No,' Syl said. 'Only in Stockholm.'

'Just one?'

'Three. One's a baby out in Farsta. Another one is in Year 4 at Alvik School. The third is thirty-six years old and lives near Odenplan.'

'Bloody hell,' Berger said. 'What else?'

'Not much. I haven't had time. But there doesn't seem to be much about her. She's got an apartment on Vidargatan, wherever that is. Surveillance?'

'Right away. And email me everything you've got on her. Passport? Driving licence? Date of birth and ID number?'

'I'll send you all I've got,' Syl said. 'But none of the above.'

'We'll have to instigate a large-scale search,' Berger said, and then left.

A couple of seconds later he stuck his head back into Syl's cubbyhole and said: 'Thanks.'

11

Monday 26 October, 12.01

Then time entered two phases. At first it went improbably, almost unmanageably, quickly. Berger was standing at the whiteboard while his ever-expanding team ran back and forth with information. He tried to summarise it as best he could on the old-fashioned whiteboard, attaching notes with magnets and drawing lines and arrows.

No passport, no driving licence, no photographs beyond those they'd already found. But a date of birth and ID number linked to the apartment on Vidargatan. And a floor plan of the flat.

'She doesn't seem to be particularly digital,' Deer said. 'No Facebook, no Twitter, no Instagram, at least not under her own name. No immediately accessible email address. No blog, and no website.'

'Is that even possible these days?' Berger asked.

Samir came over, scratching his beard. 'Tax declarations,' he said, waving some sheets of paper.

'OK?' Berger said. 'Have we got a place of work?'

'No, she's only declared minimal income for the past four years. And nothing before that.'

'Minimal income?'

'From various sources, never more than ninety thousand kronor or so. I've tried to contact a couple of her clients but I haven't heard anything so far.'

'What sort of work?'

'Unclear. Secretarial, maybe. Possibly cleaning. It's hard to tell. A temp agency.'

'Go on,' Berger said, fixing the tax declarations to the board. He looked at them, staring intently at the neat signature, the name Nathalie Fredén perfectly legible.

'Report from Vidargatan,' a voice said behind Berger's back. He turned round and saw a young detective whose name he had suddenly forgotten.

'OK?' he said.

'No one in the flat at present,' said the young man whose name Berger was still fumbling towards.

'Don't tell me some idiot's gone and rung the bell?'

'External monitoring, et cetera. And surveillance outside, in shifts. Photographs of people going in and out.'

'Thanks,' Berger said, then added as the young man was already walking away: 'Thanks, Raymond.'

He turned towards the whiteboard and contemplated two things. The first was what 'et cetera' might mean in that context, the second was where Vidargatan actually was. In the end he was left staring into a white void. He turned round again.

'Bloody hell,' he exclaimed to the office in general. 'We must be able to find out more than this. And fast. If she doesn't work, how can she afford a flat near Odenplan? Bank accounts? How has she managed to get to her thirties without earning any money? Has she been in a care home? An institution? Prison? Give me something!'

'No criminal record,' Deer said from somewhere. 'But you already knew that.'

Maja was suddenly standing beside him, big and solid, and said in her steady way: 'Nathalie Fredén is listed as unmarried, and was born in Umeå thirty-six years ago. Her parents' names were John and Erica, and they're both dead. I've managed to find a primary school there, the Mariehem School. They're busy digging out all the information they've got. Including a class photo. Apparently she was only there up to Year 3.'

'And how the hell is a class photograph from Year 3 going to help us?' Berger bellowed.

Deer appeared next to Maja, making her look even smaller than usual.

'Now you sound like Allan,' Deer said, giving him her most innocent – in other words, her most evil – look.

He looked at her and took a couple of deep breaths through his nose.

'Yoga breathing,' Deer declared.

'I get it,' Berger said eventually. 'We can check to see if it really is her.'

'There are obvious holes in Nathalie Fredén's biography,' Maja said calmly. 'It would be good if we could at least confirm that it's the same person. And, maybe even more so, if it *isn't*.'

'Good,' Berger nodded. 'I'm sorry. Carry on.'

Maja returned to her desk.

Samir came back and stood beside Deer. He seemed to be waiting his turn, so Deer went on: 'I think I might have a Facebook account. Belongs to an N Freden, no accent. No posts and no friends. Dormant, clearly. But when it was registered, both a mobile number and email address were listed. I've called the mobile but the number's not in use.'

'Get a trace on it anyway,' Berger said. 'And the email?'

'I've sent it to Forensics.'

'Good work, Deer. Keep looking. Samir?'

'Initial conversation with a temp agency who employed Nathalie Fredén four years ago. She's on their books, but no one there remembers her. She was sent to a now defunct car-hire company in Ulvsunda.'

'Hmm,' Berger said. 'The obvious holes in Nathalie Fredén's biography are becoming increasingly obvious. Keep working. Find some former employees of the car-hire company.'

Samir turned on his heels and went back to his place.

A sudden pause arose. Berger stared at the whiteboard. He was looking at the gaps on it.

'The most likely explanation is that she hasn't actually been spending that much time in Sweden,' Deer said.

He had forgotten she was still standing there.

'Maybe,' he said.

'Swedish mobile number, though, and obvious traces of her presence here in the past . . . '

'. . . four years,' Berger concluded.

'But possibly not before that,' Deer said.

'Maybe not,' Berger agreed.

Then Maja was back again. Without a word she held out a sheet of paper. It featured a photograph, clearly cropped from a group picture, its colour faded. And the face was very young.

'A bit of a snub nose,' Deer said.

'And blonde,' Maja said. 'It could be her.'

'Year 3,' Berger said. 'Year 3. What age is that? Nine? Ten? What does puberty do to people? Some people look pretty recognisable afterwards, while others change completely. So what about Nathalie Fredén?'

The three of them stood there staring at the class photograph, which Berger had already pinned up between the two sharpest pictures of bicycle-woman's face.

'Possible,' Deer said after a while.

'Good summary,' Berger said. 'Possible, no more than that. Which makes it pretty much useless. Neither true nor false. I'd have preferred it if nine-year-old Nathalie Fredén had been adopted from Biafra.'

'Biafra?' Deer said.

At that moment Berger glanced out of the window for the first time in a very long while. It had started to rain again, hard, heavy drops blowing against the windows of the large office space. That was when time entered its second phase. Everything slowed down. None of the paths led any further. It was apparent that Nathalie Fredén had always been employed through temp agencies, and that her Swedish employment history seemed to have begun a mere four years ago. But it wasn't possible to find out more detailed information from any of the companies. It didn't seem to be in their nature to have any form of personal contact with their staff. The email belonging to 'N Freden' didn't lead anywhere, nor did the defunct car-hire company in Ulvsunda. No bank accounts of any kind were identified, nothing like that. And no trace of a single person in the entire universe who remembers bumping into Nathalie Fredén just once during her thirty-six years on the planet. No classmates, no neighbours, no colleagues, no friends.

In the end Berger had had enough. On his way out of the office he heard Deer's extremely tentative question: 'Dentist?'

He turned and gestured towards the whiteboard. 'Good idea. We're pretty toothless right now.'

12

Monday 26 October, 18.47

Dusk had long since fallen, but the rain just went on falling.

There were two street lamps on the easily overlooked side street. They were both suspended from what looked like lethal cables strung across the street, from building to building, and the evening showed its true character in the constantly shifting pools of light. Beyond these pools it was hard to see how hard the downpour was, but even in the darkness it could be felt and, not least, heard. The rain was hammering all the car roofs along the street in a variety of tones, but it seemed to be making an extra effort with the dark blue Volvo. The downpour was drowned out by retaliatory heavy metal. Meaning that the two men in the car weren't at all prepared for the knock.

Berger saw the men's hands fumble across jackets that had been buttoned all too carefully. But he understood; he had sat in his share of surveillance vehicles, and the thing that was engraved in his marrow wasn't the boredom, the tiredness, the hunger, the need to pee, or even the smells – it was the cold.

'You need to turn the volume down,' he said through the opening window. 'I can hear your music from the pavement.'

'Sam,' the older man said in a measured voice, then lowered the volume with purposeful slowness.

'Any signs of life?' Berger said.

'Is that really what I think it is?' the man said. 'Do you have any idea how ridiculous a cop with an umbrella looks?'

'Signs of life?' Sam repeated from under his umbrella.

'We'd have been in touch if there were.'

'And you've taken photographs of everyone going in and out?'

The younger man in the passenger seat raised a disproportionately large camera in response.

'Many people?' Berger went on.

'Not really,' the older man said. 'About ten since we took over.'

'You can see inside the building as well,' the younger one said, pointing. 'Through the windows in the stairwell.'

Berger nodded. 'If she shows up in the next half an hour, leave her be, and don't report it. Just shadow her up the stairs but don't intervene unless the situation is critical. Understood?'

The older officer raised his left eyebrow and said: 'I take that to mean that you . . . '

'Understood?'

'Understood.'

The umbrella blew apart as he crossed Vidargatan. He ditched the remains on the pavement and walked up to the unremarkable door, tapped in the code, made his way up the stairs and stopped outside the still-untouched door.

It was a conscious decision on the part of the police, taken by Allan, of course: not to enter a flat that could be rigged. Or at least alarmed. Wired with surveillance cameras. There was thought to be a significant risk that a raid would warn Nathalie Fredén, whereupon she would in all likelihood disappear, leaving no more than the smattering of evidence that her identity had provided thus far.

Berger studied the stone floor of the stairwell. A number of wet footprints were visible, and a small puddle had already formed around his feet. Evidence that was going to linger for quite some time.

Everything was telling him not to go in.

Not least that Allan's words could no longer be treated as a joke. If Berger did warn Nathalie Fredén in any way, he really would be fired.

Even so, his lock-pick was out.

Even so, it slipped into the lock.

He studied the gap between the door and frame all the way round. There was nothing obvious, no classic strand of hair or piece of paper, nothing that should have stopped him from breaking in.

He paused to consider one last time. And he considered very seriously.

Even if all their external assessments suggested that it was unlikely, there was a slim chance that Ellen Savinger was behind that door. Berger simply couldn't hold back any longer. His entire being fought against all this waiting.

Leaving the pick in the lock, he went and looked out through the window in the stairwell. Sure enough, he could see straight down onto the surveillance car. He raised his hand and the younger officer raised the camera in response. Berger pulled back. Fragments of weak street lighting flashed in the black trickles of rain competing to hit Vidargatan first.

And he was back in the rain. He was standing behind a ruined building in the middle of a downpour, the wooden planks behind his back so rotten they felt spongy. Police officers disappeared, one after the other, into the rainstorm, swallowed up by the grey soup. He set off, followed by Deer's whimpering breath. The house from hell was hidden from view.

It was entirely possible that hell was waiting behind this unprepossessing door as well.

He had to be prepared for that. Mentally, physically, and as a police officer. The realisation actually came as a shock. He had been blinded by the speed of his actions for too long.

He looked at his hand as it rested on the lock-pick. But it was no longer resting. It was moving. As if it only partially belonged to him. His hand was a little rodent, or a newborn rabbit, all pink and trembling, ready for a life as someone else's prey.

The wounds on his right knuckles had opened up again. He felt exposed.

The rain thudded against the nearly pitch-black windows.

The lights, which were on a timer, went out. The character of the stairwell changed. A different sort of darkness fell on the previously mundane landing. He was in a different universe, the real universe, where darkness reigned. All light is an illusion, a reassuring veneer of lies to help us stay alive, to help us bear growing up. He was in a different era now, one that was still governed by barbarism, where the chimaera of civilisation had not yet made its entrance.

He was in a raw, unadorned world.

There was no getting away from it.

He could see the switch glowing red through the darkness. It was only a few metres away. All he had to do was pull the pick from the lock, switch the lights on and go back out into Vidargatan. Around the corner people were thronging under the artificial lights of Odenplan. It was all just half a minute away.

Yet somehow not. It seemed to be on the other side of the universe. Billions of light years away.

And Berger was here. Caught in the darkness. Captivated by the darkness.

He heard a click as the pick caught. He pulled out his pistol, raised his torch and opened the door.

There was a faint tugging draught, as if the air pressure was much lower inside the flat than in the world outside. And it was utterly dark.

He focused his attention inside the flat and listened. Not a sound, in fact no real sensory impressions at all. No smell. And no booby trap. A peculiar emptiness. Two rooms and a kitchen. He had a quick look around the bathroom. Clean but spartan. No stains in the bowl. No toothbrush. The kitchen was just as clean, but there was a mug in the sink with deeply engrained coffee residue. The dishwasher was empty. The bedroom: sheets on the bed, no bedspread, no duvet. And at this time of year you really needed a duvet. Finally the living room. No dust on the flat-screen television. The remote left neatly on top of the entertainment unit. A stereo that was a fair few years old. CD player. When did people stop using CD players? The leather sofa was hard, didn't seem to have been worn in. He sniffed a couple of cushions on the sofa and a neatly folded blanket. They all smelled more of a factory than a home. And the books on the shelves were so commonplace that it was almost absurd: travel writing, international bestsellers, nothing that gave the slightest indication of individual taste.

When he had glanced through all the rooms he shone the torch over the walls. He was looking for two things: signs of alarms or surveillance cameras, and any shift in the colour of the walls. He found nothing. At least not in the subdued glow of the torch. Everything looked far too normal. The coffee mug in the sink was the only indication that anyone lived here.

It worried him. It suggested an asceticism which in turn suggested a degree of fixation, focus on a task that was more important than life itself. Life wasn't just something that happened while you were planning something else. And in this instance there simply wasn't a life to uncover – at least not here.

He pulled the floor plan from his pocket. Wandered round, trying to identify all the internal and external walls of the flat. It didn't take long. Unless Nathalie Fredén had got hold of one of the neighbouring flats, there were no hidden compartments here. No labyrinths.

He pulled on a pair of plastic gloves and returned to the bathroom. He ran his hand along the skirting board and found a quantity of dust. Then he looked behind the shower curtain again. Nothing but a bathtub. A shower set at a height that would have been enough for him to wash his chest but no higher than that. No shampoo, no shower gel. And, again, no toothbrush.

No one lived anywhere without a toothbrush. Either you were away and had your toothbrush with you, or you spent most of your time somewhere else. Ordinarily at your partner's home.

Which means that there's somewhere else.

And possibly even a partner . . .

He'd had enough. There was nothing else to discover. No hidden corners. Nothing lurking just below the surface. Or at least nothing that could be found without the help of the person in question.

He sat down at the kitchen table, with a view in two directions: the hall and front door, and the window looking out onto the courtyard. The storm was whipping the almost bare branches of a scarcely visible aspen tree, but the clatter of the rain drowned out everything else. He positioned the torch so that it was shining straight up at the ceiling and put his service pistol down on the table in front of him. He ran his gloved finger over the shiny wood surface and smelled it. Finally, a smell: his own plastic glove. Nothing else.

He remained seated there beneath an umbrella of weak torchlight. Perhaps he was thinking. Perhaps time was merely passing. Although he glanced down at his Rolex every so often he lost track of how much time passed. Even if he had made a real effort, it wouldn't have been possible to see the time; the face of the watch was by now almost completely obscured by condensation.

Berger didn't particularly react to the footsteps out in the stairwell. The likelihood of their belonging to Nathalie Fredén was infinitesimal. She had flown the coop, all this shit was in vain.

He felt like crying.

He wished he could remember how.

Fifteen-year-old Ellen Savinger was lost.

The steps were right outside now. Inside himself he heard them shuffle past, carrying on to the next floor. Like a hope flaring up and then vanishing again, instantly forgotten, leaving nothing but a vacuum.

But inside wasn't the same as outside.

When the key was inserted into the lock he was somewhere else.

Berger only just managed to turn the torch off before the door opened. A figure slipped in, darker than the darkness for a couple of seconds until it reached the switch and sharp light stripped away his night vision.

The woman was wearing an off-white raincoat, and she was squinting towards the kitchen, as if she could sense something she couldn't see. And when she turned slightly her snub nose came into view.

He grabbed his pistol and roared: 'Nathalie Fredén! Hands on your head!'

She jumped. Yet *she didn't really jump.* He would never seriously be able to analyse that feeling.

When she put her hands on her head he pulled out his mobile phone and took a picture. He didn't really know why.

'Who are you?' she asked in her deep voice.

'The dentist,' Berger said.

Then the surveillance officers crashed in with their weapons raised. The younger one forced Nathalie Fredén down onto the floor. The older one did a quick pat-down.

Berger watched the inverted form of events. He saw them reflected in the kitchen window. All sound had disappeared; he didn't hear a word of what the surveillance officers were shouting out in the hall. There was a strange rustling sound instead. It came from the almost bare aspen tree out in the courtyard. He looked at the remaining leaves. They were trembling. The aspen leaves were trembling hard in the rainstorm, sending their rustling song into his ears.

As if someone were trying to get through from another time.

Berger turned his gaze to the flat again. Returned from the badlands. One word took hold in his head. *Micrometeorology.* He met Nathalie Fredén's crystal-clear gaze from where she lay on the floor. Then he said: 'You're very dry.'

13

They've run a long way, first along the increasingly desolate road from the bus stop, then out onto the meadow with the unfeasibly tall grass that is now thinning out to the point where the sparkle of the water is coming into view. He feels almost breathless as he gets closer to the fluttering golden-yellow hair slowing down in front of him.

As his mane of hair settles back into place, the boy turns round and is touched by a light so radiant he seems to be surrounded by a huge halo. It makes his face even more striking.

He's never stopped being astonished at that face, will never stop being astonished.

They stand eye to eye and hug each other briefly, out of breath, panting. He leans over, hands on knees, can hardly get enough air, but he's fifteen years old and his breathing is soon back to normal. When he looks up again, when his field of vision is no longer filled by green grass, he sees the other boy disappear into the copse by the shore, where the boathouse is, green-brown and ugly and quite wonderful.

He stumbles in that direction, hears the gulls screech in the distance, feels the high sea air sweep in and merge with the smell of grass. It carries a hint of decay on it.

He reaches the copse, makes his way through the increasingly tangled undergrowth, and there it is, the big boathouse. In one direction it stretches out into the lake, and there's a door there; that's where he sees the fluttering golden-yellow hair disappear. He heads to the other side, climbs up the always slippery rock to peer in through the window. It's high because the boathouse stands on pillars, a short way off the ground.

It's hard for him to find a foothold. The moss comes loose, taking his feet with it. In the end they find purchase. He stands still at last.

It's tricky to see in. It's completely dark inside the boathouse, and the window is extremely dirty. He can't see anything at all. But he doesn't give up. His sweaty hand gradually clears a small gap in the dirt. And in the end he can actually see in.

That's when time stops.

That's when it really does stop.

14

Monday 26 October, 22.06

Berger stepped inside. The door closed behind him. The room was extremely clinical. The woven wallpaper was as bland as the empty birch-veneer table. On a side table stood an unidentifiable piece of electronic equipment. There were no windows in the room, but there were two chairs. One of them was empty.

On the other sat Nathalie Fredén.

She was wearing the same simple, vaguely sporty clothes she had been wearing in her flat on Vidargatan, minus the off-white raincoat, and her clear blue eyes followed him the whole way from the door to the other chair. He sat down and studied her. It was only a few hours since they had last seen each other. Since then a prosecutor had been brought in and had instigated a preliminary investigation into her activities.

Without a word Berger removed a number of items from his rucksack. Three thick files, a laptop and a mobile phone. He opened one of the files and said as he leafed through its various contents: 'I know you're something of a mystery, and ordinarily that might have roused my interest. But right now I don't give a damn about you. This is all about one thing. This.'

And he put a photograph down in front of her. It showed

fifteen-year-old Ellen Savinger with a smile that hinted at a future of unlimited possibilities.

Berger watched Nathalie Fredén. She looked at the picture without the slightest change in her expression. Her face, which had shown itself to be so expressive before, registered no reaction whatsoever.

'It's all about this,' he repeated.

She merely went on looking at the photograph.

'Have I understood correctly?' he went on. 'You've waived your right to a lawyer?'

'I don't even know why I'm here,' Fredén said in her dark, slow voice. 'Let alone why I would need a lawyer.'

'Is that a yes?'

'Yes.'

Berger took a deep breath and turned to the electronic device on the side table.

'Red light,' he said, pointing. 'When it's lit the audio and video are on. So that everything is official and can be recorded. The light is off at the moment. Is there anything you want to say to me, and me alone, before we start doing this formally? Just between the two of us?'

'That your mobile phone is already recording,' Nathalie Fredén said.

It was lying upside down on the table between them. No lights, no sound. He smiled faintly, leaned over to the side table and pressed the record button. The red light came on.

He said the day's date. He said where they were. He said who was present. He said: 'Nathalie Fredén, you are primarily suspected of withholding information regarding the kidnap of Ellen Savinger, fifteen years old. I have now informed you of the nature of the suspicions against you. Do you understand these suspicions?'

'Yes. But not what I might have to do with any of it.'

Berger put three photographs on the table in front of her. Two were enlarged, cleaned-up pictures from his mobile phone, taken from the porch in Märsta. The third was a press photograph that Syl had only just got hold of. It showed Nathalie Fredén even more clearly. Even the brand of her bicycle was clearly visible. Rex.

'Is this you?' Berger asked.

'It looks like it,' Fredén said calmly.

'Do you know where that is?'

'Not really. I cycle a lot. It looks like it's raining.'

'You cycle a lot?'

'Yes. I like cycling.'

'What, thirty kilometres to Märsta in the rain?'

'Märsta? OK, now I know where that is. The police were there. And the media. This is a press photograph, isn't it?'

'What were you doing there?'

'Cycling. A Sunday excursion north of the city.'

'And what happened?'

'I saw flashing blue lights and followed them.'

'Has that happened before?'

'What?'

'That you saw flashing blue lights and followed them?'

'Now and again, yes. When you cycle as much as I do.'

'Can you give me an example?'

'No idea. Now and again.'

'Here, for instance?'

And then three photographs from the wintry forest between Karlskoga and Kristinehamn, all with Nathalie Fredén and her bicycle in their centre.

'That looks like winter,' she said calmly.

Berger looked at her very seriously for the first time. If he had ever been under the illusion that this would be easy – which he probably hadn't – then that illusion had long since blown away now. He would have to delve deeper.

He looked into her blue eyes and tried to get a real sense of who she was. Either she lied very easily, always had a good excuse to hand, or she was almost implausibly naive. It was incredibly difficult to determine which.

Then it dawned on him. He'd had an idea at the back of his mind, but this was the first time he managed to formulate it. Nearly two years ago she had made preparations to end up here, right here, when she gave her name to the reporter. Now he understood. *She is where she wants to be.* But why?

In a different world he might even have realised how beautiful she was. And now, when he understood how difficult this was going to be, how deep he would have to delve to get anywhere, he realised also that he would have to get to know her better. This was his only chance.

'Yes,' he said. 'It's winter.'

'I don't know where that is,' she said. 'A lot of unexpected things happen when I'm out cycling. That's part of the charm of it.'

'Of these long bike rides?'

'Yes. They can take weeks. I cycle all round Sweden.'

'Aimlessly?'

'Mostly, yes. I try to be a free person.'

'A free person.'

'Yes, actually. I don't think you're as cynical as you sounded when you said that.'

'Why not?'

'It shows in your eyes.'

'So you consider yourself to be a free person?'

'We all follow a whole load of laws, not least the laws of

nature. No one can be properly free. But you can seek freedom. That's much harder than being cynical. Cynicism is the cheap version.'

'A whole load of laws . . . Financial as well?'

'Yes, those too.'

'You have no income to speak of, no Swedish bank account. How do you finance your free life?'

'It doesn't cost that much. If it did, I wouldn't be free. And I was given my bicycle by an ex.'

'But a flat near Odenplan costs money.'

'I inherited it from my grandfather.'

'What was his name?'

'Arvid Hammarström.'

'And your parents?'

'John and Erica Fredén.'

'Erica, born Hammarström?'

'Yes, but . . . '

'Where were you born?'

'Umeå.'

'Which primary school did you go to?'

'The Mariehem School, I think it was called. But why do you want to know so much about me? I thought this was all about that.'

She pointed at the photograph of Ellen Savinger.

There was something in the gesture that really got to him. Nonchalance, ambivalence, whatever. He shut his eyes for a couple of seconds. Controlled himself. As best he could. The tick of his watch seemed to grow stronger. It was as if his wrist were on fire.

He said, with as much restraint as he could muster: 'She isn't a "that". She's a girl with her whole life ahead of her. She's spent three weeks shut inside that fucking house in Märsta, captive in that horrific basement, subjected to a whole load of unfathomable shit. I emerged from that basement and you were standing outside afterwards. And in Kristinehamn some eight months earlier, when the police thought that another fifteen-year-old girl had been buried in the forest, you were standing there as well. And you were standing *here*, outside a biker gang's clubhouse in Västerås a year before that, when yet another fifteen-year-old girl was thought to be held, like a lamb to the slaughter, on the premises. How the hell can you just happen to be standing there at all three crime scenes?'

All the pictures had been revealed. All the cards were on the table. Yet really just *one*, one card that he had staked everything on. He ought to get something out of it, a reaction at the very least. He had to get through the wall. Even a small crack would do.

He focused all of his attention on her. She maintained a neutral expression, yet there was still something playing across her face. That type of reaction wasn't particularly common in interview rooms, but he had seen it on a few rare occasions. It had its own special place in the internal register of human reactions that Sam Berger had compiled over the years. He just couldn't quite place it.

It was a long way from Västerås and the television camera which had unwittingly captured her two decisions. On that occasion a lot had played out on her forehead. Two clear decisions. The first was whether or not to speak to local media at all, the second whether or not to say her name.

If she hadn't done that a year and a half ago they wouldn't be sitting there. Neither of them.

No, this reaction was much smaller, yet unmistakable. Not on her forehead but under her eyes.

Her brow was quite smooth.

'Botox?' Berger said instinctively.

Nathalie Fredén looked at him. For the first time there was no immediate response. And no perceptible reaction.

'Your forehead,' Berger went on, touching the top of her face with his index finger. 'It was much more expressive in Västerås.'

'Västerås?'

'You know what I'm talking about. The interview with local television in Västerås. When you made your decision.'

'I have no idea what you're talking about.'

'Of course not,' Berger said, leaning back. 'So it is Botox? Why would you need that? Why would you want to be less expressive?'

Now she just shook her head.

He waited and reflected. What was the reaction he had seen? He ran it through his internal register. What had he said that had prompted that reaction? A fusillade of information. *When* had the reaction happened? When precisely?

He found the right location in the archive. It was a reaction that said she really wanted to comment on something he had said. She was forcing herself not to. Comment? No, not comment. Correct. Yes, that was it. He had said something that she wanted to *correct*. He felt like breaking off at once to go and check the video recording of the interrogation.

The Botox discussion was just a way of getting time to think.

Even so, she replied: 'Botox wasn't produced to make skin smoother. Not to start with.'

'It's a neurotoxin, isn't it?' he said without really caring.

'A diluted form of the botulinum toxin,' she said. 'It's one of the strongest poisons known to man. One millilitre would be enough to kill everyone in Sweden.'

'And people inject that just a centimetre away from their eyes?'

'Botox was originally used to treat the spasms associated with brain damage.'

She was talking. She was talking of her own volition. That in itself was something new. He let her go on.

'And of course to treat migraines,' she continued.

He looked at her altered fae. 'So, migraines? You had Botox injected into your forehead to treat migraines?'

'Yes,' she said.

'Hmm,' he said. 'Serious migraines?'

'Fairly.'

He cast a pointed glance at the video camera in the left-hand corner of the ceiling. Deer had probably already picked up on it. He lowered his head and met Nathalie's eyes.

'What did I get wrong earlier?' he finally asked.

'What do you mean?'

He sighed and tried again, but after that he'd have to move on. 'I said a whole load of things about how you just happened to be standing there at the three crime scenes. I got something wrong. What was it?'

When she merely looked at him with that same smooth forehead, he slapped some more photographs on the table.

'March last year, fifteen-year-old girl missing, the police mount an operation in Västerås – bang, there you are. February this year, fifteen-year-old girl missing, police mount an operation in Kristinehamn – bang, there you are. Yesterday morning, fifteen-year-old girl missing, police mount an operation in Märsta – bang, there you are. How the hell can you have been in all three places?'

'Coincidence,' Nathalie Fredén said. 'I cycle all over Sweden. That's my life. Sometimes I have to work the odd month here and there, simple office work, but apart from that I keep on the move. Sometimes I run into things. There's nothing strange about that.'

'But do you really not understand that it *is* strange? That it's *seriously* strange? Are you mentally handicapped? Have you been shut away in an institution?'

'Ugh,' she said with distaste and pushed the pictures away.

'I'm serious,' Berger said, taking hold of her wrists. 'You're not in any databases, you live completely outside of society. Your social pattern is that of a criminal, a homeless person, or someone who's mentally ill. But it's all a persona.'

'A what?'

'A persona, a mask. You're pretending to be something you're not.'

'You don't get it,' she said, pulling her hands free. 'You can't handle it. I'm nothing more strange than a free person. That's what I do, I cycle, in complete freedom. I have no credit card, no internet access, no mobile phone. I tried once, I got a mobile phone, tried to join Facebook. But I let it drop. What's the point?'

The terrible thing was that what she was saying was sounding more and more plausible. For the first time a hint of doubt entered Berger's resistant consciousness. Serious migraines, constant cycling all round Sweden, probable first-hand knowledge of mental institutions, the inherited flat, maybe a shoebox full of inherited cash she'd been living off. And then that lame phrase, 'it shows in your eyes'. Taken as a whole, an asocial existence, completely outside of society.

The perfect assistant.

The subordinate helpmeet.

A master's slave.

'Who is he?' Berger exclaimed, standing up. 'Who the hell

is the scum who's got you in his power? Who is it you're ready to lie for? Lie until you're blue in the face? Who's your master, your ruler? Who sent you?'

The door opened behind Berger's back. Deer came in and half whispered in his ear, very slowly: 'Sam, you have an important call.'

She led him out of the interview room through one of the two doors and closed it firmly but gently behind them. Then she turned round in the soundproofed observation room and barked at Samir over at the computer: 'Watch her every move. If she so much as lifts a finger, you rush in.'

Then she fixed her very sharpest look on Berger, shook her head and moved aside. Behind her stood Allan. It was as if his bushy eyebrows were saying: And it was looking so promising.

Berger managed to stop himself exploding, formulated the words very carefully and said: 'You saw where it was heading, Allan.'

'Of course,' Allan said. 'But I also saw that it was heading off the rails. You need to take a break.'

'She's a puppet,' Berger said. 'She has a specially selected, damaged psyche that the Scum is directing from a distance. She's the shell, surrounding another person's will. She was placed here for a reason. Has she been through a metal detector? She could have a whole fucking bomb in her stomach. Or at the very least a transmitter, a recording device.'

'Of course she has,' Allan said.

'Did you spot the three critical moments, Deer?'

'Botox treatment for migraines,' Deer said, looking down at her notepad. 'I've got people on it already. It can't be that common a treatment, and she must have started treatment after her television debut a year and a half ago. And I saw her reaction when you revealed our three crime scenes. Maja and Syl are working on that, trying to find the exact moment the reaction occurred. Because she wanted to *correct* you, didn't she?'

'I've trained you well, Deer,' Berger said.

'You haven't trained me at all. You said three? I'm not sure about the third critical moment. Arvid Hammarström and the inheritance? If that's it, we've got people looking into it. But the Mariehem School was accurate.'

'No,' Berger said. 'I meant the bicycle. Have you found it?'

'Not sure. We've seized three women's Rex bicycles in the vicinity. She didn't have a key to a bike lock on her, and those three were all locked. We're dusting them for prints and comparing them with the photographs.'

'Good,' Berger said. 'She was given the bicycle by an ex. Rex from an ex. With a bit of luck we'll manage to find the ex. And with a bit more luck, the ex is our man.'

'The perp?' Deer exclaimed.

'Check the number on the frame. Maybe we can figure out when and where the bike was bought. And by whom.'

'What the hell is this?' he asked straight out.

Berger in turn was watching Allan. He did look genuinely curious. Had a trace of police instinct returned to the old bureaucrat?

'Samir?' Berger said.

Without taking his eyes from the screen, the young man said: 'What?'

'Strongest impression from the interview?'

Samir looked up and said: 'I'm looking at her now, and I've been looking at her the whole time. If she had a serious mental health condition, wouldn't it be more obvious?'

'There is such a range of disorders,' Berger said.

'I know,' Samir said, gesturing towards the screen. 'But there's nothing. I'm not seeing a troubled soul.'

They gathered round the computer screen, leaning in. Nathalie Fredén was sitting perfectly still at the table in the interview room. There was no movement. It might as well have been frozen.

'No curiosity about the things I left in the room?' Berger asked.

'None,' Samir said. Not a flicker of movement.'

'That in itself strikes me as an indication of mental illness,' Allan said. 'Isn't she just a complete lunatic with a thin veneer of social competence that we simply have to drill through? Isn't that what you were starting to do in there, Sam, before you got overexcited? For my part I don't care if you destroy her. Peel off layer after layer and see how empty she is inside. I can't help wondering if she's a dead end. A psycho who has a habit of showing up in the crowd whenever there's a major operation. She cycles round the country with a police radio at the ready, then dashes off to exciting places to get her pulse racing. Have you actually checked to see how many police photographs she appears in?'

Berger straightened up and stared at the ceiling of the small room.

'*How many*,' he repeated in a completely different voice.

Allan and Samir looked up at him with two different generations' expressions of scepticism. Then Berger's mobile rang. It sounded like a pig, mid-slaughter. He answered it.

'Hello,' a sharp voice said. 'This is Sylvia.'

'Syl,' Berger said. 'What have you got?'

'Maja and I have been scrutinising the recording. We think we've found the moment when Fredén wants to correct you.'

'I'm listening.'

'It's right at the end of your long speech. You start by saying "She's isn't a 'that'. She's a girl with her whole life ahead of her." Do you remember?'

'Vaguely, yes. Go on.'

'Then you put all the pictures on the table and get to Västerås.'

'But it wasn't then?'

'That's the dilemma,' Syl said sharply. 'For a while we thought that was it, when you mentioned the biker gang in Västerås. You hadn't talked about that before. But then we got the impression that it was when you talked about a lamb to the slaughter. Do you remember the phrase?'

'More or less. That was when she reacted?'

'Like I said, we thought so for a while. But then came your last salvo. I quote: "How the hell can you just happen to be standing there at all three crime scenes?" And that's when the reaction actually comes.'

'*How many*,' Berger said, looking up at the ceiling.

'Yes, now that we've looked carefully and compared the results from all four cameras, that seems to have been the moment.'

'More precisely?'

'When you say "all three crime scenes".'

'Interpretation?'

'When you say the number. Three.'

'Yes,' Berger said, clenching his fist.

15

Tuesday 27 October, 01.26

Berger stepped inside after the break imposed on him. The door closed. Nathalie Fredén watched him. Without a word he switched on the recording equipment. The red light came on. He uttered the required phrases and then said: 'Tell me, who did you get your bicycle from?'

'It was a long time ago. I think his name was Charles.'

'Wasn't it an ex? Don't you remember your former lover's name?'

'Like I said, it was a long time ago.'

'But your Rex can't be more than four years old?'

'You really want to talk about my bicycle?'

'I really want to talk about your Rex . . . your ruler, king. That's what I really want to talk about. But we can start somewhere else. Although I can promise that we'll come back to it. Have you ever lived abroad?'

'Abroad? No.'

'Never?'

'No.'

'Where did you disappear to after Year 3 in Mariehem School

in Umeå? According to your teacher, your family was going abroad.'

'I don't know anything about that.'

'No, there's no indication that you actually went. Your parents remained registered at the same address in the forest outside Umeå for another fifteen years. But you vanished from school records. Where did you get to when you were ten years old?'

Nathalie Fredén fell silent and met Berger's gaze in a new way. While he pushed across the enlarged photograph of the ten-year-old Nathalie Fredén, he tried to figure out what it was that felt new.

'Do you recognise yourself?' he asked.

She turned away and stared at the wall beside them.

'That smile,' Berger went on. 'Anyone would think you had your whole life ahead of you, that anything was possible, don't you think? Look at the picture, Nathalie. I want you to remember who you were then. Ten years old. Look at that smile. You were happy. But could you see a future of unlimited possibilities?'

'I don't know what you want.'

'I'm looking at that smile, Nathalie, those disproportionately large front teeth, the sort everyone has when they're ten; those teeth seem to be there to tell the rest of the body: hurry up and catch up with us. But I know that neither you nor I see a future of unlimited possibilities in that smile. It's something else, isn't it? What do you see, Nathalie?'

The same silence. Which was different from the first interview. He went on: 'Just before I came in here the staff at Mariehem School managed to dig out some files from their pre-digital archive. Someone had to physically hunt through a basement up in Västerbotten. Do you know what they found, Nathalie? It wasn't that you moved abroad.'

'I don't know what you're talking about.'

'No. No, of course not. But if I put it like this: in those days there used to be counsellors in schools. Even the occasional school psychologist.'

Nathalie Fredén was present in a different way now; it was as if she was suddenly crash-landing into her own body. She fixed her eyes on him in a way that he hadn't experienced up to now. She became a different person. But she said nothing.

He went on, his eyes on a sheet of paper: 'There are three visits to the counsellor in fairly quick succession, and then – just a few days after the last one – a visit to the school psychologist. That takes place four days before the end of the school year, in June. Then you don't come back for the autumn term, because you've moved abroad, according to your teacher. How much of this do you remember?'

'The betrayal.'

It came so abruptly, so distinctly, with a sharp and very clear stare, straight into Berger's own eyes. He held her gaze for a while, and was then held by hers. He found himself thinking about the balance of power, about the interrogator's indisputable upper hand in the interview room. In the end he looked away and, to his immense irritation, found himself moving his papers around the table.

'Whose betrayal?' he said without raising his eyes.

When she didn't answer he was obliged to look up, ready to regain control of the conversation. But the look in her eyes was too strong, too sharp; it was as if she was delving deep inside him, even though he had no idea why. He had to alter the situation. He let his eyes drift towards the wall instead. She hummed and leaned back hard in her chair, as if she had gained some sort of insight.

'Who betrayed you?' he tried again, looking back at her once more. But she was no longer looking at him, her gaze was turned inward.

He paused for a moment. There had been contact, a strong, peculiar contact, and now it was gone again. He didn't have time to get to the bottom of it, and falling silent was hardly an option. Some sort of breakthrough had taken place, and he had to find his way back to it.

'The school psychologist, a Hans-Ove Carlsson, is dead now,' he said, 'but the counsellor is still alive. It won't take us long to track her down. What's she going to say, Nathalie?'

Fredén sighed heavily and said nothing.

Berger pushed the enlarged photograph of the ten-year-old Nathalie Fredén forward and put another picture next to it.

'The class photo,' he said. 'Your happy smile in context.'

No response at all.

'Group photographs are always interesting,' he went on. 'Even formulaic ones like class pictures. Can they tell you anything about the dynamics within a group? Are the individuals merely positioned by a jaded photographer who once had grand ambitions? Or do these compositions reflect real relationships?'

Still no response, except possibly a hint of derision at the corners of her mouth. He continued: 'There's a tiny gap around you. All the others are standing close together, their bodies touching. But it looks like no one wants to touch you, Nathalie.'

The same unfocused, neutral gaze, now with a trace of scepticism.

'Did your classmates think you were disgusting, Nathalie?' Berger asked gently.

He saw something flare up in her eyes and slowly move towards him. Before it found its target he went on: 'You were ten years old, Nathalie. What had happened to you to make them think you were disgusting?'

A light was shining out from her half-closed eyelids, a tremulous light that for a moment or so replaced all sound.

'You know *exactly* what happened,' she said sharply.

For a fleeting moment Berger felt something course through him. Surprise, yes, definitely, but more than that. Discomfort, a short jolt of discomfort. And something else, something that lingered, a feeling that her words were on a completely different plane to his. He didn't understand who she was, what she was doing, and that was so unusual that for a few moments he actually felt at a complete loss.

Even so, he was on a path, and at the end of it was fifteen-year-old Ellen Savinger, and she was alive, and nothing could make him stray from it.

'I actually think I do,' he said gently. 'What you remember of that time, Nathalie, is the "betrayal", you said that very clearly. I assume that you were betrayed by the world around you, the whole world, from parents to friends to teachers. There wasn't much talk of bullying in those days, Nathalie. A lot of people in the older generation still thought bullying was a useful trial for life as an adult. But you couldn't bear your classmates thinking you were disgusting; you were in such a bad way that you were sent to the counsellor, once, twice, three times, and in the end the counsellor wasn't up to the job and had to send you to the school psychologist. The school psychologist organised a place for you in a private clinic. What sort of place was it, Nathalie?'

But Nathalie Fredén was no longer within reach. She was just staring at the wall.

'You were ten years old,' Berger continued. 'The evidence seems to suggest that you were there for some twenty years.

Then you were suddenly let out into a world you didn't recognise. Everything was unfamiliar. You had become a grown-up in a protected environment, had no contact with the outside world. What did you feel when you got out?'

Fredén turned her gaze towards him, but there wasn't much in it. She said nothing.

He went on: 'During those twenty years your parents had died. Your grandfather died around the time of your release, and in the absence of other heirs he left you not only the flat on Vidargatan but also a tidy sum of money.'

'But you said I didn't have a bank account.'

It came out of nowhere. Berger had pretty much given up all hope of getting any response whatsoever. He touched his ear instinctively, hoping to get additional information quickly. Deer was on the case, and her voice echoed immediately in his ear: 'Shoebox containing a few hundred kronor found under a floorboard in the kitchen in Vidargatan.'

'No bank account, no,' Berger said. 'I don't know if you distrust banks or if you simply don't know how they work. But I'm pleased that you're trying to mislead me with lies. It shows that you're keeping up.'

'Have you really got one of those earpieces?' Nathalie Fredén asked, pointing.

Always poking his ear, Berger thought. Why did he do that? Had she got to him in a way that he couldn't yet recognise? It was an unpleasant feeling. He shook it off, as he managed to shake off most things.

'The money's gone now,' he said. 'There are a few notes left in the shoebox. What do you usually do when the money runs out?'

'Work. Get a shitty temporary job. But we've already talked about that.'

'But you haven't worked in over a year now. And even then you didn't earn anywhere near enough to survive for a whole year.'

'I had some of Grandfather's money left.'

'No, I don't think so; there wasn't that much. Where do you get your money, Nathalie? How do you pay the service charge for the flat, just over two thousand kronor a month? Always paid in cash, at different banks around the city. Are you even the one paying? Is it someone else? Is it the man you got the bicycle from?'

She shook her head, nothing more.

'Who helped you when you got out of the clinic?' he asked.

She didn't answer.

He went on: 'Was it Charles? Who ended up as your boyfriend? The man who gave you your bicycle? Your Rex?'

To make up for the lack of an answer, Deer's voice sounded in his ear: 'A four-year-old Rex has just been identified. Matching prints. Also matches the photographs. We've got the frame number, but we don't know where it was bought and who bought it.'

Berger felt himself nod slightly. He was off balance but didn't really understand how and why. He had to complete his line of questioning, but there was something troubling him. The whole situation troubled him. She was reacting to the wrong things, as if she really did live in a different reality. As if she had an entirely different approach to the truth.

Unless it was a different truth. In a different world, a completely unhinged world.

He said, without much hope: 'Did you have another bicycle before your Rex?'

She had a different light in her eyes. 'I've always cycled.'

And suddenly there was the glimmer of hope. He continued: 'At the clinic as well?'

'I don't know what clinic you're talking about.'

'When you were ten years old and you mum and dad betrayed you and put you in the clinic, did you have a bicycle then?'

'I don't know . . . '

'Perhaps that was the only genuinely nice thing about the clinic? Cycling? Did you cycle much back then?'

'I've always cycled a lot.'

'How did you get your first bicycle when you got out of the clinic? Did you buy it?'

'Yes, with Grandfather's money.'

'What happened to that bicycle?'

'I rode it until it fell apart.'

'And then Charles appeared and gave you another one?'

'I think so.'

'You *think* so?'

'I don't remember. I have a feeling that's what happened.'

'How did you meet Charles?'

'I don't remember. When I was cycling.'

'Was it in the city? In Stockholm?'

'He cycled up beside me at a traffic light, and said my bicycle looked really rubbish.'

'Was that how your relationship began?'

'Yes.'

'Was he kind to you?'

'I got the bicycle . . . '

'And apart from that?'

'I don't know . . . '

'What did you do together? Apart from cycling.'

'We didn't cycle together.'

'But he used to send you out on bike rides, didn't he? Not always short ones, either?'

'I don't know . . . '

'Did you and Charles have a sexual relationship?'

'I don't know . . . '

'Of course you know, Nathalie. Did you have sex?'

'Yes . . . '

'What sort of sex?'

'I don't know . . . Quite . . . hard . . . '

'How do you mean? Did he tie you up? Did he hit you?'

'A bit . . . '

'A bit? Were you a virgin when you got out of the clinic?'

No answer.

He went on: 'So that was it? You didn't know what sex was. You thought it was supposed to be like that. That he was supposed to hit you. And give you orders. That's it, isn't it? He dominated you.'

No answer this time either. Was he losing contact?

'What happened the first time he dominated you?'

'How do you mean?'

Yes. A response. Some sort of response. 'What did he want you to do, Nathalie?'

'I don't want to talk about it.'

'We have two choices, Nathalie. Either we go into detail about what you did in the bedroom, and then you'll have to describe everything in great detail, no matter how intimate or embarrassing it is. Or we talk about what he ordered you to do *outside* the bedroom. Which would you prefer?'

'The second option.'

'Fine,' Berger said. 'What was the first thing he wanted you to do? If we ignore sex?'

'Cycle to a particular place at a particular time.'

'Did he say why?'

'If I was anywhere nearby it would be easy to find. There would be flashing blue lights, and I should follow them.'

'Did he say why?'

'No.'

'Did you understand why?'

'No.'

Berger leaned back.

In his ear he heard a perfectly timed voice: 'Don't touch you ear this time, Sam. I've got Cary here. So you know what's at stake.'

Cary? Berger thought. *Who the hell is Cary?*

'The sound technician,' a male voice explained. 'Comprehensive voice analysis shows that there's a ninety-eight per cent probability that Nathalie Fredén made the call about the house in Märsta under the name Lina Vikström.'

Berger sat quietly and let both the conversation and the information sink in. In the end he thought: *Yes, Deer, I understand what's at stake.*

But he said: 'The first time wasn't Västerås, was it?'

He pushed the picture of the bikers' clubhouse towards Fredén. She looked at it but said nothing.

He went on: 'There were more than three occasions, weren't there? More than three kidnapped fifteen-year-old girls?'

'I don't know anything about any kidnapped girls.'

'I didn't think you did. I thought you were just remote-controlled by your master, an empty shell. But now I know better. When was the first time?'

'I don't keep track of time.'

'But there was at least one occasion before Västerås. Västerås was in March, a year and a half ago. It was winter, a biker gang's clubhouse. You said your name on television. Do you remember?'

'Yes.'

'But Västerås wasn't the first time Charles told you to cycle out to the country to stand by a police cordon. When was the first time?'

'I don't know. It was summer.'

'Summer. And *where* was it?'

'I don't remember. Closer to Stockholm.'

'Try to remember. It's important.'

Nathalie Fredén paused. A real pause, as if to think properly. 'Sollentuna.'

In Berger's ear Deer said: 'We're on it.'

Berger took a deep breath. 'Can you describe what happened on that occasion?'

'Charles told me to cycle there.'

'What did he say exactly?'

'I can't remember that.'

'I think you can. Try. It was the first time. Didn't you wonder why?'

'Yes. But I wasn't allowed to ask.'

'You just had to do what Charles said?'

'Yes, that's what we'd agreed.'

'And what were you supposed to do there?'

'I just had to stand and watch.'

'And whereabouts was it? Do you remember where in Sollentuna?'

'There were big blocks of flats, lots of big blocks of flats. Flashing blue lights in the car park below. They'd cordoned it off. That's where I stood. Not much happened.'

'Lots of big block of flats? Malmvägen? Stupvägen?'

'I don't know the name of the street.'

'Do you remember how you got there? Did you cycle alongside the railway line? Under the motorway?'

'It was over two years ago.'

'You said you don't keep track of time.'

'Yes, beside the railway, under the motorway, up a hill. Then away from the railway. A roundabout. Two. It wasn't far after that.'

'Stupvägen,' Berger said. 'The shopping centre at Helenelund. That fits with the car park under the blocks of flats.'

'There were steps up to the buildings.'

'And when was this? Do you remember anything else, other than that it was summer?'

'No. It was hot.'

Berger stopped. It had been going astonishingly well. But the spark seemed to have gone out in Nathalie Fredén's eyes. He had a few moments left before they needed to take a break. 'What's Charles's surname?'

'Don't remember. Something common.'

'Something-son? Andersson, Johansson?'

'No . . . More like one of those Bergström names . . . '

'Bergström names? You mean like Lundberg, Lindström, Berglund, Sandberg?'

'Yes, but none of those.'

Deer was on the ball and prompted in his ear: 'Sjöberg? Forsberg? Åkerlund?'

Nope.

'Bergman? Lundgren? Holmberg? Sandström?'

No.

'Lindqvist? Engström? Eklund?'

'Maybe,' Fredén said. 'Something like that.'

'Which one?'

'The first.'

'Lindqvist?'

'But not quite . . . '

'Lundqvist? Lindgren?'

'He said it should have an h at the end.'

'An h? Strömbergh? Lindbergh?'

'Yes, that was it. Lindbergh. With an h.'

Berger fell back in his chair with a deep sigh. 'Charles Lindbergh,' he said in an American accent. 'There you go. Lucky Lindy. *The Spirit of St. Louis.* Did you ever see the name Charles Lindbergh written down? Did you ever see his driving licence or passport?'

'No. But he was very particular about the h.'

'I can imagine,' Berger said. 'Charles Lindbergh was an American who was the first man to fly across the Atlantic. In 1927, to be precise. Your master stole an existing identity and made it his own. Just like you did with Lina Vikström.'

'What?'

'We know you made the call saying that you'd seen Ellen Savinger in a house in Märsta. You assumed the role of a neighbour, Lina Vikström, who was away travelling. You know more than you're letting on, Nathalie.'

'I don't know what you're talking about.'

'No,' Berger said. 'Of course you don't.'

Then he pressed a button on his mobile phone. It said, in a female voice: *'Look, I'm pretty sure I saw her just now, you know, her, that girl, through the window . . . Well, I'm not sure it was her, but she had that thing, I don't know, that pink leather strap round her neck with that crooked cross, the Greek one, I don't know if it's Orthodox, but she's a genuine blonde, for God's sake, can't have any Greek roots.'*

Berger pressed the button again and it fell silent.

He sat for a while and just looked at the woman who went by the name of Nathalie Fredén. She didn't meet his gaze. He tried to get all the information – everything that had been said there in the interview room, and everything they knew from elsewhere – to fit together. To form a unified whole. It wasn't possible. It simply wasn't possible.

'It's now been scientifically proven that this is your voice, Nathalie,' he said in the end.

She wouldn't look at him.

He carried on: 'Even so, the person who called the police and said that is a completely different person from the one I've met here. Which makes me think that this is a role as well, just like Lina Vikström was a role. You're someone else altogether.'

She was still looking away.

'I want you to look at me now, Nathalie,' he said calmly. 'I want you to look me in the eye.'

Still nothing.

'Now,' he said. 'Do it now.'

Slowly she looked towards him. In the end he was looking straight into those blue eyes. Eyes could conceal things, but they could never lie, in his experience. So what was he seeing now? Something neutral, apparently untroubled, and certainly beyond reach. This person was completely different from the person he had believed her to be. The one he had been lulled into believing in.

Had allowed himself to be lulled into believing in.

'You called to tell us about the house in Märsta when Charles Lindbergh – or Erik Johansson, as we know him – had already abandoned it four days before. Why did you wait four days? Why did he want you to wait four days?'

'Erik Johansson?'

'Why did you wait four days? Why did you have to stand outside the cordon this time, in Märsta?'

No answer. Her expression suggested that a frown would have appeared in her forehead if the Botox hadn't prevented it.

'If you weren't just reading out loud when you called the police, Nathalie, then what you say proves that you not only knew that Ellen Savinger was in the house, but also that you had access to information that no one but the police and the perpetrator were aware of. No one apart from us knew about the pink leather strap with the Orthodox cross. Just us and the Scum.'

'Scum?'

'Charles Lindbergh and Erik Johansson are merely aliases. His real name is the Scum. And you know that too. It's not as if he was nice to you. So tell me.'

'Tell you what?'

'Have you been inside the house in Märsta? Did you see Ellen sitting there chained up and bleeding? Did you see her scrape the nails off her fingers and toes on the ice-cold cement floor? Did you help to torture her?'

'No! No, I don't know what you're talking about.'

'Yes, you do. You know exactly what I'm fucking talking about. That's quite enough bullshit now. Did you help to torture her?'

'Stop it.'

'Stop it? Stop it?'

'Sam,' a voice said calmly and quietly in his ear.

That was all it took. Berger fell silent. He felt time pass, his heart's sharp stabs at itself. Always one beat closer to death.

Always.

'Tell me about the phone call,' he said calmly.

'I didn't make a phone call,' she said.

'You don't understand, Nathalie. We *know* you made that phone call. We *know* you were playing a role, and with a lot of flair, by the way. That's not what I'm asking you. Just tell me about the phone call.'

She sat in silence. He let her, even though he couldn't really tell which direction she would take.

Eventually she said: 'I didn't make a phone call.'

He let out a deep sigh and pulled two sketches from a folder. He pushed them towards her. One showed a man in a van in Östermalm. The other was from the person who had seen their odd neighbour on the edge of the forest in Märsta.

'Does either of these drawings look like Charles?'

Nathalie Fredén looked at them and shook her head.

'Not much,' she said.

'OK,' Berger said, pulling the drawings back. 'We're going to take a break now. As soon as I leave the room you'll be joined by a police artist who will help you to come up with a portrait of Charles Lindbergh. And I want you to think about that phone call, and about anything else that springs to mind when you think about him.'

He looked down at his wrist.

A hole had opened up in the pervasive condensation inside his watch. He could see about a third of the top left quadrant of the face. But no hands.

Time was still unfamiliar to him.

16

Tuesday 27 October, 02.42

Everyone wanted to put as much distance between them and the interview room as possible. They gathered round Berger's desk in the far corner of the office. Berger and Deer, Allan and Samir. Much as he would have liked to, Berger couldn't just curl up in a foetal position and try to understand why everything felt so distorted. It had been pretty successful, actually.

The darkness was broken by screen-lit faces. The rain was hammering invisibly but in no way inaudibly against the many windows. It was the middle of the night.

Close to the hour of the wolf.

Samir was fast-forwarding through the recording from the interview room. As he was about to hit *play* Berger put his hand on Samir's. He didn't feel ready, not yet.

Instead Deer said: 'We've found out a number of things. Not least, we have the toxicology analysis from the National Forensic Centre. Ellen Savinger's blood did indeed contain high quantities of an as yet unidentified blood-thinning substance.'

'And you had some homework to do, didn't you, Deer?'

'I know.' Deer sighed. 'Why pump Ellen full of blood

thinners? And I can't come up with any answer except to make her bleed a lot . . . '

'And last a long time,' Berger said. 'Utter torment. What else?'

'A whole list. It's growing all the time. Considering how hard it is to inject Botox to combat the symptoms of migraines, there's a surprising number of people doing it. And bearing in mind that it's the middle of the night, we've had a surprising number of responses to our enquiries.'

'Responses to your enquiries about what, exactly?'

'About female clients in the right age range and in the right time period. We've heard back from a few clinics that seem to work nights. They've probably outsourced their customer service operations to countries where it isn't night.'

'Good,' Berger said. 'Although the big question is what we want all that information for.'

'That's the big question about *all* this,' Allan exclaimed. 'Aren't we complicating things unnecessarily?'

'It's one line of inquiry,' Deer said. 'We need to expand our understanding of who Nathalie Fredén is. The Botox is part of that. The migraines are part of that.'

'It's a fuck of a long shot,' Allan bellowed. 'Surely it's obvious what we're looking at? Occam's razor, for God's sake. Cut away all the dead flesh. The simplest solution often turns out to be the right one.'

'I'm having trouble seeing anything simple here,' Berger muttered.

'She's the murderer, for fuck's sake!' Allan roared.

'To start with you said she was a lunatic, a dead end, a psycho,' Berger said.

'And now it turns out instead that she's a brilliant actor. Who's *playing* a lunatic. You ripped her mask off, Sam. You should have kept up the barrage. Blow after blow. She would have collapsed.'

'If she'd fallen apart I wouldn't have got anything else out of her at all,' Berger said. 'And she was close to collapse at the end. Now we've got another chance, and we're better prepared than ever.'

Allan straightened up and said with the full force of his baritone: 'For God's sake, there is no Charles Lindbergh. She made him up. She's sitting there having fun. This crime isn't in the past. She *didn't* do it. She's *still doing it*. Usually you find yourself interviewing a suspect when the crime has already been committed. Afterwards. Not this time. This is extremely rare. The crime is happening, this very moment. You're sitting there questioning her while she's still committing it. Every second she drags things out means another perverse little bit of sexual gratification for that bitch, and more torment for Ellen Savinger, as well as yet another gob of saliva right in our faces.'

'So now we really do have Sweden's first serial killer in that interview room?'

'Call her whatever the hell you want to. Go up on the roof and scream "serial killer" right across Kungsholmen, across the whole city, I don't care. You were too soft, Sam.'

'Last time I was too pushy. Now I'm too soft. You're a hard boss to please, Allan.'

'I'm going to the toilet,' Allan said and turned away abruptly.

They watched as he was quickly swallowed by the darkness.

'He has a point,' Deer said.

'I know,' Berger muttered. 'Have you got anything else?'

'We know who she bought the bike from. Syl got hold of a register of serial numbers. Something called Wiborg Supplies

Ltd. No idea what that is. Anonymous client, 24 May, three years ago.

'OK. Hmm,' Berger said. 'Sold new?'

'Yes. No trace of the serial number since then.'

'That rings some sort of bell. Wiborg?'

'Isn't that a town in Denmark?' Deer said.

Berger felt himself frowning. 'Go ahead, Samir.'

The recording of the interview began to play.

'The name Charles comes up almost immediately,' Samir said, pointing at the screen.

'A lot of different sides to Charles Lindbergh,' Berger said, asking Samir to pause. 'She's showing off again. *Pretentiously* showing off, Deer. Facts: first to fly across the Atlantic. His son was kidnapped and murdered. Said to have been a Nazi at the start of the war. A notorious womaniser. The kidnap and murder of his son is presumably the most pertinent.'

'I don't think that means a great deal,' Deer said. 'Go on.'

Samir started the film again. Something unidentifiable fell from his beard as he scratched it. 'Childhood. Some peculiar reactions there.'

'Where exactly?' Berger asked.

'There,' Samir said. '"Betrayal."'

'That look,' Deer said. 'She's really staring at you, as if she wants to emphasise the betrayal.'

'Which seemed out of place at the time,' Berger said. 'What do you think about her reaction to the bullying hypothesis? There?'

'Growing disinterest,' Deer said. 'It was hot, then it went cold.'

'Strange,' Berger said simply.

He could have said much more. Unfortunately he couldn't put it into words.

'But there's one more thing,' Samir said.

'The most peculiar,' Deer said.

The film reached the class photograph, Berger's comments on the gap around the ten-year-old Nathalie. Then he said: *'You were ten years old, Nathalie. What had happened to you to make them think you were disgusting?'*

And Fredén said very sharply: *'You know* exactly *what happened.'*

Samir paused.

'What's going on here?' Deer mused.

'It's like you were there in Umeå all those years ago,' Samir said.

'What do you mean?' Berger said.

'It just felt so . . . personal,' Samir said.

'I agree,' Berger said. 'And I've never even been to sodding Umeå.'

'It doesn't make sense,' Deer said. 'It means something else.'

'And it's driving me mad,' Berger said.

The trio stared for a while at the dead screen.

Then Berger said: 'Run that sequence again.'

'You were ten years old, Nathalie. What had happened to you to make them think you were disgusting?'

And then Fredén's sharp retort: *'You know* exactly *what happened.'*

Samir paused again.

'Bloody hell,' Berger said, let out a deep sigh. 'Keep going.'

Now his on-screen self was talking about returning to the world outside after twenty years in the clinic. He moved on to the inheritance, her inheritance from her grandfather. The reaction: *'But you said I didn't have a bank account.'*

'If she is playing a role,' Deer said, 'then this is where she falls out of character.'

The film kept rolling.

'Fast-forward,' Berger said.

Samir clicked ahead until Deer put her hand on his. The film slowed to normal speed and Nathalie Fredén said: *'I don't remember. Closer to Stockholm.'*

Berger said: *'Try to remember. It's important.'*

After an unusually long pause Nathalie Fredén said: *'Sollentuna.'*

'How are we getting on with Sollentuna?' Berger asked, speaking over the recording.

'Nothing yet,' Deer said. 'Syl's working on it. If a fifteen-year-old girl disappeared there she'll find it.'

'If that's true, then I managed to miss it. It must be hidden behind something else. Look for other crimes in Helenelund the summer before last.'

'That's a pretty wide search, I promise you. But what struck me most about that was your in-depth knowledge of Sollentuna.'

Deer pointed at the screen. Berger was just saying: *'Stupvägen. The shopping centre at Helenelund. That fits with the car park under the blocks of flats.'*

Berger nodded. 'I grew up there.'

Then Allan returned, smelling of smoke. Berger had just been thinking to himself that it was remarkable Allan had never smoked a single cigarette in his life. He chuckled as he detected a smell of wet fabric alongside the smoke. In all likelihood Allan hadn't been to the toilet at all, but on one of Police Headquarters' smoking balconies. He was soaked.

Berger saw a pool of water start to form around Allan's beautifully polished shoes, and something fell into place inside him.

When you're out in the rain you get wet.

He took out his mobile phone and swiped to find the most

recent photograph. Nathalie Fredén standing inside the front door of her flat on Vidargatan, having just switched the light on. And the floor around her feet was completely dry. Not a single raindrop shimmered on her off-white raincoat. It was completely dry.

Micrometeorology.

'OK,' he said, getting to his feet. 'My turn to go to the toilet.'

He left the office and hurried down the stairs and along the deserted corridors. After a few more sets of stairs and corridors he reached the media room and stormed through it. He yanked open one of the inner doors.

Syl looked up from her computer screens with her thin hair sticking up above a pair of bloodshot eyes and said, actually sounding surprised: 'Sambo? Aren't you in the interview room?'

'Later,' Berger said. The office chair next to Syl had been reclined as far as it would go, and on it was a Winnie-the-Pooh pillow and duvet. A small head with thin, mousy hair stuck out from the gap between them. The little panting breaths had a dampening effect on Berger's agitated state.

'My daughter, Moira,' Syl said, smiling a smile that Berger had never seen before. 'I had to bring her in with me; there's been a hell of a lot of overtime lately.'

'I didn't even know you were married,' Berger whispered, bewildered.

'Is that obligatory?' Syl said with a wry smile. 'You and Freja were never married, were you?'

Berger looked at the peacefully sleeping child and couldn't help smiling softly. Whoever the father was, his genes hadn't stood a chance. Moira was the spitting image of her mother, Sylvia Andersson.

'But Syl,' Berger exclaimed. 'How old is she?'

'Five,' Syl said. 'Don't tell Allan.'

'The day I start gossiping to Allan you'll know I'm just seconds away from smelling burning hair,' Berger said. 'She's beautiful, take good care of her.'

Syl looked at him for a moment. Something like sympathy appeared on her face. It disappeared as she said: 'What did you want, Sambo?'

'Yes, what did I want?' Berger said, unable to take his eyes off Moira. 'Oh yes, have you checked out Wiborg Supplies?'

'I think Maja's doing that. But where the bike was bought is hardly that big a deal . . . '

'It's just that Wiborg sounds familiar somehow. It's not ringing any bells?'

Syl slowly shook her head.

'Can you do an anonymous search?' Berger said.

Syl looked distinctly disapproving. 'What did we agree when I helped you dig out the investigations into Julia and Jonna?'

'That it was the last time you'd do anything illicit for me. But I also happen to know that not only can you do it, but you also find it quite exciting.'

'It's risky . . . '

'Do it. I'll take any flak.'

He walked out, taking one last look at Moira's peacefully sleeping form. He went and got his car from the deserted police garage and drove through the black, rain-drenched city. He reached Vidargatan, and double-parked as close as he could. To save getting wet.

As if that were possible.

It was just after three o'clock when he entered the stairwell, turned the lights on and climbed the stairs. The door was sealed with police tape. He looked at it for a moment; there was no sign that it had been touched, let alone broken. He tore it off, picked the lock, stepped inside and stopped in the darkness behind the door, caught his breath.

Yes, he could tell. Someone had been there. But that wasn't enough, obviously.

He switched his torch on and shone it over the walls of the small hallway. Now that he knew what he was looking for it was easy enough to find. It hadn't been there the last time he was in the flat.

The centimetre-wide hole just above the door to the kitchen seemed to radiate a sort of luminous darkness. A few tiny grains of white lay on the threshold. Berger crouched down and ascertained that it was plaster. He found a stool and climbed on top of it. Poked the hole.

Yes, there had almost certainly been a camera there. A microscopic camera.

He climbed down and went into the kitchen. There were barely any yellow leaves left on the big aspen tree in the courtyard, but even so their rustling seemed to drown out the rain. He sat down at the kitchen table and looked out into the hall, trying to process the fact that it was only a few hours since he had last sat there. It felt like a lifetime ago.

OK, think. Think, at last. Undisturbed.

In the solitude that he knew he always needed.

Nathalie Fredén was dry when she walked through the door. She couldn't have come from the street. She must have come from somewhere inside the building. She must have been sitting somewhere in the building waiting until – via the hidden camera – she saw the police enter her flat. Then she headed towards it and was seen through the windows of the stairwell by the surveillance officers in their car. She could have been operating on her own at that point.

But not now that the camera had been removed.

That had been done by someone else.

Someone who had presumably been waiting with her in another flat.

Where they could well have had a third guest.

Ellen Savinger.

But why would Nathalie Fredén hand herself over to the police? Why would she walk straight into the trap?

In a nutshell: what did Charles or Erik or the Scum have in mind by sacrificing his slave?

A sacrifice which had been planned for more than two years.

There was clearly something that didn't make sense.

And Sam Berger couldn't figure it out.

Was he being selectively blind? Was he stuck in a corner, unable to see a truth that was obvious from every other angle?

He stood up. Lit his way to the front door. Went out into the stairwell again. Found the glowing red switch. Went down the stairs. Stopped in front of the list of residents. He read the names, nothing that stood out. There were ten fairly common Swedish surnames, and one of them concealed the flat where that bastard and Fredén had sat and waited, just a few metres away, just a few hours ago.

If Berger had been firing on all cylinders they would have had the bastard, all wrapped up in a box.

Literally.

Of course there was a slim chance that he was still there, that he was still in one of the flats, just a few metres away from Berger. At that very moment. But it wasn't very likely. Obviously Berger would see to it that all the flats were searched as soon as possible, but the bastard was probably gone. Leaving just a faint but lingering laugh.

Why had he thrown Nathalie Fredén to the wolves?

Berger aimed his mobile phone at the list of names and took

a picture. It suddenly started to sound like a piglet being ritually slaughtered.

He quickly silenced the ring tone and was about to whisper back to Deer, who had presumably begun to suspect that he wasn't in the toilet after all. But then he saw that it was an unknown number beginning 0915. Before he got the door open and threw himself out into Vidargatan he also noticed that the time was now 3.27. The hour of the wolf, and the rain was still tipping down relentlessly.

'Yes,' he answered, pulling his jacket collar up. 'Sam Berger.'

'I'm sorry to call at such an unusual hour,' said a female, elderly voice in a northern accent.

'Who is this?' Berger asked.

'They said it was urgent, and I never sleep very well after three in the morning anyway.'

'Who am I speaking to?'

'Yes, sorry,' the tremulous voice said. 'My name is Britt-Marie Bengtsson. I'm calling from Bastuträsk.'

'I see,' Berger said impatiently. 'Who told you it was urgent?'

'The police in Umeå. Apparently they've been trying to reach me since last night. They gave me Constable Berger's telephone number.'

Berger had a feeling that a penny should be dropping. Sadly there was no penny, and no dropping.

'I'm listening,' he said simply.

'I worked as a counsellor in Mariehem School in Umeå in the late eighties and early nineties.'

'Ah,' Berger said, hearing the rattle as the penny finally dropped.

'I understand that you're interested in one of my former clients?'

'If you call a ten-year-old girl a client.'

'What would you suggest, constable? Patient? Pupil?'

'Anything but constable. That title disappeared from the police force in the early seventies.'

'Which says quite a lot about my age,' Britt-Marie Bengtsson said calmly.

'They evidently had quite a job finding you,' Berger said.

'I remarried and moved to Bastuträsk after I retired.'

'OK,' Berger said. 'As you know, this concerns Nathalie Fredén, who was in Year 3 at Mariehem School in the late 1980s.'

'Poor Nathalie, yes,' Britt-Marie Bengtsson said. 'She came to see me because she was being badly bullied in class.'

'That's what I imagined,' Berger said. 'What happened?'

'It remains a mystery why some people are picked out as victims, I'm afraid. Nathalie came to me of her own volition. She wasn't at all happy. We met a few times, but nothing I was able to suggest seemed to help; the situation just got worse and worse. I had to turn to Hans-Ove for help.'

'The school psychologist, yes,' Berger said. 'And evidently he managed to find a place for Nathalie in a psychiatric clinic.'

'Hans-Ove?' Britt-Marie Bengtsson exclaimed. 'Really? Well, I never. He wasn't exactly the most sensitive psychologist in the country . . . '

'You didn't know about that?'

'No, and I don't understand how things could have turned out the way they did in that case. Mind you, that's no guarantee. The point was that her mother worked in the registry office, and back then all the records were kept manually. You could say it was before the age of computers. At least, they weren't widespread.'

'Wait a moment,' Berger said, stopping on the pavement. The rain was lashing against him.

'I'm waiting,' Britt-Marie Bengtsson said obediently.

'Just tell me what happened in your own words.'

'Yes, well, it was all very unofficial. For the mother's sake we accepted the official story. That little Nathalie had moved abroad to live with relatives.'

'What are you saying?'

'Nathalie Fredén is dead,' Britt-Marie Bengtsson said. 'She committed suicide that summer.'

17

Tuesday 27 October, 03.58

Deer was waiting for him outside the main entrance to Police Headquarters. It was almost four o'clock in the morning, and her presence was balm for the soul. She didn't say anything, but her brown eyes – which bore absolutely no resemblance to a deer's – were sharper than ever. From her pocket she fished an earpiece that she fastened to his right ear a little too carefully. Then she looked him in the eye, acknowledging the less than perfect circumstances, and gave him a little pat on the cheek. Then she was gone. Without a word.

He didn't want to have to pass his colleagues in the control room. He only wanted to meet one person. And she didn't exist.

So he stood in the gloomy corridor, entirely alone, in front of a characterless door. His clothes were dripping.

He took a deep breath, ran his card through the reader and tapped in the code.

Nathalie Fredén wasn't alone in the interview room. A guard was standing by the wall, and at the desk sat a woman with a laptop. When she saw Berger she sent an email with the characteristic little whooshing sound, closed the computer, then stood up and left with a nod, closely followed by the guard.

There was a ping from Berger's own reserve laptop, which was facing away from Fredén. Before he sat down he opened the newly arrived email. In contained a sketch. The male face looked like an utterly bland mixture of the two older pictures of Erik Johansson. He glanced at the equipment on the side table and noted that the light was already glowing red. He turned the laptop round and sat down.

'So you're seriously claiming that this is your version of Charles?'

'It's not easy,' Nathalie Fredén said.

'Especially if the whole thing is a lie.'

She looked at him. Her eyes were sharp but expressionless.

'Maybe you spent more time looking at his cock than his face,' Berger said, slamming the laptop closed.

'What?' Nathalie Fredén said.

'The show is over,' Berger said. 'Nice performance. But now it's over.'

She watched him, and suddenly he found himself wondering how he could ever have been taken in by her feigned naivety. The look in her eyes now was something entirely different.

'How come you were completely dry when you came into your flat earlier this evening? It was pouring outside.'

'Was I dry?'

'Bone dry. Like your performance. Your neighbours on Vidargatan aren't going to be too delighted when the police – as we speak, in fact – wake them up to find out which flat you were hiding in while you waited. The real question is whether or not you were alone.'

She went on looking at him. She said nothing. He didn't like that look.

'What do you have to say about that?' he asked.

'I don't understand. I came home. You were sitting at my

kitchen table. Two men came in from behind and threw themselves on me.'

'But you were dry when you came in. You came from another flat in the building. Who was with you, watching the feed from the surveillance camera in the hall?'

'Was there a surveillance camera? In my flat?'

'It's gone now. Charles came to get it. Then he went home to Ellen and carried on torturing her.'

'There was a surveillance camera inside my flat and you didn't spot it?'

And that was when he saw the smile in the left-hand corner of her mouth.

Everything went black inside him. The way it occasionally did. It was something that came from deep down. He had learned to control it, but it demanded absolute stillness, what used to be called counting to ten. When he was younger he would sometimes wake up with busted knuckles and loose teeth, once with half his bicep bitten off.

The fucking bitch had been toying with him the whole time. He wanted to lash out. Hard. Wipe her out.

Instead he went into the darkness. Found a calm point. Returned to the still point of the turning world. Saw Marcus and Oscar in front of him. Remembered what sort of person he had been. Wanted to be that person again, to take strength from that, from the depths.

Time passed. He felt her eyes drill into his downturned head. Then he looked up again and said with studied calm: 'One beautiful day nearly a quarter of a century ago, a young girl went up to the hayloft of the farm where she lived with her parents. She'd rigged up a pitchfork so that it was pointing straight up, firmly anchored between the floorboards. Calmly and methodically she made her way up the steep ladder to the hayloft, and instead of jumping into the hay and bursting out laughing, she jumped straight onto the pitchfork. The doctors concluded that she lived another half an hour.'

Fredén's gaze didn't flinch at all, her face showed no emotion.

Berger went on: 'The farm was outside Umeå, the girl was ten years old, and her name was Nathalie Fredén. She simply didn't want to be alive any more.'

He looked down again, at the floor, looked deep down. Rage was building up inside him, red hot, white hot. He stood up quickly, grabbed hold of the laptop, heard it crunch between his fingers, felt the scabs on his right knuckles crack, lurched across the table and roared in a voice he hadn't heard for years: 'Who the hell are you really?'

She was no longer looking at him. Her gaze was steady, but focused elsewhere. Berger heard Deer talking soothingly in his ear, and he tore the earpiece out.

Then he saw what Nathalie Fredén was looking at. A glowing red light. Their eyes met briefly. The air between them was toxic.

He threw his right hand out towards the switch. Blood spattered the wall. The little red light went out.

Nathalie Fredén leaned towards him and snarled: 'Trust me, you don't want to know who I am.'

The door from the control room opened. Deer and Allan rushed in. Berger picked up the laptop and sent it crashing against the wall. Its keys shot across the interview room.

'Take this piece of shit down to the cells,' Berger yelled. 'Total isolation, no contact with anyone. Now!'

Then he stormed out. He landed with a thud on his desk chair. Sat still in the darkness. Staring into space.

Soon he felt a light hand on his shoulder. After the initial irritation the hand connected directly with his heart, took hold of it, calmed it.

'I feel the same, Sam,' Deer said. 'She's bloody clever.'

'Far too clever, for fuck's sake,' Berger snapped. 'She's a fucking professional. That's the missing piece.'

He stood up. Realisations shot wordlessly through him.

'Stay here,' he said, and walked out. He ran through corridors and down stairs. Completely out of breath he ran through the media room and opened the door to Syl's cubbyhole. Five-year-old Moira was sleeping just as peacefully as she had been before – she didn't seem to have moved in her bed fashioned from a reclined office chair – but her mother looked different. Syl looked pale, her thin hair hanging in clumps, and she seemed to have been waiting for him for a long time.

'You bastard,' she said.

'Wiborg Supplies Ltd,' he said. 'What the hell is it?'

'It's . . . not good.'

'I bloody well knew I'd heard it before somewhere. The Security Service?'

'I don't know if it *is* the Security Service, but it's where the Security Service's agents get their material. They've got everything. And by that I mean everything.'

'Even bicycles made by a mediocre brand like Rex. The Security Service's fucking undercover agents. Fuck!'

Syl nodded and looked shaken. 'When I made my way in through a hidden back door I found a whole series of anomalies. I presume that's to do with the fact that the Security Service split from the Police Authority on 1 January. The whole set-up seemed rather chaotic. The whole network's security was pretty weak, and I was able to work my way back through time.'

'Anomalies?'

'First and foremost a list,' Syl said quietly. 'Just a few clicks away. Clicks that probably mean the end of my career. Or worse . . . '

'Come on, Syl. A list?'

'The identities of their agents. Divided into "internal resources" and "external resources".'

'What the hell?' Berger exclaimed. 'They've got a *list*? What sort of amateur crap is that?'

'Christ . . . I think I was sufficiently camouflaged,' Syl groaned, glancing in terror at her sleeping daughter. 'I must have been sufficiently camouflaged. There can't be any footprints. There can't be.'

Berger breathed out. Looked around. Saw nothing. Didn't even see Moira in the stretched-out office chair. Definitely didn't see that she had opened her eyes and was looking at him as if he were something from a nightmare.

'OK,' he said. 'OK, calm down, Syl, take a few deep breaths and all that sort of thing. We'll have to make the best of the situation. Have you got that bloody Botox list here?'

'What? What are you on about now?'

'Botox. The list of clients who've had Botox injections to treat migraines. That's the only thing that can't be fake. No wrinkles on her forehead. No one could fake that.'

'OK. Yes, it's here. What exactly do you want?'

'Cross-check the Botox list with the list of agents.'

'Ah,' Syl said, a hint of colour returning to her face. She typed quickly, then abruptly let go of the keyboard.

'What is this, Sambo? Is Nathalie Fredén from the Security Service? An agent?'

'I don't know,' Berger said. 'I have no fucking clue.'

They looked at each other for a moment. Then the computer let out a bleep. Syl turned sharply back towards it and typed some more.

'I've actually got a name,' she said in a thin voice. 'From "internal resources". Started Botox treatment for chronic migraines at something called the Eriksberg Clinic. April, eighteen months ago. Female, thirty-seven years old.'

'What does "internal resources" mean? Is she on the payroll?'

'Yes, "external" can be anything from mercenaries to pickpockets. "Internal" is police officers who work undercover. But in this case she also works *with* Internal.'

'Now I'm not following.'

'With Internal. Internal Investigations.'

Berger felt he was in free fall. There was no protection, no solid ground anywhere. The claustrophobic little room started to spin, and from the edges of his dizziness he saw Nathalie Fredén's eyes focusing very distinctly on the little red light. He saw her lean towards him and heard her snarl: 'Trust me, you don't want to know who I am.'

And everything fell into place. Almost everything.

'OK,' he said. 'OK. What's her name?'

'Molly Blom. Originally an actress, in fact.'

'Home address?'

'Sam . . . '

'Is there a home address?'

'Stenbocksgatan 4, Östermalm.'

Berger walked around Syl's little room, filled with the smell of human beings. He was breathing heavily, trying to think. It didn't really work. Even so, he said: 'You need to get rid of every last trace, Syl. Nothing must lead back to you. This isn't about you, and I won't mention you. Get rid of it all, and go back to the daily grind. And take it nice and easy.'

'But what the hell is this all about?' Syl exclaimed.

'It's about me,' Berger said, and walked out.

The last thing he saw was five-year-old Moira's inquisitive eyes staring out from her improvised bed. They followed him through a Stockholm in which the rain refused to stop tormenting him. There was still no trace of any dawn. It was just as dark as earlier in that peculiar, impossibly long night.

Berger's car threw cascades of water at the city's few nocturnal pedestrians. He spent more time looking in the rear-view mirror than ahead. So far he couldn't see anything.

But he realised they were there.

18

Tuesday 27 October, 04.47

Stenbocksgatan was a forgotten side street between Engelbrektsgatan and Eriksbergsgatan, right next to Humlegården. He parked a couple of blocks away and soon found number 4, an imposing brick facade with bay windows. The actual entrance was low and not particularly difficult to get into. As he put the lock-pick back in his pocket he looked around the rain-streaked darkness of the street.

Nothing.

Even so, he knew his time was limited.

Answers, he needed answers. He wasn't sure if he could formulate a single question, but he knew he'd recognise an answer. Perhaps the answer would formulate the question for him. Anything at all that could turn the tide. Because his life was on its way to becoming a different life.

He just didn't understand why.

He quickly found the name Blom on the list of residents and set off up the unremarkable stairs. He had his lock-pick out again as he walked up the last few steps. He turned and looked back. He had left some serious puddles behind him.

As if that made the slightest difference, he thought as he fiddled with the pick.

The person who lived there was no ordinary citizen; he felt that at once. The locks were unusually difficult to pick, three of them, one on top of the other. For a fleeting moment he actually feared he wasn't going to succeed, for the first time in his career. But then the third and final lock clicked and the door slid open. He closed it behind him, locked it securely and stood still for a moment. He looked at the pile of post by his feet. Two days' worth of newspapers, no more. Molly Blom had been home two days ago. A couple of windowed envelopes, nothing personal.

The flat was scarcely more furnished than Vidargatan, but the atmosphere was completely different. Where Vidargatan gave off a sense of abandonment, Stenbocksgatan seemed to be a lived-in, almost comfortable abode. The occupant was happy there, if she was actually capable of feeling happy anywhere in the world.

He didn't really know where that impression came from, but he decided to validate it. He validated all his impressions, storing them up in case they could serve as ammunition during the undoubtedly less than pleasant days ahead.

The kitchen seemed to have been refurbished recently, not cheaply, and of course it was clinically clean. He opened the fridge but all he found was a large selection of protein drinks and some cut fruit wrapped in cling film.

That was the overriding impression as he walked through the two-room flat: order, cleanliness, neatness, absolute control.

In the living room was a perfectly white sofa. He ran his hand over the soothing and doubtless very expensive fabric.

Anyone daring to have a white sofa had to be certain of being immaculate. On the surface. And probably not have many visitors. Or at least carefully selected ones, just as clean, just as proper. If there were any lovers, then they were *neat* lovers.

The bathroom seemed almost sterile, including the obviously expensive spray shower, and everything smelled faintly perfumed with a sophisticated scent. On a chest of drawers in the airy, fresh bedroom were a number of framed photographs. He picked them up, one after the other. The first was of three people wearing bathing suits with exactly the same striped pattern. Between two beaming and very evidently upper-middle-class parents stood a thin girl of about ten – the age when the real Nathalie Fredén had killed herself – and there were certainly external similarities with the class photograph from Mariehem School in Umeå. Including the snub nose. Three more photographs showed the adult Molly Blom in various sporting settings, always on her own. In one she was running, presumably a marathon, and in the others she was wearing climbing equipment. In one of the climbing pictures she was dangling from a rope by a sheer rock face, waving happily at the camera.

In the interview room he had never seen her smile. Only now did he realise just how beautiful she was.

Berger put the rock-face photograph down with a bang. Why the hell would anyone have pictures of themselves lined up in the bedroom?

He went back to the living room and felt that his image of Molly Blom was growing clearer. Fucking Security Service. He'd vaguely heard about these teams. Half-external elite units that could just as easily be deployed against corrupt police officers as international mafias. Only used when they were truly needed.

And now they were evidently needed.

Against Sam Berger, of all people.

The living room bulged out in a bay window. There was a desk in it. It was just as tidy as the rest of the flat. No computer in sight. A few pens, six pads of Post-it notes, different colours. He spent a while looking at them. Then he turned round to get an overview of the room.

Above the white sofa hung a piece of art two metres wide, an astonishing photograph of a group of mountain climbers heading up a snow-covered peak. You could just see their black silhouettes against the extraordinary sunset, its colours reflecting off the snow. What occurred to Berger, apart from the breathtaking beauty of the picture, was how bulky it was: it stuck out almost ten centimetres from the wall.

Just as he was struck by the irrelevant thought that it must have been very heavy for the removal men, he heard a muffled noise from the street door, as if someone was trying to move around very quietly. He let out a deep sigh and scanned the room again in the hope of spotting something, anything at all.

Beside the sofa, beneath the picture, he saw a crumpled Post-it note. Pink. He darted over and picked it up, saw that there was handwriting on it. He scanned it and thought for a couple of seconds. There was no time for anything more.

But it was enough to make him clench his right fist so hard that the scabs opened up again.

Then he heard footsteps on the stairs.

Two men, no more.

He pulled a tiny plastic bag from his pocket, the smallest type of evidence bag, tucked the little pink note inside and tugged his jeans down. Then, with a certain degree of force, he pushed the bag into his rectum. He heard the locks on the door open, one after the other, and only just had time to do up his jeans before they stormed into the flat.

He purposefully splashed blood from his wounded knuckles

over the white sofa, and finished off by wiping his bloody right hand on it. Then they were on him. One of them punched him in the solar plexus and he buckled – the pain leaving him unable to breathe – and countered the blow by headbutting the man in the groin. The man flew backwards with a heavy groan, hitting the small of his back against the doorframe. As Berger straightened up and managed to draw breath again, he was struck from behind, a heavy punch to his kidney that made him kick out furiously behind him. His foot found nothing but air and he lost his balance. As he fell, his flailing foot managed to connect with something, and the second attacker staggered back. The other one stood up in the doorway and rushed at Berger, intending to accomplish something as elegant as stamping on his face. Berger rolled out of the way, grabbed the raised leg and punched the shin hard, sending this attacker off on one leg as well. Berger got to his feet and threw himself at the second man, aiming for a classic armlock. He succeeded and heard pain spread through the flat, along with a cry that sounded like: 'Roy!'

But with more of a sob.

Berger saw an arm sporting a big, cheap diver's watch sweep past with a syringe in its hand. Then he felt a prick in his neck. His field of vision collapsed in a peculiar way, and the last thing he saw before his consciousness was cut off was the pattern of bloodstains on the lovely white sofa.

19

Tuesday 27 October, 14.37

Even before he opened his eyes, Berger knew he was in an interview room.

Sight is our most instinctive sense. When we wake up, we want to open our eyes at once. It's a gut reaction, and our newly woken consciousness is rarely sharp enough to make us disobey a gut reaction.

But on this occasion it was.

Berger had been awake for a couple of minutes and was trying to gather as much information as he could without opening his eyes. His whole body ached, but that didn't really matter.

First and foremost, he was sitting up. He had been placed, unconscious, on a hard chair, and his arms were resting on what felt like metal armrests. It took him a while to realise that they were held in place by leather straps around his wrists. The chair felt so stable that it might well be fastened to the floor, and a faint cellar smell was finding its way into his nose.

And everything was spinning. The world was spinning.

Just before Berger's synapses settled down his brain was overwhelmed by the chill suspicion that he had been captured by the Scum.

That he was sitting in a cellar, waiting for some extreme form of torture.

That Ellen Savinger's mutilated corpse was nailed to the wall in front of him.

But then he remembered.

The last thing he grasped before he decided to open his eyes was that there was someone else in the room, someone who in all likelihood was watching him carefully.

'Molly Blom,' he said and waited three seconds before opening his eyes.

Sure enough, she was sitting in front of him. The same blonde hair, the same snub nose, the same blue eyes, but with a very different expression in them.

'Sam Berger,' she replied, staring hard at him.

The woman he had had in the interview room under the name Nathalie Fredén was now sitting before him in a very different sort of interview room. Were they even in Police Headquarters?

'A syringe in the neck?' he said. 'Seriously?'

'Apparently you were fighting like a three-term jailbird,' Molly Blom said quietly. 'And you were in the process of demolishing my home. What would have been more appropriate? A quiet telling-off?'

'Appropriate? You mean like appreciating the effect of a deliberate red herring in a serial murder investigation?'

'Nicely formulated,' Molly Blom commended coolly.

'If you hadn't sent a decoy into the system, the time could have been spent trying to rescue Ellen Savinger.'

'And *why* do you suppose we sent a decoy into the system?' Molly Blom asked.

The room detached itself from her. He had been focusing so hard that the rest of his field of vision hadn't existed until now, not until the need to think arose. The room was featureless and bare, and apart from the cellar smell there was no indication of where it might be. Berger could see a side table that was exactly the same as the one in his interview room, including the recording apparatus and red light.

The light was on.

His eyes moved past his wrists, which were indeed held down by leather straps. The table he couldn't reach or touch. On it were – apart from his watch, a laptop, a number of files and various documents and notes – two picture frames, facing away from him, one of them bright blue, and a box. A rectangular wooden box with a gilded catch.

A box for watches.

He smiled grimly. 'An eye for an eye?'

She didn't smile. And she didn't say anything.

He went on: 'I went into your home, so you went into mine?'

'You spattered blood over my sofa. Why did you do that?'

'Because it was so disgustingly white. It needed messing up.'

'Hmm.'

'Whereas you yourself are as black as sin. The Security Service's unofficial "internal resource". Bloody hell. And then you broke into my home and snooped about.'

'But unlike you, I didn't demolish anything.'

He was still thinking of her as Nathalie Fredén. He had to stop that. Apart from their appearance there were very few similarities between Nathalie Fredén and Molly Blom. Above all, the power balance was completely different.

'You've demolished my life,' he said. 'That's possibly rather worse that a stained sofa.'

'But not worse than a stained and demolished fifteen-year-old,' Molly Blom said.

'And what's that supposed to mean?'

'Everything, of course. Everything that all this is about. But I don't think you want to start there, Sam Berger. I think you'd rather start somewhere else instead. "Although I can promise that we'll come back to it".'

'Undercover operatives always borrow other people's words,' Berger said. 'Because they have no identity of their own. Now you've proved that you can borrow mine. Clever. But where is your identity, Nathalie Fredén?'

'You're in good shape considering you were unconscious a minute ago,' Molly Blom said. 'Clever. But watch out, dizziness can strike at any moment. And your eyelids are thin.'

'What?'

'"What?" is good. "What?" is a reasonable attempt to buy more thinking time. Especially if you thought I might provide a fairly long answer. Have you had enough time, Sam?'

'No. Talk some more.'

'Your eyelids aren't just thin, they're also revealing. You were awake for three minutes and eight seconds. Did you manage to work out where you were?'

'Yes,' Berger said. 'In the badlands.'

'In a way, yes,' Molly Blom said. 'Nothing's official any more. We're in a different place now. A different time. But you realised that before you opened your eyes.'

'Even so, there's a whole group, a whole fucking *police force* even, that must have started to miss me by now.'

'"Miss" is a very loaded term, Sam. Are you sure that Allan Gudmundsson and Desiré Rosenkvist miss you?'

'Allan probably won't miss me. But Deer will.'

'The detective inspector you consistently undervalue? She'll miss you? With that doe-eyed look of hers, full of longing?'

'OK, I'm tired of this now,' Berger said, tugging at the straps.

'It's been fun, a very successful prank, but now we've got a fucking serial killer to catch. Let me go.'

'Hmm,' Molly Blom said. 'So I have to let you go now, do I? Now that my prank is finished?'

Her eyes were darker than ever.

He opted for silence. It seemed simpler than choosing words.

'Yes,' she said eventually. 'We really do have a serial killer to catch. As quickly as possible. And the quickest way to do that is through you, Sam Berger. We've been watching you very closely ever since you secretly pulled the investigations into Julia Almström and Jonna Eriksson.'

'But that was only a few weeks ago,' Berger exclaimed. 'You've been fucking about at crime scenes on that damn bicycle since Sollentuna, two years ago.'

'I wasn't in Sollentuna,' Blom said. 'I just told you I was.'

'Why?'

'Because that was where it started. I needed to figure out exactly what you, Sam Berger, knew about that. Analyse your reactions.'

'But I don't know anything.'

'You were very quick to identify Helenelund shopping centre, Stupvägen. As if you already knew about it.'

'I know about Helenelund,' Berger said. 'I grew up near there.'

'And that's one of the things that makes it so interesting,' Blom said, leafing through her papers.

'What happened there?' Berger asked. 'Two summers ago?'

'In April that year a gang of Iraqi rebels crossed the border with Syria to join in the civil war. The group had already started calling itself the Islamic State of Iraq and Syria.'

'ISIS,' Berger said, astonished.

'Or IS, as we call them these days. Or Daesh, which they

hate being called. Sunni Muslim youths had already been heading there to fight against the Syrian dictator, Bashar al-Assad. We regarded them mostly as naive freedom fighters. But with the appearance of IS it became clear that the young men going down there were jihadists, and we received the first indications that IS was recruiting in Sweden. One such indication was found in Helenelund, in the Pachachi family, to be precise. A twenty-one-year-old man, Yazid Pachachi – born in Sweden to Sunni Muslim, Iraqi parents – was one of the very first confirmed links to IS. It looked like his fifteen-year-old sister Aisha had gone with him. We infiltrated the neighbourhood and figured out that that probably wasn't the case, and that Aisha was actually missing, here in Sweden. The parents were paralysed by Yazid's unexpected radicalisation and militarisation, and Aisha's disappearance got caught in the shadow of the son's, not altogether surprisingly. But all the evidence suggests that she disappeared on Friday 7 June two and half years ago, after the last day of school. She simply never came home from the celebration to mark the end of the school year.'

'But you didn't realise that until it was too late?'

'Far too late, yes. At first we spent several weeks thinking she was living in Syria as the child-bride of some IS monster. Then we wasted far too much time on the hypothesis that it was some sort of honour killing. But now I'm sure Aisha Pachachi was this serial killer's first victim.'

'But why the hell didn't you let us know, in the *real* Crime Unit?'

'Because the next victim was also a Muslim girl.'

'Oh fuck.'

'The Berwari family in Vivalla, Örebro. Kurdish. At the end of November that same year, the daughter, Nefel Berwari, fifteen years old, vanished without a trace. But her parents didn't report it to the police either, they hushed it up – apparently for reasons of honour – and tried to solve it among themselves. After all, Vivalla already had one of the highest Muslim populations in Sweden, and it was as a result of our infiltration of Örebro mosque that we heard that Nefel Berwari was missing. Only then did we look back at Helenelund and Aisha Pachachi and start to suspect that we were dealing with one and the same perpetrator. Either a serial kidnapper or a serial killer. Or both.'

'Who was either . . . '

'Racist or Muslim, yes. Either it was something internal – honour-related or Islamist – or something to do with the far right – a lone John Ausonius-style nutter or something more organised. In both instances there was good reason for the Security Service to classify the investigation.'

'Six months between Aisha and Nefel,' Berger said. 'Then four months before Julia Almström in Västerås. Quick – and accelerating. But then a break, almost a year until Jonna Eriksson in Kristinehamn. And then eight months until Ellen Savinger. Don't serial killers usually speed up their activities once they get a taste for what they're doing?'

'Unless we've missed a victim,' Molly Blom said.

Berger paused and leaned back as best he could. He looked at the woman on the other side of the table. She was wearing different clothes, a tight, sporty white T-shirt, black trousers that were practically sweatpants, and bright pink trainers.

A completely different person.

One who bore a far greater resemblance to the mountain climber in the photographs in her flat.

He decided not to mention that. 'Is that what you think? That there are other victims?'

'Yes. And that's why you're sitting here, Sam Berger.'

He let out a laugh. 'And there was me thinking this was starting to sound like a productive conversation between two talented police officers. But that was obviously too good to be true . . . '

'Your contribution to the conversation has been pretty negligible so far. But that's about to change. So, a tentative premise: let's pretend this is the first time you've heard about Aisha Pachachi and Nefel Berwari. What would your conclusion be, Sam Berger?'

Berger looked deep into Molly Blom's eyes and said, after prolonged reflection: 'Up until Ellen Savinger it's a matter of concealing the fact that a girl has gone missing at all. It's perfectly possible that there are other victims; it was sheer coincidence that you found Nefel Berwari and picked up on the possibility of a recurrent offence. I didn't know about either of them – on that point your "tentative premise" is correct – but I still managed to grasp that we were dealing with a serial killer. Yet working from your assumptions – five victims – the conclusion has to be that there are two separate series. Up until Ellen the crimes have to be concealed. For some reason the Scum starts murdering fifteen-year-old Muslim girls specifically – why, we don't know. It's possible that he's got something to do with an ancient, patriarchal, honour-based culture, but it's more likely that he just figured out that that's a good way to conceal the crimes; the most successful crimes are always the ones that no one knows have been committed. It's even possible to see poor Aisha Pachachi and Nefel Berwari as practice. The next step is more difficult. The Scum has realised that if a girl from an immigrant family disappears there's no media frenzy; prejudice suggests that any such disappearance is "honour-related", and not even the evening tabloids have the stomach for that. But if a blonde fifteen-year-old Swedish girl goes missing, things liven up considerably. Everything is easier for the public to deal with. Which means it's harder to hide. How do you hide the fact that a fifteen-year-old Swedish girl disappears? By making it look like she's run away. Which is what happens to Julia Almström. Have you found the young man who was emailing her? The one who'd done time and wanted to move abroad?'

'No,' Molly Blom said. 'He doesn't exist.'

'Roughly six months between Aisha and Nefel. Not quite four months until Julia, a temporary increase in pace. Then what?'

'Almost a year until Jonna Eriksson. I know. It doesn't make sense. What happens in between?'

'How should I know?' Berger said. 'I found Julia and Jonna, that's all. But now I see that Julia and the biker gang in Västerås marked a shift. A shift on the part of the Security Service. You broke from your previous strategy. Did you realise that was the start of a new phase, a change of tactic on his part? Why did you show up on your bicycle precisely then? What the hell was the thing with the bike anyway? And why did you talk to that television reporter? Why did you give the name of your bizarre alter ego, Nathalie Fredén? I saw you hesitate; your not yet entirely smooth forehead actually frowned.'

Berger looked at her forehead. There really wasn't much going on there. But that made the activity in the rest of her face all the more pronounced. It was as if her whole system of emotional markers had shifted down her cheeks.

Eventually she said: 'I appreciate that things must seem a little confusing to you right now, Sam. It's not that long since you broke into my flat and got beaten up by my men. Even so, it feels like you still think you're sitting on this side of the table. Was that five questions you just asked?'

'Answer one of them, at least,' Berger said.

'Nathalie Fredén was a well developed identity that I occasionally used undercover. You torched it.'

'For good, I hope.'

'It's only torched in terms of the police, and both Allan Gudmundsson and Desiré Rosenkvist know where their true loyalties lie. They're both loyal to authority. You aren't, Sam.'

'But why use that identity there and then? In Västerås?'

'The killer led us to the biker gang in a conscious attempt to mislead us. We used a bicycle I'd requisitioned for a previous job, drove to Västerås with the bike in the back of the car and tried to make me look as little like a police officer as possible. There was a chance the murderer would show up, so I was simply there to do some surveillance. But then that reporter appeared, and I had to make a quick decision. Were there advantages to the perpetrator seeing me on television? Might I catch his interest somehow? It wasn't an easy decision to give my fake name and risk blowing a well established alias, but I thought the advantages outweighed the disadvantages.'

'Did you get into trouble as a result?'

Molly Blom laughed.

'I'm not you, Sam. Don't get us mixed up.'

'There's not much risk of that . . . '

'And above all, don't underestimate me.'

A sharp glare. Berger realised that he was unlikely ever to underestimate Molly Blom again.

'Does Deer know I'm here?' he asked.

She looked at him, in a different way. Possibly a slightly more human way. Although that probably wasn't the right word.

'*I'm* here, aren't I?' Molly Blom said.

'Well you've clearly been released,' Berger said. 'But does she know I'm here? And where is "here"? Am I even in Police

Headquarters? And these damn straps . . . what sort of fucking Guantánamo is this?'

'Calm down,' she said, and looked him in the eye.

And the strange thing was that he calmed down. Or grew calmer, at least. Curiosity got the better of anger. It was possible that he had never been more curious in his life.

Where the hell was he?

Who the hell was she?

What the hell was going on?

'At least tell me this is all legit,' he said. 'That you are a Swedish police officer.'

'All this has been sanctioned,' she said. 'Don't worry. Do you remember I said I'd get back to where we started?'

'I'm a detective,' Berger said. 'I remember things.'

'What do you remember?'

'I said: "You've demolished my life. That's possibly rather worse that a stained sofa." You said: "But not worse than a stained and demolished fifteen-year-old." So the Security Service suspect me of . . . well, what, exactly?'

Molly Blom's eyebrows frowned. Her forehead remained flat.

'It's the timing,' she said.

'The timing?' he said.

'When exactly did you procure the regional police's files on Julia Almström and Jonna Eriksson?'

Berger sat in silence, thinking. Produced wordless thoughts. Tried to make sense of everything.

'If you don't remember, I'll tell you,' Molly Blom continued. 'Ellen Savinger was abducted from her school in Östermalm on 7 October, almost three weeks ago. But you requested the files on 3 October, Sam. As if you already knew that Ellen was going to be kidnapped.'

Berger sat there, motionless.

Blom went on: 'I can't understand it, Sam. How did you know in advance that Ellen Savinger was going to be kidnapped?'

He remained silent. She watched him. Intently.

The look in her eyes had changed. It was odd: not only was she sharing a large amount of information with him after getting someone to stick a syringe in his neck, but her expression wasn't full of hate. It was more questioning than that.

On closer inspection, the whole thing was actually very peculiar.

'Is it true that you were originally an actress?' he asked.

She looked disappointed.

Then she took a deep breath. 'Four days before Ellen Savinger was kidnapped, you secretly acquired the files covering the investigations into Julia Almström and Jonna Eriksson from two different regional police forces, Central and Bergslagen. Do you really not understand that that act is a lot more suspicious than standing at different police cordons with a bicycle between your legs?'

'That's not true,' he said.

The room started to spin. Either the sedative from the injection hadn't completely left his system, or reality was catching up with him – an awareness of why he was actually sitting there.

It wasn't because he'd exceeded his authority.

It was something much worse.

'Not true?' Molly Blom said.

'The reorganisation,' Berger said, while everything was spinning.

'I have no idea what you're talking about.'

'The chaos at the start of the year,' Berger went on, but the spinning didn't stop. A wave of nausea washed over him.

'The Security Service became an independent body and everything else was gathered together under the Police Authority. And?'

'Have you got any water?'

'No,' Molly Blom said calmly. 'Carry on.'

'Julia Almström wasn't investigated by the Central Police District,' Berger said. 'But the biker gang in Västerås was, before the reorganisation. It was the local Västmanland police who were in charge of the original investigation. But a month or so after the reorganisation, the newly formed Bergslagen Police District took over Julia Almström's disappearance.'

'And you managed to say all that even though the whole room is spinning?'

'How do you know about that?'

'I can tell by looking at you,' Molly Blom said calmly. 'What are you trying to say?'

'That at the beginning of October is was relatively easy to extract files without leaving any trace. Things were still in a state of chaos following the reorganisation.'

'But you did leave a trace,' Blom said. 'And I don't think you were alone.'

'I was alone,' Berger said, unexpectedly sharply.

'We'll come back to that,' Blom said, giving him a hard stare. 'We found a trail, anyway. The files relating to the investigations were pulled four days before Ellen Savinger disappeared.'

'No,' Berger said. The room really didn't seem to want to stop spinning. 'I didn't leave a trail, at least no dates. Things were chaotic, it was fairly easy. If there's a trail, it's been planted.'

'Planted?'

'Yes. I didn't leave a trail. And I pulled the files five days after Ellen went missing, Monday 12 October. I'd spent the whole weekend looking for parallels. Other fifteen-year-old girls who'd disappeared.'

'The whole weekend?' Blom exclaimed, her voice dripping with sarcasm. 'Two whole days?'

'I didn't have longer than that. I found two new victims. Given more time I'd have found Aisha Pachachi and Nefel Berwari as well, in spite of your attempts to cover them up. And you were the one who informed me that there were more, Nathalie Fredén. When you reacted so strongly to me saying "three crime scenes".'

'Let's set that peculiar lie to one side,' Molly Blom said. 'It's a lie that implies that someone with access to all the police material – a police officer – would have brought forward your incursion into regional police records to a time before Ellen's disappearance. A lie which is far too crazy to be properly thought out, so I'm consigning that to the category of wild excuses. And that's why it isn't really the main point. The main point – as you know all too well, Sam – is this.'

With that, she put her hand on his box of watches. Slowly she slid the little gilded catch to one side, opened the lid, revealing the velvet-lined compartments.

'Here we have no fewer that four watches, made by Jaeger-LeCoultre, Rolex and IWC, all from the fifties and sixties. The fifth ought to be on your wrist, but then we wouldn't have been able to strap your wrists. It's in front of you.'

Berger looked at his Rolex Oyster Perpetual Datejust on the interview-room table. The tiny drops of condensation had moved, so he could only see the centre of the dial, with the two hands pointing in different directions. There was no way of working out how long he'd been unconscious.

Molly Blom looked at him. 'In a more traditional internal investigation, I would have been very interested in the fact that the combined value of these watches exceeds half a million kronor.'

'They were inherited,' Berger said. 'From my grandfather. His name was Arvid Hammarström.'

'Good to hear you haven't lost your sense of humour,' Blom said in an expressionless voice. 'That suggests we've got energy for the next session. Which will be very different, I can assure you. But, as I say, your improbably expensive watches would only have been of interest if this had been a traditional case. Which of course it isn't. There's nothing traditional about this.'

'I'm good with watches,' Berger said, holding on to the metallic armrest with half-immobilised hands.

'You're good with watches?'

'I buy broken ones and repair them.'

'And you think I'm interested in your pathetic little hobby? You think that's why I'm talking about your watches?'

'I don't know what you mean now.'

'Oh, but you do,' Blom said, grabbing hold of a couple of the box's velvet-lined dividing walls and pulling upwards.

In the little space beneath the watches was a jumble of plastic. Molly Blom picked up one of a number of extremely small ziplock bags and carefully read the label that was stuck to it. '"Ellen Savinger". Goodness,' she said. 'What could this mean?'

Berger said nothing. But his breathing was perfectly audible.

'The more innocent explanation is that this is something you found in the house in Märsta and withheld from the investigation. Shall we take a look at what it is?'

She opened the little zip and tipped the contents of the bag out onto the table, between the two photograph frames. What fell out was a tiny cog, no more than a centimetre in diameter.

'Where did you find this?' she asked.

Berger remained silent. It was a long time since he'd felt his brain cells work so hard.

'OK,' Molly Blom said after a while. 'This could be written off as the traditional hubris of a burned-out detective inspector. "I've found something no one else found, and I'm going to solve this much more quickly than the official investigation can." That would obviously be misconduct, but not misconduct of the worst sort. But then we have this.'

Two more of the little plastic bags were pulled out. Outwardly they looked just the same, including the labels with the tiny writing in ballpoint pen.

Molly Blom laid the three bags out so that they were in a line, the open one marked *Ellen Savinger* on the right, with the cog in front of it. Then she picked up the middle one and said as she opened it: 'Jonna Eriksson.'

And she tipped out a similar minute cog onto the table. Without a word she repeated the same manoeuvre with the last bag, marked *Julia Almström*. Another cog, slightly larger this time, rolled out.

'If you stole Ellen's cog from the house in Märsta, where do the other two come from?'

Berger's silence hung heavily in the room, as inescapable a car alarm.

Blom went on: 'The cases before Ellen Savinger's featured neither a body nor a crime scene. There were two failed attempts to find Julia and Jonna – the bikers' clubhouse in Västerås and the buried elk in Kristinehamn – but neither of those crime scenes turned out to be connected to these offences. Let me ask once more: Where do these cogs come from?'

Because Berger's silence had entered a new and apparently final phase, Molly Blom said. 'But we're not done yet. There's more. Are you ready for more, Sam Berger?'

She picked his Rolex up from the table and put it next to the others in his watch box. She looked at it pointedly.

'Six compartments. But only five watches. That empty compartment looks rather sad, doesn't it?'

Then she leaned over and removed a bundle of old papers from her bag. She tapped them together on the desk. 'Every watch of this quality has an individual guarantee. I'll count those guarantees. One, two, three, four, five . . . six. Hang on, that isn't right. There are only five watches. I'll count again. One, two, three, four, five, six.'

'Stop it,' Berger said.

'Two Rolexes,' Blom went on mercilessly while she looked through the dog-eared guarantees. 'Two IWCs. One Jaeger-LeCoultre. And one Patek Philippe, apparently. Where's your Patek Philippe watch, Sam?'

'It was stolen.'

'It seems to be the jewel in the crown, Sam. A – what does it say? – Patek Philippe 2508 Calatrava. We've just heard back from a watchmaker who's supposed to be Sweden's foremost expert on wristwatches, and he wasn't even prepared to hazard a guess at the value of a watch of that description. He said it was priceless.'

Blom paused and looked at Berger. He really did look pretty feeble.

'Are you seriously suggesting that this priceless watch was stolen and you didn't bother to report it to the police?'

'You need special insurance for it,' Berger said quietly. 'I couldn't afford it. And I'm familiar with how a stolen-property report is dealt with by the police. Not at all, usually.'

'So where and when are you saying it was stolen?'

'A couple of years ago,' Berger said. 'At the gym.'

'Two and a half, perhaps? In June, two years ago?'

'Something like that, yes.'

Blom nodded for a while.

'The watchmaker in question may have refused to value your missing Patek Philippe 2508 Calatrava, but he did say a lot of other interesting things. For one, he identified these three cogs. There's a high probability that they come from a Patek Philippe 2508 Calatrava.'

20

Tuesday 27 October, 16.24

Molly Blom stepped into a room where two men were sitting staring at computer screens. They nodded to her, as if to acknowledge that everything was under control.

'I'll be gone an hour,' she said. 'An hour and a half at most.'

The man closest to the wall glanced at a large, cheap diver's watch on his wrist. 'And Berger?'

'Let him rest,' Blom said. 'Take him to the cell, Roy.'

Then she opened the other door in the small room and went out into a featureless corridor. She followed it until she came to a lift that blended in to the beige wall. Inside the lift she ran a card through a reader and tapped in a six-digit code, after which the lift began to rise.

Molly Blom looked at her reflection in the hopeless lift mirror. She had been involved in a lot of undercover jobs, played loads of roles, and on one level this was one of the simplest. She moved closer and looked into her own eyes, and actually thought that deep inside that blue stare she could catch a glimpse of the other level. The one telling her that this was the very hardest role she had ever played.

The lift reached the ground floor, G. There was no button below G.

She got out and found herself in a perfectly ordinary stairwell. On the other side of the door she could see Bergsgatan through the curtains of rain, but set off in the opposite direction, into a courtyard containing a dozen parked cars. She clicked her key fob and a dark van, a Mercedes Vito, flashed its lights. She jumped in and lifted up the passenger seat. In a compartment beneath the seat was a shoulder bag. She opened it and fished out a brown envelope and a mobile phone, which she switched on. She set a timer for one hour. She manoeuvred the bulky van around the small courtyard and drove out through the gates before they had opened fully. She headed down to Norr Mälarstrand, then to the hideous roundabout at Lindhagensplan and onto Traneberg Bridge. She carried on towards Brommaplan, then along Bergslagsvägen. She turned off towards Vinsta, one of Stockholm's most soulless industrial estates, found a parking space in front of an anonymous and apparently dilapidated facade where a grimy sign announced that the building was the home of Wiborg Supplies Ltd.

She didn't have time to get seriously wet before stepping into what was supposed to be the reception area. The few samples on display in the glass cabinets consisted of indefinable, dust-covered pieces of piping with unreasonable price tags. Taken as a whole, the reception area made a genuinely unwelcoming impression, which was only enhanced by the fact that the dour receptionist smelled of methanol. She caught sight of Blom and jerked her thumb towards the door to one side behind her. The lock whirred and Molly Blom walked through.

At first glance the industrial premises confirmed the impression made by reception. The combination of warehouse and workshop contained four men sitting at computers that only a very trained eye would have been able to distinguish from slow old desktops of the nineties. One of the men stood up and walked towards her.

'Is it ready?' she asked.

The man was wearing blue overalls, appeared to be in his forties, and the look in his clear blue eyes was very different from the rest of his appearance. He nodded. 'Part-paid and ready for delivery. And no receipt?'

'No receipt this time,' Blom confirmed.

He nodded slowly, as if nothing could surprise him, and went over to his desk. He heaved a parcel out of a drawer and held it out towards her. She in turn handed him the brown envelope. He took it and put it back in the same desk drawer.

'Thanks, Olle,' she said, but he had already returned to his computer.

She drove back the same way, but at Lindhagensplan she carried on along Drottningholmsvägen, drove right across Kungsholmen, across Barnhus Bridge, and all the way along Tegnérgatan until she reached the narrow street that linked Engelbrektsgatan and Eriksbergsgatan.

She left the van double-parked and went into number 4, Stenbocksgatan. She took the stairs in just a few strides, undid all the locks, went in and soaked up the atmosphere. It felt defiled, dirty. As if the atoms of a nasty fight were still in the air. Then she went into the living room and looked at what had once been a brilliantly white sofa.

Four of the six cushions were spoiled, as was one armrest. Splatters of blood from Berger's wounded right knuckles. It must have taken a hell of a lot of effort to produce that much blood.

Berger must have been clenching his fist very hard.

Molly Blom shook her head. She wasn't sure if she'd be able

to get the sofa replaced. And she wouldn't be able to stay there as long as it was present.

She went into the kitchen and opened the fridge, took out two protein drinks, gulped them down, and ate half an apple that she unwrapped from its cling film.

Then she did a quick search of her own home. She would have preferred to go through it more thoroughly, but what had she said to the guys in the observation room? 'I'll be gone an hour. An hour and a half at most.' It would have to do. She hated when things didn't work perfectly. The way she did. These days.

The kitchen. OK, no obvious peculiarities. Nothing in the fridge, nothing in the cupboards, nothing on the worktop, nothing in the bin. He had evidently been in a hurry. The blood was hardly planned. Obviously it could have happened during his fight with Kent and Roy, but her gut said Berger had clenched his fist hard enough to reopen his wounds because he was livid and stressed. When he saw his knuckles and saw the whiteness of the sofa, temptation got the better of him. OK, she could buy that. He wasn't a man who appreciated the finer things in life. When he saw the sofa he reacted instinctively. White things need messing up.

The bedroom. Quickly. Yes, the photographs on the chest of drawers had been moved. He had picked up or at least moved the pictures of her climbing. What had he been thinking? He had believed that she was a fundamentally damaged person – the Nathalie Fredén she had wanted him to see – and then he was confronted instead with this new personality. A mountain-climbing personality. The opposite of losing control.

That was probably Berger's reaction. She changed from someone who had lost control to someone in complete control. And vice versa, in his case: from full control to losing control.

Everything he had assumed about his suspect had turned out to be the exact opposite.

He must have been surprised to get so much out of her when he himself was being questioned. But she really did need him to know about Aisha Pachachi and Nefel Berwari.

Otherwise there wouldn't be any point to any of it. Otherwise he wouldn't have been able to draw any conclusions at all. Otherwise she wouldn't have had any use for him.

And she really did need him.

Precisely how he had managed to find her real identity remained something of a mystery. Yet at the same time it was promising. This was a man who knew what he was doing. Had he also known what he was doing when he had been wandering recklessly through her apartment? Or had he been panicking?

He was looking for the most important things, trying desperately to find the essentials. Trying to think things through with a knife to his throat.

Just as she had planned.

He must have put down the picture of her hanging from a rope beside a sheer rock face – that seemed most likely, seeing as that photograph had been moved furthest – and then gone back into the living room. There he had turned to the bay window containing a desk. What could he have seen there?

The six pads of Post-it notes in assorted colours. Had he actually been able to draw any conclusions from those? If he had, then he really was sharp.

She turned and stared at the huge photograph of the climbers heading up a snow-covered mountain. She looked at their black silhouettes against the colourful sunset. Had he stood there? Had Berger walked this way, out into the bay window, and then turned round?

A sharp, intense ringtone broke the silence. Molly Blom was

jolted from her reflections and eventually managed to pull her mobile out of her bag. An hour had passed. And she still had one more stop to make.

Even though the rush-hour traffic had started to build up, she managed to get back to Kungsholmen in reasonable time. She parked in the usual courtyard and opened up the parcel from Wiborg Supplies Ltd. Inside lay something that looked like an ordinary white smartphone, but when she switched it on the screen looked completely different. She gave a quick nod, then headed out onto Bergsgatan. She walked up towards Police Headquarters, went in through the main entrance on Polhemsgatan and tapped in codes to get through a number of doors until she reached the domain of the Security Service. It took a few more codes, swipe cards and fingerprints before she reached the headquarters of the various departments. Eventually she reached the right place, the Intelligence Unit, and, as the sign on his door suggested, Steen, the head of the unit. She knocked. After an appropriate interval there was a dull whirr to indicate that the door had been unlocked.

She went in. Behind the desk sat a well preserved, steel-grey man in his sixties. He pushed his reading glasses up onto his forehead and looked at her.

'Well, I never,' Steen said. 'Miss Blom. How have you been getting on?'

'I'm reporting as agreed,' Molly Blom said stiffly. 'Questioning is proceeding according to plan.'

'Has Berger confessed his involvement?'

'No. But the picture is getting clearer.'

'And is it as we anticipated?'

'To a large extent, yes.'

'Imagine that something planted so long ago could bear fruit,' Steen said. 'That gives us something to think about.'

'Berger is a police officer, in spite of everything,' Blom said. 'That means we have to be doubly sure of everything.'

'As agreed,' Steen said. 'Nothing goes to the prosecutor until we're sure.'

'Then, August, there's something that you might have forgotten.'

'And what might that be?'

'Ellen Savinger.'

August Steen looked astonished. 'What?' he said.

'Ellen Savinger,' Molly Blom repeated, holding her ground.

'I don't understand what you mean,' Steen declared.

'The missing fifteen-year-old,' Blom clarified in a neutral voice.

'Oh. Yes. Of course. But presumably the Islamic line of inquiry now looks considerably cooler?'

'It does. But Ellen is still alive.'

'She's *at least* the fifth victim,' August Steen said. 'Of course she isn't alive.'

'We can't make that assumption. On the contrary, the situation is in all likelihood urgent.'

'But that's a matter for the regular criminal police. Once the jihadist trail vanished and the whole thing mutated into an internal investigation, we became hired hands. With one specific task: to investigate Berger's involvement.'

'On the other hand, we've been hiding things from the criminal police,' Molly Blom said. 'They've had to work from false assumptions.'

'The Islamic trail may have gone cold,' Steen said, 'but the internal one is red hot. *We're* red hot. If we can get Sam Berger to confess his involvement, we will have made a significant contribution which will make any earlier cover-ups conveniently disappear. We'll look like heroes. Especially you, Molly.'

'And Ellen Savinger?'

'Dead,' Steen said. 'But the final victim.'

'We don't know that.'

'I know you're deeply engaged in this, Molly,' Steen said in a different tone. 'I know you've been trying to flush out the killer since the third murder. I know that the whole bicycle project was your baby. It was an ingenious but, in my opinion, rather too protracted and even fanciful method of attracting the perpetrator's attention, but of course it turned out to be an exemplary piece of planning. He found you in the end. And now you've made it, Molly. The seed has borne fruit. Because you're an internal resource, you won't be able to bask in the glory, but here, within the service, you'll be a hero. Berger is, however, not a threat to Sweden's democratic system, its citizens' freedoms and rights, or national security.'

'Then I request permission to bring this project to a close as soon as possible.'

'Request granted. Thank you for your verbal report. In this time of change I need you on other cases, cases which really threaten Sweden's democratic system, et cetera.'

Molly Blom left her boss's office and walked down the corridor. She wasn't entirely happy with August Steen's tone. It implied an indifference towards Ellen Savinger's fate that couldn't only be attributed to Steen's trademark professionalism.

When she reached the lift a man was already waiting, someone she vaguely recognised. They nodded to each other. When the lift arrived the man pointed questioningly at the button marked G. She gave a brief nod. He pressed G. The lift sank through Police Headquarters. They got out at G, and the man walked towards the exit. She took her time, tied her shoelace, and waited until he was out of sight. Then she got back in the lift, ran her card through the reader and tapped in the six-digit code. The lift started to move down.

When it arrived she made her way along the beige corridors until an almost invisible door emerged from the homogeneity. She went in. The two thickset men were no longer staring at their computers. One was eating a banana; the other was taking a nap.

She nodded to the banana-eater and called out sharply: 'Wake up, Roy.'

The sleeping man jerked awake in front of his computer, and his diver's watch knocked against the wall.

'Get him,' Molly said.

They went out.

Molly Blom sat down on one of the chairs in the control room and pulled the white smartphone from her bag. She looked at it for a while. Then she calibrated it, stood up, took a deep breath and thought: *It's time.*

It really is time.

21

Time has stopped. It really has stopped.

He is balancing on the slippery rock, his feet are slipping, but even so his sweaty hand has slowly but surely managed to clear a peephole in the window.

The door glides open. Light shoots into the absolute darkness of the boathouse. It falls across the interior, right into its depths. It streams past boat engines and life jackets, past stranded buoys and rusty anchors; it rolls past the eyes of mooring rings and hawsers and sails; it catches chains and cogs and cables that are no longer merely randomly scattered about the old boathouse but are actually joined together.

But none of that is important. Everything else vanishes when he realises what the narrow beam of light falls across. It's a face.

It's a girl's face.

The patch of strong spring light seems to blind her. Her face twists from side to side; she pulls back from the light. For a long time she seems unable to see. Eventually she opens her eyes. They turn towards the door. And at that moment the other boy steps into the light. His friend's blond fringe looks luminous in the sunlight, his whole head glowing. Then he turns sideways, and the light falls across his face at an angle, making it seem even more irregular and misshapen than usual. Then he reaches for the door and begins to pull it shut.

Outside on his rock he sees the girl's eyes in the slowly narrowing light. They're full of something he can't understand. Is it happiness? Is it desire? Is it . . . terror?

Then she twists her head back and catches sight of him through the window. Their eyes meet. It's a moment of peculiar contact. The look in her eyes changes, and he doesn't understand what it is. He's too young, too immature, too unprepared to understand it, but her eyes open wide, and only then does he see the tape covering her mouth. He sees her push at the tape with her tongue, and he sees something moving down her forehead. Only when the drop reaches her left eye does he realise that it's blood, a drop of blood that's trickled down from her hair. And only when her eye is completely red does he hear the heartrending scream through the tape. It makes him lose his footing, and, just as the other boy closes the door completely and darkness returns to the boathouse, he falls off the rock.

He gets to his feet. The heartrending scream is still echoing, and he can't blame the fact that he's hit his head or twisted his ankle, but he runs away.

He runs. As fast as his legs will carry him.

Once he's built up speed through the chest-high grass, the scream stops abruptly.

22

Tuesday 27 October, 18.10

When Berger was roughly yanked to a sitting position on the hard bunk he had no idea what had woken him. A dream, perhaps, a memory, a message from the depths of his unconscious. Perhaps it was – on closer reflection – simply the fact that there were two men standing in his cell gripping his arms. When they got him to his feet his eyes were still flaring from the world of dreams. As they dragged him through the gloomy corridor he still couldn't see straight. And as they strapped him into the metal chair in the interview room he had trouble fixing his gaze on Molly Blom. She was sitting in her place, with her elbows on the table, staring into his eyes. He looked at the table and tried not only to focus but also to see if anything had changed. It had. His eyes settled on his Rolex. The condensation was almost gone from the face now, the hands showed that the time was almost quarter past six; he just didn't know if it was morning or evening. And beneath one of the many folders, Berger noticed a mobile sticking out, a white smartphone that he hadn't seen before. He was on the point of commenting on it when Blom turned one of the two picture frames so that he was staring into the happy faces of two ten-year-old boys. The Arc de Triomphe rose up behind them.

Paris.

'Marcus and Oscar,' Molly Blom said.

'But what . . . ?' Berger said, taken aback.

'The photograph is from your desk in Police Headquarters,' Blom interrupted. 'It shows your twins, Marcus and Oscar. When did you last see them?'

'Like hell am I going to answer questions like that.'

'This is nothing compared to what you subjected me to.'

'Not you. Nathalie Fredén. You aren't Nathalie Fredén. And there was a purpose to that.'

'And you don't think there's a purpose to this?' Blom said.

'Yes, to frame me, of all people, for a crime I haven't committed. Me. The person who's been hunting the Scum harder than anyone.'

'You're wrong there. And I promised you that this session would be different. It will be, Sam, and there's no point in you pretending otherwise or trying to obstruct the proceedings. This fight is already lost. Do you understand?'

'Because you have two "external resources" out there in the control room? Because they don't have to obey the same laws as us? What are they going to do? Waterboard me? Is it really true that one of them's called Roy? I don't suppose the other's called Roger?'

Blom gave Berger a long, disappointed look. In the end she shook her head. 'We'll start again. When did you last see Marcus and Oscar?'

'How can that be even remotely relevant?'

'When?'

'Go to hell.'

'When they were this old, or thereabouts?'

Blom pushed a printed photograph towards him. It was the one from his mobile. The one everything stemmed from. The fixed point, the pole star, the still point of the turning world.

'Our experts have concluded that this is the most regularly used item in your entire mobile phone. You seem to keep going back to it.'

'For fuck's sake,' Berger said.

He didn't even have enough energy to feel angry any more. He felt hopelessly lost. Exposed. And at the same time something else was going on inside him. A process. A process that involved a pink Post-it note.

'Winter clothes, I'd say,' Blom went on, unconcerned. 'Winter clothes, even though it looks rather springlike in that ditch with all that coltsfoot. What's the old peasants' saying? Bring in the spring with a sweat, and the autumn with a shiver? I'd guess the second half of April. What year?'

Berger remained silent.

Blom slammed her fist down on the table, then fixed her flaring eyes on him and roared: 'There's no way you're going to sit there and sulk, you pathetic excuse for a cop! The clock's ticking for Ellen Savinger.'

'If I was the murderer,' Berger muttered in surprise, 'why would I care about that?'

'Answer my questions. That's all you have to do. Answer the questions as quickly as possible. Don't say anything else.'

He wondered how many times he thought he'd seen his first glimpse of the real Molly Blom.

'You know exactly when the picture was taken,' Berger muttered. 'You just have to look at my phone; it'll tell you, down to the minute.'

He looked up and met her gaze. It hadn't changed at all.

'If you really do want to save Ellen,' he went on, forcing

himself to meet that stony gaze, 'why did you spend so long on all that mysterious Nathalie Fredén crap? To see what I knew? You could have done it this way instead, with a bit of standard-issue torture from your external resources; it would have gone much faster. No, that's not true. You're the sharpest instrument Internal has got – the sharpest those clowns have ever had – and you weren't putting on that performance for my benefit. You don't think I'm guilty at all. This is another performance. I wonder what kind.'

Blom's eyes were on fire now. She clenched her fist and looked off to the side, up towards one of the small cameras embedded in the ceiling. Two seconds later the man called Roy yanked open the door and stared at Blom with his nostrils flaring. She shook her head briefly. Roy returned to the control room, apparently disappointed.

'Next time I'll let him do what he likes,' Blom said with strained calm. 'Are you ready to give precise answers to my questions?'

Berger looked into her eyes. They were different now. He tried to put together the barest outline of what was going on. Whatever was happening was completely out of his control, and didn't seem to have anything to do with Roy either. He nodded.

'When did you last see your twins?' Blom asked.

'Like you said, that picture was taken in April, two years ago, two and a half. One month later that scum took them from school, three weeks before the end of term. Year 2. They were eight then, they're eleven now.'

'I assume you're aware of how much information your reply contained, Sam?'

He made a grudging gesture with his head but remained silent.

Blom went on: 'You use the term *scum* to refer to your ex-wife? The same name you've given our kidnapper?'

'She is scum,' Berger said. 'And we were never married, thank God.'

'Well, at least it's refreshing that you don't call her a whore,' Blom said. 'After all, you've turned poor Desiré Rosenkvist into your Madonna, your little Deer.'

Before Berger had time to respond Blom flipped the second frame, the bright blue one, revealing a picture of Berger's former partner. It was a wonderful picture, taken on the beach in Fort Lauderdale, Florida, and he still couldn't quite bring himself to look at it. It was always turned the wrong way round on his desk at home. But now he looked away too late.

'Here we have "scum" number two,' Molly Blom said. 'Originally known as Freja Lindström. You lived together for eleven years. During those years you had Oscar and Marcus together. Freja didn't marry you during those eleven years, Sam, but when she met French businessman Jean she got married after just six months. The whole family now lives in Paris. Freja is now Freja Babineaux, and your sons are now Marcus and Oscar Babineaux. Is it true that you haven't seen them since that April day two years ago? When she took them and ran?'

Berger's eyes had been closed for a while. Now he opened them.

'Ran?' he said.

'There's a police report from Arlanda Airport,' Blom said. 'Some sort of altercation with the security personnel, committed by a Samuel Berger. Came to blows. But Freja, Marcus and Oscar Lindström were all on the next flight to Paris. Little more than a month later they were Freja, Marcus and Oscar Babineaux. So yes, "ran" seems to be the correct word.'

'No,' Berger said quietly. 'My life fell apart when she left, I wasn't in a fit state to look after two unruly eight-year-olds. I let her have custody. But I'd hardly have done that if I'd known she was going to take the twins out of the country. When I found out, I went to Arlanda to try to persuade her to stay.'

'And instead you assaulted the staff at the security check?'

'Hardly assaulted . . . '

Berger closed his eyes again. He was trying to stop them overflowing. But he couldn't hide the situation with his hands. Nothing to wipe the inevitable tears with.

Blom continued mercilessly: 'Obviously your hatred of women didn't start when your partner left you in February almost three years ago, taking the twins with her – Freja had no doubt been the target of that for a while – but after that you took it to a new level. Then in May, when she perfectly legally picked Marcus and Oscar from Sofia School and took them with her to Paris, your hatred of women grew, Sam. After the incident at Arlanda you started referring to your ex as "scum", and became outright dangerous. Barely a month later, on 7 June, fifteen-year-old Aisha Pachachi went missing from Helenelund in Sollentuna, where you grew up. It was the end of the school year, right in the middle of all those celebrations you could no longer be a part of. You only got to attend one end-of-year celebration with them, Sam, and that was when your sons were in their first year of school. How crazy must that have made you?'

Berger remained silent and stared down at the table. Blom carried on, without taking her eyes off him: 'That summer you started taking your revenge on a whole gender, Sam. You wanted to make sure those fifteen-year-old girls didn't grow up into treacherous adult women. You're on a crusade against evil women of the future who steal men's sons from them. You grab them before they have a chance to harm any men. You vent your fury on these young girls. When you make your activities public, as with Ellen's kidnapping, you also make sure you're in charge of the investigation – that's why you suddenly made the kidnappings public after keeping them hidden for so long. The fact that you transfer the grotesque term you use for the mother of your children – *scum* – to the murderer, who happens to be you, makes the whole thing so perverse that it's almost intriguing.'

After a heavy silence Berger looked up at her. Tears were streaming from his eyes. 'I love my children. I want them back.'

'I'm sure they'd love to come back to their serial-killer father,' Blom said brutally.

Ordinarily Berger would have been able to wipe his tears away in a matter of seconds and start again. That wasn't possible this time. They just ran, like they would down a little girl's cheeks, or the cheeks of a psychiatric patient.

It was almost like a revelation. It had been a long time since he had seen himself in such a clear light.

In far too many ways, Molly Blom was right.

In every respect except the vital one, in fact.

And it was as if she knew that. As if she were punishing him for something else. For being who he was.

'You know I haven't done this,' he said.

'Why did you requisition the files on Julia Almström and Jonna Eriksson four days before Ellen Savinger was kidnapped?'

'That's not right . . . '

'I'll tell you why,' Blom said pointedly. 'Because you wanted to show off, make yourself out to be smarter than you are. You could calmly lead us to Julia and Jonna without risking anything. Desiré Rosenkvist and the others would be so impressed. You could show off while keeping your own role concealed. You neglected to say anything about the first two victims, Aisha

Pachachi and Nefel Berwari, and any evidence relating to Julia and Jonna was already long gone. But not entirely.'

She pointed at the little cogs that were still lying on the table, next to their small plastic bags.

'There are no crime scenes for Julia and Jonna,' Molly Blom went on. 'Yet these little cogs belonging to a Patek Philippe 2508 Calatrava have been gathered from two crime scenes. No one in the world knows where Julia Almström and Jonna Eriksson were held captive and killed. No one except the murderer. These aren't clues, Sam Berger, they're trophies. These cogs are trophies of the sort that serial killers almost always collect. Really sick serial killers. And you're a really sick serial killer. You want to stop women from growing up. You're scum. You're the Scum.'

Molly Blom paused. She looked intently at Sam Berger. She owned him.

He nodded slowly.

'Yes,' he said. 'It really does look atrocious.'

'You sacrificed your best watch,' Blom said. 'You took your finest possession apart and started putting one cog from the watch in each of the places where you murdered the girls. If a single cog disappeared for good, you would have sacrificed your favourite object in the whole wide world. It was all about raising the stakes. Not a single cog was to be found by the police, not a single crime scene, not a single girl's body. You're gathering your Patek Philippe 2508 Calatrava back together, Sam. Soon time will be running smoothly again. When you've murdered enough girls.'

Berger was breathing heavily. After a while he said, as calmly as possibly: 'I'll have to come back to the cogs. In a minute. But first I need an answer to a question.'

'You need an answer? You don't have the right to anything, scum, least of all a question.'

'But otherwise nothing makes sense. Lina Vikström?'

'What?'

'You called the police as Lina Vikström from Märsta,' Berger said. 'You had an almost impeccable Security Service mask on your voice. You said you'd seen Ellen Savinger through the window of a ramshackle house in the neighbourhood. You said you'd seen a pink leather strap round her neck, with an Orthodox cross. Because the Security Service had full access to the police investigation, and were actually ahead of it, the pink strap wasn't that strange. But the strange thing is that you knew *where* Ellen was being held captive. We'd been looking for her for almost three weeks: it was top priority. How the hell did the Security Service find her before we did? And why didn't you want to go in? Why put us on the Märsta trail?'

Blom looked at him.

'You purposefully concealed a clear line of inquiry,' she said.

'What the hell?' he said. 'I didn't do that.'

'Of course not,' she said with icy chill. 'So you checked car rentals? All the car rentals within something like a two-hundred-kilometre radius?'

'I had three officers on it,' Berger said. 'They found a few possibilities, but nothing sufficiently promising. Every fifth car hired in the Stockholm area is apparently picked up using fake documents. Very difficult to pin down.'

'But you were sloppy,' Blom said. 'If I can put it like that. A report came in from the Märsta Police about a van that had been hidden in one of the derelict buildings on the neighbouring land. An old lady walking her dog, an Asta Granström, came across it early one morning. It was a van that had been rented from Statoil in Gävle back in the spring.'

'Like hell,' Berger said. 'We'd have found her.'

'She died before you found her,' Blom said. 'My theory is that you murdered her. You were in Märsta. You were the one who rented that van, Sam Berger. You were leading the investigation by day and creeping around Märsta by night. When you tortured Ellen. And you killed the old woman and managed to stop her report from getting any further than the Märsta Police. It never found its way into the investigation.'

'Because the Security Service prevented it,' Berger shouted. 'Because you allowed it to leak into the investigation indirectly, via Lina Vikström. Christ – you managed to keep the Märsta Police quiet? But you can't have killed the old woman. I don't remember an old woman from the investigation.'

'Because you killed her,' Blom said. 'Then put a lid on it.'

'But I don't even know who you're talking about, Molly. Who was this old woman? How did she die?'

'Don't call me Molly, you bastard. I don't want my first name in your mouth. Now, try to explain away those cogs from your very favourite watch. If you can.'

Berger felt the whole world spinning. Pain was burning through every nerve cell in his body.

'The cog,' he wheezed. 'Yes. Bloody hell. When I got hold of the files on Julia Almström and Jonna Eriksson – five days *after* Ellen's disappearance, not four days before – I realised that the local police couldn't have conducted a thorough search of Julia and Jonna's homes. It was a chaotic time, both before and after the reorganisation. The soon-to-be defunct local force in Västmanland didn't make much of an effort with Julia, and the completely new regional Bergslagen Police was largely incompetent when it came to Jonna. I simply went to their homes. The Almström family in Malmaberg in north-east Västerås was very accommodating; they were in pieces. Julia's room remained exactly as she had left it, and there – tucked in beside the skirting board next to Julia's wardrobe – I found the first cog. That one.'

Berger pointed at the largest of the cogs on the interview-room table between them.

'Tucked in beside the skirting board?' Blom said, with heavy sarcasm.

'Then there was Jonna Eriksson,' Berger went on. 'She was a foster child with a notorious family in Kristinehamn. A new girl had already moved into her room. But there it was, nonetheless, at the back of a bookcase, another cog. That one. And I found Ellen's beside one of the pillars in the basement. Sort of tucked in under the post.'

'But you'd found both Julia and Jonna's cogs before you found Ellen's?'

'Yes.'

'How the hell did you know that you were supposed to be looking for *cogs*?'

Berger leaned back and closed his eyes. After a while he said: 'Because he knows who I am.'

But Blom stood up and slammed her fist down on the table as soon as Berger started to speak, completely drowning him out with a roar: 'Now shut up and think before you tell any more lies!'

He stared at her.

She went on: 'Now we're just going to sit here and stare at each other until you tell the truth, you pathetic piece of shit. I don't care if it takes half an hour.'

Then she sat down again and stared at him. He stared back. He was trying desperately to grasp what was happening, but he understood nothing, except that he should remain silent.

Time passed. They remained completely motionless for five seconds, ten. Fifteen, then Berger saw Blom slide her hand under one of the files and touch the new white smartphone beneath it.

Without turning his head, he let his eyes slide over to the recording equipment on the side table. The red light flickered but went on glowing.

Molly Blom leaned forward and said quietly: 'Twenty seconds exactly. Listen carefully now, don't say anything. This isn't a mobile phone. It's a remote control that lets the last twenty seconds run on a loop for a while. We can't take more than a few minutes or they'll notice out in the control room. Nothing we say now is being recorded. But we don't have much time. You know who the killer is?'

Berger stared at her wildly for two seconds. That's all they could afford.

'Yes,' he said. 'I think we grew up together.'

'And the cogs?'

'Several things. He likes clocks. He *loves* clocks. Big ones, like you get in clock towers. It's likely that he's torturing these girls using clocks. Perfect, intractable mechanisms.'

'But the cogs from your Patek Philippe are small.'

'In part he wants to show the world that this is about clocks. And in part he's leaving clues for you, implicating me. I realised that as soon as I found the first cog. That he was the one who had stolen my watch. Now he's distributing the cogs to incriminate me. That's why I've been collecting them and keeping them away from the investigation. They're his way of getting back at me.'

'Evidence?' Blom said.

'You left several lines of inquiry for me,' Berger said. 'Two things that stuck out from my interviews with you. When you said "The betrayal" so distinctly and your comment "You know *exactly* what happened". Those were the two times you emerged from your role as Nathalie Fredén. I've been racking my brains.

Was *I* the one who betrayed *you*? When, where, how? I don't know you.'

'Don't play dumb, Sam Berger,' Molly Blom said. 'You know exactly what happened.'

He stared at her, overwhelmed by the rustling of aspen leaves, and felt himself turning pale.

'Bloody hell,' he said.

'I became a cop for reasons of justice,' she said. 'What happened to me should never happen to anyone else. Especially not a woman. A girl.'

'You were there? At Helenelund School? I don't remember you.'

'I was in the year below,' she said. 'Your lunatic of a friend grabbed me one day. He strapped me into that sick contraption. And you saw me. You saw me through the window, you bastard. And you ran away. You fucking coward.'

Berger was perfectly silent. He couldn't get a single word out.

'Your betrayal in that moment,' Molly Blom said, 'still leaves me utterly speechless. From that second on I couldn't trust anyone in the whole world.'

'Fucking hell,' Berger said.

'Not much time left,' Blom said. 'They'll be starting to wonder out there.'

The sound of aspen leaves in Berger's ears was deafening. Even so, he knew there was one question that had to be asked. 'I retrieved the investigations five days after Ellen Savinger went missing. Why are you saying it was four days before?'

'Because that was my opportunity to attack you. To get to this point.'

'You changed the dates?'

'So that the Security Service could go in as hired hands for Internal Investigations. It was my chance to get to meet you. Under the right circumstances. Once I'd punished you enough.'

'And why did you want to meet me under the right circumstances? Because you know who the killer is as well?'

'I've suspected it for a while,' Blom said, moving her neck from side to side. 'His name is William Larsson.'

'Yes,' Berger said. 'William Larsson. He joined my class in Year 9. His face was all crooked, misshapen. He had some sort of rare disorder, some inherited variant of something like Proteus Syndrome, I think; it wasn't entirely clear. His mother, who was on her own with him, had to keep moving around Stockholm because he kept getting bullied. At Helenelund School, among others. The girls weren't kind to him.'

'The fifteen-year-old girls,' Blom said. 'And one of them was me.'

'I'd have sounded the alarm if I'd found him,' Blom said. 'Then of course it would all have ended up in the investigation. But he no longer exists. William Larsson has ceased to exist. I was forced to look underground.'

'Me too,' Blom said. 'I've been working on this for a long time, considerably longer than you. I wanted to find him, at any cost. But he ceased to exist after Year 9. I managed to break out of that mechanism of his before it pulled me apart, quite by chance, but I never said anything to anyone. Not a word to a single person. It was too painful; I was eaten up with shame and anxiety. And then he vanished. I've looked everywhere, but he flew away. Like Charles Lindbergh.'

'Do you think it's really William, then?' Berger said. 'Is that possible?'

'It's possible, if he's undergone plastic surgery abroad. And now he's back, externally patched up, but more warped than ever inside. And with an appearance that no one recognises.'

'I understand you wanting to punish me,' Berger said. 'There's nothing in my life I've regretted as much as that moment when I fled from you and the boathouse.'

Blom looked at him. 'You took something from my flat, didn't you?'

Berger blinked hard. Then he opened his mouth and managed to extract a rolled-up piece of paper from the innermost crevice between his top teeth and right cheek. A pink, rather damp piece of paper.

A Post-it note.

'It was on the floor,' he said. 'Next to the sofa.'

Blom leaned forward and read it out loud: 'WL pl. surg. Saudi?'

'It made me suspect a thing or two about you,' Berger said. 'WL had to be William Larsson. Then the rest: "pl. surg. Saudi?" Plastic surgery in Saudi Arabia?'

'Yes. The Saudis are very good at plastic surgery, which might seem odd in light of Wahhabism and in a society where women aren't even allowed to drive. But behind the veil there's a lot of scope for plastic surgery. Because it's unofficial it would be very difficult to trace. Hence the question mark.'

'But you must have got further than that. Otherwise you wouldn't have written it down.'

'Think about where it started. But our time's up. I can tell they're starting to wonder over in the control room.'

'So what the hell happens now?' Berger asked.

'I honestly don't know,' Blom said. 'It's possible that you are actually William Larsson's accomplice. You were very close. Perhaps you are just being remote-controlled by your master, Sam Berger. You were his only real friend. But we have to stop now. Sit still.'

Her hand slipped beneath the file again.

Just before she clicked the white remote control Sam Berger said: 'I became a cop because I had a guilty conscience.'

She smiled grimly; the red light on the recording apparatus flickered. Then Molly Blom said, loudly and clearly: 'OK, this is getting us nowhere. We'll take a break.'

23

Tuesday 27 October, 18.43

Molly Blom watched him being taken away. When Roy and Kent dragged Sam Berger out she wondered what had disappeared with them. Her career?

She pulled the fake mobile phone towards her and dropped it into her bag with a silent prayer that it had worked. Everything from Wiborg Supplies Ltd always worked. That was the whole point.

She looked at her real mobile phone. The day was completely out of joint. It was almost seven o'clock. Molly Blom had a feeling she wasn't going to get any sleep that night either. But on the other hand she was used to that; she'd arranged her life around it. She compensated for her irregular professional life with an extremely disciplined private life.

What mattered right now was re-establishing a degree of control. Order and structure. She had laid it all on the table for Berger, but there wasn't much chance of him saying anything, partly because he had enough of his own to hide, and partly because he was in fact locked up. It looked like everything hinged on Molly Blom.

No, don't go there. Not now. Don't fall into that pit. Not until it was clear what the next step would be.

And of course that was precisely the pit she fell into.

Life. She had tried so hard to suppress it. Suppress everything. She had tried to pretend everything was normal, that her past was completely unremarkable. It had worked well: the end of the school year, then Year 9, without William Larsson, without gorgeous Samuel Berger, the embodiment of betrayal. Everything was fine, good grades, nice-enough friends, good parents, nothing out of the ordinary.

At the time, she had no idea where they had gone next, either William or Sam. They just disappeared.

She remained seated in the interview room off the top-secret passageway, buried deep within Police Headquarters. She opened her laptop and stared at the screen. She went through the case, both the official and unofficial versions, and found nothing that she didn't already know.

Instead the past came back with inexorable force.

She had told Berger the truth: from the moment he snuck away from the boathouse she hadn't been able to trust anyone in the whole world.

There was only one person to trust. Herself. Everything depended on Molly Blom. No one else would help her succeed in life. There was nothing to fall back on.

Except herself.

Her life became a miracle of control and self-control. She played the part of a successful person. She did it so well that she realised she had a genuine talent for playing roles. In Year 9 she started acting, most likely to keep her real self at a distance, and when she took a gamble and applied to the Royal Dramatic Theatre's vocational school after finishing her studies she was accepted, and was one of their youngest students ever.

She appeared in some short films, student projects; she played a couple of the biggest female theatrical roles, Ophelia and Masha, during her final term. Everyone predicted a bright future for her. And she loved the theatre. But other forces had begun to take over. Playing roles was no longer enough, the result was never anything that bore any resemblance to justice. And justice was what she wanted in life, tangible justice. It was becoming increasingly clear what she wanted to do: she wanted to join the police. She wanted to protect the world from every imaginable type of William Larsson. And Sam Berger too, for that matter.

She wanted to protect the world from injustice.

It didn't take long at Police Academy for her to realise that that wasn't quite what was on offer. Police Academy promised something very practical: the ability to arrest suspects, catch crooks, but there was far too little about moral labyrinths.

Yet for the first time since the boathouse she wasn't playing a role. She *was* a police officer. She was a trainee police officer, then a police officer; she went on courses; she specialised and became a detective inspector. She was given a number of indications that her theatrical background made her highly attractive to the Security Service, and it didn't take long for her to be recruited personally by August Steen and transformed into the perfect undercover agent. By this point she had been doing the job for almost a decade. And it was obviously taking its toll.

Time passed at that lonely interview-room table. She had been awake for so long; she had played Nathalie Fredén for so long. That really had taken its toll. And it was as if time had caught up with her, grabbed hold of her, and she fell asleep in front of her computer, her face slumped onto the keyboard.

When she saw, much later, the immense document that her

sleeping head had written, she wondered for a moment if it had sprung from the depths of her unconscious.

She had no idea how long she had been asleep when her mobile began to shout at her. Half-asleep, she couldn't remember having set the alarm clock.

She hadn't.

It was ringing. Unknown number. As always.

All calls of any importance came from unknown numbers. The story of her life.

She woke up, quickly, as ever. Ever ready.

'How's it going?' asked a voice that she'd recognise anywhere. It ran like a thread through her life. But it was also slightly alarming that the head of the Security Service's Intelligence Unit was calling her in the middle of the night. It was the middle of the night, wasn't it?

'We're moving in the right direction, August,' she said tentatively.

'Good to hear it,' August Steen said. 'Can you come up to my office for a bit, Molly?'

'Are you in the building?' Blom couldn't help sounding surprised.

'There's quite a lot happening on other fronts,' Steen said. 'I'm not here for your sake, if that's what you're thinking. But I'd like a briefing, if it's not too much to ask.'

'On my way,' she said, standing up and wishing she could still frown. She stopped and thought for half a minute. Then she packed away everything from the table. She stopped abruptly with her hand in her bag. The fake smartphone had caught her attention. She took it out and looked at it, then put it in the back pocket of her black sweatpants, tossed her bag over her shoulder and headed out into the corridor via the control room. Kent was sitting there immersed in the recordings of the interview.

'Where's Roy?' she asked.

'He's gone to the toilet,' Kent said, pausing the film. 'We didn't want to wake you.'

'OK. Tell him we're taking a break for a couple of hours. You look pretty wiped out too.'

Kent gave her a quick glance, nodded curtly and went back to the recording.

Molly Blom wasn't at all happy about that look. She took a right in the corridor instead of a left and soon reached a different lift. Before it came to a halt she slid her hand into her back pocket, pushed one of the lift's ceiling panels aside and placed the fake mobile phone inside. She slipped the panel back before the lift had climbed up into the public realm of Police Headquarters. Then she started the process of coding her way forward, closer and closer to the absolute centre of power.

The leadership area seemed completely empty until she entered the last corridor. There she saw a figure sweep into one of the toilets. All she could see of the figure as the door closed was a wrist bearing a large diver's watch.

Too much fell into place too quickly. She was good at infiltration, used to taking quick, improvised decisions, and a strategy had already begun to form. It was almost ready by the time she knocked on the door marked with Steen's name and position, and heard the cold whirr of the lock.

August Steen looked up from his computer, impassive, clicked his mouse, pushed his reading glasses up onto his forehead and looked at her.

Molly Blom said: 'Considering that there's quite a lot happening on other fronts the corridors are surprisingly empty. And you've got toothpaste at the corner of your mouth.'

Steen wiped the left side of his mouth instinctively.

'Right,' she said.

He wrinkled his nose and cast a sharp glance at her. Then he wiped the right side of his mouth.

There was no toothpaste there.

'So, you rushed over here,' she said. 'What for?'

'I felt that we needed to talk,' August Steen said.

'About what?'

'About the most recent session. You pushed Berger hard.'

'I thought that was the point.'

'"I'm sure they'd love to come back to their serial-killer father" was perhaps a little extreme . . . '

'You didn't rush here all the way from Äppelviken at this time of night because of a clumsy choice of words, August.'

'Very true, Molly,' Steen said, watching her carefully. 'I rushed here because something seems to have disturbed our recording equipment. And that sort of thing disturbs me as well. Possibly even more, actually. We are, after all, the Security Service. If someone disturbs our equipment, that's a definite threat to the security of the realm.'

'What do you mean?'

'I have to acknowledge that the long staring contest at the end of the session was ingenious. Absolute silence. What was it you said? "Now we're just going to sit here and stare at each other until you tell the truth, you pathetic piece of shit. I don't care if it takes half an hour." Then the two of you really do sit there for more than ten minutes and just stare at each other. And then you conclude with the phrase "OK, this is getting us nowhere. We'll take a break." Splendid. Now he knows that there are no limits to our patience.'

'Why do I detect a note of sarcasm in your voice?'

'Because this happened,' Steen said, turning his screen. He clicked the mouse and fixed his gaze on Blom's face, which was lit by the glow of the monitor.

What she saw was a fairly long clip of her and Berger sitting and staring at each other. A minute and a half passed, then the picture jumped, and Berger and Blom's body language was suddenly very different, considerably more active. Voices emerged from the computer.

Molly Blom said: '. . . back, externally patched up, but more warped than ever inside. And with an appearance that no one recognises.'

Sam Berger said: 'I understand you wanting to punish me. There's nothing in my life I've regretted as much as that moment when I fled from . . . '

The film cut out abruptly, and Berger and Blom returned just as abruptly to their staring.

August Steen turned the screen back, and looked at Blom with absolute neutrality. 'I'm trying to understand this. Can you explain it to me, Molly?'

Blom quickly evaluated the amount of information in the short clip. At least it played to her advantage.

'That's very odd,' she said.

'I think so too. And so did Kent and Roy when they called me. Need I tell you that I was in the middle of my very deepest beauty sleep?'

'Yes.'

'I was in the middle of my very deepest beauty sleep.'

'Shame. Now that I come to think about it, Berger did break the long silence once. But it was more than that. Is the rest missing?'

'That's how it looks,' Steen said, opening his hands.

Blom nodded and her eyebrows frowned.

'Berger was completely exhausted,' she said. 'I'd pushed him hard, after all. Suddenly he came out with some weird story about how he suspected that his ex, Freja, had come back to

Sweden in secret, with a new appearance. Then he claimed that I was in league with her and that was why I wanted to punish him. There was some story about him having walked away from his family during one of the twins' football matches, and that he regretted it more than anything else in his life. Is the rest really missing? I could have done with some help interpreting it. Was he on the point of losing his grip completely? Or was he just playing a game? If the equipment's on the blink, the technicians had better examine it closely. Don't tell me I've been wasting my time.'

'Anders Karlberg, our senior technician, has just been down to collect it,' Steen said. 'He seemed to agree with you, not for the first time, I might add. Are you still seeing each other?'

'What did he say about the equipment?'

'That it looks like some sort of technical fault. Not necessarily a disruptive transmitter.'

'Good,' Blom said. 'But we lost quite a bit there. Mostly crazy talk from an overtired suspect, but, still, things that could be important.'

'I'm convinced of that,' Steen said with a sideways glance. 'He didn't seem crazy before.'

'I assume I stared him to pieces.'

Steen frowned, nodded, then drummed his fingers on his desk.

'Hmm,' he said. 'This doesn't feel good at all.'

'I completely agree,' Blom said.

'It feels odd that Berger should enter some sort of psychosis without any warning, and then just go back to staring. And not least because you conclude by saying wearily "this is getting us nowhere".'

'I don't think it was a psychosis, exactly . . . '

'I'm not at all convinced that we're hearing a mentally

unstable man here,' Steen said. 'I'm not happy with your explanation, Molly.'

'It's the truth,' Blom said, as calmly as she could. 'And it's hardly my fault that the equipment didn't work.'

August Steen ran a hand over his neatly combed grey hair, then eventually nodded. 'OK, this sequence will be analysed in minute detail. And Karlberg says his technicians might be able to restore the rest. I'm sending Kent and Roy to the technical team now, they'll have to spend all night working on it.'

'I'll go with them,' Blom said, making a move towards the door.

'No,' Steen said, raising his hand.

'No?' Blom said.

'I don't think that's a good idea, Molly. I think it would be best if you went home at once and got some sleep. Be here at nine o'clock tomorrow morning.'

She looked at him and conjured up her most insulted expression.

'What the hell?' she said. 'You think I'm that exhausted? I've been through considerably worse.'

'I know,' Steen said distantly. 'But this is what's happening. No argument. Straight home, Molly. Bed. Nine o'clock sharp tomorrow morning. OK?'

She made a suitably indignant exit and wandered through the corridors with suitably slumped shoulders. Only when she was back at the lift did she raise them again.

OK, she thought, trying to cool down her brain. *OK, you've always known you really didn't want to be on the wrong side of August Steen*. Rarely had she been on the receiving end of so many passive-aggressive threats. With icy clarity she realised that he had come very close to asking to look in her bag.

She nudged the ceiling hatch aside and retrieved the device.

Then she turned to the mirror, looked deep into her eyes and thought: *Is it over now? Is my career over? Who would touch a disgraced cop?*

She looked down at the fake smartphone. How the hell was it possible that the fucking gizmo hadn't worked the way it should?

The lift stopped. She stepped out into the corridor and resumed the same miserable posture. She passed the door of Berger's cell, the door to the interview room, then, round a corner in the corridor, the door to the control room.

She took a deep breath, it was unavoidable. She opened the door.

Kent and Roy were gone, sure enough. There was no one to check the images from the surveillance cameras. They had taken almost all the technical equipment with them. Which meant there was a tiny sliver of hope for the drastic plan she had come up with.

She grabbed Berger's abandoned rucksack from one corner and went back out into the corridor, retracing her steps until she reached his cell. She sighed deeply and reached out the hand clutching her security card to the reader.

Then she heard a snorting sound coming from the other side of the door.

As if he were having nightmares.

24

Wednesday 28 October, 00.05

Berger was lying on the hard bunk in the tiny isolation cell, and he wasn't alone. There was quite a crowd around him. The floodgates had opened, the memories were building up. Everything was hazy, yet so very clear. He could see the details of faces he hadn't consciously thought about for decades. He saw his nursery teachers' hairstyles. He saw his great-grandmother's liver spots. He saw every player in his under-twelve football team. He saw his dad at his carpentry bench and his mum by the stove, as if they had merged with the age-old gender roles he had grown up with. Out of the walls came classmates from every year, relatives who had long since emigrated or died, gangs of friends enveloped in clouds of off-piste snow, colleagues with different ranks of uniform, a bared set of teeth approaching his bicep, a group of girls he had slept with all on the same day in Koh Phangan, and then a dark-haired girl from a bar in Barcelona whose face he couldn't remember ever having seen. The women in his life kept popping up and sweeping past with impassive faces. Misogyny? Sam Berger? He *loved* these women, or at least he had at the time. *Never misogyny*, he thought as he tried to catch their elusive gazes. Then came Freja, their first encounter. Freja Lindström – the party where she suddenly showed up with her stiff business boyfriend, their immediate, obvious connection, the same raucous laughter at life's peculiarities. Exactly the same sense of humour. Was it the similarities that led to the death of the relationship eleven years later? He felt like asking her as she walked across the floor of the cell – time after time, in an endless loop – and cast a fleeting, *frightened* glance over her shoulder when she caught sight of him. That was the walk towards security at Arlanda, the very last time he saw her. He was stopped at the barrier, guards were called, Freja shielded the twins with her body and gentle words; he heard their laughter, but they never saw him that last time. And he only caught a glimpse of them, and here in the cell he could just make out their hands in hers at Arlanda. But then the twins grew out of their freed hands and appeared in an accelerating succession of flickering images. The fuck that he *knew* created them, the quivering heat as he shot his sperm deeper that usual into Freja's orgasm-rocked body. Sitting in the twin buggy, and only Daddy Sam could tell them apart, even Mummy Freja often said the wrong name, but never Daddy Sam. Swimming with their armbands in the Adriatic Sea; fishing for cod in the sea off Halmstad; testing each other on their homework while they pretended to play a video game; running the children's race at the Midnight Marathon and waiting for each other the whole way, and crossing the line at exactly the same moment; singing so loudly that the neighbours in Ploggatan eventually filed a formal protest with the housing association; standing in their winter clothes in a ditch one spring, picking coltsfoot; and at Arlanda, as nothing but disjointed hands in their mother's as she cast a *frightened* glance over her shoulder at him. And the other women in his life gathered around her, and the looks in their eyes were no longer impassive and elusive, but just as he dared to meet their gaze the women started to inflate like balloons, one after the other, and disappear in separate, soundless explosions. Towards the end Deer appeared, she inflated and disappeared. Then Freja inflated and disappeared.

In the end there was only one woman left.

Sam ran through the tall grass that reached his chest. He was following a blond halo of hair visible just above the grass, a floating halo moving over a green sea. He was panting. In the end he caught up with the halo; the long blond hair settled into place, and William Larsson turned round. Sam had never stopped, would never stop being astonished at his friend's misshapen face, all its cubistic protruding nodules. They were standing eye to eye now; they exchanged a quick hug, breathless. Then William raced off again. Sam didn't follow him. He went to the rock instead, the stone was smooth, but he held on. Cleared a circle of the filthy glass.

With a backdrop of rustling aspen leaves, which sounded louder and louder, he met the fifteen-year-old girl's gaze. Their eyes locked until the little drop of blood ran down her forehead and into her eye, turning it red. And yes, he saw more among the stranded buoys and rusty anchors, among the mooring rings, hawsers and sails. He saw the whole, tirelessly ticking mechanism that he had seen so often, been impressed by, fascinated by. He saw the perfectly coordinated constellation of cogs and pinions and springs, axles and pins, shafts, flywheels and spindles, pendulums, clicks and weights.

But that wasn't all.

In the middle of the mechanism stood the girl. Wrapped in chains. The powerful clock ticked relentlessly on, slowly, slowly pulling her apart.

Through the decades he met the girl's gaze. He met Molly Blom's pleading gaze. And he woke up.

And stared into Molly Blom's far from pleading gaze.

She was crouching beside his bunk. 'Get up. We're in a hurry.'

She helped him, his legs felt unsteady.

'A hurry?' he said groggily.

'Hands behind your back,' she said.

He did as she said. She fastened a zip tie around them, made it plain that she had her pistol in her shoulder holster, and pushed him out through the door. In silence they walked through the dismal corridors. They reached the now familiar door to the interview room, but she walked past it. They turned a corner and passed another door, in all likelihood the door to the control room.

'Where the hell are we going?' he whispered. Given the number of surveillance cameras mounted in the ceiling of the corridor, hidden microphones seemed likely.

She didn't answer, just pushed him straight. After a bewilderingly long walk, they reached an almost invisible lift door. She pressed the button, ran her card through a reader and tapped in a six-digit code.

She still didn't say anything.

Berger saw the two of them in the grimy lift mirror. It was the first time he'd seen them together. Prisoner and guard. Crook and cop. Molly and Sam. Berger and Blom. Everything felt distorted.

'Are you taking me up to the department now?' Berger said. 'To make me run the gauntlet in front of my betrayed and disappointed colleagues?'

'I doubt even Desiré Rosenkvist is there now,' Blom said just as the lift doors opened, revealing the pitch-black of night. She pressed a glowing red button and a merciless fluorescent glare lit up an unremarkable stairwell. Berger could just make out a street lamp through the window in the door.

'Are we even in Stockholm?' he said.

Without a word she pulled him after her, away from the door. She opened another door that led to a large courtyard containing a number of parked cars, among them a dark Mercedes Vito van. It flashed its lights through the rain as Berger heard the locks click. She pushed him in across the driver's seat; he slid over the gear stick and handbrake and glanced over his shoulder into the back of the van. It contained a couple of aluminium suitcases. She placed her shoulder bag there, and beside it the rucksack containing his laptop, watch box, files, the framed photographs – he even glimpsed his mobile phone. When he turned round, about to speak, she held his Rolex Oyster Perpetual Datejust out to him. All the condensation was gone. The watch case looked completely dry. And the hands were pointing very clearly at eighteen minutes past twelve.

'You like watches?' she said, dangling the timepiece. 'Clocks?'

'William taught me,' he said.

'That's why I need you,' she said, tucking the watch into his jacket pocket and strapping him into the passenger seat with two large zip ties. He couldn't move.

She started the engine, and as she began to manoeuvre the van out of its tight parking space she said: 'I need you, but I don't know if I can trust you.'

A gate opened in the narrow archway and the van slipped smoothly out onto a deserted Bergsgatan. Above them Stockholm Police Headquarters loomed up like a medieval fortress.

'We're in Stockholm,' he confirmed.

She drove fast. He approved.

'What about Roy and Roger?' he said.

She just shook her head.

They said nothing. As they passed Tegnérlunden the illuminated statue of the titanic Strindberg stared down at them from his block of stone. A couple of well oiled nocturnal wanderers on the pedestrianised zone of Drottninggatan failed to cross Tegnérgatan properly. Molly Blom blasted the horn, forcing them up into a bike rack. They drove across Sveavägen and turned into Birger Jarlsgatan. Still in silence.

Berger even managed to keep his trap shut when Blom did a handbrake turn into Eriksbergsgatan. But a few moments later he nodded through the window and said: 'The Eriksberg Clinic.'

She glanced at him and took the next turn even harder.

'The Botox,' he went on. 'You didn't have to say anything. Why did you?'

'I thought you were smarter than you are,' Molly Blom said.

'Was it true, about the migraines?'

'Do you really think I want a baby-smooth forehead? But it does help.'

He frowned but said nothing more. He didn't even say a word when they drove into Stenbocksgatan and double-parked outside number 4. She jumped out; he sat there, unable to move. She went round the van, opened the passenger door and looked at him all tied up. She had a knife in her hand. 'So, am I going to regret this for the rest of my life?'

'Definitely,' he said. 'If you're thinking of stabbing me.'

She sighed and cut the two zip ties. But when he got out onto the pavement his hands were still fastened behind his back.

She pushed him ahead of her up the stairs, undid the locks and said: 'You did well to pick all these.'

'Thanks,' he said. 'Years of training.'

They went inside. She on switched the lights. A gentle, soothing glow spread across the flat. They went into the living room. The once immaculate white sofa was covered in stains. Ugly, rust-red stains. He felt like a villain. Like the villain he was. She led him over to the bay window and half sat on the desk, looking at the sofa.

'You stood here,' she said, picking up the various blocks of Post-it notes. 'You'd seen these. Maybe you could already hear Kent and Roy down by the front door. Then what happened?'

Berger sighed and thought. Above the sofa hung the huge picture of the mountaineers.

'I thought about how thick that picture was,' he said, nodding. 'How heavy it must have been for the removal men. Then I saw the scrap of paper on the floor and thought about the six different colours of Post-it notes. I picked it up and read it, pulled out the smallest evidence bag I had and shoved it up my backside.'

'Fitting,' Blom said. 'Do you know how much that sofa cost?'

They walked towards the picture, and Berger said: 'That's probably why I wanted to mess it up.'

'Hmm,' she said.

They reached the sofa. He pointed at the floor.

'That's where the note was,' he said.

She took the rolled-up, still slightly damp pink Post-it note from her pocket, unrolled it and said: 'It's probably best if we put it back in its place, then.'

She slid her hand behind the large photograph. There was a small click as a previously invisible crack opened down the snow-covered mountain. She leaned across the sofa. Then she folded back both sides of the picture. It was now twice as wide, about four metres from end to end, and inside an entire police investigation was mapped out in exquisite detail. Photographs, notes, receipts, forms, extracts from official registers, copies of certificates, airline tickets, and – above all – a confusion of Post-it notes in every imaginable colour.

Molly Blom attached the missing pink Post-it note with a magnet and said: 'I shall try to forget where that note has been.'

Berger looked at the impenetrable pattern. He could tell that his eyes were the size of saucers.

'Fucking hell,' he said. 'You really *are* crazy.'

'Do you still think you've been chasing this piece of scum harder than anyone else?' Blom asked, adjusting some of the notes.

Berger moved closer and looked to the left, where he found a photograph of himself from the start of Year 9. What struck him was the innocence in those eyes. Back then he hadn't yet seen a girl get tortured by his crazy friend in a rotting boathouse. Or crept away with his tail between his legs. Or consciously tried to suppress the whole thing.

'Who has framed photographs of themselves lined up in their bedroom? Who only has pictures of themselves in doing extreme sports? Who has migraines so terrible that they can only be treated with Botox? Who has nothing but protein drinks and plastic-wrapped fruit in their fridge? I'll tell you: a *manic* person. A control freak.'

'Not manic,' Blom said calmly, pointing at one of the photographs towards the middle of the display, a young, uniformed Molly Blom on a podium. 'Not manic, but determined. I'm a year younger than you, and I became a police officer two years before you did, and by then I already had an acting career behind me. While you were bumming about south-east Asia and taking random courses at university. Philosophy, wasn't it?'

'I thought it was going to give me the answer to all of life's riddles,' Berger said, looking at a photograph of the fifteen-year-old William Larsson. His face really was misshapen.

'He vanished without trace after Year 9,' Blom said with a nod.

'What are we doing here?' Berger asked.

'There are gaps,' Blom said, pointing at the display. 'And you're going to help me fill them.'

'Well we've wasted a fuck load of time on this charade, time Ellen Savinger doesn't have.'

Then it struck. All the tension he thought he'd seen in her face from the moment she fetched him from his cell erupted into sheer fury. She forced him up against the wall.

'Now listen very carefully, you bastard!' she roared. 'We've just confessed, both of us, that we've been running unsanctioned parallel investigations. We've both confessed that we already know who the murderer is. We've already confessed that our pasts are woven together with his. We're both utterly fucked. Do you understand? Can you get that into your head, you pathetic excuse for a cop?'

Berger felt himself just staring at her.

'Your loop was supposed to conceal that,' he said eventually.

'There was some sort of glitch, I don't know what. Some of our confidential conversation got picked up, and they're now hard at work trying to dig out the rest. Do you understand what that means?'

'Oh, fuck,' he said.

They said nothing for a while, just looked at each other.

In the end Berger said: 'As far as I'm concerned, it doesn't change that much. Things can't really get much worse. I'm already suspected of being a serial killer. But things really don't look good for you.'

Blom shoved him down onto the stained sofa and started walking round her flat. Berger watched patterns emerge inside her. He could see her weighing up pros and cons. He could see her making decisions that would affect the rest of her life.

'You've already removed me from custody of your own volition,' he said. 'You brought me here and showed me your secret investigation. You've already made your decision. You've broken more laws than I have.'

She breathed out. Stared at him, blaming him for messing up her controlled life. And he could see that it made sense. Then, understanding just how much sense it made, something even heavier hit him. The features of his face all seemed to slump.

She saw it. And pulled back.

He huddled up and sank down with his hands still tied behind his back. He hid his face against his knees, pressed it against his knees.

She heard him whimper. She crouched down.

'Oh, God,' he gasped. 'How many do you think there are?'

'We've got five,' she said. 'I think there are seven.'

'Seven fifteen-year-old girls,' he said. 'And none of them would have got hurt if I hadn't been such a coward. If I'd rescued you William Larsson would have been caught. And he wouldn't have come back now and become a serial killer. I – cowardly, pathetic Sam Berger – created him.'

'But you've been aware of that the whole time, surely?'

He whimpered some more. With great effort she overcame her instincts and reached a hand out towards him. It landed on his shoulder. They sat like that for a while.

Then she said: 'I feel pretty similar. I was a coward as well. I got free, but I didn't say a thing to anyone. I didn't tell anyone at all. I've lived with this on my own all these years.'

He snorted. 'But even that was my fault.'

'Yes,' she said. 'But I could have stopped him too.'

'Bloody hell,' he said. 'We don't have much time, do we?'

'I don't know how far they've got with the recording from

the interview room. My boss, August Steen, doesn't believe me. He *really* doesn't believe me. Kent and Roy could already be on their way up the stairs.'

'Again,' he said, and got to his feet. 'No, fuck that.'

She stood up, stretched and said: 'Well, one thing's clear. This frame can't stay here.'

'But it must weigh a ton.'

'It's supposed to look like it does.'

Berger looked at Blom. She returned his gaze. Their eyes locked.

'OK,' Berger said eventually. 'William Larsson is scattering clues to get me put away for his monstrous crimes. But does he know that you're on his trail?'

'There's no reason to think that, no.'

'There is.'

'There is?'

'How tall are you?'

She paused and stared at him.

'One metre sixty-nine,' she said in the end.

'Yes,' he said. 'The booby trap.'

'What?'

'The knives in the house in Märsta. They weren't designed for a normal-height cop, not even a short one, like Ekman. They were meant for a slightly taller than average woman. Or possibly you specifically, Molly. If I'm allowed to use your first name . . . '

If it had been possible, she would have frowned. She thought for a moment.

'OK,' she nodded, taking her knife out once more. He could see her wrestling with her thoughts.

Then she sighed and cut through the zip tie behind his back.

Their eyes met. He gestured towards the picture frame.

'So it doesn't weigh a ton?'

'No,' she said. 'I carried it up with the help of just one other person when I moved in.'

He nodded and started to push the stained sofa out of the way. Then he pointed at the pink Post-it note bearing the words *WL pl. surg. Saudi?* 'Just don't tell me you left that on the floor on purpose?'

She went to other end of the frame. 'That's something you'll never know.'

Then she slowly closed her end of the picture. He did the same. And what was hanging on the wall was nothing more than a very large picture of a gang of mountaineers heading up a snow-covered mountain. Together they gently lifted it down from the wall. It really wasn't particularly heavy. It felt more like polystyrene, or perhaps balsa wood. They carried it out into the hall. She opened the door to the stairs and the autumn darkness. Yelling in the stairwell in the dead of the night would obviously be a terrible move, so Berger sat on all the things he wanted to say while Blom locked the door and they manoeuvred the picture down the stairs and hurried to get it into the van before the frame got too wet, then jumped in themselves.

They sat there for a while. The weak glow of the street lamps shifted in patterns down the windscreen, spreading out, disappearing, re-emerging.

Berger breathed in deeply and looked at Blom. Eventually she looked away from the play of light on the windscreen and met his gaze.

'It's not just that we've tried to destroy each other in our respective interview rooms,' Berger said. 'We also have backgrounds that make us deeply unsuitable for each other. Are you seriously suggesting that we work together?'

It felt like the first time she had truly met his gaze, without any role play. In the end she looked away and made an impatient gesture.

'It's our only chance,' she said to the windscreen.

'Is there really no chance we could explain this and go back? Make a proper police investigation out of it?'

She paused. 'You and I are both guilty of disloyalty to our bosses. We'd be asked to hand over our IDs and weapons with immediate effect. We'd get the sack and a bunch of detached outsiders would take over our investigations. That's not going to help Ellen Savinger.'

'You're thinking of Allan?'

'I'm thinking of Allan, and I'm thinking of August. Allan and August. August doesn't give a damn about all this. For him the Security Service looks after the security of the realm and nothing else; his only move would be to throw the book at me. You know Allan's thoughts on the case better than I do. He's fallen for the fine old Social Democratic adage that Sweden doesn't have serial killers, and scarcely any intelligent killers at all. His desire to believe in Swedish innocence will turn William into a clumsy, mentally challenged kidnapper who is doing this sort of thing for the first time. And while you may not get fired quite as forcefully as I will, you're hardly going to be trusted with particularly challenging work. The archive, perhaps? A junior clerk in the police archive?'

'So you're suggesting that we . . . freelance?'

'Isn't that supposed to be the next big thing?' Molly Blom said, and even if it wasn't the first time he saw her smile, and even if was an extremely wry smile, it was at least a smile aimed directly at Sam Berger. He smiled back, probably also rather wryly.

'OK,' he said after a pause. 'I presume you've got some fancy

Security Service hideout in mind for us? Some smart CIA safe house that's conveniently off the grid?'

'Sadly they're very carefully controlled.'

'We're on the run with no idea of where we're running to? And you were the one thinking I was smarter than I am? Not the other way round?'

'It was hard enough to get this far,' she said morosely. 'We can go to a motel.'

Their eyes met and they stared at each other. It was strangely obvious that they both wanted the other to say what they were thinking. What they were both thinking.

Berger rubbed his forehead and decided that it was up to him. 'Sure, we could go to a motel. Of course we could.'

Blom just looked at him.

He groaned. 'Or we could go straight for William . . . '

The look in her eyes didn't change. She wasn't about to make this easy for him.

'The boathouse,' he said.

She went on staring at him.

He continued: 'The situation changed after Märsta. Now he knows we're on to him. Doesn't everything we know about this case tell us that he's got Ellen in the boathouse?'

Molly Blom finally turned away from him. She gazed off into the distance, far beyond Stenbocksgatan.

Eventually she said: 'There's no way I'm ever going back there.'

Berger waited a while before going on. 'We've both suspected William Larsson for a while. We both know that there's a place directly connected to our suspicions. Don't try to tell me you haven't been there.'

She was silent, still gazing far into the distance.

'Well, I've been there. It was quiet. Dead and deserted for God knows how many years.'

She nodded slowly and said reluctantly: 'I've been there too. It was empty.'

'Do you know anything about it?'

'It's still there, on the shore of Edsviken,' she said. 'It's fenced off, untouched. There's some kind of drawn-out legal dispute between two companies that both claim to own it.'

Berger looked at her. 'Isn't there a mad, perverse logic in the idea that William would go back to where it all started? And hasn't he actually invited the two of us? Isn't he sitting there with Ellen strapped to that clock he once tied you to? Sitting there waiting for us?'

Once again, so much emotion was coursing through Blom's body that it was visible everywhere except her forehead, which she was now resting against her left hand.

'Well, then,' he went on. 'Let's go to the boathouse. To pick up William Larsson.'

She looked at him for a little too long before starting the engine. The windscreen wipers began to move. She carried on along Stenbocksgatan and out into Engelbrektsgatan, past the pitch-blackness of Humlegården. The van had almost reached the junction with Birger Jarlsgatan when she pulled halfway up onto the pavement and stopped. Apart from a few sporadic taxis there was no traffic at all on the streets around Stureplan. Berger pointed towards the junction.

'This really is Hercules at the crossroads,' he said.

She pulled a face.

He went on: 'Left to Kungsholmen and Police Headquarters, where we'll have to fight impossible odds to keep our jobs and force our bosses to confront the truth. Right towards Sollentuna and the boathouse, towards William Larsson, towards Ellen Savinger. Towards terrible freedom.'

She stared out through the windscreen. The wipers were

sweeping across the windscreen feverishly. Some of the time it was perfectly clear, some of the time completely impenetrable. But she could see the choice of routes.

An unusually tangible life choice.

'Left or right?' Berger said. 'Last chance. Safe territory or . . . the badlands?'

She put the van in first gear and accelerated away from the pavement.

Then she turned right and roared off northwards up Birger Jarlsgatan.

Towards the badlands.

III

25

Sam gathered up his schoolbooks, dropped them in his rucksack and ran out so fast that dust flew up from the fitted carpet. He saw just the backs of his parents' heads as they huddled in front of the television in the kitchen. It was shouting the news that someone called Bill Clinton had won the US presidential election. He called out a quick bye and just glimpsed their raised hands before he shut the back door with a thud and saw that the first snow of winter had settled on his bicycle. And he only had eight minutes. He sighed and shook the bike as best he could, then slid down the garden path as the snow beneath his buttocks melted. He was going to look like shit at school. Out on the road it was seriously slippery, cars were parked along the road, abandoned. As he cycled under the railway bridge the train roared above his head. That wasn't good; now he was properly late. He emerged onto Sollentunavägen and raced along the pavement, turned in to the school, rode straight into the bicycle rack and quickly locked up his bike. He rushed through the deserted hall and heard the bell ring as he took the stairs three at a time. The door to the chemistry room was about to close, and just as he got his stiff, frozen fingers in the gap he saw a figure a few metres off, facing away from him, someone staring out through the window at the building next door. All he managed to see before he was sucked into the chemistry room was a long mane of blond hair. He sat down at one of the desks, next to

Pia, who gave him a smile that meant the day had got off to a good start after all.

The young chemistry teacher, also their form teacher, cleared his throat and said: 'We've got a new pupil joining the class today. It's very important that you're nice to him.' Anton called out from the back row: 'We're always nice, what the hell's wrong with you?' and gave the chemistry teacher his typical, wide Anton smile.

The chemistry teacher frowned. 'It's more important than usual that you're nice now. He has a . . . deformity . . . '

As the teacher abandoned his sentence and left the classroom, leaving the door open, the class started chattering. What's he talking about? A deformity? What's going on? Then the chemistry teacher returned. He had with him a boy with long blond hair.

'This is William,' the chemistry teacher said in a loud voice.

The class fell silent. So silent that the ticking of the clock on the wall sounded like the ringing of a church bell.

'Hello,' William said.

It was break. She wasn't very fond of breaks. Apart from the outsiders, the girls gathered in two groups. Molly would rather have hung out at the smoking corner, but if there was even a whiff of smoke about her when she got home her mum would have gone mental at her, and she couldn't handle that, not again. And she didn't want to be one of the outsiders, the swots or outcasts or few brave souls who simply couldn't be bothered with the whole social game; she wasn't strong enough for that. So she headed towards the same old group loitering on the bench right outside the school doors. Even though it had snowed for the first time that winter, the gang was outside without coats. It was as if their bodies were wiser than they were, as if they instinctively realised that they needed oxygen to get through the day. And maybe cool down. It was noisy and playfully combative and all pretty pointless. But Linda had got a mobile phone from her rich dad, and after a while everyone was staring at it.

'It's a Nokia 1011, with GSM,' Linda said with genuine pride. No one understood what she was saying, but they all wanted to hold the magnificent dark-grey gadget. It went from Alma to Layla to Eva to Salma, and then suddenly it was in Molly's hand, and she needed to come up with something funny, she couldn't just stand there looking lost. So she raised the mobile phone to her ear and said: 'Yes, this is Linda Bergting, I'd like to order a gigolo.'

And they laughed and Maria cried out: 'Bloody hell, Molly!'

Linda snatched it back and yelled: 'Now it's going to stink of your sex-starved breath all fucking day'.

They laughed, all of them, but then Molly suddenly saw Alma stop laughing and open her eyes wide. 'Wow,' she said so quietly it was just a movement of her lips.

The group fell silent, one by one, as head after head turned towards the doors. The guy with the long blond hair stopped for a moment and turned his face towards them. It was all misshapen. His chin was crooked, a horn-like bulge stuck out from one side of his forehead, his right cheekbone poked up, the left was sunken. Then he turned and walked away.

'Shit,' Linda said, and dropped her mobile phone.

When the pupils gathered in the school hall stupidly early in the morning, the coolest of them still smelled of drink. It had been a long Lucia night. But not for Sam. He had been invited but hadn't bothered to go. He couldn't be bothered with much these days, had given up most things. He'd stopped playing football, no longer practised the guitar, and had even given up his electronics. Everything was boring these days, including school. He couldn't even really be bothered with girls, he realised when he looked down at Pia sitting next to him.

And soon it would be Christmas, not that that felt very exciting, celebrating with Grandma and Granddad and Dad and Mum and his brother all playing happy families. The Year 9s sat right at the front of the hall, waiting for the Lucia procession. Another fucking Lucia procession, with candles and singing and shit. Sam just wanted to sleep. The curtain behind the stage began to move, presumably the headmaster on his way to give yet another meaningless speech. But the person who came out onto the stage was Anton from Sam's class. He grabbed the microphone, and at the same moment Sam saw their chemistry teacher stand up a few rows away.

Anton smiled his usual big Anton grin, and his voice rang out around the hall: 'You're expecting a Lucia procession, you fucking peasants, but here comes the real Lucia.' A couple of Anton's friends, Micke and Freddan, dragged a Lucia out through the curtain. This Lucia had on a fluttering white dress, and wax candles were burning from the crown perched on long blond hair, which had been combed to cover the whole head. The chemistry teacher pushed his way forward, more urgently now, while Anton laughed loudly and brushed the hair away from the Lucia's face. The mouth was covered by duct tape, and the face was crooked, misshapen. It was now apparent that the Lucia's arms had been tied with more tape.

Anton smiled again and said into the microphone: 'Come on then, sing, for fuck's sake, don't be shy.'

As the chemistry teacher tumbled onto the stage, Freddan pulled the tape from the Lucia's face and Anton held out the microphone. The only sound that echoed round the hall was long, drawn-out whimper. The chemistry teacher was there now. He pushed Anton and Micke and Freddan out of the way and tried to lift the burning Lucia crown, but it had been glued onto the blond hair. The chemistry teacher blew out the candles and tried to tease the crown off, but only ended up pulling at the hair as wax ran down into it. William screamed loudly, straight into the microphone. And while Anton and Micke and Freddan ran laughing down the side aisle and out of the hall, Sam realised just how sick he felt.

Sam was sitting on a bench some way into the schoolyard, and he took out the little radio he had got for Christmas and tried to find the new station. He had actually been hoping for a Sony Discman – it would have been brilliant to be able to take your CDs with you – but his parents had given him a radio. He pretended to be more annoyed than he was, because he actually quite liked listening to the radio. He adjusted the dial but kept getting it wrong and didn't even notice when someone sat down on the bench beside him. He only turned round when he heard someone clear their throat. Even though a couple of months had passed, he was taken aback. He had never stopped being astonished, would never stop being astonished. And he had probably never seen William's jagged face this close before.

'Radio?' William said.

'P4 is starting to broadcast today,' Sam managed to say. 'I don't really know which frequency.'

William nodded. 'You like technical things, don't you?' And then he held something out to Sam.

It was a circle, almost ten centimetres in diameter, and inside a large number of cogs and pinions were moving in remarkable patterns. Instinctively, Sam put the radio down on the snowy bench and looked closer. It was a magical feeling, seeing all those little wheels spin at different speeds.

'What it is?' he asked.

'A pocket watch from the turn of the century,' William said. 'I've taken the back off. Do you want to hold it?'

Sam nodded.

William carefully placed the watch in his frozen hands. 'It's

American,' he said. 'An Elgin. Otherwise all the best watchmakers are from Switzerland.'

Sam just stared.

William went on: 'I've got lots.'

'How the hell can you afford that?'

'I buy broken ones and repair them. You just need to understand how they work.'

'Cool,' Sam said. 'Why me?'

'I heard you were interested in technical stuff, electronics.'

'I've given that up,' Sam said sullenly.

'This was before electronics. You have to wind this watch, but there are also self-winding watches.' Sam looked up from the hypnotic cogs and for the first time met William's gaze in that jagged face.

'OK,' William said, instinctively retreating. 'That's not the only reason I showed you this.'

'OK. Why, then?'

'Because you've never been mean to me.'

Sam sat motionless for a while. Then something happened; he didn't understand what. The watch flew from his hand, and he was left holding nothing but snow. He heard giggling and saw several of the tiny cogs roll across the snow before being swallowed up by it. He looked up and saw a gang of girls scattering. He recognised the girl at the front, the one who appeared to have thrown the snowball. She was one of the toughest in Year 8; he thought her name might be Linda. Before she ran off she shouted: 'Why don't you give the abortion a blow job instead?' Sam shook his head and saw William sink to his knees, searching the snow for the vanished cogs. Their eyes met. Sam had never seen such a black look in all his life. Then they hunted through the snow together.

Molly was sitting by herself on the bench near the door, trying to skim her geography textbook. She had forgotten they were having a test. She tried to make sense of the west coast of Africa beyond the dodgy bit that was Western Sahara. Was it Mauritania, Senegal, Gambia – Gambia was sort of squeezed inside Senegal – and then Guinea-Bissau, Guinea, Sierra Leone, Liberia? Then Ivory Coast, Ghana . . . Then a snowball hit the west coast of Africa and quickly melted, ruining the whole page. Molly looked up and saw Linda hurrying to form another snowball. She tucked her book away in her bag and made a snowball as fast as she could. She threw it, but it missed Linda and hit Maria behind her. Maria screamed and rushed forward to rub Molly's face in the snow, but by then Molly had already taken cover behind the bench with Layla. Alma in turn attacked Maria from behind while Linda turned on Salma instead, with some pretty useless snowballs. In the end they were just laughing.

Then Salma stiffened and pointed: 'Look over there. Isn't that Samuel from Year 9? Sexy Sam?' Their voices wove together, triggering each other: 'What the shit, is that really the abortion next to him? What are they doing? Doesn't he know ugliness is catching? That's disgusting, being that close. Imagine having to touch that face. So fucking disgusting.' By the time they crept towards them there were seven of them. Molly went with them but kept in the background. It didn't feel good. But Sam and William didn't notice a thing; they were just staring at something that looked like a little tub of chewing tobacco. Was that all they were doing, chewing tobacco for the first time? In the end the gang was close enough to launch a snowball. Everyone looked at Linda, their unofficial leader. Slowly and carefully she shaped a snowball, and in the background Molly heard some muffled giggling, though she couldn't claim to be entirely innocent of that herself. But when Linda's snowball struck and something that clearly wasn't chewing tobacco rolled away from the tub – and both William and Sam started searching the snow – Molly suddenly saw an image of the Lucia celebrations, saw the chemistry teacher lead William from the stage, where, with the help of the school cleaner, he eventually had to cut off his long blond hair, his pride and joy, hacking off great clumps of it from his deformed head. Admittedly, she was running from the scene faster than all the other girls, but unlike them she couldn't bring herself to laugh.

Sam avoided William at school as winter turned to spring, but when there were no witnesses he would occasionally go over to his house. William's hair had started to grow out again, and they would lock themselves in his room in the flat in the centre of Helenelund where he lived with his mum, who smelled sort of sweet and always looked stressed. Sam was struck by a mark on the door of William's room, four impressions, as from the knuckles of a fist, but he never asked about them. William would get his watches out. He kept them in threes, and when Sam asked why he replied: 'The Ramans do everything in threes,' and explained that it came from Arthur C. Clarke's science-fiction novel Rendezvous with Rama. *Then he started to show Sam his collection, everything from big wall clocks to the one that was probably Sam's favourite, the ring clock. It was a very small timepiece placed on a ring that would fit a woman's finger. But then William would show him plans and photographs of the complete opposite: gigantic tower clocks with big chains and heavy cogs, big pinions and springs, axles and pins, shafts, flywheels and spindles, pendulums, clicks and weights. When William showed him the pictures from inside the clock tower in Cremona in Italy – the largest medieval clock in the world – his eyes lit up. And Sam's probably did the same.*

Then one day William said: 'The snow's gone now.' Sam must have given some sort of indication that he didn't understand, because William went on: 'Do you want to come and look at something I've made?'

Sam wasn't sure if he wanted to be seen with William, so he pulled a hesitant face.

'You can follow at a distance,' William said, as if he understood exactly what Sam meant.

And they cycled off. William first, on his crappy bike with the ridiculously high handlebars, Sam two hundred metres behind on his extremely staid Crescent, which he had increasingly come to loathe. Then they arrived. They left their bicycles by a bus stop that seemed to have been forgotten about and ran out into a meadow where the tall grass had been flattened by the rain, and squelched past the aspen trees until a small building came into view by the water. A boathouse among the trees, right on the shore, greenish-brown and ugly and quite wonderful.

William went up to it and said: 'It's been abandoned.'

'Are you really sure?'

William nodded and went down to the door by the water's edge. Two steps up, then a padlock that he had the key to, and then in. Old-fashioned boating equipment lay strewn about, rusty boat engines and stiffened life jackets, stranded buoys and rusty anchors, but beyond all that was something that looked far newer. Chains. Cogs. Pinions. Springs. Axles. Pins. Shafts. Flywheels. Clicks. Weights. Dripping oil. The entire mechanism was fixed to two sturdy posts that were in turn attached to the floor of the boathouse and reached all the way to the roof. And somewhere in the middle of the confusion was a clock face. When Sam looked closer he saw that the minute hand was moving the whole time, slowly, clockwise. It showed a couple of minutes to three.

William said: 'Just wait.'

Sam waited. They waited, for what felt like a long time, but was really only two minutes. When the clock chimed a heavy weight fell from above and made a circular depression in the wooden floor.

Molly was thinking about the exams. She squinted up at the strong spring sun and thought that there was one more year. One more year of childhood, then it would be over, right there, in that big schoolyard.

She had just turned fifteen, in March, and life was moving in the right direction. On the way to adulthood. She had lost all interest in the boys at school. After thinking about it for a while – a good while, to be honest – she had come to the conclusion that she was not interested in the male sex after all. There may have been the odd boy at school who was still interesting – a Micke, an Alex, a Sam, a Svante – but mainly she was focused on the future. There were other things that appealed to her. She might not have wanted to call it politics, but social issues, certainly. She had become aware of something very recently: people were so different and it really didn't matter. Difference was a good thing; interest in things we didn't know about was what helped us to develop as people. She'd heard that somewhere in the world there was a big investigation into human genes, and it was unclear if you could actually speak about the human race, or if we ought instead to be talking about many races, several races, the way racism always had. Perhaps something was going on, a scientific investigation that could prove that we all – all five billion of us – belonged to exactly the same human race, in spite of minor variations in colour and culture. It was incredibly interesting that there had actually been human races that had become extinct. What were they called? Neanderthals, Java Man? Once they too had migrated from Africa and had their own civilisations, or at least tribal societies, and they had disappeared. They had simply been wiped out; there was no trace of them left. Except bones. The important thing was that it meant the rest of us were connected, regardless of our differences. And that was precisely the sort of thing she was thinking when the big, empty schoolyard was no longer completely empty, when a figure came into view, a figure that only just looked like it belonged to the collective human race she had been dreaming of. And she managed to force a smile when William sat down on the bench beside her and said: 'Hello! Do you want to come and see something I found?'

⋆ ⋆ ⋆

The early summer that prevails in a desolate, grit-covered football pitch is strangely remorseless, no wind, the air laced with dust, the sun sharp and prickly. Sam sees a group of people at the other end of the pitch, by the far goal. He sees that they're girls, lots of girls; he can hear their shrill voices but can't make out any words. The emptiness above the dusty grit seems to filter out everything resembling language. Sam has become a different person; time has changed. It feels as if he's aged a couple of years in just a few weeks. These days he avoids this sort of gathering. He can feel that he has become a loner. But there's something about the unarticulated yelling that draws him in. Against all his instincts he is drawn in that direction, and sees the back of one girl after another. They're wearing summery clothes, dresses, skirts, and the merciless sun makes their long hair shine in all manner of hues. The dust swirls around them, and as they move Sam can see that they aren't alone. Behind them a taller head rises up. Anton's, and it's moving. It disappears behind the curtain of girls, reappears, still moving. Then the curtain parts a little more, and against the goalpost, tied to the post, stands a figure. Its long blond hair hangs like another curtain in front of the figure's face. His trousers have been pulled down, the lower half of his body exposed, and Sam turns abruptly and leaves before William has a chance to see him. All Sam can think, over and over again, manically, is: It's almost the summer holidays. All this crap will soon be over.

26

Wednesday 28 October, 01.53

In spite of the downpour the aspen leaves were rustling. And even if the rain had flattened the occasional clump of grass, it remained almost head-high. It was lit up, jerkily, by the sweeping beams of two pocket torches. If anyone had seen the scene from above, it would have looked like two bioluminescent fish playing in the unexplored depths of the ocean.

It was unclear if anyone did see it from above.

A hand rose up above the grass. Berger ducked and moved towards it at a crouch. Blom's index finger was pointing towards one of the aspens, and eventually Berger caught sight of the large security camera.

'It looks ancient,' he whispered.

'Who knows?' Blom whispered back, adjusting her bulletproof vest. Then she gave him a sharp look, as if she were evaluating his mental state. With evident reluctance, she held something out towards him.

Only when she snatched the object back from his outstretched hand did he realise that it was a pistol.

'The way I see it, you could still be in league with William,' she whispered, aiming her own gun at him. 'You could have led me here so you can strap me to that fucking contraption one more time.'

'Is that what you really think?' Berger said.

Blom wrinkled her nose, then she handed him the weapon. He took it and weighed it in his hand, then nodded. Her face was wet, her blonde hair streaked with rain – and her eyes very clear. Then she set off, torch and pistol raised. Soon she was nothing more than a flickering beam of light winding its way through the greenery. He followed it.

Sometimes he lost sight of her, but she always popped up again, a light like elusive quicksilver through the still green grass.

Out of the darkness the clump of aspen trees rose up. He could detect the faintly brackish smell of open water, and behind the trees he could just make out a greenish-brown building.

The boathouse.

It shouldn't be visible, he was thinking as he walked straight into her. She was crouching low in the grass with her torch switched off.

'Turn it off,' she whispered.

He did as she said.

'Light,' she said, pointing towards the trees.

He could see the vague outline of the boathouse but couldn't make much sense of what he was looking at.

'Where from?' he asked.

'Don't know,' she said. 'But we shouldn't be able to see it yet. It ought to be pitch-black.'

'Is it coming from inside?'

She just shook her head and sharpened her gaze.

They were about fifty metres away, and it was their last chance to hide in the tall grass. Just a metre or so in front of them the grass gave way to bare rock before the trees took over. Berger looked at her carefully and had to admit that Blom was more used to being out in the field than he was. He saw her reach a decision.

'There's a lot at stake,' she whispered.

He nodded and stared at the faintly illuminated boathouse. Something seemed to linger there, life, perhaps death. Perhaps their deaths. He shuddered.

'We need to split up,' Blom said. 'I'll take this side. You go round to the lake.'

'Look out for booby traps,' Berger said. 'You know how he likes contraptions.'

'That hasn't slipped my mind,' she said darkly, and disappeared.

He set off. Felt himself get swallowed up.

He turned away from the water and entered the trees, keeping his torch switched off. He could just make out the short pillars the boathouse rested on. Saw the rock. Saw the slippery rock. Saw the window above the rock. Even thought he could see a twenty-two-year-old mark on the window. He had to ignore his feelings and act rationally.

If William Larsson had returned to where it all started, he was waiting in the pitch-black. Maybe he'd seen them coming a while back.

Maybe he was looking at Berger right now.

Berger had been frozen up until that moment. The tumultuous events of the past twenty-four hours had left him detached from the present. It was like he was moving through a really sick dream. But now, deep among the trees beside the boathouse of his childhood, reality caught up with him. He woke up. His frozen heart thawed; his pulse beat faster. He felt himself shaking. Suddenly he realised with his whole being, his whole body, what might actually be hidden behind that oddly luminous facade.

It could be hell itself.

Everything was in his hands, however much they were shaking. There was no shortcut. Concentration, focus. Clarity of vision. The ability to look evil in the eye. His hand stopped shaking.

Berger went down to the stony shore. A definite chill was coming from the black water. Pointing his torch at the ground, he managed to avoid the most slippery stones. He approached the boathouse from the water's edge. He could see a window in a door, nothing more, but there was a crooked flight of steps leading up to the jetty that stretched from the building into the lake.

Berger was almost at the boathouse. His left hand aimed the torch straight at the ground while his gun rested in his right hand.

As he reached the steps he heard a rattling sound from the jetty above. It penetrated the night, followed by silence. He took the safety off his gun, shone the torch at the steps and went up with slow, silent footsteps. He pressed himself against the wall of the boathouse and paused. Cast a quick glance round the corner.

Nothing there. All he could see was some maritime junk on the jetty. On the far side of the building there was no equivalent flight of steps, only a half-metre-high railing and a two-metre drop to the rocks at the water's edge.

No one had jumped down; he would have heard them. That left the door.

It was closed.

Berger heard his rapidly accelerating pulse like the ticking of a clock. A large clock, with a powerful clapper.

He snuck round the corner, treading cautiously on the planks of the jetty. They felt strong enough, didn't creak. He took a couple of steps towards the door. Stopped. Listened.

Nothing but the rain.

A diamond-shaped window in the door was considerably darker than the door itself.

Then he heard the rattling sound again. It was coming from inside the boathouse. It was time. No way back now.

The sound wasn't coming from the door itself, but from the side of it. There was a hole. The first thing he saw were odd pinpricks of light that his accumulated experience tried in vain to associate with known weapons. It didn't work. A portal opened through time – into absolute chaos.

Then he saw teeth, sharp, bared teeth, and heard a strangely aggressive wheezing sound.

Then he saw the spines.

A hedgehog emerged from the hole. It spines were raised. It wheezed again, then turned and went back inside the boathouse with a rattling sound. Something inside shrieked. It didn't sound human.

Berger reached his hand towards the door. He tried the handle. Locked. He backed away towards the railing and raised his foot to kick the door in. Then it was thrown open.

At the edge of his field of vision he saw his lowered weapon rise up. He saw it in an absurd series of images, a slightly blacker crooked line through the darkness until all he saw was an unexpectedly solid Glock at chest height. Only afterwards did he see the bare, raised hand.

Molly Blom didn't lower it, even when she saw that he had lowered his weapon. Instead she gestured with her hand for him to follow her. He went over and stepped inside the boathouse. It stank of tar. He followed the beam of her torch to the corner. There were four small hedgehogs. Nearby an agitated parent hedgehog was moving about, wheezing and rattling.

He laughed, an unplanned laugh of relief.

'No one here,' Molly Blom said.

Their torches moved round the rest of the boathouse. Apart from the abandoned boat engines, buoys and a number of beer cans of varying vintage, there were a couple of carpentry benches and two tables, a crumpled tarpaulin, some cables and ropes in various shades of green.

But what made the strongest impression were the two pillars stretching from floor to roof some way from the wall. In the wall closest to the jetty were six mooring rings in two vertical columns, three in each, so that the two columns formed an imaginary cube with the pillars as the two other uprights.

Blom's torch jerked and the circle of light sank lower.

'Dear God,' she said.

Berger stepped between the posts and looked away from the wall. On the opposite wall, some seven metres away, was a window. In the window he could see an ancient greasy mark. A wave of deep shame washed over him, and the shame quickly turned to pain. The gnawing, shooting pain of a wrecked conscience.

She came over to him. She was holding something in her hand. After a while he saw that it was a strand of hair. A long, blond hair.

'The worst thing,' Molly Blom said, 'is that I can't tell if it's mine or William's.'

They sat there together on the floor of the boathouse listening to the rustling of the hedgehogs. Time passed in peculiar phases. The trees rustled non-stop. There was someone trying to get through from another time.

'The light,' Berger said. 'Why did it feel like the building was lit up?'

'It didn't matter in the end,' Blom said.

'I'm just wondering why.'

'Probably fluorescent paint. Probably old. Probably painted by William himself twenty-two years ago.'

'But why?'

'He captured this abandoned boathouse. He made it his own. He wanted to find it easily at night. There was already decent fluorescent paint back then.'

'That would last until now?'

There was a sudden burst of rustling from the hedgehogs in the corner. Berger started, breathed out, shrugged off his bulletproof vest and stood up. He went over to a cobweb-covered light switch and pressed it. A lamp lit up over by the jetty door.

'Bloody hell,' Berger said. 'Electricity.'

Blom raised her head with a look from a completely different decade and said: 'Presumably one of the warring companies is paying without realising.'

Then she tugged off her own bulletproof vest. 'We need to get going as soon as possible.'

Berger nodded, then kept nodding for a few moments. 'Do we have to?'

Blom paused and stared at him.

'We've got nowhere to go tonight,' Berger said. 'And time's passing. Maybe we should try to get something done. Do some thinking.'

'You mean I should stay in the building where I was tortured? And where you betrayed me so cruelly?'

'That is probably what I mean.'

* * *

It took several hours to create some sort of order. They worked through dawn, clearing, tidying, hanging, organising, fixing, until it was actually light enough for them to switch the lights off. At that point they carried in a huge package draped in a stiffened military-green tarpaulin. They leaned the package against the two pillars and, exhausted, folded back the rain-drenched tarpaulin. Slowly a wonderful photograph of a gang of mountaineers climbing a snow-covered mountain was revealed. They hammered a couple of nails in the pillars and hung the picture up. Then they unfolded the sides and doubled the width of the frame. It was covered with Post-it notes and other papers which, against all the odds, had remained dry.

Blom went over to one of the carpentry benches and sat down on a now tolerably clean chair. The carpentry bench now held nothing but protein drinks. Then she started to unpack things from her suitcases, laying out cables and connecting her computer to numerous different devices.

Berger said: 'Are those Security Service cases?'

'Survival equipment for undercover jobs,' Blom said. 'They're always in the van.'

'And are you sure they're not wired? Are they really untraceable?'

'Seeing as I removed the SIM card from your mobile, we ought to be OK,' she said. 'This is my untraceable equipment, including a perfectly acceptable 4G connection.'

'But we still won't be able to access databases and internal networks?'

'We will. The idea with this equipment is that I should be able to do precisely that from obscure locations, with total anonymity. One of the few advantages of working undercover.'

Berger nodded and assessed the interior of the boathouse. It was still filthy, and definitely ascetic, but it might actually work.

'The basics, then?' he said. 'Running water, places to sleep, toilet, fridge, cooker, food?'

'Running water?' Blom said. 'When we've got a lake right outside the door?'

'That's the sea. Salt water.'

'OK, so we'll have to pick up some bottles of water. And some sort of mini-fridge and a microwave. Sleeping bags and food. We'll sort it later this morning. Don't get hung up on details.'

'Money doesn't feel like a detail,' Berger said. 'Our bank cards are screwed.'

Molly Blom leaned down towards the suitcase again. She fished up a thick bundle of five-hundred-krona notes.

'Undercover cash,' she said. 'Have a protein drink. Stop whining, start working.'

27

Wednesday 28 October, 12.14

Berger looked down at her legs from the van's passenger seat.

'Army trousers?' he said. 'Are we doing national service?'

She pulled a face and concentrated on driving.

'Seriously, though,' he said. 'I didn't see you buy them.'

'You shop like a woman,' Blom said. 'I shop like a man. It took forever for you to choose underpants.'

'It's a sensitive piece of clothing,' Berger said.

The rain was tipping down on Norrortsleden. They were passing beneath the E18, north of Ullnasjön, heading out to the sticks.

'Do you think changing the number plates will be enough?' Berger asked.

'I know there are rumours about some experimental method of reverse-tracking GPS,' Blom said, 'but I doubt they'd resort to that in this situation. We aren't exactly a direct threat to Sweden's democratic system, its citizens' freedoms and rights or national security.'

'No?' Berger said. 'What a disappointment.'

They were silent for a while. Then he changed the subject.

'What do you think happened when William vanished after

school? He went up in smoke, disappeared off the face of the earth.'

'I think our shared hypothesis is correct,' Blom said. 'He must have had help.'

'He was completely helpless right from the start, all the way through primary school,' Berger said. 'He and his mum kept moving round the suburbs of Stockholm because of the bullying. You haven't got kids, Molly, you can't begin to imagine the pain of seeing your child bullied everywhere they go. Being turned into a nomad because of cruelty. Knowing that in every new place you arrive, the same hell would be repeated.'

'What do you remember about his mother?' Blom asked.

'Not much,' Berger said. 'She was pretty twitchy.'

'Twitchy?' Blom said.

'Nervous, always doing something, couldn't sit still. Smelled funny.'

'Funny?'

'Are you my psychologist?'

'Focus now. Funny, how? Disgusting?'

'No, not at all. More like nice. Sweet, perhaps.'

'Alcohol?'

Berger paused. Then nodded slowly.

'I hadn't really been exposed to that back then. But that's probably what it was.'

'She died in rehab in Kista twelve years ago.'

Berger nodded again.

'There's a horrible logic to that,' he said.

'Do you remember what she looked like?' Blom asked. 'I've only seen a passport photograph. Blonde?'

'No,' Berger said. 'Mind you, that really blond hair is usually a childhood thing. Nordic childhood, anyway. Then you end up with brown hair. I was blond when I was little. I bet you were too.'

'What do you mean?' Blom exclaimed. 'I'm blonde now!'

'Yeah, except for a couple of millimetres of roots.'

Blom wrenched the van to the left. The tyres shrieked, saving her the trouble. Åkersberga, which had appeared like a mirage, vanished again as they headed on into the countryside.

'And no sign of a father?' she said. 'You don't remember anything?'

'You've spent a couple of years on this,' Berger said. 'I've had a few hours, and I haven't got any further. William never wanted to talk about his dad.'

'From William's birth, Stina Larsson was registered as a single parent. No dad at all. No siblings.'

'Should we assume that the father was blond?' Berger said. 'Now I come to think of it, his mum was more of a classic brunette.'

In the distance the harsh red walls of Österåker Prison rose up, concertinaed like some crazy giant's accordion.

'You still don't feel like telling me what we're doing here?' Berger said.

'It's a gamble,' Blom said, giving him a sideways glance.

'What are you looking for?'

'Surveillance cameras. We'd better stop here.'

'So I'm going to sit with the engine running just out of range and wait?'

'Exactly,' Blom said, and pulled up. 'A getaway van.'

The interview room in Österåker Prison was as bland every other interview room: table, security cameras, chairs, nothing else. The prisoner on the other side of the table was bland as well, in his grey prison tracksuit. He was in his early forties, and if it weren't for the evidence time had left on his face, he would have been completely transparent.

'I assume there's similar evidence on the rest of your body?' Molly Blom said.

'The usual paedophile treatment,' the prisoner said, touching his latest black eye.

'Only you, Axel Jansson, aren't just a paedophile, you're a murderer as well.'

'And you, Eva Lindkvist, are a cop asking seriously stale fucking questions. You'd be a really shit cop if you hadn't read the verdict.'

'Where you strategically confessed to all counts of sexual assault against children and consistently denied murder. To escape a murder conviction. Child-killers get extra special treatment in here, I bet.'

'I'm not a violent person.'

'Of course not, Axel. Sunisa Phetwiset was a Thai sex-slave, only just fifteen, owned by the Albanian mafia. No violence involved there.'

'That wasn't even paedophilia,' Axel Jansson said. 'She was legal.'

'In the other confirmed cases the girls were eight, eleven, four and twelve. Four?'

'It was a moment of weakness. But never violence.'

'Of course not, Axel. Tell me about the night with Sunisa Phetwiset.'

'You must have read the whole fucking file. The interviews are in there. What I said then hasn't changed at all.'

'The young Thai girl was delivered to your home by the Albanians. You had sex. She left your flat at quarter past eleven that evening.'

'And she got a tip!'

'The problem is the blood found in your flat, the stairwell, and in the boot of your car. The problem is the fragments of skin and blood found under your fingernails. All containing Sunisa Phetwiset's DNA.'

'There was no body,' Axel Jansson said angrily. 'They dragged every stretch of water imaginable. No body, no murder.'

'You know it's not as simple as that.'

'What are you doing here, Eva Lindkvist? And who the fuck are you really?'

'Calm down, Axel. I'm following up on a completely different case; it's got nothing to do with you. You're not risking anything by talking to me.'

'Every time I talk to a cop I'm risking my life.'

Molly Blom paused, then leaned across the table and whispered: 'So you still haven't realised that I'm the best and most undeserved chance you've ever had in the whole of your pathetic life?'

Axel Jansson actually jerked back. Eventually he asked: 'What are you saying?'

'That there might be a different murderer. What did you leave out when you were questioned?'

'Nothing. It really happened like I said. We fucked, I paid, she left. Nothing else. A different murderer?'

'And the blood in the flat and under your nails?'

'Under my nails isn't that odd. I was a bit rougher than I admitted.'

'And the flat?'

'No idea. It was just scratch marks on her buttocks. But there were several decilitres of blood found throughout the flat.'

'I'm really not doing myself any favours sitting here

whispering with you, Axel. They'll soon come in and intervene. I need more. How did the blood get into your flat? Were you there the whole time until the police arrived?'

'No, because they didn't show up until a couple of days later.'

Blom leaned back and felt a wave of nausea ripple through her body. She inhaled deeply and stood up. Even though she tried not to turn round, she saw the whole of Axel Jansson's body shrink as he prepared for the next round of paedophile-bashing.

Molly Blom was led back through metal detectors and heavy gates until she regained her freedom. She stared up at the grey, metallic Roslagen sky and let the heavy raindrops hit her face. She stood like that for a while. As if the rain could wash the shit from her face.

Against her will she found herself thinking about Axel Jansson, and about the deep misfortune of having been born with such a warped inclination. Then she thought about the possibility of helping to shorten his sentence. She thought about four-year-old girls and felt that she probably needed to think it all through one more time. Then she reached the van. It was facing the other direction, ready to escape. Berger was sitting in the driver's seat with the engine running.

She got into the passenger seat. 'I think we've got another victim.'

Berger set the van moving and said. 'If we're going to do this, we can't have any more secrets.'

Blom found herself nodding. 'A fifteen-year-old victim of trafficking, a Sunisa Phetwiset, was murdered during the period between Julia Almström and Jonna Eriksson, on 9 October last year. Axel Jansson, a paedophile, was convicted of her murder. But I don't think he's guilty of that particular offence. Her body was never found. Someone set him up to hide the real murderer's identity. I think it was William.'

'And you found that out this morning?'

'I was looking for victims between Julia and Jonna. I haven't focused on it properly before now, hadn't considered the possibility that he might conceal an act of murder with another murder. Now we need to fill the gap between Jonna and Ellen. The missing victim. Head towards the city. What did you get up to this morning?'

'I found an aunt,' Berger muttered. He pulled onto the E18. 'Do you feel like telling me about when you were strapped to the clock? I need to know how it works.'

Something slid across Blom's face, slipping over her smooth forehead.

'It had a ticking clock face,' she said. 'I could see time passing. And got terrified every half an hour.'

'What would happen then?'

'I was stretched a bit more, like on a rack. But he seemed to be able to adjust it however he wanted.'

As they drove past Arninge, Berger asked: 'Did you get the feeling that you were meant to die?'

'You ask such lovely questions.'

They sat in silence for a while. He glanced at her. She looked gloomy and withdrawn.

'How did you escape?' he eventually asked.

'I managed to get my left hand out of the handcuff. Then I freed my right hand and my feet.'

'You were standing upright while chains pulled your legs and arms?'

'No,' Blom said, closing her eyes. 'Not my legs. Just my arms. I was standing with my legs tied together and lashed to the floor. Your arms get pulled apart, and start to bleed when the skin breaks. I stood there for eight hours, and I think my skin would have split if I'd been there for another hour. Ellen Savinger has been missing for three weeks. What could he have done to her in all that time?'

'Somehow he lets his victims rest,' Berger said. 'So they can sit down and reach the floor with their nails. There are marks from fingernails and toenails in Märsta.'

'In the floor?'

'Yes,' Berger said. 'In the cement floor.'

Blom grimaced and stared out through the side window.

They sat in silence until they reached Västerbroplan. The rain had more or less stopped by then. Berger followed Blom's directions and parked. A man was standing beside the parking space, waiting. He was in his early forties, and the bags under his eyes were both darker and larger than the rest of his features.

'Bertil Brandt,' he said, holding his hand out to them.

'Eva Lindkvist,' Molly Blom said.

She looked expectantly at Berger, who said: 'Charles Lindbergh.'

He regretted that for a long time.

They walked out across Västerbron. Didn't say much. Up at the crown of the bridge they stopped and looked out across Stockholm in the harsh grey light.

'It's probably going to start raining again soon,' Brandt said.

'Maybe,' Blom said.

They stood like that for a while. An unsettling gloom lay over the city.

'It was raining that night,' Berger said eventually.

'You know that, Bertil?'

'Oh, yes. I know all about that night.'

'There aren't many people who've cut through that fence . . . '

Bertil Brandt smiled weakly. It was a hardened smile. He would survive, but he'd never be himself again.

'Three years ago they erected the fence. But only on this side, the eastern side, towards the city. And the funny thing is, I understand why they did that.'

'Can you explain it?' Blom said.

'You come up here, with tunnel vision, intoxicated with suicidal euphoria. There's a certain romance to the eastern side of the bridge – leaving all that crap in your life behind and jumping towards beauty, with the whole of Stockholm at your feet. And if there's a two-metre-high fence here, the romance diminishes. Then you have to climb over barriers and cross what's still a very busy road, even at night, to get to the west side. And all the romance disappears, taking with it your tunnel vision. Reality catches up with your dreams, you feel stupid, see yourself in a more honest light. The whole glorious project looks pathetic, feeble. Only the ones who are really determined go through with it.'

'But now there's a fence on the western side as well.'

'And it's helped. People still climb over, but far fewer. And, like you said, very few people cut through the fence.'

'But Emma did,' Molly Blom said. 'She had a sturdy set of bolt cutters with her, left behind on the bridge with her fingerprints all over them.'

'Yes,' Bertil Brandt said. 'She had it all thought through.'

'But no one saw her actually jump?'

'And no body was found. I think she just floated out to sea. She liked the sea.'

'No witnesses?'

'Not to the act itself, no. It was Midsummer's Day, a bright night, but there was no one about. Anyone left in the city was probably recovering from Midsummer's Eve. Even so, there are two separate accounts of her walking across the bridge with the bolt cutters in her hand, walking very purposefully. And there's one surveillance camera.'

'A surveillance camera?'

'Down by Hornstull. That's the direction she came from. The bolt cutters are clearly visible. And her face.'

'How did she look?'

'How did she look?'

'Yes. You said you know all about that night.'

Brandt laughed, an intensely desolate laugh, and shook his head. 'You might be the least sensitive cop I've ever come across.'

'Possibly the one with the least amount of time.'

'That doesn't matter to Emma. Or me.'

'There's a good chance it's more urgent than you think . . . '

'Tense. Tense to the point of bursting.'

'Her face?'

'Surveillance camera footage isn't exactly high resolution. But she was pale, and looked very, very tense. My little . . . '

Brandt tailed off. Blom waited. Felt a lump in her throat.

One night, twenty-two years ago, she herself had been on her way up Västerbron. And back then there was no fence, just a metre-high railing. She had stopped on the way up the eastern side, looked out across the city and suddenly felt that some sort of meaning might be able to return to the life that William Larsson had taken from her. If not at that precise moment.

'The anguish,' Brandt said. 'The anguish of being impotent.'

'Impotent in the face of suicide?'

'We'd been so close. Then she slipped away. It was horrible to watch. Emma's mum was dead. It was just her and me.'

'Why did she slip away?'

'I never really made sense of it. I think there was a lot of crap at school, but she never said anything, just retreated into herself.'

'It was that impotence you were referring to?'

'Yes,' the man said. 'Against the nightmare of bullying.'

A few minutes later they were heading south. Berger was behind the wheel again.

After driving all the way along Ringvägen he said: 'It's impossible to imagine. Having a daughter who kills herself with such determination.'

'And is stopped,' Blom said. 'Stopped just as she's about to jump.'

'You think Emma Brandt was William's sixth victim?'

'Late on Midsummer's Day this year,' Blom said. 'Right between Jonna Eriksson and Ellen Savinger. Yes, that's what I think. Pretty much everyone who jumps from Västerbron ends up being found, sooner or later. Emma Brandt was the exception, her body just disappeared. It's four months ago now.'

'So you think we've got our seven victims now?'

'Yes,' Molly Blom said, gazing out across the water of Årstaviken as they crossed Skanstull Bridge. 'Those are my strongest candidates.'

'But the idea of William Larsson, a victim of bullying, taking revenge on Emma Brandt, a victim of bullying, seems odd.'

'And how did he find her? How did he know she was planning to kill herself? I'm not saying I have the answer, I'm just looking for things that seem likely. William seems to have been well informed in the other cases. He snatched Aisha Pachachi the day she finished her last exam, and Ellen Savinger just after she'd left school. He planted a load of false evidence in Sunisa Phetwiset's case and managed to take Julia Almström from her home in Västerås in the middle of the night. Each kidnapping seems to have been preceded by a hell of a lot of research.'

'And there's no real evidence,' Berger said, turning off Nynäsvägen, going round the roundabout and setting off along Tyresövägen.

'Where are we going?' Blom finally asked.

'Wait and see,' Berger said.

28

Wednesday 28 October, 15.13

Without really being aware of it, they turned off Tyresövägen and onto Gudöbroleden in Vendelsö. Lupinstigen was a short, diagonal link between Gudöbroleden and Vendelsö gårdsväg, which in turn led down towards the waters of Drevviken. Berger let the van roll down Lupinstigen and parked outside Vendelsögården, a home for people with dementia. Blom wrinkled her nose but said nothing. She followed him up to the top floor. He knocked on an unmarked door. Nothing happened.

In the end a carer appeared out of nowhere and said: 'Are you looking for Alicia?'

Berger looked at her name badge. 'Hello, Mia. Yes, we're looking for Alicia Anger. Is she here?'

'I'd be very surprised if she wasn't,' Mia Arvidsson said, unlocking the door. 'She never goes anywhere else.'

Berger put his hand on the door just before it opened. 'A quick status report would be useful.'

'Police?' the carer said, smiling to herself. 'Good luck.'

'"Good luck." So she's pretty far gone?'

'Let's just say that you need a bit of patience to reach the moment of clarity,' Mia Arvidsson said, opening the door wide. 'But you need to be ready for it when it comes.'

The old lady was sitting in a rocking chair, and she wasn't particularly old, just distant. They waited until the carer had gone. Berger introduced himself and Blom with imaginative names. He sat down on an armchair in front of the woman, while Blom stayed standing by the wall, her arms folded sceptically across her chest.

Afterwards Berger found himself fascinated by the creative potential of language once all barriers had been removed. He understood the words the old woman said, but their context remained obscure. The tragic thing was that she was no older than sixty-six, her name was Alicia Anger, she was William Larsson's mother's sister, and suffered badly from what Berger assumed was Alzheimer's.

He tried again: 'Did you have any contact with your sister Stina when she was pregnant? Almost forty years ago now?'

'The second breath always beat grey grains of truth for little Adelia. The nice sister, the one with a beard, says the archivists eat ants' eggs. Every quarter. You too, Gundersen, not least you.'

'Gundersen?'

'You too. With your Valkyrie's legs. The ones you fly with. You were courageous in battle, but not in life. Like Anger.'

'Anger, your husband?'

'He ran away. Away from me. I kept his name to make mischief. I think it killed him.'

And suddenly the sentences held together. Was the moment of clarity on its way?

'Do you remember when your sister Stina had a big tummy?'

'We don't have children in our family.'

Berger fell silent for a moment and considered the nuances

behind that sentence. Then he went on: 'William was the exception, wasn't he?'

'Poor William,' Alicia Anger said, as she stopped rocking and found solid ground in the late seventies. 'He was the best argument for why the Larsson family shouldn't have children. And you ran when you saw him . . '

'*I* ran?'

'You know you did. You ran *before* you even saw him.'

'Didn't I ever see my son?' Berger gambled.

'If you had, you would have died. His face . . . '

'When did you last see me?'

'Now you're being cheeky. I've never met you.'

'But Stina talked about me?'

'Maybe not talked. Vomited. Spewed.'

'What did she spew? That I was courageous in battle, but not in life?'

'I realised that for myself, thank you very much. You scum.'

Scum, Berger thought, feeling his heart pounding.

'What does "battle" mean, Alicia?'

'You were a warrior, and I've heard that warriors often suppress the fact that they are warriors.'

'Where was I a warrior?'

'For money, you scum.'

'Where? Do you know where, Alicia?'

'I don't know. Some ruddy Arab country.'

'In the mid-seventies. Lebanon?'

'Shut up, you bastard.'

'And what's the rest of my name, apart from Gundersen?'

'Don't you know? Nils. The way she used to bang on about that bloody name as soon as she got a drink inside her. The few times she was sober she tried to forget it.'

'I was blonder in those days, wasn't I, Alicia?'

'White blond. And you just walked out. How the hell could you just walk out?'

'I went on fighting. Did I come back?'

'The first Valkyrie sings the sweetest. Skögul, the one who filled Odin's horn with mead. Hrist, Mist, Hildr, Göndul. God, they could fight, those women. So, Señor Cortado, have you ever heard about *the red girl*?'

'No,' Berger said, almost speechless.

'Ulster, Ireland. *Ingen ruaidh*. Led a gang of Vikings in the tenth century. Much feared. Don't say anything to the bearded lady, but *I'm the red girl*. Call me *Ingen*.'

'Do you know if William ever met his father?'

'From time to time the cockerels crowed, Nils. Your blood curdled.'

When Berger shut the door on the red girl, alias Alicia Anger, the rocking chair was moving again. He met Blom's gaze. They stood there for a moment, reaching for words. It was as if language was barely possible any more.

In the end Berger managed to say: 'What do you think?'

'Very hard to say,' Blom said. 'It could be nothing but senile nonsense. But it's probably worth checking if there's a blond mercenary by the name of Nils Gundersen. How did you find her?'

'She was on the edge of William's family tree on your whiteboard. You were the one who found her.'

Blom pulled a grim face and set off down the stairs. Berger lingered and watched her go. That oddly energetic stride. He saw her reach the window at the turn in the stairs. He saw her stop abruptly and draw back from the window. He saw her look up at him and beckon him closer.

It was a big window, facing the road. He stood close beside her as she pointed up Lupinstigen. He had noted of all the parked cars when they entered Vendelsögården Care Home.

Something had changed. There was a new car parked across the street, a graphite-coloured Volvo. It was raining again, pouring, and no matter how Berger tried he couldn't see if there were one or two people sitting in the front. He looked at their Mercedes Vito, which was parked right in front of the home, just a dozen metres from the Volvo. They'd never be able to reach it without being seen.

They held back, waiting for more obvious signs. After a minute or so the driver's window opened and a piece of chewing gum was thrown out. Berger wasn't sure if he was imagining things, but he'd thought he'd seen a big, cheap diver's watch on the wrist before it quickly disappeared.

He let out a deep sigh and turned round. She had already walked away. They found a kitchen door at the back of the building, crossed the gardens of a number of identical apartment blocks, emerged onto Vendelsö gårdsväg, ran west through the pouring rain, away from Lupinstigen and reached a car park, checked for security cameras and failed to find any. Berger identified a suitably antiquated car, put his old tricks to good use and jimmied the lock. They got in and waited. None of the neighbours appeared; there was no reaction. He leaned over and pulled the cables free, then touched them together. The old car rumbled into life.

'I was very fond of my Vito,' Blom sighed.

Berger moved off towards Vendelsö gårdsväg, then paused briefly before heading left, towards the lake. They both looked right and saw a rain-drenched figure.

There was no doubt that it was Roy's colleague, Kent. He had evidently been hidden from view.

They saw him turn round and gesticulate frantically towards Lupinstigen. Berger let slip another deep sigh and put his foot down.

'And we had to take this piece of shit,' Blom said.

'If you'd been able to break into a newer model, we could have taken that,' Berger said pointedly.

He turned left into Vendelsö allé and roared out onto the main road by pretty much ignoring a roundabout. Blom kept her eye on the rear-view mirror.

'They're gaining on us,' she said.

Piece of shit it might be, but it had a bit of go in it, Berger concluded with his foot on the floor. Even so, it was obvious that Roy and Kent were getting closer and closer in their souped-up graphite-grey Security Service car. Berger tried to focus. They were on a typical main road in the outer suburbs. What was Roy thinking? Was he seriously going to ram them on a busy major road? Shoot at them, even? They were probably safer on main roads and open spaces, sticking to an inconspicuous speed. But then they wouldn't have any chance of shaking Roy and Kent, and the Volvo was bound to have a tank twice the size of theirs. And backup was undoubtedly on the way. Something needed to happen. Fast.

Berger cast a brief glance at Blom. She looked like her thoughts were running in the same direction. Gudöbroleden would soon dive beneath the motorway. They could get up onto the larger Nynäsvägen and hope for enough traffic to allow them to make their escape.

'Up here or not?' Berger roared.

'Not,' Blom said, and pointed to the left. Some way off a number of high-rise apartment blocks loomed above what was probably Haninge shopping centre. He heard the distant sound of a train heading south, and he ran a red light by the junction with Gamla Nynäsvägen. A state of mild chaos broke out in the traffic behind them, putting another hundred metres between them and the Volvo. Vital metres. Then he jerked the wheel abruptly and raced into the jungle of Haninge's apartment blocks. He found what looked like a full car park and drove into the last free space.

Blom nodded and threw herself out. They ran from the car, keeping low. From a distance it looked comfortably anonymous. They ran into the housing estate and saw the graphite-grey Volvo drive past out on Gamla Nynäsvägen. They saw it brake sharply, as Roy looked for somewhere to turn round, but the carriageways were separated by a stretch of grass that was too high to drive across without wrecking the car.

Blom suddenly grabbed his hand and took off. They crossed Gamla Nynäsvägen between angry, horn-blaring cars, and then Berger realised why Blom had run. He too could hear a train in the distance, and it sounded different, as if it was slowing down. They ran along a quieter street and saw, a few hundred metres away, a covered footbridge. That ought to signify a railway station. Through the rain they could soon see the storm-lashed water of a lake, and, this side of it, an embankment, a platform, a railway line, a fence that didn't look too high, even if the barbed wire looked vicious. The sound of the train grew louder and louder as a local commuter service pulled slowly in along the far set of tracks.

Blom set off towards the fence. She grabbed the wire between barbs and turned a full somersault to reach the embankment. It was rush hour and the platform was full of commuters. People stared at her, someone took a picture with a mobile phone. Berger in turn glanced quickly over his shoulder and saw a grey Volvo speeding along the station road. Instinctively he rushed at the fence and grabbed it, ignoring the fact that a barb pierced his left palm. The southbound local train pulled up at the platform and the doors slid slowly open.

'Come on!' Blom yelled from the embankment.

The sound of the Volvo's engine was very clear now, a subdued growl. People streamed out of the open doors of the train, others started to get on. The driver's voice rang out. Berger couldn't get a firm grip with his feet; they kept slipping in the gaps in the fence. Blom grabbed his jacket and pulled him over, and he tumbled into a puddle. The Volvo caught up with them, stopping just a few metres behind Berger's back, but he was over now. He got to his feet and rushed wildly after Blom, who had just leapt onto the platform from the rails closest to them. The train's doors began to close, and she jumped in and reached one hand out through the diminishing gap. He just managed to catch her hand and let himself be pulled in before the doors closed and the train set off. The last they saw of Handen station was Roy punching the fence. His whole arm recoiled.

The carriage was fairly full. People were looking at them with distaste. There were a couple of raised mobiles. It hadn't exactly been a subtle escape. Something needed to be done.

Blom got there first. She held up her ID. 'Sorry about that. Police. There's nothing to see.'

The seasoned commuters went back to whatever they had been doing with suspicious expressions. Berger breathed out and looked at his bleeding hand.

'How the hell did they find us?' he whispered.

'Later,' Blom said. 'Right now the question is whether or not they're going to get to the next station in time.'

'Jordbro,' Berger groaned.

'There's quite a lot of traffic,' Blom said, 'but all they have to do is keep driving down Gamla Nynäsvägen. We're not safe yet.'

Berger felt his bleeding palm. 'Oh well. I injured my hand in Handen. Which is something.'

The train picked up speed; it seemed unlikely that the Volvo could drive any faster. Three minutes later they were at Jordbro station. They couldn't see the Volvo through the train windows. They got out, rushed through the barriers and evaluated the situation. It was a noticeably less urban station, but on the other side of the tracks was a familiar logo. Possibly the most familiar logo in the world. Coca-Cola's headquarters in Sweden, a vast industrial building with a hell of a lot of cars parked outside. They set off in that direction, through the wretched, never-ending rain.

'Shift workers,' Blom said. 'No one will miss anything until first thing tomorrow morning.'

'Do you fancy something a little more modern?' Berger said.

She flashed him a dark look, and soon they were sitting in another similar vehicle from the nineties in the traffic heading back towards Stockholm.

'Stay away from the congestion charge zone,' Blom said.

'No cameras.' Berger nodded.

Only when they reached Farsta did he start to feel safe. Then he repeated: 'How the hell did they find us?'

'They can't have had a transmitter on my van,' Blom said. 'They'd have picked us up last night. Or this morning when we were out shopping.'

'So what, then? Have I got some fucking chip in my body? Have you?'

'Hardly,' Blom said. 'My guess is that they've managed to reverse the GPS signal after all. I didn't really think that was possible yet, you need to fix at least four satellites to do it.'

'Are we safe in the boathouse? Can we go back there? Or will Roy and Roger be sitting there waiting for us?'

'That depends on when they managed to pick up the signal.'

Berger sighed.

'OK,' he said. 'We're just going to have to find out.'

29

Wednesday 28 October, 19.04

The rain was scattering myriad fleeting rings across the dark surface of Edsviken.

There had been no one waiting for them in the boathouse.

There was no evidence to suggest that they had been discovered.

Berger was leaning on the railing out on the jetty, breathing out at last. He was soaked and was trying his best not to fall asleep where he stood. There was a break in the middle of the railing where a ladder led straight down into the water. Even the thought that it might be necessary to climb down there before long made the blood run cold in his veins.

Blom came and stood next to him. She was just as wet as he was.

'Done?' she asked.

He nodded. 'I've rigged up four cameras at strategic points,' he confirmed. 'Are they really the same kind you used in Vidargatan?'

She nodded. 'And I've changed the plates on our stolen Mazda.'

'How much stuff have you actually got in those Security Service cases?' he asked.

She didn't answer. They stood for a while looking out over the dark inlet.

'Sometimes I wish I still smoked,' Berger said.

Then they went back inside. They sat down at their respective carpentry benches, at their respective computers. Next to each bench lay a sleeping bag and camping mat. Completely untouched.

Berger was drinking coffee, Blom tea. They were both trying to ignore how tired they were.

Berger tried typing with his damaged left hand. It worked surprisingly well. He was following up an idea that had occurred to him up on Västerbron, while he was feeling ashamed at having introduced himself as Charles Lindbergh.

Blom had begun by checking the most obvious thing. After a while she said: 'There's no national alert.'

He looked at her in silence.

'The police aren't looking for us,' she clarified. 'The Security Service hasn't gone public about our disappearance. No press conferences.'

'Good,' Berger said. 'So just the sharpest cops in Sweden hunting us in the utmost secrecy, then.'

Blom flashed him a bitter look.

He went on: 'What do Deer and Allan know?'

'They know I'm Security Service and that we pulled you in for questioning on behalf of Internal Investigations. Not much more than that.'

'And where do they think I am now?'

'In our custody, I presume. Unless August Steen has fabricated some story about you being on holiday. To be honest, I don't know.'

Berger muttered something and they both went back to their computers. Blom sat quietly, typing her way deeper and deeper into the Security Service's endless archives. Berger was digging into an abandoned police investigation, trying to find connections. At one point he got up and went over to the big whiteboard. Eventually he found what he was looking for. A video clip had been running for a while on his computer before Blom folded the screen of her laptop down with a groan.

'No luck?' Berger said.

'No Nils Gundersen in any Security Service files,' Blom said.

'It was a gamble,' Berger said, shrugging. 'Gundersen may be no more than a character from Alicia Anger's confused imagination.'

Blom nodded. 'There might be another option, but it's considerably more complicated.'

Berger thought for a moment. 'I don't know if I dare activate Syl . . . '

Blom looked at him. 'Now you're being almost ridiculously mysterious.'

'Syl,' Berger said slowly, 'is the reason I was able to find you.'

'I've been wondering how you managed that,' Blom said. 'So Syl is some sort of program?'

Berger laughed. 'Not far off, really.'

'Stop being difficult.'

'I shouldn't be saying this even now.' Berger sighed. 'But you and I have ended up in a tricky position of reluctant but unavoidable trust. Syl's real name is Sylvia Andersson, and I've worked with her pretty much since Police Academy. She conducted an anonymous search for Wiborg Supplies Ltd and found your name on a list that we then cross-referenced with Botox clinics.'

'A list?' Blom exclaimed. 'What sort of list?'

'The Security Service's "internal" and "external" resources.'

'What? All of them?'

'There was something about weak security around the time of the reorganisation at the end of last year. Syl said she'd found several anomalies there. Maybe she found her way down to the very deepest levels.'

'There may well be files I don't have clearance for,' Blom said, 'but I'd still prefer not to have to rely on this Syl of yours. After all, we are on the run from justice. Let me try my way first.'

'Your considerably more complicated way,' Berger nodded. 'So what is it, then? No secrets, now.'

'MISS,' Blom said bluntly.

Berger looked at her and slowly shook his head.

'The Military Intelligence and Security Service?' he said. 'Have you got friends there? An old lover, perhaps?'

'Not old at all,' Blom said calmly. 'So what have you been up to? "No secrets, now."'

'This,' Berger said, turning his laptop round.

It was security footage from a cash machine somewhere in the city centre. It was raining gently, but the scene was well lit, and deserted. Eventually a young girl walked past. In her hand she had a pair of bolt cutters. Berger froze the film when the girl turned her face towards the camera. She really did look tense. Tense to the point of bursting.

'Emma Brandt, fifteen years old,' Berger said. 'Hornstull, late on Midsummer's Day this year.'

'Good,' Blom said. 'Take a screenshot. I want a printout.'

'A printout?'

'I want pictures of all the kidnapped girls,' she said, pointing at the whiteboard.

Berger nodded, took a screenshot and went on playing the clip. Once again, the scene was completely deserted. He pressed fast-forward. If it weren't for a moonlighting sparrow, the footage would have looked like a still picture. Then he slowed the playback to normal again. Soon a van swept past. He froze the picture again. On the side of the white van the word *Statoil* stood out clearly, above a line of much smaller writing.

'Ah,' Molly Blom said.

'Ah,' Berger echoed, and zoomed in on the writing below.

The picture was badly pixelated and barely legible, but the letters spelled out the name Gävle.

'Here comes William,' Berger said. 'Seven minutes later. By now Emma Brandt has made it all the way to the crown of the bridge. Maybe she's also started to cut the fence.'

The van flickered past, frame by frame. When Berger stopped the clip again it was possible to read a couple of letters and at least one digit on the number plate.

'You lot kept the information about the Statoil van secret from us,' Berger said. 'But I just found it on your board. The number matches.'

Blom nodded. 'Nice,' she said. 'That's it, isn't it? Statoil in Gävle. The one at Sätrahöjden. We checked it out thoroughly. Hired in May by a Johan Eriksson.'

'Brother of Erik Johansson?'

'Hmm,' Blom said. 'We followed it up carefully. There was no trace of it. And the security footage from the petrol station had long since been wiped.'

'It wouldn't surprise me if this was the same van that was seen outside Ellen Savinger's school in Östermalm.'

'At least we're getting closer to some real evidence,' Blom said.

They went back to their respective laptops. The darkness outside the boathouse couldn't get any darker. The passage of time, though impossible to tell from the world around them, showed on their increasingly tired faces.

After a couple of hours a crooked smile spread across Berger's face, and he snatched up Blom's untraceable mobile phone and went out onto the jetty.

During the relatively long call Blom printed pictures of Sunisa Phetwiset and Emma Brandt, the two potential new victims. She went over to the whiteboard and put them up next to the older pictures. There were now seven of them, and as she looked at the row of young faces – all victims of an insane serial killer who had tried to murder her nearly a quarter of a century ago – she felt not only revulsion and a terrible sorrow, but something else. A vague insight that quickly evaporated.

But she had seen something.

Something in the seven faces. And now it was gone.

Berger came in from the jetty, held the phone up and said, unnecessarily cheerfully: 'Tomorrow we're going to Kristinehamn.'

'That's, what, three hundred kilometres away?'

'Only 250. Just think, you cycled all that way once upon a time.'

He was expecting a very sharp glare. But she merely said: 'Tell me.'

'Jonna Eriksson went missing together with her boyfriend, Simon Lundberg, on 12 February this year from her foster home in Kristinehamn. The newly established Bergslagen Police Authority conducted a large number of interviews with past and present foster parents, friends, teachers, you name it. They didn't come up with anything of note, except that Jonna and Simon often ran away from their respective foster homes together. No one was particularly interested in them. But there was a significant date marked in their files – when Jonna's best friend Sandra was due to come home after a long stay in Australia. That date has just passed. She's home now. And she had quite a bit to say.'

'Worth a round trip of five hundred kilometres?'

'I think so. Sandra knows of a secret place in the Värmland forests where Jonna and Simon could have gone to hide away from the world. No one else knows about it. And no one contacted Sandra when she was travelling through the Australian outback.'

Blom nodded and gave a brief smile. It was a remarkable smile.

Then she stood up and went over to the whiteboard. She looked at the faces once more. They were almost all smiling.

Aisha Pachachi, Nefel Berwari, Julia Almström, Sunisa Phetwiset, Jonna Eriksson, Emma Brandt and Ellen Savinger.

'I was standing here a little while ago, and I had some sort of revelation. It's gone now, but I'm seeing something. When did William rent the house in Märsta, in the name of Erik Johansson?'

'Over two years ago,' Berger said, watching her intently. 'From March, two and a half years ago. The owners live in Argentina.'

'March,' Blom said. 'And he kidnaps the first victim, Aisha, at the end of the school year on 7 June. He obviously took her to the house in Märsta. The wall. Why were the mooring rings so deeply embedded? I haven't been inside the house, of course. But that whole business of the labyrinth in the basement: is that his work?'

'Don't know,' Berger said. 'It seems crazy enough.'

Molly Blom scratched her head hard, as if she were trying to wake her brain cells up. Then she said: 'He's taken seven girls in two and a half years, if our hypothesis is correct. The Märsta house is the only crime scene we've got. Has he had seven similarly elaborate buildings at his disposal? Where he could calmly take his time constructing his torture clock? There can't be that many, surely? Wouldn't it be logical for there to be just one clock, *one* crime scene? Where he took all the girls?'

'OK,' Berger said. 'You mean the Märsta house was the headquarters? That Ellen wasn't the first girl held there? Even though only her DNA was found?'

'How about this,' Blom said, with the light of revelation shining in her eyes. 'For each girl he tortured, he added a new layer of wall. Which works because the mooring rings are ten centimetres in diameter. In the end there can't have been much left of the rings. He's *walled up* all the DNA evidence.'

Berger felt his churning thoughts contort his face.

'Shit, we have to go to Märsta tomorrow,' he said. 'I was hoping we'd get to Kristinehamn.'

'Tomorrow?' Blom said, pulling on her tracksuit top.

30

Thursday 29 October, 00.01

Berger pressed his back against the wooden planks. They were really so rotten they felt soft. He looked over at the remains of the next building. Blom was crouched there in the darkness; he couldn't see her, just saw the play of her torch on the grass. Up among the aspen trees there were no leaves left, no rustling to perforate the night.

And it wasn't raining.

He cast a glance at his watch. Behind the almost condensation-free glass the hands were pointing at midnight.

They were entering the ghosting hour.

Blom was suddenly gone. When he looked up from his watch she wasn't there. His torch swept the grass, the trees, the rotting walls of the ruined outbuilding, a small, half-collapsed door in its facade.

Then the door was thrown open. The interior was illuminated, the light shining straight through to the road behind.

Blom appeared in the opening. She waved him towards her. He went over. He saw that the wall opposite was completely open, as in a garage. Her finger pointed into the beam of light, at the clay that acted as a floor. There were clear, relatively fresh, tyre marks.

They set off. How long had it actually been since Berger first laid eyes on this place? He had caught up with his advancing colleagues, seeing them emerge from the downpour, one by one, crouched figures which, even though he could only see them from behind, exuded an unmistakable focus.

Before long one of them would have his upper arms punctured by flying knives. So his first visit wasn't actually that long ago; Ekman was probably still in hospital. Berger tried in vain to count the days before his thoughts went off in a different direction.

Towards evidence. Allan's perspective.

A lot had happened during the last, very few days, an absurd amount had been ploughed up from the dirt of the past. They had now sniffed out seven possible victims of their mad perpetrator, who, judging by everything they knew, was William Larsson. But the fact remained that there was only one piece of evidence that a violent kidnapper was at work, and none at all to suggest a serial killer. The only physical evidence was still the DNA found in the basement of the house that was looming up in front of them. Ellen Savinger's blood.

Aisha Pachachi could very well have followed her brother and become a child-bride of IS in Syria.

Nefel Berwari could very well have fallen victim to an honour killing in Vivala, Örebro.

Julia Almström could very well have fled the country with her unidentified ex-con boyfriend.

Sunisa Phetwiset could very well have been murdered by paedophile Axel Jansson.

Jonna Eriksson could very well have run away with her boyfriend and fellow unfortunate, Simon Lundberg.

Emma Brandt could very well have jumped from Västerbron and been carried out to sea by the current.

And William Larsson could very well be nothing more than a ghost conjured up from the darkest parts of Sam Berger and Molly Blom's pasts, taking form without actually existing. Looked at dispassionately, it seemed pretty likely that he had died in the nineties as a result of his severe deformities.

The whole thing could very well turn out to be ghosts in the machine, which were now, in the ghosting hour, about to reveal their true nature.

Apart from Ellen Savinger. She was, beyond all doubt, a kidnapped and possibly murdered fifteen-year-old girl.

And perhaps there was evidence behind the bloodstain on the wall that they weren't dealing with ghosts after all, but with the very real victims of a serial killer.

Really real. Really behind the wall.

By the steps up to the porch blue and white plastic tape was still fluttering in the imperceptible night breeze. Berger went first, Blom followed. The likelihood of there being anyone inside the house was extremely small, but they both instinctively drew their pistols at the same time.

Berger pushed the door open and crouched down. He shone his torch at the knife-throwing mechanism. Nothing seemed to have changed. He slipped inside, followed by Blom.

Left, into the living room, everything was the same. A quick glance into the bedroom, then into the kitchen. The hatch in the floor was open, the police tape was where it had been when he was last there. There was nothing to indicate that anyone had been in the house since then.

Berger shone his torch on the steps and went down, then lit up the walls of the labyrinth. He turned and saw the focused look on Blom's pale face through the darkness. They made their way through the maze of rooms to reach the hole hacked in the wall. Berger got down on his knees and shuffled through, holding his gun raised. His torch played across the bare but by no means mute walls while Blom slipped into the cell. Some white powder fell on her as she passed through the opening, as if the wall was slowly giving way. She spat out crumbs of plasterboard. Then she looked around and went over to the far wall. Her hand slowly traced the outer edge of the bloodstain, and she crouched down and found the nail marks in the floor with the torch. Toenails. Fingernails. Then she looked at the two posts and felt the mooring rings in the wall.

Berger saw that she too could feel the walls scream. Feel rather than hear. He had been overwhelmed by it the first time. She was probably overwhelmed as well, but in her own way. And the question now was how many screams there were.

Was it a whole girls' choir?

'Yes,' she said eventually. 'It must be the same clock.'

'A big, tower clock,' he said. 'Much more powerful than you'd think.'

'Not me,' she said sharply, and went back to the wall to the left of the bloodstain. She pointed at the hacked-out indentation around the middle mooring ring.

'It's hard to tell,' she said. 'There *could* be different layers, but it's been very roughly cut.'

'I apologise that my work doesn't meet with your approval, ma'am,' Berger said sullenly.

'Well, we're just going to have to be more gentle this time,' Blom said calmly, pulling a hammer and chisel from a couple of her army trousers' many pockets. She held the chisel against the centre of the bloodstain and turned to look at Berger. He nodded.

'It's more solid than you think,' he said.

She hit the chisel with the hammer. Nothing happened. Again. A few chips broke off.

After a while she had cut out the sides of a square three centimetres across. Then inside it she started carefully chipping off as thin a layer of the wall as she could.

One centimetre in, the wall changed colour. Blom struck once more and a larger piece of cement came loose and fell to the floor, revealing a small section of wall that was clearly a brownish-red colour.

'Bloody hell,' Berger said, pulling an evidence bag from his jacket pocket.

Blom pulled on a pair of plastic gloves, broke off a piece of the rust-brown wall and dropped it into Berger's opened bag. He sealed it and wrote *Layer 1* on it in permanent pen. Then he put it back in his pocket and carried on watching as Blom worked.

After a good stretch of precision chiselling a new layer emerged. Two clenched fists, and the same procedure was repeated. But this time Blom passed the hammer and chisel to Berger, who took a moment before accepting the tools.

A while later he held up an evidence bag bearing the label *Layer 3*, shone his torch at it and said: 'The only thing is, how are we going to get any DNA from these?'

'I may have a solution to that,' Blom said, watching the little plastic bag as it slipped into Berger's pocket.

'Let me guess,' Berger said. 'An external resource?'

He put the tools down on the floor and looked at his hands. It was strange: he had more calluses on his hands this time than when he uncovered the large mooring rings.

Blom picked up the hammer and chisel and went on working at the square. Soon a further rust-red layer appeared.

Time passed. Berger took over. He spent a long time chiselling.

Eventually they were both staring at a plastic bag labelled *Layer 6* in very unsteady handwriting.

'Six layers plus Ellen,' Blom said. 'Seven girls.'

Then the screams rose up from the cell walls again, and Berger actually thought he could make out seven voices. Seven voices from purgatory.

Berger tried to think rationally. It wasn't altogether easy.

'It's not necessarily seven girls,' he said. 'There may be others. There could be more victims.'

Then they heard something. It was barely a scrape, but it still made Molly Blom go utterly rigid. With a quick glance at Berger she managed to hush him before he even thought about saying anything.

The front door opening?

Or just the sounds of the building, lingering from the ghosting hour?

Blom and Berger stood stock-still.

They heard nothing else. Just an echoing silence.

Blom switched her torch off and pushed Berger's aside. Then they heard a faint scraping sound.

Like a foot on the cellar steps.

Berger silently drew his pistol from his shoulder holster and raised one finger in the air, then two, with a questioning look. Blom shook her head, as if she couldn't tell either, and started to move towards the opening without making a sound. Even when they heard the next step, not far from the opening, they still couldn't tell if they were dealing with one or two visitors.

Either way, only one person would be able to crawl into the cell at a time.

They took up strategic positions around the opening, both aiming their weapons at the hole. Berger switched his torch off. Everything turned pitch-black. There was the sound of someone getting down on their knees, lying on their stomach.

The sound of someone crawling through the opening.

Berger switched his torch back on and kicked the wall above the opening. The figure that had just slid into the cell was completely covered by greyish-white powder.

Blom yelled: 'Don't move!'

A cloud of finer dust settled slowly on the figure. Its face was entirely greyish-white until a pair of brown eyes opened with an expression of utter terror.

A deer's eyes.

'What the fuck, Deer?' Berger cried out, lowering his pistol.

'OK,' Desiré Rosenkvist said hoarsely. 'Now this really is a nightmare.'

'Are you alone?' Blom shouted.

'Horribly alone,' Deer said.

Berger took her hand and pulled her to her feet.

Blom finally lowered her pistol and asked: 'What are you doing here?'

'That's my line, surely?' Deer said, brushing herself down. 'I've been trying to get hold of you for ages, Sam, and Allan keeps saying that you're still being questioned. What the hell is going on?'

'Long story,' Berger said.

Deer pointed at Blom. 'Nathalie Fredén. Wow. And you've both got guns. Christ, this really *is* a nightmare.'

'It's hard to give you a short version,' Berger said. 'You're going to have to decide if you trust me or not.'

Deer looked at him sceptically.

'She's a cop, then?' she said. 'All we heard from Allan was that she'd been released and you'd been taken in for questioning by Internal Investigations. But I can't deny that I had a strong feeling that the Security Service was involved.'

'I'm a cop, yes,' Blom said, without putting her pistol away. 'What are you doing here?'

'A nocturnal thought,' Deer said. 'The wall. Why was it so thick? Wasn't it a bit unlikely that the perpetrator had extended the wall by ten centimetres all in one go? Wasn't it more likely that it was done in stages? Maybe Julia Almström and Jonna Eriksson were held against this wall as well.'

'I've trained you well, Deer,' Berger said, passing over one of the small evidence bags.

'You haven't trained me at all, Sam, and you know it,' Deer said, then read the label. '"Layer 6"? *Six*?'

'Six layers beneath this one, all with definite traces of blood. Seven girls have been held here.'

'Fucking hell,' Deer said. 'What is this? Some sort of secret parallel investigation? By the Security Service? Have they recruited you, Sam?'

'It's more complicated than that,' Blom said. 'The question is, can we trust you?'

Berger cast a quick glance at Blom, and thought he got some sort of acknowledgement in return.

'We don't exist,' he said. 'You haven't seen us here. You chiselled this little square out yourself. You took these six evidence bags to Robin at the National Forensic Centre.'

Deer snorted and shook her head briefly.

'I thought this smelled funny,' she said. 'So you're on the run?'

'We're working below the radar,' Blom said. She still had her gun in her hand.

'Sam?' Deer said, questioningly.

'Undercover,' Berger confirmed. 'Have you still got your old pay-as-you-go mobile?'

'It's at home. Not charged up, though,' Deer said.

'I'll text you a list of four names. Check if they match. Julia, Jonna and Ellen's DNA is already part of the investigation, but you need to get hold of DNA from the other four old investigations: desk drawers, combs, toothbrushes, clothes, locks of hair, anything.'

'To be honest, there isn't much of an investigation now,' Deer said gloomily. 'There's hardly anything left. My guess is that the Security Service is going to take it over soon.'

'This will probably inject a bit of life into it. You'll understand the connections when you get the names. Then you can follow them up. Reply to my text when the analysis is done. Never use official channels.'

Deer sighed and looked like she was thinking hard.

'So it was true? This is a serial killer?'

'And all seven victims seem to have been held here,' Berger said.

'I felt it the first time I came into this horrific little cell,' Deer said. 'A lot of things have happened here.'

'We're leaving now,' Berger said, handing over the other evidence bags. 'Like I said, you haven't seen us.'

'I don't even know who you are,' Deer said, going over to the wall. She inspected the carefully chiselled hole and shook her head. 'Above all, I don't know who *you* are, Sam. You lied to me. You really were running a parallel investigation. And you obstructed the real investigation. I can't honestly believe you've got much of a future in the force.'

'The only thing that matters right now is that you trust me, Deer. I'm going to have to apologise for the rest of it under more normal circumstances.'

Berger kneeled down and crept backwards through the hole.

Deer turned to Blom and said: 'And I don't actually know you at all. Who are you?'

'Eva Lindkvist,' Molly Blom said, finally tucking her pistol back in her shoulder holster.

Once they'd gone Deer put her hands to her ears and pressed hard.

But the screams only got louder and louder.

31

Thursday 29 October, 07.02

They waited for it. It didn't take long.

It started as a creeping change. The world raised itself laboriously out of the darkness, split in two, then the red dawn managed to separate above from below, sky from water. Out of the gap between them, colours seeped through and spread across the surface of the water.

They were standing out on the jetty after a couple of hours' sleep. Berger was feeling his bandaged left palm, and could tell that Blom was watching him.

'What happened after you ran away?' she said. 'Back then. Twenty-two years ago.'

Berger shook his head. 'When I had run some way through the grass your screaming stopped. I didn't even turn back then. I ran home with my tail between my legs, and I hid. Nothing should be quite as worrying as a teenager overplaying normality. But my parents didn't notice a thing.'

'And William?'

'I just avoided him,' Berger said. 'For the rest of term. And I still didn't know who you were. I never saw you clearly enough.'

'Do you think he hated us?' Blom asked.

Berger looked into the sun as it grew with unexpected speed. 'To understand any of this you have to understand who William was. We're talking about a mother and son who were forced to move from Huvudsta, Hässelby, Stuvsta, Bandhagen, because the son was being bullied so badly. He struggled through life with his lumpy face; he clung to his clocks even though all hell kept breaking loose around him. Eventually something snapped. It could have been that snowball you threw at the pocket watch he was showing me, it could have been something else.'

'That snowball,' Blom said. 'I didn't throw it.'

'You were there, weren't you?' Berger said. 'You were in that gang when it happened. He loved his clocks, and attacking them was like attacking the most precious thing in the world to him. He loved wristwatches, pocket watches, wall clocks, but now he was building the most difficult one of all: a tower clock. But without a tower. Just a boathouse. So he set about modifying his construction, so it could be used to take revenge. The fact that it ended up being you, Molly, was probably just a coincidence.'

'Not any more. Nothing's coincidental now.'

'On a completely different level, maybe. When he showed me his clocks he wanted to be admired, judged for his talents not his face. He wanted to share something. Going through the things he went through, well . . . what doesn't kill you makes you stronger. Yet anyone who becomes a murderer is as good as dead.'

'You mean it's suicide by proxy?'

'Yes, he just doesn't have the right make-up, I guess.'

'And what would be the right make-up?'

'I don't know,' Berger said. 'Forgiveness isn't my area of expertise.'

'That would have been the only solution, you mean?'

'Maybe. Learning from evil in order to understand it and be able to counteract it, both within yourself and out in the world. I've failed to do that.'

'I didn't forgive either,' Blom said. 'Does anyone, truly?'

'But you did manage to go on.'

'By acting my way through my life, yes.'

'That feels like what we all do,' Berger said with a snort. 'When I was a son I played the part of a son. When I was a father I played the part of a father. I'll play the part of an old man too. Hell, I'll end up playing dead.'

'But not a police officer?'

'I don't think I've ever played the part of a police officer, no. Have you?'

'It's the only role I've never played,' Blom said.

They stood there for a while. The redness turned into morning light and spread relentlessly across Edsviken. Day had come.

'That role will probably be over and done with soon,' Berger said.

Blom nodded slowly; then in the end shook her head. She went back into the boathouse. Berger waited a while longer. Then he followed her.

Blom pulled on her tracksuit top and drank a protein drink as she looked through the previous day's security footage. The screen was divided into four. Four rectangles displayed shots from around the boathouse, and nothing happening in any of them.

'A quiet night,' she said, zipping up her top.

She watched sceptically as he picked up his old jacket and slowly pulled it on.

'We're an odd couple,' she declared, and walked out.

He caught up with her by the fence.

'I'll drive,' she said.

He didn't object: he had no great desire to drive a stolen 1994 Mazda with false plates all the way to Kristinehamn.

The rain held off, more or less, for the first 250 kilometres. They had just one significant exchange throughout the entire journey.

'Tell me about mountain climbing,' Berger said.

'Mountain climbing?' Blom said. The car wobbled on the irritating 90 km/h stretch near Örebro.

'It seems to be your one real passion in life.'

'You're seriously suggesting we talk about our lives?'

He laughed. 'Don't bother, then. But it's a bit uneven.'

'What do you mean?'

'I know you much better as Nathalie Fredén than as Molly Blom. Whereas you've already drilled pretty deep into Sam Berger's boringly stable psyche.'

It looked as if the smooth forehead actually frowned, but it was probably a result of the sun suddenly breaking through the clouds.

'Yes,' she eventually said. 'I like climbing.'

'I always imagine that undercover officers would relax by doing something that didn't remind them of work. Crocheting, maybe? Growing geraniums?'

'You think climbing reminds me of work?'

'Doesn't it? Aren't they both about precision and control on the brink of the abyss?'

'In some ways,' she conceded. 'But when I'm dangling there with nature stretching out to infinity, the only thing I feel is a vast, overwhelming sense of freedom.'

He nodded. 'I'm scared of heights,' Berger said. 'And I don't really trust myself. I might get a sudden impulse and just let go.'

'Tell me about the watches.'

He smiled. 'The watches make me calm. There's something remarkable about the way all those tiny cogs interact. I enter a different world and recharge my strength. Time is always the same there. Calm and straightforward. Because of the complexity.'

'Oddly enough, it sounds a bit like mountain climbing,' Blom said.

'Mountain climbing with a safety net,' Berger said.

They were silent the rest of the way to Kristinehamn.

At one corner of Södra Torget a moody-looking girl was sitting in the worsening rain. Her tattoos were clearly visible through her far-too-thin clothes. As she peered inside the car she looked extremely suspicious.

'Sandra,' Berger said.

'Hmm,' the girl said. 'Who's she?'

Blom held up her fake police ID. 'Jump in the back.'

'I don't think so,' Sandra said. 'Isn't that what Jonna and Simon did?'

'Weren't you in Australia then?' Berger said. 'Don't worry, we are police officers. And we only want to talk to you. On the phone yesterday you said something about a secret hideout . . . ?'

Sandra let out a deep sigh and got in the back seat. Blom drove off slowly and parked nearby.

'Our cave,' Sandra said. 'It was our secret place when we were younger. I don't know for sure if she ever showed it to Simon.'

'You were close when you were younger?' Blom said.

'Yes,' Sandra said. 'We lived with the same foster family for a couple of years. The cave was where we used to hide from the world. Then Jonna was moved on and we didn't see each other so much. I've only met Simon a couple of times.'

'Do you think she's likely to have shown Simon the cave?'

Sandra nodded. 'I think that's where they escaped to, every so often,' Sandra said. 'When there was too much shit going on. Like we used to.'

'Have you been there recently?'

'I've only just got back from Australia. I was away for nearly a year. And before that it had probably been a couple of years. I don't run away any more.'

'Can you show us the cave, Sandra?' Berger asked.

She nodded and they set off, heading into the forests of Värmland on narrowing roads. The increasingly heavy rain hammered on the car roof. They reached a hillier part of the forest, where waterlogged roads rolled up and down the hills. They nearly got stuck several times.

Eventually Sandra pointed straight ahead, towards a sign indicating a passing place.

'That's where the path starts,' she said.

Blom drove the car halfway into the bushes next to the sign, where the muddy road was slightly wider. The front wheels span their way a few centimetres into the mud before she stopped.

'It's about five hundred metres in from here,' Sandra said. 'The path isn't very obvious.'

'It's very wet out there,' Blom said. 'You stay in the car.'

'Fuck that,' Sandra said, and opened the door.

She led them along a track they would barely have noticed without her. The wet branches kept hitting them or dripping water. After just a dozen metres their clothes were soaked. The only consolation was that they couldn't get any wetter.

After a while the terrain got more hilly. They were walking along the side of a fairly steep rock face where even the moss and algae seemed to have trouble finding a foothold. The rock face veered away from the track and they followed it. Eventually Sandra stopped and pointed. An improbable amount of mascara was running down her cheeks.

'The bushes have grown a lot,' she said.

They followed her finger. In one place the even growth along the base of the rock became irregular.

Sandra started to walk towards the uneven bushes. Blom put a hand on her shoulder, and Sandra turned round with a look of irritation.

'Wait here,' Blom said.

'You can take cover under that pine,' Berger said, gesturing towards a tall tree that he hoped was a pine.

With obvious reluctance, Sandra went and stood by the trunk of the pine as Blom and Berger set off. When Berger cast a quick glance back over his shoulder she looked like a ghost from Norse mythology. Her pale face was streaked with black, her big eyes wide open.

The bushes, whatever kind they were, were covered in thorns and in places were so tall that it was hard to imagine two young girls – on the run from a hostile world – managing to get through them. The bushes must have grown like mad in the past few years.

The question was whether *someone* had managed to get through, not half a decade ago, but about eight months ago. In the middle of February.

When Jonna Eriksson and Simon Lundberg vanished without trace from the face of the earth.

The fact that Berger was leading the way was more than Blom could bear. She made her own way through the thick undergrowth instead. When lightning flashed across the metallic sky Berger considered shouting back to Sandra, telling her to move away from the tree, but when the first clap of thunder rang out, heavy and deep, it struck him that she was probably far more confident in the wild than he was. Besides, it felt wrong to shout. Only when he could make out the opening to the cave did he realise why. It felt peculiarly occupied.

It was entirely possible that William Larsson was hiding in there with Ellen Savinger strapped to a huge clock mechanism.

As he drew his pistol, Berger saw that Blom, positioned further along in the undergrowth, already had hers out. By the time the next crack of lightning shot its branching pattern across the sky she had disappeared into the oddly hostile greenery. And when the thunder came – louder this time, right after the lightning – he realised that she was going to get there first. As if that mattered.

She was waiting for him by the entrance to the cave. It wasn't much more than head-high, and rain-damaged spiders' webs hung in front of the dark opening like a natural curtain. Faint chirping noises were coming from the gloom. The barely perceptible walls appeared to move slightly in the unsteady shadows. Berger raised his torch to get a closer look, but Blom grabbed his hand and pushed it down.

'Not a good idea,' she whispered.

Then she set off into the cave with the beam of her torch aimed carefully at the ground. Berger followed her, doing the same. The floor of the cave was covered with stones that had come loose from the roof over the years, sucked down inexorably by gravity. But there was something else as well. It looked like droppings of some sort. Small ones. Possibly rats' droppings.

The narrow passageway went on for ten metres or so. Berger took care not to shine his torch up the walls. Then the cave opened out abruptly. They suddenly found themselves in a cavern. Dim light was filtering in through a hidden crack five metres above them. And the play of shadows suddenly became clear.

The walls of the cave were covered with bats. They hung there, moving gently, as if they were breathing in a strange, jerky, collective rhythm.

But overwhelmingly the bats were swarming around a metre-high formation at the back of the cavern. And they weren't just hanging there. They were moving, crawling, creeping across each other in a peculiar pattern. It was as if a relief in a Roman bath had come to life.

Berger heard himself groan. He glanced at Blom. She too was staring at the formation. Both torches were pointing at the floor, the only thing illuminating the bats was the daylight from the crack above.

'On the count of three,' Blom whispered. 'Then we shine our torches right at it and take cover immediately, flat on the ground. OK?'

Something inside Berger understood instinctively. But he just stood there, completely bewildered. He heard himself whisper: 'OK.'

Blom looked at him in the dim light. It was as if she was evaluating his mental state again.

Then she whispered: 'One. Two. Three!'

The torch beams swept towards the teeming bats. Then everything switched to freeze-frame. As Berger threw himself on the ground he saw the bats lift off like a single mass, a flying manta ray. The chirping increased exponentially as he fell, and before Berger hit the ground the immense sweeping wing flew over their heads and out of the cave, presumably rising like a huge plume through the rain outside. Pain transmitted itself with unusual slowness from his knees to his brain as the object deserted by the bats became visible in the twin torch beams. A couple of the ancient creatures remained; one bat was clinging to one of the ribs, another was peering groggily from between the teeth of the almost stripped-bare skull.

The jaw moved; it looked like the skeleton was chewing on a bat.

'Fucking hell,' Berger said, getting to his feet.

The skeleton was crouched against the wall of the cave. Remnants of rotten, dried flesh clung to a few of the white bones. The bat freed itself from the skeleton's mouth like an embodied scream and flew off in search of the others.

Berger reached for Blom's hand in the gloom. It responded by grasping his. Hand in hand they went over to the huddled remains of a human body. In the quivering light of their torches the whole scene looked archaic, as if they were visiting the time of cave dwellers.

The skeleton really was crouching down, as if it were resting after a run with a mammoth.

In a loose circle around the skeleton lay the remains of clothes that had fallen off the body as its size diminished. A wallet was peeping out from beneath the drifts of bat droppings.

Blom freed her hand from Berger's and pulled on a pair of plastic gloves. She extracted the wallet and, with trembling fingers, found an ID card.

Simon Lundberg's.

They looked at the skeleton. Yes, it could be the remains of a fifteen-year-old boy.

They shone their torches around the rest of the cavern. There wasn't a lot else to see.

'No Jonna Eriksson,' Berger concluded.

'No,' Blom said, moving her torch closer to the scraps of clothing around the skeleton. She picked them up, one by one, from the piles of droppings. Eventually a shimmering object was uncovered.

It wasn't much more than a centimetre in diameter, had tiny teeth and was perfectly round.

It was a very small cog.

32

Thursday 29 October, 13.12

Molly Blom dozed off twice at the wheel on the drive home. Fortunately it happened in the fleeting moments when Sam Berger was in full command of his faculties. Beyond that, he wasn't much help. His general condition couldn't really be described as anything other that half-dead.

When they hurried back into the boathouse early that afternoon – after checking the security footage from the car park by the nearest row houses – they agreed it was time to get into their sleeping bags. Neither of them could be bothered to work out how long they had been awake over the past few days.

Berger removed a very small plastic bag from his pocket and wrote a few words on a label, which he stuck on the bag. Then he put it with the others beneath the watches in their box. The last thing he saw were the words *Jonna Eriksson, cave.*

'Just a couple of hours,' Blom said from her side of the bench, pulling off her tracksuit top. She unbuttoned her army trousers and stood for a moment.

Berger had, without really thinking about it, pulled off his top and was in the middle of removing his jeans. He stopped and met her sharp gaze.

'I know,' he said. 'Sooner or later I'm going to have to get in that bastard water. But first some sleep.'

'I wasn't reacting to your body odour,' Blom said, pointing. 'What happened to your arm?'

Berger felt the five-centimetre-wide indentation in his left arm. It was just as numb as always.

'An old injury,' he said, pulling his jeans off.

'It looks like someone took a real bite out of you,' Blom said.

But by then Berger had already lain down and fallen asleep.

The early summer that prevails in a desolate, grit-covered football pitch is strangely remorseless, no wind, the air laced with dust, the sun sharp and prickly. Sam sees a group of people at the other end of the pitch, by the far goal. He sees that they're girls, lots of girls; he can hear their shrill voices but can't make out any words. The emptiness above the dusty grit seems to filter out everything resembling language. Sam has become a different person; time has changed. It feels as if he's aged a couple of years in just a few weeks. These days he avoids this sort of gathering. He can feel that he has become a loner. But there's something about the unarticulated yelling that draws him in. Against all his instincts he is drawn in that direction, and sees the back of one girl after another. They're wearing summery clothes, dresses, skirts, and the merciless sun makes their long hair shine in all manner of hues. The dust swirls around them, and as they move Sam can see that they aren't alone. Behind them a taller head rises up. Anton's, and it's moving. It disappears behind the curtain of girls, reappears, still moving. Then the curtain parts a little more, and against the goalpost, tied to the post, stands a figure. Its long blond hair hangs like another curtain in front of the figure's face. His trousers have been pulled down, the lower half of his body exposed.

Then Anton sees Sam. He smiles his typical Anton grin and calls out, 'Well hello there! Come and say hi to your friend!'

Sam would rather have turned on his heel and fled before William saw him, but it's too late now. All Sam can think as he moves through the curtain of girls is: It's almost the summer holidays. All this crap will soon be over. *But it isn't over for Anton. Not by a long shot. He passes something to Sam, and it takes a few moments before Sam realises that it's a towel, a damp towel.*

'Whip him!'

And only then does Sam see how badly William's been whipped. And he suddenly sees the boathouse before him; he sees the girl's tongue push at the duct tape, hears her wild screaming that cuts off abruptly after he takes off like a frightened rabbit through the grass that reaches up to his chest. And he whips and lashes out, and he sees William's body shrink with pain, but not a sound emerges from his lips. He looks up for the first time and meets Sam's gaze.

Sam goes closer, is standing very close now, and whispers: 'That was for the boathouse, you fucking lunatic.'

Unknown forces propelled Sam into a sitting position. He stared blindly across the boathouse until his vision returned. And in his field of vision was Molly Blom. She took a photograph from the printer and held it up in front of him. It showed Simon Lundberg's crouching skeleton.

'It's me he's after,' Berger said groggily.

Blom stuck the photograph to the whiteboard and looked at him. But she didn't say anything.

Berger stood up, climbed out of the sleeping bag and went on: 'He hates me more than I remembered. I'd sanitised my memories.'

'That's how we survive,' Blom said. 'What did you dream?'

Blom was wearing her army trousers and tracksuit top again. But she looked slightly different. Berger ignored the impression and stumbled over towards the whiteboard. He stood there, looking at the pictures of William Larsson's victims.

'Were you there at the goalposts?' he asked.

Blom went on looking at him with penetrating intensity. 'I don't know what you're talking about,' she said.

'William was tied to the post,' he said. 'It was after the boathouse, early summer. There was gang of girls. Were you one of them?'

Blom shook her head.

'I kept to myself as much as I could until the end of term,' she said.

'I think the rest of your friends were there,' Berger said. 'And I whipped his cock. With a damp towel.'

'William?'

'Yes. Bloody hell.'

For the first time he met her gaze. There was a hint of sympathy in there.

He wasn't sure he wanted her sympathy.

Then she nodded, as if to break the silence, once and for all, and gestured towards Berger's largely naked body.

'Go and have a wash,' she said. 'There's shampoo out there.'

Then he saw what was different about her. Her hair was still wet.

He stood under the protruding roof for a while, looking out at the curtain of rain shrouding the whole of Edsviken. Then he let out a deep sigh, snatched up the bottle of shampoo from the railing and took three steps down the ladder until a stabbing pain spread up through his body from his big toe. Then he jumped in. The water came up to his navel. As if in a flash of lightning it was like he could see his brain, every minuscule activity in any given moment. He lowered the rest of his body under the water and felt through the paralysing cold – more clearly than ever – that William wanted something from them. He wanted to talk to them. He wanted to tell a story. And that story ended with a great deal of pain and a great deal of death.

Death as a full stop.

But then his lungs told him a different story, about having to get out of the icy cold, and as he broke the surface a different name was in his mind. And a realisation. As he washed he tried to get the meandering impulses in his brain to pin the realisation down.

A few minutes later he stormed inside, wrapped in a towel, and called out: 'Anton.'

Blom was standing looking at the seven victims. He saw her quickly brush a tear from her eye before turning towards him.

'What?'

'Anton,' he repeated. 'Worst bully in the class. Do you remember him?'

'I wasn't in your class, as you know. I was in Year 8 when you were in Year 9.'

'But you remember the Lucia celebration? When they glued the Lucia crown to William's hair?'

He watched as she was transported back in time through years that she really didn't want to revisit.

'Yes, I remember,' she said. 'It was three Year 9s.'

'Anton, Micke and Freddan,' Berger said. 'Anton was the one who told William to sing.'

'Ah. "Come on then, sing, for fuck's sake, don't be shy." '

'Word for word, no less,' Berger said.

'I remember far too much,' Blom said. 'What about Anton?'

'He was the one who tied William to the goalpost and pulled

his trousers down, and then got the girls there somehow, to watch his humiliation.'

'And he asked you to join in?'

'I saw red,' Berger said. 'Maybe I was whipping myself, deep down. Trying to whip the cowardice out.'

'In a way that was even more cowardly.'

'I know,' Berger said quietly. 'But if William has come back to Helenelund, if this is all about taking revenge for the injustices of childhood in a really sick way, would he leave Anton untouched?'

'Ah,' Blom said. 'Can you find him?'

'I'll try,' Berger said, throwing himself at his laptop.

He had a name, he had a year of birth, he even had a vague idea of when his birthday was. It didn't take long to find Anton Bergmark.

'Plumber,' Berger said. 'Stayed in Sollentuna. Worked in his dad's business for ten years. Took over from him. Called himself managing director. Then declared unfit for work.'

'Unfit for work?' Blom said. 'When?'

'Almost three years ago. Took early retirement six months later.'

'That's quite a change. From managing director to unfit for work to early retirement in the space of six months. The obvious interpretation is substance abuse of some kind.'

'Too many business dinners with cocaine dessert?' Berger said. 'Not out of the question. The business fell apart, went bankrupt. Divorced from his second wife not long before. She got custody of the three children, one of whom wasn't even hers but Anton's from his first marriage.'

'Restraining order?'

'Can't find anything like that. But there's an address.'

'Let me guess,' Blom said. 'A rehab centre?'

'The Svalan Care Home,' Berger said. 'In the centre of Sollentuna.'

They began to sense that things weren't quite right when they were on their way in. The Svalan Care Home occupied a couple of floors in one of the huge blocks on Malmvägen in Sollentuna, and the walls of the long corridor were adorned with rather too many cross-stitched samplers with phrases like *My home is my castle* and *East, west, home is best* to signify a rehab centre for addicts. When the first wheelchair rolled out and a woman who had to be in her late nineties greeted them with the words 'Ah, the Elfenben couple! Is it already time to empty the latrines?' that sense only grew stronger. A nurse appeared with a quizzical look on her face, and Berger held up his ID.

'What sort of care home is Svalan?'

The odd thing was that the nurse laughed before replying. 'It's what used to be called long-stay.'

'Senile elderly patients waiting to die?'

'Not only them. We have a number of younger patients as well.'

'Including Anton Bergmark?'

The nurse nodded and led them along the corridor until they reached a larger room with a view of the other apartment blocks. There were about a dozen people scattered around the room. A television was on, but no one seemed to be watching it. Everyone Berger and Blom saw looked elderly; they were in wheelchairs and weren't doing much. The nurse walked past them to the window. There was a man sitting in a wheelchair, looking out through the rain. He had his back to them, but his posture was slumped, his arms were hanging down, and the reflection in the big window was too indistinct to tell them anything.

'Anton?' the nurse said.

That didn't prompt any reaction at all.

The nurse grabbed the handle of the wheelchair and slowly turned it round.

And Berger was suddenly fifteen-year-old Sam, running like he had never run before, through meadow grass which reached up to his chest. The figure in front of him slowed down and slowly turned round.

The face that was turned towards Berger and Blom in Svalan Care Home in the centre of Sollentuna was crooked and misshapen. The bumps seemed to stick out in an almost cubist fashion from his head.

They stared at the deformed face. It stared back, dark, sceptical, dismissive.

Sam would rather have turned on his heel and fled before William saw him, but it's too late now. All Sam can think as he moves through the curtain of girls is: It's almost the summer holidays. All this crap will soon be over. *But it isn't over for Anton. Not by a long shot. He passes something to Sam, and it takes a few moments before Sam realises that it's a towel, a damp towel.*

'Whip him!'

And only then does Sam see how badly William's been whipped. And he suddenly sees the boathouse before him; he sees the girl's tongue push at the duct tape, hears her wild screaming that cuts off abruptly after he takes off like a frightened rabbit through the grass that reaches up to his chest. And he whips and lashes out, and he sees William's body shrink with pain, but not a sound emerges from his lips. He looks up for the first time and meets Sam's gaze.

Sam goes closer, is standing very close now, and whispers: 'That was for the boathouse, you fucking lunatic.'

William stares into his eyes. Sam has never seen such a black look in his whole life. Then there's movement. It's extremely slow. Sam sees it almost frame by frame. The long, blond hair lifts and is tossed back. The crooked, misshapen features emerge from below the hair, and out of that crookedness two rows of bared teeth emerge. They part. They approach Sam's upper arm. He never feels the teeth penetrate his skin and then his flesh. He never hears the teeth meet, deep in his arm. He doesn't hear it and he doesn't feel it. And the pain radiating from his bicep doesn't gain momentum before he sees the piece of flesh fall from William's mouth, followed by a steady stream of blood. With distorted slowness the piece of flesh drifts down towards the dry grit of the football pitch.

33

Thursday 29 October, 14.54

Berger and Blom stared at the deformed face. It stared back, dark, sceptical, dismissive. Berger felt his insides lurch.

'William?' he said, and didn't recognise his own voice.

He saw Blom out of the corner of his eye. He could see that she was shaking.

To her very core.

The figure in the wheelchair didn't reply. He just sat still and stared at Berger, completely blank. A trickle of saliva slowly ran down his chin.

Had they been utterly wrong?

Had both Berger and Blom allowed themselves to be deceived by their damaged childhoods? Had they thrown away their careers on a whim?

Were they back to square one?

Traces of rationality returned to Berger. Was this really William? And why would he be sitting here, tucked away in a care home under the name of his former tormentor, Anton Bergmark?

There were signs of age, lines, wrinkles, redness to indicate the passage of years. But the swellings and lumps, all the jagged angles, were in the same places as twenty-two years ago.

In exactly the same places.

Blom came to her senses first. She looked at the nurse. 'Can you fetch all the documentation you have about Anton?'

The nurse nodded and went away.

It wasn't William Larsson's gaze. If it was, it was utterly wrecked. The eyes were watery, absent.

'Are you William Larsson?' Berger asked with exaggerated clarity.

The watery gaze rose through the cratered landscape of the face and latched onto him. Berger looked back, but didn't know what he was seeing.

'Hello, Sam,' the figure said, and produced a crooked smile. When the left corner of the mouth turned upward a string of saliva dribbled from the right side.

Berger turned towards Blom. He had been recognised. The question was: what did that mean? He saw that Blom had stopped shaking. She was already deep in thought. What did it mean, if William Larsson had never left the country? Who was behind the kidnappings if William's deformities had finally reached his brain and left him pretty much a vegetable? How had he come to assume Anton Bergmark's identity? Blom's shaking had been replaced by whirring. Berger could see her mind whirring – as clearly as if it were his own.

'Hello, William,' he asked. 'How are you?'

The figure produced a hiss that was probably intended to be a laugh.

'How are you, Sam?' the figure said. 'How's your arm?'

Berger's right hand instinctively reached for his left arm. Even through the fabric of his jacket he could clearly feel the indentation in his bicep.

'You bit me,' he said. 'You bit me badly.'

Now the figure just stared at him, and somewhere in the

midst of that stare his consciousness seemed to fade. The look in his eyes was no longer clear. It was somewhere else.

The nurse appeared with a bundle of medical notes. 'There's a police report here as well, from the Sollentuna Police. That's in the bottom file.'

She handed the two files to Blom and left them. They took one each, went to the other end of the day room and read them standing up. After an indeterminate amount of time they swapped. When Berger was finished with the second file he looked over at Blom. Her eyes were closed.

In the end Berger said. 'Fucking hell.'

'We were wrong,' Blom said. 'But not as wrong as we thought.'

'Less wrong than we feared,' Berger said, and felt himself smiling wryly.

'Aisha Pachachi wasn't William's first victim,' Blom said. 'Anton Bergmark was.'

Berger nodded and cleared his throat.

'Let me try to summarise what we just read,' he said. 'One winter's evening in February almost three years ago the recently divorced Anton Bergmark was sitting at home in his villa in Häggvik in Sollentuna, drinking. Someone came to the door, and all the evidence suggests that he let the visitor in voluntarily. The marks on his wrists and ankles, as well as on the legs of the dining table in the living room, indicate that Anton was strapped to the table, lying on his back. Further marks suggest that some sort of vice was attached to one end of the table, holding Anton's head in place before the assault began. According to the medical report, the assault was carried out using four different hammers, all different sizes. The grotesque torture went on for almost two days. Somewhere during the process Anton Bergmark literally lost his mind. He was declared very obviously unfit to work, and was granted early retirement six months later. Because Bergmark had done business with numerous criminal gangs, the assault was assumed to be connected with unpaid debts. The investigation focused exclusively on those groups, and in the absence of evidence, ran out of steam. The Sollentuna Police managed to keep it fairly quiet; the media barely mentioned the case and no pictures of Bergmark were ever published following the assault. There was no one who could draw any connection between William's face twenty years before and Anton's face today.'

Blom grimaced and nodded.

'A reversal of roles,' she said after a pause.

Berger summarised: 'William smashed up Anton's face in order to make it look like his own, the way it looked when he was being bullied; he probably doesn't look like that now. The determination, precision and emotional detachment required to use a vice and four hammers to turn Anton into William means that we need to re-evaluate William. He's a bloody professional. How can he be such a pro?'

'Professional, yet still utterly mad,' Blom said. 'You'd have to be utterly mad to exact such an elaborate revenge on your old tormentor.'

'He was sixteen years old, physically and mentally wrecked after years of the worst bullying you can imagine. Over the next twenty years he became some sort of professional torturer. How?'

'This is all hypothetical,' Blom said. 'We're fumbling in the dark. You don't necessarily need training to excel at torture.'

'You mean he was just a natural?'

'I don't know. Driven by a relentless desire for vengeance?'

'I don't buy that,' Berger said, pointing towards the figure in the wheelchair ten metres away. 'You've seen Anton, Molly.

That was done by a man who's tortured people before, probably on a regular basis. He's been trained in either the criminal or military world, and I think what we're looking at here strengthens the hypothesis that there really was a father called Nils Gundersen who was a mercenary in "some ruddy Arab country". We need to find him.'

Blom looked troubled.

'I don't know,' she said hesitantly. 'But I'm worried that it's time for a serious conversation . . . '

'MISS?'

'It's not that simple . . . '

'For fuck's sake, just grab the bull by the horns,' Berger said. 'I promise not to listen.'

'I need more than that,' Blom said, taking her phone out. 'You need to be out of earshot.'

While Blom went round the corner Berger walked around the day room. He counted fifteen people absorbed in absolute inactivity scattered around the room. The television was still on, showing a football match with no sound; no one seemed to be watching it. It was as if time had stopped, as if he was in a small gap in the violently rushing flow of time. As if a cog had fallen out of the clock.

Over by the window sat the figure in his wheelchair. The unseeing eyes stared out at the miserable apartment blocks, and he was lolling in a position that would probably leave him completely bedridden within a couple of years.

Berger crouched down beside him. 'Anton?'

Anton Bergmark turned to look at him. Something resembling consciousness returned to his watery eyes. 'Fuck, you really hit him.'

Berger jerked back.

'What did you say, Anton?' he said.

But the man in the wheelchair had already disappeared off somewhere.

Berger stood up and stroked Anton's head gently. He saw his reflection in the window, streaked with rain, dissolving. It wasn't that different from Anton's.

Then he wandered the corridors, his mind elsewhere. On an isolated sofa Molly Blom was sitting with her laptop on her knees.

She was staring at the screen and said without looking up: 'Well, that went better than expected.'

'MISS remembered you with great fondness?' Berger suggested.

She ignored him. 'MISS actually has a Nils Gundersen in their register. Wanted internationally for various types of war crime. Born 1948. Norwegian citizen up to the millennium, when he became a Lebanese citizen. Said to live in the city of Jbeil, better known as Byblos.'

'Bloody hell,' Berger said.

'Gundersen became an officer in the Norwegian army at the age of twenty-two, rose quickly through the ranks, then went off to the Foreign Legion in 1973 at the age of twenty-five. Disappeared two years later, abruptly, illegal desertion. Probably recruited as a mercenary by one of the many factions involved in the Lebanese Civil War at the time. Cropped up in a news report from Beirut around Christmas '76, in a tank. Right tangle of foreign and domestic interest groups: the USA was involved, along with Israel, Syria, Iran, Iraq. And the Lebanese factions were Sunni, Shiite, Palestinian, Druze and Maronite. MISS doesn't know which group Gundersen fought for. Because he was a wanted man, they paid attention to his subsequent trips to Europe. The general conclusion is that he was recruiting, and his presence was documented in ten European cities or so between '76 and '84. One of the first was Stockholm.'

'Wow,' Berger said. '1976?'

'Gundersen never stayed long in the same place. Only afterwards was it confirmed that he had actually been in Stockholm for a little less than a week in the middle of April 1976. And William Larsson was born more or less exactly nine months later, on Monday 17 January.'

'Fucking hell,' Berger said.

'That still doesn't prove anything,' Blom said. 'And there's no photographic evidence of the visit either. But there is this.'

Blom turned the computer round. The screen displayed a whole series of pictures. She clicked on the first, a fairly grainy portrait of a stocky, bearded, weather-beaten man in his fifties. He looked like he was walking through a bazaar.

'According to MISS, this is the last known picture of Nils Gundersen,' Blom said. 'Taken by the CIA in Marrakesh. He was only identified when he was already long gone. At that point he was already wanted for war crimes in Lebanon, Afghanistan and Iraq.'

'The CIA,' Berger said coolly.

Blom clicked through a number of pictures of an increasingly young Gundersen in various settings. They got more and more warlike.

'Yes,' Blom said, pointing at the screen. 'Gundersen on the side of the Iraqis in the first Gulf War. Operation Desert Storm.'

'The Gulf War?' Berger asked, staring at the picture of the now moustachioed and very blond officer in front of his men.

'Yes,' Blom said. 'This picture's from '91. If they've got the rank right, he's a colonel.'

'Brought in by Saddam Hussein?'

'Looks that way. And this colonel showed up two years later to collect his son from Sweden.'

'You're actually saying *son*?'

'Hang on,' Blom said, clicking through the pictures. Nils Gundersen kept on getting younger. In the first picture he was standing in a mountainous landscape, had a full beard and was leaning against a bazooka.

'Afghanistan?' Berger said.

'The Mujahedin,' Blom said. 'It looks like Gundersen had links with the CIA and trained Mujahedin fighters in the eighties. The Soviet Union's last war.'

'Hmm,' Berger said.

The slideshow went on. Nils Gundersen as a stylish young officer with the Norwegian flag neatly sewn onto his breast pocket. As a high-school student with a sparkling smile. As a rosy-cheeked adolescent on skis. In one yellowed black-and-white photograph he was sitting in a sandpit throwing sand. And he was in his mother's arms on a sturdy armchair. Behind the chair stood a man.

'This is the only known photograph of Gundersen's father,' Blom said, and began to zoom in on the man's face. 'Genetic traits often skip a generation.'

Eventually Berger could see that the man's chin was crooked, and there was a bony protrusion on one side of his forehead.

William Larsson's grandfather had a very angular, misshapen face. It bore a strong resemblance to a cubist sculpture.

34

Thursday 29 October, 16.12

That afternoon the hedgehogs went into hibernation. The whole family withdrew to the far corner of the boathouse. It was apparent that the mother had constructed a winter abode for them. She wandered over towards the unhappy figures by the whiteboard, as if to say: Goodnight, we're off for the winter, into the infinite world of dreams, so much better than your world.

Then she went back and settled down with her little ones.

One of the unhappy figures by the whiteboard was half undressed. The second was touching the first one's arm.

'You can see teeth marks,' Molly Blom said.

'I know,' Berger said. 'They don't seem to want to fade.'

As he pulled his top back on, Blom turned round and attached another photograph to the board. Beside the picture of the fifteen-year-old William Larsson there was now a new snap of Anton Bergmark. The facial deformities were amazingly similar.

'A precision job,' Berger said.

Blom stood next to him, looking at the two pictures. Eventually she said: 'If we assume that William managed to leave

Sweden with the help of his father, a blond mercenary active in the Arab world, then we can probably assume that was where he underwent pretty comprehensive plastic surgery. That would have been 1993, the Lebanese Civil War had ended a few years before and the Gulf War was over. In those slightly more peaceful times, maybe Nils Gundersen finally found out he had a son, and discovered the sort of life he was living. He heard about the bullying, decided to rescue his son and took him back to his own world, a secret world below the radar. Off in the badlands.'

'But wouldn't Gundersen have needed some sort of help in Sweden?' Berger said. 'I mean, he was an internationally wanted war criminal. It can't have been that easy to remove an injured and highly conspicuous sixteen-year-old from Sweden to Lebanon without anyone noticing.'

'He probably had contacts in Sweden from his visit here in '76, when William was conceived.'

Berger walked closer to the board and looked carefully at the picture of the young William Larsson.

'Gundersen was a fighter,' he said. 'He wasn't the sort of man who turned the other cheek. I think we can assume that he didn't exactly preach the value of forgiveness.'

Blom nodded.

'A man schooled in torture and violence,' she said. 'And some twenty years later the son returns, after plastic surgery and military training, and embarks on his revenge with a decisive blow against the worst of the bullies, Anton Bergmark. William tortures him with a hammer for two crazed, nightmarish days, transforming him into a person who no longer exists except in his own head. And even this crime is disguised, to make it look like a different sort of attack. But then he stops attacking the guilty and goes after innocent girls. Why?'

'We're outside the realm of logic,' Berger said. 'He isn't interested in taking out his revenge on grown women. It was fifteen-year-old girls who witnessed his humiliation. That's what stayed with him, and maybe made him completely incapable of interacting normally with women. They're the ones who have to be wiped out. I agree that when it comes down to it, he's basically a psychopath His mass-murdering father may have taught him how to give his actions a rational and professional veneer, but William's motives are genuinely sick. If a man gets in the way, like Simon Lundberg in the cave, he just gets rid of him. It's the girls that interest him.'

'Seven layers of blood in the cellar in Märsta,' Blom said. 'He tortured all of them. And thanks to Anton we know William has both the ability and detachment to carry it out. He spent two whole days with him.'

'Bloody hell,' Berger said.

They paused. Looked at the increasingly bizarre pattern on the board. Thought.

After a while Blom said: 'When his dad came to fetch his sixteen-year-old son, he would have informed the mother, right? Unless he just took him?'

'Good,' Berger said. 'We've got two different pictures of Nils Gundersen. The obvious one: the tough guy. Deserts the Foreign Legion to become a mercenary. Fights in Lebanon, Afghanistan, Iraq. Wanted for war crimes and for breaking international law. The less obvious picture is the dad who finds out he's got a son, that the son is being bullied and having a hard time, and rescues him. Which of these two Gundersens did the mother, Stina Larsson, see? Probably the latter, don't you think? The dad coming back to rescue his son?'

'I agree,' Blom said. 'They probably had some degree of contact. In theory, Stina would have consented to the move.'

'Which means that Stina's sister, Alicia Anger over in Vendelsögården Care Home, might be able to tell us more.'

'If we can find our way through the fog of language.'

'It's worth a try,' Berger said, holding out his hand. It took a while before Blom placed her mobile phone in it.

'Vendelsögården, Mia Arvidsson,' a female voice answered.

'Hello, Mia,' Berger said. 'I believe we spoke when I visited one of your patients, Alicia Anger, the other day.'

'Possibly,' Mia Arvidsson said drily. 'Who am I speaking to?'

'My name is . . . Charles Lindbergh. I'm the policeman who came to talk to Alicia yesterday I don't know if you remember. I was wondering if it was possible to talk to her over the phone?'

'Yes. And no.'

'Can you expand on that?'

'Yes, I remember. And no, it's not possible to speak to her.'

'I know communication can be a bit tricky . . . '

'The communication difficulties I'm referring to are absolute,' Mia Arvidsson said. 'Alicia Anger is dead.'

Berger fell silent. Everything was silent.

Arvidsson went on: 'The police have been here. They concluded that it was a natural but unconventional death. "A feeding error," if I remember the phrase correctly.'

'A . . . feeding error . . . ?'

'It's difficult to describe,' Mia Arvidsson said. 'You'd almost have to see it for yourself.'

Berger reflected. Then he took a chance. 'You don't happen to have a picture?'

'Yes,' Mia Arvidsson said. 'But it's not something I have any intention of sharing.'

'I'm a police officer. I'm not going to publish it.'

'But the police have already got it . . . '

'Not me,' Berger said. 'And I really do need to see it. Right away.'

He clearly heard the nurse sigh.

'Have you got an email address?' she asked.

Berger glanced towards Blom. She was already busy tapping at her computer. Then she turned the screen towards him and he read out an email address.

The email arrived three minutes later, to the newly created and very temporary email address. The picture showed Alicia Anger in her rocking chair in Vendelsögården Care Home. With the exception of one detail: she looked more peaceful than she had in life.

Out of her mouth hung a black sock, like a blackened tongue.

There was a caption as well, probably supplied by Mia Arvidsson: *Given Mrs Anger's eating habits and daily accidents at mealtimes, the likelihood that she simply mistook the sock for food and choked on it is so high that the case has been closed and written off as an accident.*

Most likely a quote from the police report.

'It could be true, of course,' Blom said, looking at the grotesque picture. 'She wasn't exactly in full command of her faculties.'

'*Ingen ruaidh*,' Berger said. 'Now "the red girl" is filling Odin's horn with mead. But she was damn well murdered.'

'By William?' Blom said. 'Why would he murder his own senile aunt?'

'It happened this morning, apparently,' Berger read. 'So the day after Roy and Roger tracked us down. Are we really going to believe that's a coincidence?'

'His name's Kent,' Blom said. 'And I've worked with Kent and Roy for a long time. I doubt they'd have murdered her.'

'Even so, she wouldn't have died if we hadn't gone to see her,' Berger said.

Then Blom's secure mobile rang. It had never rung before.

They both stared at it warily. Blom looked at the screen: *Unknown*. The story of her life.

Then she answered.

'Yes?'

Berger was watching her. Her expression didn't change; she just passed the phone to him without a word.

'Yes?'

'Sam,' Deer's unmistakable voice said. 'We need to meet.'

'Text messages aren't good enough?' Berger said.

'The buttons on my backup mobile are too small. The bench on Norr Mälarstrand in half an hour. OK?'

'OK,' Berger said. 'Bring Syl.'

'Syl?' Deer said. 'Why?'

'Tell her she knows why. And tell her it's completely OK if she refuses.'

The conversation was over. Berger looked at the time. Just past four.

Molly said: 'The bench?'

The park bench next to the little jetty along the northern shore of Riddarfjärden didn't have the same feel as when Berger and Deer used to sit there to escape the occasionally oppressive atmosphere of Police Headquarters with coffee, conversation and a nice view.

Then it provided a breathing space. Now all it provided was a very wet space.

Even so, Deer was sitting there beneath an umbrella. And she wasn't alone. Under a second umbrella they could make out a taller and considerably sharper profile.

Berger and Blom circled the bench for a while to make sure that Deer hadn't been tempted to temper mercy with justice.

There was no sign that she was being watched. They sat down on either side of Deer and Syl, without umbrellas.

They were pretty much alone between the sparse street lamps on Norr Mälarstrand.

'You're both wanted now,' Deer said. 'The Security Service issued an alert at lunchtime. Looks like they made their minds up. And apparently you, Nathalie Fredén, aren't called Eva Lindkvist, but Molly Blom. It's a fairly drastic step to reveal the identity of an "internal resource". That suggests serious criminality.'

'OK,' Berger said. 'Are you wearing recording devices?'

'Of course,' Deer said in a perfectly neutral voice.

'Why else did you summon me here?' Berger said. 'What was it that couldn't be dealt with over the phone?'

She handed him a file.

'I assumed you'd want hard copies of everything,' Deer said.

Berger slipped the file inside his jacket and smiled.

'I've trained you well, Deer,' he said.

'As we all know, you haven't trained me at all,' Deer said. 'The DNA samples were a match. I got strands of hair from a number of places, and it all fitted. Seven girls with the names, birth dates and ID numbers that you sent in your text have been held in that hellish cellar in Märsta. One after the other.'

Berger nodded and glanced at Blom. She was nodding too.

'Not just ghosts in the machine,' he said after a brief pause.

'I've got a couple more things,' Deer said. 'First a message from Vira. You remember Vira?'

'Medical Officer Höög's assistant? The twenty-one-year-old? Of course, crystal clear.'

'On closer examination it turns out that the blood-thinning

agent wasn't a blood-thinning agent at all, but a sedative that isn't available in Sweden.'

'And the other thing?' Blom said.

Deer turned towards Blom and looked at her for a few moments.

'Security Service,' Deer finally said, in a peculiar tone of voice.

'Yes?' Berger said, pouring oil on troubled waters.

Deer turned back to him and said, with the same sceptical expression: 'Are you sure you know what you're doing, Sam? I don't want to see you end up in prison. It would spoil my CV.'

'Out with it,' Berger said.

Deer cleared her throat. 'Today, when the Security Service issued the alert, the explanations were so vague, so evasive, that I tried to look into it more closely. I had a quiet word with an old friend who works for the Security Service now. He said it had something to do with new information the technical team had managed to extract from an interview recording. Does that mean anything to you?'

Berger looked at Blom. She nodded anxiously.

'Thanks again,' Berger said. 'Thanks very much.'

'And why am I here?' Syl asked, clearly concerned.

'I presume Deer has explained the situation to you?'

'For God's sake, there's an alert out for you as of today, Sambo,' Syl spluttered. 'The fact that I'm talking to you without arresting you makes me an accomplice.'

'But you're here anyway,' Berger said.

'I understand that it was you, Sylvia, who managed to find my name,' Blom said.

'Which we swore a solemn oath not to tell anyone,' Syl said, flashing a cutting glance at Berger.

'Anomalies,' Berger said. 'When you found the Security

Service list during that unofficial search you mentioned anomalies. You found more than the list . . . ?'

'And then I closed my eyes,' Syl said.

'I want you to open them again,' Berger said. 'What sort of anomalies?'

Syl frowned and ran her hand through her thin, mousy hair. 'There were signs that security had been intentionally weakened for an hour or so around the turn of the year. It looks like secret documents weren't just accessed.'

'But . . . ?'

'I don't know,' Syl said, shrugging. 'Erased, maybe.'

'So there were signs that things had been *erased* from the Security Service's top-secret archive?' Blom exclaimed.

'Signs,' Syl said. 'Nothing more.'

'Can you take a closer look?' Berger asked.

'We've already agreed a couple of times that this is all over now,' Syl said. 'And you were still a police officer then.'

Berger laughed. 'Can you take a closer look?' he repeated.

'If you insist,' Syl said sullenly.

'Thanks,' Berger said. 'Well, we won't detain you any longer.'

Deer and Syl stood up. Syl began to walk away, but Deer waited a moment longer, looking at Berger. Then she shook her head, turned and walked off beneath her umbrella. Soon they had both disappeared into the rain, as though swallowed up for good.

Molly Blom said: 'I know their rota.'

'What?' Berger said, his eyes focused on the distant past.

'The technical guys' rota. I know it. I know where one of them comes out, and roughly when. We need to find out what they've managed to extract from our looped footage. We said things there that could wreck our whole investigation.'

'So you're thinking of adding "violence against a public servant" to our already impressive list of achievements?'

'Anders Karlberg is a friend,' Blom said. 'I think we can talk to him. Without resorting to violence.'

'A friend?'

'OK,' Molly Blom said, shrugging. 'A bit more than a friend.'

35

Thursday 29 October, 17.45

They tapped in the code and entered the stairwell on Bergsgatan, walked past the lift that led down to hell, and stepped out into the courtyard where Blom's Mercedes Vito was actually parked once more. Now under new ownership, she presumed. She pressed against the wall to her left to evade the security cameras and crept over to a brand-new Tesla. Berger crouched down beside her.

'A Tesla. Wow,' he whispered.

'Anders really likes the latest technology,' she whispered.

'In bed as well?'

'Well, he's not in the same league as your Madame X, of course.'

Then they were mercifully silent for half an hour. The Security Service really had delved into his personal life. Berger couldn't even be bothered to feel embarrassed.

They stayed crouched in the miserable courtyard until their joints seized up and their muscles started to cramp. Two people appeared and drove off in their own cars. Three.

When time seemed to have been rained into submission and washed away they heard a fourth set of footsteps. Blom looked at Berger's watch and nodded. The Tesla's doors clicked open. When the driver was behind the wheel, they jumped in, Blom in the passenger seat, Berger in the back.

'Fucking hell!' the slightly greying driver yelled after hitting his head on the roof of the car.

'Why wasn't an alert issued sooner, Anders?' Blom asked.

'Molly, for God's sake,' Anders Karlberg said, casting a quick glance over his shoulder at Berger. 'Try to remember that I'm old enough to have a heart attack.'

'I know,' Blom said. 'But I'm not old enough to be fired on less than clear grounds. What happened?'

'Shit,' Karlberg groaned quietly, and rubbed his bald patch. 'And to top it all off you drag your partner in crime into my Tesla, too.'

'I promise not to make a mess,' Berger said, looking at the mud he'd inadvertently deposited on the seat.

'You know me, Anders,' Molly Blom said. 'You know I'm not a criminal. Tell me.'

'Oh, I know you, alright. You're a tough woman.'

'Come on, Anders.'

'Something disrupted the recording equipment,' Karlberg said. 'It took a while before we realised we were dealing with a loop. A transmitter inserted a piece of code and created a loop that repeated every twenty seconds. To keep it simple let's call it a virus. But the loop failed for a few seconds. We didn't understand why that only happened once, even though the loop repeated more than thirty times. It turned out that it had been done with an impressively well concealed piece of code. We only managed to crack it at lunchtime today.'

'And why did that trigger a nationwide alert?'

'Because we realised that the glitch was intentional. A little miracle of coding. August Steen reckoned you'd done that on purpose. So that you'd get found out. Which got him wondering why. He needs to bring you in, Molly. You've got to explain what you're up to.'

'Hang on,' Blom said. 'The breach in the loop was *intentional*?'

'Yes,' Anders Karlberg said. 'Almost like a microscopic alarm clock.'

Sam Berger crunched the gears as he put the clapped-out Mazda into first, accelerated along Norr Mälarstrand and said: 'Wiborg Supplies Ltd?'

'Yes,' Blom said, shaking her head. 'I should have guessed. Everything they do is usually so perfect.'

'And the guy who made the gizmo at Wiborg is called Olle? So what do you know about this Olle?'

'Nothing, really,' Blom said. 'Olle Nilsson. He's worked at Wiborg Supplies for a while now. Smart, doesn't say much, extremely professional. But I don't actually know anything about him.'

'But you still commissioned him to do an unofficial job?'

'These guys are used to getting all kinds of jobs, more or less undercover, and they're prepared to accept payment in all sort of odd ways. Technical geniuses, all too aware of the shadowy world they're working in.'

'But something made you pick Olle Nilsson over all the other technical geniuses.'

'He seemed trustworthy, invisible, and quiet as the grave. No problem with unorthodox payment. I paid cash. No receipt.'

'So it could have been him who added that so-called microscopic alarm clock to your device. The intention could only have been to blow your cover. Maybe even *our* cover. In which case Olle Nilsson must have some connection to William.'

'We should certainly talk to him,' Blom said. 'It could have been a mistake.'

'Hardly, though, surely?'

'No,' Blom said. 'Hardly.'

They passed the roundabout at Lindhagensplan, Traneberg Bridge and Brommaplan in silence. The Mazda headed down the length of Bergslagsvägen until it reached the run-down Vinsta industrial estate. Berger glanced at the time as he pulled up in front of the apparently ramshackle Wiborg Supplies. It was almost seven o'clock, and there was no indication that there was any work being done anywhere in the desolate estate. They stopped on the loading bay and looked around the car park. There was no one there, no cars starting up. It was as deserted as the day after judgement day. Blom went over to a grubby keypad beside the door, tapped in a long sequence of digits, and the door, which itself looked remarkably analogue, slid open unexpectedly smoothly.

There was no sour receptionist smelling of methanol in the shabby reception area. Blom reached beneath the desk and found the button. The door behind the desk whirred and slid open with the same well oiled precision as the front door. Molly Blom and Sam Berger walked into the combined storeroom and workshop whose air of gentle shabbiness struck Berger as a facade. A solitary man in his fifties was sitting behind a pair of computers that seemed to be covered in layers of ingrained dust.

'Duty officer?' Blom said, holding her ID up at an illegible distance.

The man nodded and stood up.

'Högberg,' he said. 'And you?'

'Eva Lindkvist and Roy Grahn, Security Service. Is Olle Nilsson here today?'

Högberg shook his head and sat down again.

'Haven't seen him for a while,' he said. 'On the other hand, we never see much of him. He's on easy shifts.'

'Easy shifts?'

'Works from home, as a rule. Only comes in when it really can't be avoided.'

Berger and Blom glanced at each other.

'Have you got an address for him?' Blom asked.

'I'm not authorised to give out addresses. We like to keep a low profile.'

'I assume you know, Högberg, what sort of relationship Wiborg has with the Security Service. Obey without question. Never leak anything to anyone. So – an address?'

Högberg looked unimpressed, but clicked at his computer a few times.

'Isn't this leaking?' he said.

'You're not leaking if you're giving the Security Service what the Security Service wants,' Blom said in a tone that made Berger feel sick.

Högberg pointed to a printer. It contained a sheet of paper. Blom picked it up and read it. Then she walked out without another word. Berger followed her.

They got into the Mazda.

'Bålsta,' Blom said. 'It looks like a rural address.'

'From Märsta to Bålsta,' Berger said. 'That's plausible.'

He burned as much rubber as the Mazda was capable of. Bergslagsvägen was mercifully free of traffic, and out on the E18 they made good progress. They still had a way to go.

'We could have cracked this earlier,' Blom said in self-reproach as she typed the address into the laptop and began to zoom in on a large green area on the map. Slowly the green turned into forest, forest as seen from a satellite.

'Olle Nilsson's house is in the middle of the forest?' Berger said with a quick sideways glance at the satellite picture.

'The closest neighbour is at least a kilometre away.'

Berger stared out into the darkness streaked by useless windscreen wipers. So far the road was lit up by powerful street lamps.

The feeling that they were really getting close grew with each passing minute.

They left civilisation via the turning to Bålsta. Blom guided Berger confidently along the increasingly narrow roads. They passed fewer and fewer cars, and the gaps between street lamps kept growing. In the end there was nothing but darkness. The desolate autumnal Swedish forest was only just visible through the rain surrounding the cocoon of the car. All that existed was a dull, pattering, echoing darkness.

'Next right,' Blom said, touching her shoulder holster.

The next right couldn't even be called a road. A few hundred metres further on the track opened up a little.

'Stop here,' Blom said.

She held the laptop up towards Berger.

'If we drive any closer he'll hear us,' she said, pointing at the satellite picture of the area.

'Shitty bloody Mazda,' Berger said.

'Here,' Blom pointed. 'Forest for another four hundred metres or so, then what looks like a large clearing. It's not easy to tell, but there's open ground for two hundred metres. The house is on the far side of the clearing.'

Berger nodded and switched the engine off. Not much changed. The darkness growled around them.

They had their torches out, beams of light sweeping the trees, bouncing off the trunks, fracturing in the falling water that looked more like pins than drops.

They set off into the forest and instantly sank up to their

ankles in squelching moss. It was a waterlogged world. The trees were close together. They fought their way forward, metre by metre. A branch whipped back and caught Berger across the bridge of his nose. He didn't say anything, realised this wasn't the time for words. It was like struggling through a nightmare. The trees seemed to be clutching at them.

Sometimes Berger would think Blom had vanished, but then she would appear again, her rain-soaked jacket shining dark green.

In the end a light emerged from the forest. It was so weak that it might have been a mirage. But they both saw it, a faint break in the darkness. And the trees gradually began to thin out. Presumably they were approaching the clearing.

When they reached the final row of trees it became apparent that the light wasn't coming from the clearing, but further away. Berger switched his torch off, forced his way through the last of the vegetation and entered the clearing.

The light was coming from the far side, perhaps some two hundred metres away, illuminating the front of a shabby little house.

But that wasn't the only thing that was lit up.

At least four floodlights, a couple of metres off the ground, were focused on a central area. The area was framed by four bare tree trunks, forming a rectangle. An illuminated rectangle.

Berger couldn't see much more. He had to focus his gaze, make it cut through the water beating down on the clearing around them, which was covered by grass that was just a little too tall to be ordinary grass.

He fixed his eyes on the illuminated space, an oddly radiant, distant scene in the midst of the darkness. Four sturdy, stripped tree trunks, sawn off three metres up.

They were reminiscent of roof supports.

Thick chains ran between the four tree trunks in an intricate pattern. But not just chains. Berger thought he could also make out a couple of large cogs, some pinions and springs, a couple of shafts, a weight and a pendulum.

It was a clock.

A tower clock without a tower.

And in the middle of the clock was a human being.

Her arms were stretched out sideways, impossibly long, from an elegant, far too summery, floral dress. And the figure's long hair was perfectly blonde.

'Ellen,' Blom hissed and set off. Berger saw her sink in the tall grass. Which on closer inspection seemed more like reeds. And the clearing more like a marsh. She struggled on with the reeds up to her chest, step after laborious step.

He threw himself in behind her. He sank deeper but was considerably taller. The rain lashed at them with increasing intensity as they battled onwards. The image of the perversely illuminated clock shook and trembled in time with their uneven steps. Berger could hear a loud click cut through the darkness and saw Ellen Savinger's arms get pulled another notch further out. He heard no scream, no sound except the ones he and Blom were making as they fought their way through the marsh.

Their feet sank, got tangled in roots, then resurfaced with a sucking sound. The reeds whipped at their faces. Blom's face shone white in the night, pale but determined.

Halfway now. Berger pushed with all his might. He could hear himself roar. It was as if the sound came from somewhere else. From deep, deep inside.

Another sharp click rang out. Ellen's arms were pulled even further out from the flowery dress. They were so close now that they could see the taut figure clearly. Blonde hair covered her slumped head, and Berger realised that they were seeing Ellen from behind.

Her bare legs were lashed together under the dress; only her arms stuck out. Ellen Savinger stood there as though crucified by time itself.

Now the roaring was no longer distant. He tore his feet from the mud with all the strength he could muster. He flew past Blom. He was so close; he suddenly thought he could make out every single blonde hair on the back of Ellen's head.

Then the next click, louder than ever.

He had more or less reached the illuminated ground when he saw the heavy chains tighten one more notch. And he saw one arm come away from the body. He thought he could hear the sound of joints being wrenched from their sockets, muscles torn asunder, skin split. He watched as the right arm was pulled from the sleeve of the dress. It curved through the air and was left dangling down the bare tree trunk, swinging like a pendulum from one of the chains.

The marsh finally let go of his feet. With a roar he threw himself up onto firmer ground and rushed towards the clock. He ran around Ellen's mutilated body and looked into her eyes. They didn't look back.

Her eyes had a fixed stare.

They weren't human.

They were a doll's.

'It a fucking mannequin!' he bellowed into the night.

Blom emerged from the marsh. Small trickles of pale pink were running from the tiny cuts on her face. She said nothing, just watched the arm as it swung from the thick chain. Then she went over to the body that wasn't a body. While Berger leaned forward, hands on knees, Blom inspected the face that had never been alive. Then she reached out her hand and pulled an object from the dummy's mouth. She held it out to Berger.

It was a very small cog.

36

Thursday 29 October, 19.48

Berger looked over at Blom. She was creeping past the shattered mannequin, pistol drawn. She gestured to the side and slipped off towards the front of the little house. Berger followed. As they crouched below the porch steps the echoes of the house in Märsta felt distinctly creepy. It was like a twin.

What struck Berger at the edge of the floodlights' glare, once the voice of reason made itself heard inside him again, was that the clock must have been activated at exactly the right moment for them to fail. William must have estimated how long it would take them to fight their way across the marsh. He must have seen them arrive in the clearing and been present in order to activate the clock.

Been present.

William could have shot them at any time when they were out in the marsh. They had been live targets for several minutes. He had refrained; he had other plans for them.

And those plans were probably waiting for them inside the house.

Blom pulled out her torch and nodded towards Berger. He

got out his own and nodded back. He could see in her eyes that she was thinking the same thing.

They had to go in. There was no going back.

They made their way onto the porch, crouched beside the door, staying out of range of any booby trap. It was unlocked. Blom pushed it open.

No knives flew past in the artificial light, no infernal mechanism was lying in wait in the increased darkness across the threshold. They switched on their torches.

The hall wasn't quite like the one in Märsta; the houses weren't clones after all. A kitchen straight ahead, a flight of steps leading to the cellar on the left, a staircase leading up to the right, nothing else. They had to choose.

Berger took up position by the nearest door, with a view of both the kitchen and the hall, while Blom slipped into the kitchen. Berger wasn't at all happy when she disappeared round a corner for a moment, but she soon returned, shaking her head.

Back into the hall. Only now did they start to register the smells. They stood for a couple of moments trying to identify them. At first it seemed rancid, with traces of excrement and urine. Were there traces of death?

How many rotten corpses would they encounter in this house from hell?

No matter how much they sniffed they couldn't detect the smell of death. The far too familiar, vile, cloying stench of rotting flesh was notable by its absence.

Not that that meant anything. There could be death there anyway, hidden death, neutralised death, sterilised death. Everything in the house suggested death.

Blom paused and pointed towards the cellar stairs.

Grab the bull by the horns.

Darkness rose up from below like a solid entity. They shone their torches at the top step, but further down the stone steps turned a corner and disappeared out of sight. One of them was going to have to go first.

Berger released the safety catch of his Glock and took the lead. Blom covered him as well as she could on the cramped staircase. Particles of dust hung lazily in the beams from their torches, untouched by the misery around them. There was no sound, but the smell was getting stronger, more and more rancid, more and more foul.

Piss and shit.

Berger rounded the corner of the stairs. There was a closed door. They moved down towards it. Berger took hold of the handle, simultaneously noting how unnatural his breathing sounded. Rattling, like a dying man's. Then he pressed the handle. The door slid open.

They found themselves in a very small room containing a further two, noticeably smaller, doors. Blom could stand up in the room, but not Berger. On the floor was a bare mattress and a crumpled blanket. In one corner was a bucket with a lid on it. As they moved closer, the stench of faeces and urine grew stronger.

Piss and shit.

They stopped and took stock. It was a prison cell. There was no doubt that Ellen Savinger had also been held there. In the filthiest hellhole.

Berger saw Blom take a deep breath as she approached one of the two doors at the far end of the room. She glanced at Berger, then opened it. Berger leaned forward, covering her as she stepped inside. Blom's torch lit up the next room.

It looked very similar: a worn mattress with a blanket, a covered bucket, no bulb in the ceiling, but another two low doors at the other end of the small room.

Berger saw the surprise on Blom's face, and realised that he probably wore the same expression. It was all very odd.

Again, they picked one of the doors and found themselves in yet another tiny prison cell. Also empty.

It was becoming increasingly apparent that they had arrived too late. Neither William Larsson nor Ellen Savinger was there. William had slipped from their grasp again.

It took them a while to get their bearings in the cellar. They kept losing track of where they were, and went back to where they'd started. New doors kept appearing. They consciously left every door open when they looked behind it.

In the end all the doors were open. They wandered through the whole of the peculiar arrangement of cells. In the end they couldn't stay silent any longer.

Berger said: 'What the fuck is this? Did he keep moving her around? Seven tiny little cells, one for each day of the week?'

Blom merely shook her head. Then she headed towards what was presumably the way out. After a couple of tries they were back at the stairs again. Blom crouched down and switched her torch to its strongest setting. The bright beam of light made its way through the nearest cell, and on through the doors beyond, as far as it could reach.

Berger thought the word just as Blom said it. 'It's a labyrinth.'

'Just like Märsta,' Berger said hoarsely. 'There were cells there too. Seven fucking cells.'

'Not the days of the week,' Blom said, the glow of realisation shining in her wide eyes. 'Not seven as in the days of the week, but seven as in the number of kidnapped girls.'

They looked at each other. Blood from the scratches on their faces merged with the water dripping from their hair. Their chalk-white faces gaunt and exhausted.

'They each had a cell,' Berger said. 'Before he killed them they each had a cell.'

'He hasn't killed them,' Blom said in a voice Berger didn't recognise. 'He's kept them alive, some of them for years. He's been pumping them full of that sedative, unsurprisingly forbidden in the West, for a very long time. He's been *collecting* them.'

Berger stared at her. There wasn't just rainwater running down her face. She was crying too.

It was the first time he had seen Molly Blom cry openly.

He wondered if there would be another.

He closed his eyes. The world suddenly looked very different. Suddenly there was much more at stake, and it all depended on them. On Sam Berger and Molly Blom.

They held seven lives in their hands.

They rushed upstairs to the hall, and saw the perverse glare of the floodlights through the open front door. They could breathe again. They held onto each other, clutching each other's upper arms. Almost hugging.

'Fucking hell,' Berger said. 'Fuck. He's kept them alive. He's been waiting for us.'

'He was found out in Märsta,' Blom said. 'And in turn he must have found the woman with the dog who saw his Statoil van. He cleaned out the Märsta house, emptied it completely, removed the doors, cleaned the whole place with the utmost precision. Then he drove all the girls here, all seven of them. He's been waiting for us. And he's just driven off with them in the van. There must be another way out of here, one that's not on the map.'

And suddenly Berger could see everything with absolute clarity.

'The Ramans do everything in threes,' he said.

Blom just stared at him.

'William's favourite book,' Berger explained. 'Arthur C. Clarke's novel, *Rendezvous with Rama*.'

'OK,' Blom said, looking like she was having trouble keeping it together. 'So what are you saying?'

'There's a third house,' Berger said. 'A triplet house.'

Then he punched the wall with his fist.

The wounds on his right knuckles cracked wide open. Blood spattered the walls.

He didn't give a shit. Didn't give a shit about anything. Anything at all.

Apart from one thing.

Rescuing not one but seven girls.

The dreadful glare of the floodlights reached into the hall. He stepped out onto the porch. He shot the floodlights, one after the other, until his pistol merely clicked. He imagined he could see some of the light lingering. He stepped down from the porch and saw the front of the house shimmering, as if from some innate light.

As if painted with fluorescent paint.

He rushed back into the house. Threw himself up the stairs to the floor above. He found himself in a workshop. He saw a number of hammers of various shapes and sizes, then moulds for casting knife blades, saw a wall perforated with knife marks, and a carpenter's bench scarred by heavy hammer blows.

'Scum,' Berger said through his teeth. 'Fucking bastard scum.'

Blom nodded. Tears were trickling down her cheeks.

They were in the very centre of evil.

Berger rushed towards the next door. Behind it was a smaller room containing a bed with dirty yellow sheets. An L-shaped desk in the corner bore the impressions of computer equipment.

This was where William Larsson had sat and planned everything.

'Something's glowing,' Blom said.

Berger nodded. A very faint light seemed to be coming from below, beneath the desk. Berger yanked the desk away from the wall. A night light was plugged directly into the wall.

They crouched down.

A piece of paper had been nailed to the wall next to the dim bulb. And on the nail hung a tiny cog.

And on the sheet of paper was a message, apparently scrawled in blood.

It said: *I'm coming for you soon.*

The message ended with a smiley face.

On closer inspection, the lower part of the sheet was tucked into an envelope. Blom pulled it off and stood up. Berger got to his feet beside her. His hand was still dripping blood.

Her hands trembling, Blom opened the envelope carefully, ever so carefully, and pulled out a photograph.

It was a photograph of a building that seemed to glow with its own inner light.

It was a photograph of the boathouse.

37

Friday 30 October, 01.29

Blood streamed out into the icy cold water. It formed small tributaries that eventually flowed into a blurred delta before being swallowed up by the seas of the world. Or at least left the light, an illuminated circle in the great expanse of water.

Berger switched off his torch and pulled his hand from Edsviken. He could feel the cold making the open blood vessels of his knuckles gradually contract.

Time had passed. They had looked through every pixel of security footage before approaching the boathouse with extreme caution. There was no one there.

But they knew that William Larsson would come.

That he might come at any time.

Berger shook his head, as if to invigorate his sluggish brain cells, and looked out across the inlet, which, in its own very modest way, was attached to the world's oceans.

He went inside. Blom was standing by the open whiteboard, looking at the pictures of William Larsson's seven victims. Not for the first time.

'I almost had it,' Blom said, shaking her head. 'There's something here.'

'And you're keeping an eye on those?' Berger said, nodding towards the two open laptops as he walked to the other end of the whiteboard. Views from their security cameras, including a number of new ones, filled the screens.

'Are you?' Blom said.

'Not while I was outside,' Berger said, then pointed at a newly pinned-up photograph on the board. It sat between the fifteen-year-old William Larsson and the two photofit pictures of Erik Johansson. 'The photograph from Olle Nilsson's driving licence. It's the only one I've managed to find. Does he look like your Olle from Wiborg Supplies Ltd?'

Blom nodded. 'And alarmingly similar to the photofits from Östermalm and Märsta.'

Berger nodded in turn and pointed at the severely disfigured fifteen-year-old.

'Any similarity here?'

Blom shook her head.

'Maybe there's something about the eyes, though,' she said after a while.

'Maybe,' Berger said, trying to merge the two images on his retina. 'He appears to own the Bålsta house himself, under his Wiborg name, Olle Nilsson. It was purchased four months before he rented the house in Märsta. It all seems to have been planned carefully in advance; he would be able to move the girls between the houses at short notice, in a van on long lease from Statoil in Gävle.'

'And in order to get a job at Wiborg Supplies,' Blom said, 'he had to be a highly qualified technician, but also had to pass the Security Service's rigorous background checks. I still think that's very odd. There aren't many things harder than infiltrating the Security Service. And I say that as someone very experienced at infiltration.'

'The interest in technology has been there since the clocks,' Berger said. 'Olle Nilsson does seem to be a very skilfully constructed identity, at least as good as Nathalie Fredén. He's registered as a civil engineer with qualifications from Chalmers in Gothenburg, and has a very convincing CV that no one would ever think to question. There's nothing to suggest that he's ever travelled outside the EU. And of course no indication of *when* he took on the role of Olle Nilsson.'

'And no hint as to when William Larsson came back to Sweden,' Blom said. 'I'd still guess that he had plastic surgery in the Arab world, maybe Lebanon, maybe Saudi Arabia – my original guess – and that his dad, Nils Gundersen, managed to integrate him into society and made sure he got an excellent technical education.'

'Not only that,' Berger said. 'I think everything suggests that William followed in his father's footsteps. I think he joined the military, became a mercenary, maybe even an undercover agent of some kind.'

Blom nodded. 'Was that why he came to Sweden? But if so, who was he working for?'

'Either he returned to Sweden because the voices inside his head were getting too loud. Or the voices got too loud once he was already here – on other business,' said Berger. 'Either way, he seems to have had some kind of breakdown. I mean, he's a full-blown lunatic now.'

'Scenario one: Gundersen not only provided William with impeccable false documents, but also stoked his desire for vengeance until the time was finally right. Scenario two: William was here on a mission, but being in the country where he grew up made the past haunt him until he flipped.'

'We'll just have to ask him,' Berger said with a crooked smile.

'But how did he get into Wiborg?' Blom repeated.

'The important thing right now is that there's a third house,' Berger said. 'And we need to find it. Tonight.'

They looked at each other. There was a heavy, sombre seriousness in their eyes. Then Blom's blue eyes brightened. Berger saw something suddenly click.

Molly Blom ran back to the photographs of William's seven victims.

'It's us,' she said breathlessly.

'What?' Berger said.

'You mentioned the snowball,' Blom went on.

'Snowball?' Berger said. 'What are you talking about?'

'You and William were sitting on the bench in the schoolyard. We thought you were trying chewing tobacco for the first time. Linda threw the snowball that knocked it out of your hand. But it wasn't a tub of chewing tobacco, it was a watch.'

'A pocket watch, an Elgin,' Berger nodded, and disappeared into the past. 'That was the first time William showed me one of his watches. The cogs ended up scattered across the snow, swallowed up by it.'

'And we ran away, giggling,' Blom said. 'There were seven of us. Apart from Linda and me, there were Layla, Maria, Alma, Salma and Eva. Linda, Maria, Alma and I were born in Sweden. Layla and Salma were immigrants, both from the Middle East. And Eva was adopted from Korea.'

'Wow,' Berger said. 'You mean . . . ?'

'I think he's recreated our gang, yes. He's been collecting us. Maria and Alma were fairly anonymous Swedish brunettes, like Julia Almström and Emma Brandt. Linda was darker, more unruly, had piercings, like Jonna Eriksson. Layla was from Iraq, like Aisha Pachachi, and it wouldn't surprise me if Salma was Kurdish, like Nefel Berwari. And Eva was Asian, like Sunisa Phetwiset. Leaving me, Molly.'

'Bloody hell,' Berger said. 'The only blonde in the gang.'

'Yes,' Blom said flatly. 'Ellen Savinger is me, Molly Blom.'

'The crowning glory,' Berger said. 'The icing on the cake.'

They said nothing for a while, each of them glancing occasionally at the laptops.

Then Berger said: 'The watches were hallowed ground. That was the first time anyone had attacked what he loved most. It engraved itself deeply on his consciousness. Then most of these girls also witnessed his humiliation on the football pitch. But not you, though, Molly.'

'I had already left my mark,' Molly said. 'He'd had me strapped to his clock. There was no way he was going to forget about me.'

'Nor me,' Berger said. 'Least of all me. The traitor.'

'William Larsson is recreating his past,' Blom said. 'He's been saving all the girls for this moment, keeping them drugged until . . . '

'Until he gets the chance to destroy me,' Berger said, closing his eyes. 'Then he'll kill all seven girls in one go.'

'In other words he mustn't get the chance to destroy you,' Blom said.

They looked at each other again. Their eyes drilling deeper than ever before. Then they walked back to their computers again, as they had so many times that night.

Time took on a different shape. Everything became sluggish, slower. Even movement felt different. They weren't getting anywhere.

After a while they looked at each other again, this time with a different gaze. Blom clicked quickly at her computer and sighed. 'No, this isn't doing any good. I'm going to get a couple of hours' sleep.'

Berger nodded. 'I'm just going to get a bit of fresh air. Then I'll take first watch.'

Sam saw Molly go over to the sleeping bag on her side of the work benches. He waited for a moment, then adjusted a couple of pictures and met Ellen Savinger's gaze from the white-board. Her reserved smile hinting at a future of unlimited possibilities.

Like Molly Blom's had once done.

Then he walked away. He opened the door to the jetty and stepped out under the cover of the roof. It was pitch-black. The rain was noisily lashing the roof and churning what little Berger could see of the water's surface.

All apart from one small patch. There the surface looked completely undisturbed. He walked closer to take a look.

It wasn't the surface of the water. It was a boat.

It was a rowing boat.

Berger's hand flew up inside his jacket instinctively. His bleeding knuckles hit his shoulder holster. It was empty.

He turned and cast a quick glance through the little window in the door. His pistol was on the nearest table.

He threw the door open and rushed in. In the semi-darkness of the boathouse he saw a hand reaching for his Glock. And before he could come to a stop he found himself staring into the barrel of his own pistol.

It was odd seeing Olle Nilsson's face in real life.

It was William Larsson's. And yet it wasn't.

As if from a great distance Sam saw William turn and aim the pistol at the sleeping bag. The outline of Molly's sleeping body stood out beneath the padding, her blonde hair sticking up from the opening.

And William Larsson fired. Sam thought he saw the body jolt inside the sleeping bag. Then it didn't move again.

William shot Molly three more times. Sam threw himself at him. The shots echoed around the boathouse, deafening Sam's ears so much that he couldn't hear his own gut-wrenching roar.

Nor did he feel the blow that rendered him unconscious.

38

Friday 30 October, 02.14

Before there is a self, there is dizziness. Nothing but dizziness. A spinning that precedes everything else. And it is everything, for a long time.

Then sweating. Lots of sweating. It's not warm sweat, it's icy cold. Trickling somewhere. There's no space, no body; there's no pain, no feeling, no self. There's dizziness. There's sweating. Nothing else.

And the sweating is colder than death.

There's terror before there is a self. It's a terror that is born from nothing, and grows stronger in pumping waves. It's a primal, dark terror, without cause, without direction, and it swallows everything, consumes everything in its path.

It the end it settles in. The terror expands a brain, presses it hard against a skull. There's confinement, the confinement of the expanding brain in its minimal abode. There's a pain that has nothing to do with a body. There's an explosion of sensory impressions that eventually become a self. A self that is merely an arrowhead of pain.

There's constriction. So there must be a body. A shackled body. There are legs that can't move in any direction. There are arms that are trapped. There are arms that are sticking straight out from the body, trapped.

Then there is vision. There is a room, a dimly lit interior. There is blonde hair in a shot-up sleeping bag.

And there is a scream, a roar, a bellow.

There is a hell, and it is here, and it is now.

And the self suddenly knows that its name is Sam. But no more than that. Everything else is pain.

There are sounds. Echoing sounds, muffled sounds, metallic sounds. A dragging sound behind his back, a scraping sound, a beating sound. The sound of metal on metal. Things being constructed, arranged. But no human presence yet, no *living* presence.

Sam tries to turn his head, which is pulsating with pain. He feels something warm trickle down through the cold sweat on his forehead. He realises that it's blood.

As if that makes any difference.

He turns his head as far as it will go. He can detect movement behind him, by the floor, can see the outline of some contraption. When he looks up and starts to tilt his head back, he can see chains reaching from mooring rings in the wall. And his eyes come to rest on his own outstretched arm. His wrist is held tightly by a leather strap, and the leather strap is attached to a heavy chain that leads off into the darkness. Somewhere towards the end of it he can make out a large cog wheel.

He can hear moaning, and it takes far too long before he realises that he's the source of the moaning.

He pulls at his arm, but the chain is holding him firmly in place.

When he turns his head back, a face is there, right in front of him. It looks at him calmly, with clear blue eyes. And the unfamiliar face speaks with a very familiar voice from childhood: 'You knew we had to end up here eventually, Sam.'

He feels his own breathing, every breath a victory over himself. It would have been so much easier just to stop.

The face pulls back slightly and is sucked back into the darkness from which it came. Sam can see the body, the bulletproof vest, the wrench in his hand.

'Good timing,' William's voice goes on from the unknown face. 'There are only a couple of bolts left to tighten. I presume you've got time to wait.'

Then the face vanishes again. New sounds behind his back. A different metallic sound this time. And then the echo of a crank, followed by an emphatic ticking noise.

The face appears again. And in William's voice it says: 'I'm sorry I had to use something as banal as a crank, but I had to build the clock as quickly as possible. And because I can see you're wondering, I'll tell you: it took half an hour. Not that you'd be able to see that from your watch; the face is covered with condensation. How could you treat your watches so badly?'

The ticking sound is interrupted by a click. Sam feels his arms get pulled away from his sides. For now the pain stands no chance against all the other pain that has invaded his being.

William moves slowly backward. Now he can see further into the darkness in that direction. Sam sees him sit down on one of the carpentry benches. The one with Sam's Glock on it.

It's even lighter in the other direction. Where Molly's lying. Dead.

William sits and waits for a while. Sam understands what he's waiting for when he hears the mechanism click once more. But even this time he doesn't really feel his arms being pulled further apart.

William sees where Sam's eyes are looking. 'She's an adult. Of no interest to me. Wrong vocal pitch.'

William turns Molly's laptop towards him. He looks at the images from the security cameras. 'I enjoyed watching to see which of you would win. When I was preparing to leave the house in Märsta, I stood for a while wondering what height I should set the knives at – Sam or Molly? Molly had the Security Service behind her, and you, to be honest, seemed pretty slow, Sam. What happened to you?'

Somehow Sam gets control of his vocal cords. He hisses: 'Are they alive?'

William nods regretfully. He goes on nodding for a long while. 'There's a lot of death in the third house. But that's not what we ought to be talking about. We've got eight minutes before your first arm gets ripped off. It's usually the left arm, if you're right-handed.'

'Where's the third house, William?' Sam says.

'And we shan't talk about that either,' William says. 'We're going to talk about your betrayal. You're going to die standing face to face with your betrayal.'

'What do you mean, "betrayal"?' Sam says. 'I didn't report you.'

'You were too cowardly,' William says, with a slight smile. 'That would have been better. Then everything would have been dragged into the open. Instead it stayed in the dark and grew.'

'Your self-awareness is impressive, scum,' Sam splutters.

'But now you're being pretty brave. "Scum." A goalpost on a grit-covered football pitch. Anton, the Scum, and that nasty little gang of girls. My cock exposed. The girls giggling cretinously. And along comes the only friend I've had in the whole of my shitty life, and whips my cock over and over and over again with a damp towel. *It's a wonderful life.*'

Sam looks at William. He needs to know. If it's the last thing he hears.

'Where's the third house, William?'

The clock clicks again. Now the pain pushes past all the other pain.

'Why did you kill your aunt?' Sam shouts.

For the first time William looks at him with something like surprise.

'My what?'

'Your aunt, Alicia Anger. Why did you kill her?'

'Aunt Alice,' William says dreamily. 'She was kind. I didn't even know she was alive. But I understand.'

'What do you understand?'

'How astonishingly slow you all were. I slipped up outside the school in Östermalm, with the van. I snatched the blonde one in daylight, when there were plenty of witnesses. It was time for you to start hunting me, to make it exciting. But nothing happened. So I let an old woman walking her dog see the van in Märsta. And nothing happened then either. Not until Molly showed up at Wiborg wanting a device to disrupt recording equipment. The context wasn't quite clear, but if she wanted to hide something from the Security Service, it was probably something like this.'

William gestures to one side, towards Molly's smashed white-board. The silhouetted mountaineers are in pieces; Post-it notes are scattered across the floor.

Then William leans over and studies the laptops more closely. The far window comes into view behind him. Sam sees something red through the blood running down into his eye. Through a smudge in the glass, where a sweaty hand cleared a peephole a quarter of a century earlier, a pair of eyes appear. The clock clicks again and the pain in his shoulders becomes more intense. But Sam refuses to scream.

William straightens up; the window disappears.

'I realised that Molly was doing something that wasn't exactly by the book. So I programmed a little virus into the loop, mostly to cause a bit of trouble. The impact was considerably greater than I had anticipated.'

William stands up and walks closer.

'You're going to break soon, Sam,' he says, and smiles a proper William smile. 'I want to watch it close up. I want to see the expression on your face when you realise not only that you're dying, but that the seven perfectly innocent girls I've got to know so well in the course of the past few years will die too. Their shrill voices carried me to you. But now I've arrived. I don't need them any more.'

He stops at precisely the right distance and awaits the next tick of the clock.

At precisely the right distance.

Sam takes a deep breath, the deepest he has ever taken in his life. Then he yells with everything he has left: 'Now!'

The sounds are surprisingly muted. The world falls into slow motion.

He sees the first bullet pump through William's left foot, a second and third miss, the fourth shatters his right foot, a fifth disappears deep inside William's body. When the sixth bullet flies up through the wooden floor he is no longer standing in the same place.

William howls and throws himself towards the sleeping bag. He grabs hold of Molly's blonde hair and pulls out a shot-up shop dummy. Then he yanks open the front door and disappears into the night.

A drenched figure slips in through the door to the jetty just as the clock clicks again. Sam's arms are pulled even further apart; pain now controls his being. Molly frees him from the contraption with a few slashes to the leather straps. As she cuts his legs loose she shouts: 'Did I get him?'

'Wounded,' Sam says, rolling his shoulders. Everything seems to be in the right place. He grabs his Glock and rushes after the trail of blood into the pitch-blackness.

The rain is howling; there are no leaves left on the trees. Even so, he can clearly hear the rustling song of the aspen trees. He can hear it even though he's running, even though he's running like he's never run before, through the meadow grass that reaches up to his chest. The rustle of the aspen leaves is so oppressive, it feels like someone's trying to get through from another time.

The night feels viscous. Sam can feel how slowly he is moving. As if time isn't quite real.

The hair is no longer golden yellow, but it does slow down ahead of him. As the chalk-white head turns round, Sam knows he will never stop being astonished.

He throws himself at William. William falls. They lie in a heap. It feels almost like they're embracing.

It's as if all the blood has left William's face, and through the growing pallor the scar tissue is becoming visible, almost pulsing across his face. Sam rolls off William and sees a far too large bloodstain spreading across the crotch of his light-coloured trousers, below the bulletproof vest, and down the trouser-legs.

'Right in the cock, Sam,' William hisses. 'Just like before.'

'Where's the third house?' Sam yells.

'It's full of death, Sam. Don't forget the cogs.'

'Where is it?'

William's breathing is rattling. The rain pours mercilessly on his whitening face.

'I watched over them,' William rattles. 'I was the connection.

It took its toll. I thought Anton would get rid of it, but that wasn't enough. My knuckle marks were in the door.'

'But you don't want them to die,' Sam cries. 'You don't want that, William. Nothing is their fault. You've got to know them. You don't want to kill them. Not deep down.'

William smiles weakly. Then he hisses: 'It's not a house, Sam. It's the start of everything. Where I got *my only friend*.'

Sam hears Molly race towards them with her gun raised. When she sees William she lowers it and says hoarsely: 'Too much blood. It was the wrong ammunition.'

William points at his crotch as it grows redder and redder, and whispers: 'It's you, Sam. You've never stopped whipping me.'

Then he dies.

William stares into his eyes. Sam has never seen such a black look in his whole life. Then there's movement. It's extremely slow. Sam sees it almost frame by frame. The long, blond hair lifts and is tossed back. The crooked, misshapen features emerge from below the hair, and out of that crookedness two rows of bared teeth emerge. They part. They approach Sam's upper arm. He never feels the teeth penetrate his skin and then his flesh. He never hears the teeth meet, deep in his arm. He doesn't hear it and he doesn't feel it. And the pain radiating from his bicep doesn't gain momentum before he sees the piece of flesh fall from William's mouth, followed by a steady stream of blood. With distorted slowness the piece of flesh drifts down towards the dry grit of the football pitch. With a roar, Sam lifts the damp towel and goes on whipping. His vision goes dark, and he keeps whipping, lashing out over and over again until the blood runs freely.

39

Friday 30 October, 03.18

They could already smell the bodies from the stairwell. It wasn't strong, or at least not enough to rouse the neighbours. But the higher they climbed, the more Sam found himself in a different time.

A time that didn't smell of dead bodies.

He was fifteen years old. The door to the flat was marked *Larsson*. Behind it waited a magical world of watches and clocks. There waited his good friend with the crooked face, the boy who with a gentle hand guided him into a world of perfectly attuned cogs, pinions, springs, shafts, weights and pendulums. A world where every second was a mystery.

They had talked about how Switzerland became the centre of global clockmaking in the 1700s when the clockmakers of Paris, in their capacity as servants to the aristocracy, had to flee the French Revolution. And they had talked about the Antikythera mechanism, and how the Greeks had managed to create a mysteriously complex timepiece almost one hundred years before Christ.

It was like a door opening in Sam's brain, revealing an unknown world hidden inside the familiar everyday world, a better world that he may never have had access to without William. And it had happened behind the door which Sam, now more than twice the age he had been then, was standing front of. Molly caught up with him. She had her pistol drawn.

It didn't say *Larsson* on the letterbox, it said *Pachachi*.

The stench of bodies was stronger than before.

Sam pulled out his lock-pick and inserted it as silently as he could. He looked at his hand. It was trembling badly. He glanced over towards Molly. She was pale, and shaking. They were both aware that some version of hell awaited behind the door to William's childhood home. But there was no going back.

This was it.

They were in another universe, the real universe, where darkness reigned. All light was an illusion, a reassuring veneer of lies that allows us to live, gives us the strength to become adults. They were in a different era now, where barbarism still prevailed, where the chimaera of civilisation hadn't yet broken through.

They heard the click as the pick caught. Pistols raised, torches at the ready. The door opened.

The air seemed to get sucked into the flat, as if the pressure in there were lower than in the world outside. And it was totally dark. The smell of bodies hit them like a wall. Sam looked quickly at the material around the door. He recognised it. Odour-isolating sealant. So that as little death as possible would seep out into the stairwell.

They stood in the cramped hallway, trying to breathe the right way, the way they had been trained. As if training could fend off such extreme darkness.

From beyond the stench, Sam's childhood came back to him. He remembered every corner, every nook of the flat. The corridor to the left led to the kitchen and one of the bedrooms, the longer corridor to the right to the other bedroom and the living room. That was where William's bedroom was, the unusually large but windowless room where two teenagers had sat fiddling with their clocks and watches. Their tiny cog wheels.

William's dying words: 'Don't forget the cogs.'

They read the question in each other's eyes.

Who was dead?

Which of the seven teenage girls would never have a chance to grow up?

William's dying words: 'It's full of death.'

Sam suddenly noticed something pinned to one wall of the hall. When he shone his torch at it he realised that it was a watch. He recognised a tiny scratch in the glass.

It was his Patek Philippe 2508 Calatrava.

Ignoring it, he nodded to the left, towards the corridor that led to the kitchen and one bedroom. They took a room each.

Sam quickly ascertained that the little bedroom was empty. He noted odour-isolating material around the bedroom door again. The electronic equipment on the desk indicated that this had been William's most recent headquarters. There were bound to be a fair few answers in those computers.

He turned and met Molly's gaze. It was glassy as she nodded towards the kitchen. He left the bedroom and joined her.

At the kitchen table sat two people. They might have been engaged in a conversation, just taking a short break. They were both young men, and they had been dead a long time. The flesh had begun to fall off them, and the parts that hadn't completely dried out were crawling with maggots.

Sam heard himself groan.

'Fucking hell,' he said.

Molly was holding a handkerchief so tightly to her nose that Sam almost didn't hear what she said. 'Two young men with beards and loose-fitting clothes.'

'Brother and friend back from IS?'

She shrugged. They walked out, through the hall and past the front door. The corridor was much longer than he remembered. It was as if they were navigating a body. From somewhere far ahead shimmered an almost guttering source of light. It was as if the gloomy corridor's walls were closing in on them, contracting and getting ready to propel them into a time that had long since been lost.

As if time was ever lost.

When they reached the living room they realised where the light was coming from. There was another door, one that was simultaneously familiar and unknown to Sam. He recognised all too well the mark in the veneered surface of the door, four impressions, from the knuckles of a fist. The door to William's childhood room had always looked like that.

But it definitely hadn't given off its own light.

They went over to it.

'Fluorescent paint,' Molly said.

Sam inspected the door. It had evidently been reinforced, and there was no keyhole, just a lock that looked electronic. Beside the door sat a small box containing what appeared to be a microphone.

'I think it's rigged,' Molly said, peering at the lock.

'Explosives?' Sam asked as he went on inspecting the box.

'Definite possibility. We can't risk shooting our way in. And the lock can't be picked. It looks like it's sound-activated,' Molly said, pointing at the box.

'What sound?' Sam said.

They saw the same realisation reflected in each other's faces.

'Get it,' Sam said, and started to shrug off his rucksack.

He sat down on the sofa, took out his old watch box, opened the gilded catch, lifted out the velvet-lined compartment with the four watches and started to remove the tiny plastic bags from the tray at the bottom. He was still shaking his head when Molly returned with his Patek Philippe 2508 Calatrava. He took it, placed it on the living room table and took out his magnifying glass, tweezers and case opener from his rucksack.

'Light,' he said.

Molly shone her torch at the table. 'I just hope we've found all the cogs.'

Sam grimaced, held the case opener against the watch and took off the back. He held the magnifying glass to the exposed innards. The perfectly coordinated constellation of tiny, interacting cogs and pinions always lowered his pulse dramatically. But not this time. He sat there, assaulted by the grotesque stench of dead bodies in the terrible flat, knowing young lives were at stake, and tried to stop his hands shaking. He opened bag after bag and tipped out all the little cogs. Cogs from the flats in Kristinehamn and Västerås, from the house in Märsta, from the bat-filled cave in Värmland, from the mouth of the mannequin and from the house in Bålsta. And there was nothing to say that those were all the cogs.

Nothing but Sam's knowledge of the inner workings of watches, learned in that very flat a quarter of a century earlier. And it was telling him that there were precisely six cogs missing.

Molly was walking about the flat with her pistol drawn, radiating impatience.

'How did he get in and out?' she asked after a while.

'What?' Sam said.

'If he stole your watch and dissected it, then obviously it

couldn't be used. Couldn't he have used just any watch with that microphone?'

'Every model has a unique tick,' Sam said, carefully nudging the rotor aside so he could insert the first cog.

'So how did he do it?'

'He must have had a 2508 of his own,' Sam said. 'There aren't that many of them about.'

'Isn't it here, then? Somewhere inside the flat?'

'Hardly,' Sam said. 'This is my test. William knew there was a risk that we'd outsmart him. This was plan B. If he died, he could still test me.'

'I'm going to have a look for it anyway,' Molly said, and walked off.

'Feel free,' Sam said, to no one. 'Maybe one of the bodies is sitting on it.'

A disconcerting amount of time passed. He tried to remember everything he had ever learned, everything William had ever taught him. He was making slow progress. The tweezers kept slipping. His hands were still shaking, but not so badly. It was as if a paradoxical calm settled around him. The self-winding watch's incomparable treatment of time helped him find his way back to himself. Cog after cog slotted into place. After an indefinite period Molly came back, having failed in her mission.

'His watch collection is somewhere else,' Sam said. 'Probably in Lebanon.'

He only had the last cog left now. It was actually making sense. There was only one space left inside the watch.

The tweezers held up the cog from the house in Märsta against the light of the torch. There was still a risk that he had inserted things wrongly.

He lowered the minuscule cog towards the interior of the watch. It slotted into place with a small click. He looked at the mechanism. Nothing was moving; there was nothing to suggest that his work was done.

He replaced the back and began to shake the watch. If it was working, the rotor would activate the self-winding mechanism. He shook it for thirty seconds; his pulled shoulder stung like fire. Then he held the watch to his ear.

At first he could hear absolutely nothing. The silence of death. The echoing stillness of failure.

Then the ticking started. He breathed out, hard, and when he breathed in, just as hard, he was hit by the hideous, cloying stench of death again.

He stood up. Molly watched him. They walked together towards the fluorescent door. Sam looked at the watch, gave it a quick kiss, then held it up to the small box containing the microphone.

The seconds scraped past with infinite slowness.

Nothing happened.

Then they heard a click in the lock mechanism and the door slid slowly, slowly open, revealing absolute darkness.

Sure enough, there was a sizeable quantity of explosives attached to the door. Enough to have blown the flat sky-high if they'd tried to shoot their way in.

They both shone their torches into the room. What followed was a sequence of impressions. First they saw the ceiling, the walls, the floor, all of them covered by something thick and puffy. Sam just had time to think soundproofing before the next impression. The structure was reminiscent of the cellars in Märsta and Bålsta. There was no doubt that what lay concealed behind the fluorescent door was a labyrinth.

The third impression was a smell. A distinctly rancid smell hit them, and actually replaced the smell of dead bodies. The labyrinth did not exude a stench of death.

Impression number four was a sound.

A gentle moan was coming from a mattress on the floor of the first room. A tube from a drip stand led under the covers.

Molly stopped breathing. She crouched down beside the mattress. Slowly she pulled the covers back, and found herself looking into the eyes of a dark-haired young woman.

She was very visibly drugged, but beyond the drugs, beyond the small body's emaciated condition, there was a flash of stubborn survival instinct. The young Thai girl, Sunisa Phetwiset, had clearly decided to survive. She hadn't been murdered by Axel Jansson, the paedophile, who was serving a prison sentence for her murder, and she hadn't even been murdered by William Larsson.

She was alive.

Sam clenched his fist but managed to stop himself punching the wall. Instead he went out into the living room and opened all the windows wide. Cool, fresh night air poured into the flat from hell.

Then he went past Molly and Sunisa and kicked in another door. On a similar mattress, next to a similar drip stand, lay a young girl with piercings whom he recognised as Jonna Eriksson. She stared at him in astonishment and made some indistinct noises.

He crouched down beside her, stroked her cheek gently and said: 'Believe it or not, Jonna, you're free.'

He stood up, encouraged her to lie still, and carried on. He kicked in door after door, found girl after girl, and they were all alive. By now there were five of them.

Sometimes he would find Molly in a cell when she had come from the other direction.

'It's much bigger than it used to be,' he said.

'He must have bought the neighbouring flat as well,' Molly said.

He looked at her for a moment. Then he said: 'Call them in.'

In the end there were just two doors left. He kicked in the first of them.

It looked the same as the other cells. A crumpled mattress on the floor, the tube from a drip stand leading under the covers. But when he pulled the covers aside there was no girl lying there.

One of the cells was empty.

There was one girl missing.

He moved towards the last door. He gulped hard and kicked it in.

A girl with long blonde hair was sitting on her mattress. Around her neck she had an Orthodox cross on a pink leather strap. Judging by the expression on her face, she had heard what was going on inside the other cells. Even though her eyes were cloudy with drugs, she produced a reserved a smile that hinted at a future of unlimited possibilities.

'Ellen,' Sam said, crouching down beside the mattress.

'Are you the police?' Ellen Savinger asked.

Sam laughed. 'Yes,' he lied.

Then he hugged her and felt the fresh rainy air find its way into the innermost cell of the labyrinth.

They walked round for a while, soothing and reassuring the girls as best they could, counting the seconds until the paramedics arrived. They found themselves standing in the empty cell for a time. And suddenly they couldn't feel the fresh rainy air any longer. Everything was rancid again.

'Who's missing?' Molly asked.

'It must be Aisha,' Sam said. 'Aisha Pachachi.'

'The very first victim,' Molly said. 'The girl who lived here.'

'And whose brother is probably sitting dead at the kitchen table.'

When they heard banging at the front door they looked at each other.

'This isn't over,' Molly said.

Then they made their way out of the labyrinth. They heard Kent and Roy in the kitchen, saw them emerge from the corridor with their weapons and torches raised. Their faces were completely white.

'Lower your weapons,' Sam said. 'We'll go with you voluntarily. But look in there first. And call in everyone you have.'

They did actually lower their weapons. Roy started to retch and Kent only just moved out of the way before he threw up.

Sam went over to the wide-open windows. He stared out into the darkness. Something came towards him from out there. It may have been sullied by Aisha Pachachi's absence, but six girls were still alive, and even if he tried to fend it off, what came at him through the night could only be called happiness.

When the paramedics stormed into the flat Molly came and stood beside him.

He put his arm round her.

She put her arm round him.

It had stopped raining.

40

Friday 30 October, 16.42

Detective Superintendent Allan Gudmundsson of the Stockholm Police smelled of smoke. He was sitting at his uniquely impersonal desk, and he looked like a pensioner. He adjusted his reading glasses for the eighteenth time as he read the thick document, before eventually looking up at the odd couple on the other side of the desk. She was blonde and had a snub nose, he had brown hair flecked with grey and a week's worth of beard.

'I had been thinking of starting my weekend,' Allan Gudmundsson said.

'I vaguely remember the word,' Sam Berger said. 'But otherwise I'm drawing a complete blank.'

Allan slowly looked over at Molly Blom and stared at her critically above his reading glasses.

'So the whole Nathalie Fredén story was just an act?' he said.

'It was necessary,' Blom said curtly.

'I'm trying to understand why,' Allan said. 'Because you needed Sam's help with your own unofficial investigation? Because you realised that you had both begun to suspect that you knew the murderer? From when you were young?'

'Something like that,' Blom said. 'But that might not be the most important thing right now.'

Allan adjusted his glasses again and adopted a stern-uncle expression.

'I think I'm the one who decides what's important, young lady. Your futures are the subject of immediate investigation, and at present neither of you are even police officers. That decision rests with the Security Service and the head of the Intelligence Unit, Steen, and you'll both be called to an official meeting, probably tomorrow, Saturday. So now isn't the time to get on your high horse.'

'How are they?' Berger asked.

'Sam, Sam, Sam,' Allan said, still in uncle mode. 'As you know, I shall be retiring in just a few days' time. Everything was lined up for you to succeed me. If you hadn't been so damn stubborn.'

'Who's it going to be now?'

'Rosenkvist, of course,' Allan Gudmundsson said. 'Desiré Rosenkvist.'

Berger laughed. 'Good job I've trained Deer so well.'

'You haven't trained her at all,' Allan said bluntly.

'You're right,' Berger finally acknowledged. 'She'll be a better boss that I could ever have been.'

'How are they?' Blom echoed.

'I presume you mean the girls,' Allan said. 'On the whole, they're as well as can be expected under the circumstances. But I want some answers to my questions first. So, the reason you both took off like that was because the pair of you had been running separate unofficial, unsanctioned investigations that didn't comply with the lines taken by either the Security Service or the National Crime Unit?'

'That's right,' Blom said. 'No one would listen to our

apparently vague theories. We had no evidence. We had to find the girls. When I was caught tampering with the recording equipment in the interview room, I realised that the only option was to break Sam Berger out of custody and disappear.'

'I'm very relieved that I'm not the one who's going to decide your futures,' Allan said, tapping the bundle of papers against his knees. 'There's no doubt that you've conducted a very thorough investigation. The man you shot and killed, whose body was found on waste ground at Edsviken in Sollentuna, has been identified as a civil engineer and unofficial contractor for the Security Service going by the name of Olle Nilsson. But you claim that he was actually a murderer and serial kidnapper whose name was William Larsson. According to your story, he kidnapped seven fifteen-year-old girls over the course of two and a half years, with the intention of eventually killing them?'

'We believe that the weight of evidence is overwhelming,' Blom said. 'But what we really want to know is how the girls are.'

Allan nodded and said, with a degree of reluctance: 'What is interesting – and of course gratifying – is that there don't appear to be any signs of torture. I don't understand how that can fit with the bloodstains and nail marks in the cellar in Märsta. Or with those infernal clocks.'

'We don't understand that either,' Blom said. 'But we think William was saving the clock for Sam. Because he was the one he was after, when it came down to it.'

'He wasn't a serial killer,' Berger said. 'He was just trying to communicate with me. The traitor with a capital T.'

Allan looked at him for a while. Then he leafed through his papers and said: 'One of the girls has already made a statement about the blood. Let's see . . . Yes, the one who was kidnapped last, Ellen Savinger. She thinks she saw the perpetrator take blood from her, in a test tube, but she was drugged at the time.'

'That sounds promising,' Blom said. 'That means the blood could simply have been aimed at us, me and Sam. To put us on the right track. Maybe there never was a clock in the cellar in Märsta, and the nail marks in the floor were just one of William's special effects. But their witness statements will obviously clear that up later.'

Allan nodded and consulted his screen. 'The current state of the girls. Perhaps it would be as well if we did a full debrief. All six girls are still in hospital, but in some cases that's largely for observation and final detoxification. They've all been given a daily dose of a very strong sedative. According to the doctors, the shorter the time the girls have been subjected to that, the easier it should be for them to return to normal life. Victim number two, Nefel Berwari, is suffering from serious muscle wastage, but it should only be a matter of weeks before she's up on her feet again. Her psychological condition is rather worse, deep depression, but her cognitive and intellectual abilities are unaffected, and her family is ready to take care of her. Victim number three, Julia Almström, has – against all the odds – managed to keep herself in reasonable physical shape, and in spite of having spent a year and a half in captivity, seems almost ready to return to normal life in Västerås. Victim number four, the Thai citizen, Sunisa Phetwiset, seems to have suffered least psychological damage from captivity. Apparently she's claiming that she was looked after better in Larsson's captivity than before. She'll be given Swedish citizenship and offered protection to keep her safe from the Albanian mafia. In contrast, Jonna Eriksson, victim number five, is in the worst state. Her body is badly run-down, and she's having difficulty coming to terms with the death of her boyfriend Simon

Lundberg, whose remains were found in a cave outside Kristinehamn at your direction. But Jonna too should make a full recovery, and a highly supportive foster family in the Stockholm area has opened its doors to her. The sixth victim, Emma Brandt, has been reunited with her father and will be able to leave hospital in a couple of days. She's genuinely astonished that she was stopped from committing suicide by a murderer. They're going to be moving down to Skåne to start a new life. And finally Ellen Savinger has her family around her, and it even looks like she might be able to go back to school in Östermalm before the end of term. The Forensic Medical Unit is, however, saying that the long-term effects of the sedative are unclear.'

Blom and Berger exchanged a look; the situation was even better than they had dared to hope.

Blom said: 'And what do the girls have to say about the question of William Larsson's guilt?'

'So far questioning has been kept to a minimum,' Allan said, 'out of consideration for the girls' state of health. But the statements taken are unanimous, and match yours. All the victims have identified Olle Nilsson, and his DNA has been found in both the Bålsta house and the flat in Helenelund. The fact that Nilsson was guilty of all seven kidnappings is therefore beyond all reasonable doubt now – as well as three murders, Simon Lundberg, Yazid Pachachi and Rayhan Hamdani, and the aggravated assault of an Anton Bergmark in Sollentuna.'

'So the body sitting in the kitchen was Aisha's brother Yazid,' Berger said. 'But the name Rayhan Hamdani doesn't mean anything to me.'

'Another young man from Sollentuna who went off to fight for IS. They both died of gunshot wounds, and had serious amounts of heroin in their bodies, according to initial analysis.

They both returned to Sweden on 20 August this year. The preliminary forensic examination indicates that they've been dead just over two months, which suggests that they went to the flat more or less straight away.'

'Where a complete lunatic was busy building a labyrinth,' Berger said.

'What happened to the rest of the Pachachi family?' Blom asked. 'There's definitely a mother and father. I questioned both of them around the time of their daughter's disappearance.'

Allan nodded. 'Ali and Tahera Pachachi, yes. They've vanished into thin air as well, just like their daughter.'

'Strange,' Blom said.

'Not really,' Allan said with a shrug. 'They're presumably dead, cleared out of the way by Olle Nilsson. Because there's nothing to support your theory that his real name is William Larsson, and that he underwent plastic surgery somewhere in the Middle East. We can't find any connection to a mercenary called Nils Gundersen living in Lebanon. And your own childhood memories obviously don't count as evidence. But the Security Service are currently going through the whole of your unofficial investigation. Some evidence may of course arise from your material or from the professional scrutiny it's being subjected to – the van, or DNA from the sixteen-year-old Larsson, for instance. And the most vital work of all is still ongoing: analysis of Olle Nilsson's computers from Stupvägen, which will hopefully provide answers to a lot of questions. Mind you, it doesn't really matter who he was. Whether his name was William Larsson, Erik Johansson, Johan Eriksson or Olle Nilsson, he's been neutralised now.'

'William was a lot of people,' Berger said.

The other two looked at him for a few moments.

'Your statements have made for extremely interesting

reading. But it's clear that you don't have any detailed information about how the kidnappings took place. How did he get to know the girls? How did he know that they existed? How did he plan his actions?'

Blom cleared her throat. 'We don't actually know anything except that he seems to have snatched Aisha Pachachi right after the celebration to mark the end of the school year, broke into Julia Almström's house in the middle of the night to take her, and simply picked a blonde girl at random from the high school in Östermalm. We don't know how Nefel Berwari disappeared. The other aspects that remain unclear are how William knew that Sunisa Phetwiset, who had been forced into the sex trade, would be visiting a paedophile on a particular evening, how he found Jonna Eriksson and Simon Lundberg at their hideaway in the cave full of bats, or how he knew precisely when Emma Brandt was going to commit suicide at Midsummer. I imagine a lot of that will become clear after William's computers are analysed. The whole thing reeks of social media.'

Allan nodded. 'I also need to get to grips with your plan to capture him in the boathouse. Once you had received the message in the Bålsta house – "I'm coming for you soon" – you still went back to the boathouse. Then everything gets a bit hazy. You set up four new security cameras in the vicinity. One of them was pointing out across the water. You were anticipating that Larsson was going to come that night. You had predicted that he would strap Berger to his clock at the scene of the original crime. So you were prepared to sacrifice yourself, Sam?'

'My shoulders still hurt,' Berger said.

'We found the parts of the clock hidden under the floor,' Blom said. 'We realised that he wanted to attach Sam to the contraption. And Sam was prepared to go through that if I could render William harmless without killing him. We needed him to tell us where the third house was. The third labyrinth. Everything hinged on that.'

'We had a number of different strategies, depending on which direction he came from,' Berger said. 'But the mannequin that we'd dragged back from Bålsta was part of all of them.'

'He came from the water,' Blom said. 'In a rowing boat. That was unexpected, but not unmanageable. At best he would regard me as so irrelevant that he would merely get rid of me without closer inspection.'

'That was obviously an element of uncertainty,' Berger said. 'But we would have stuck to the plan even if he had discovered the dummy.'

'Then what?' Allan said.

'We picked him up on the jetty camera,' Blom said, 'as the rowing boat glided in. We quickly got ready; the dummy was already inside my sleeping bag. The fact that William was wearing a bulletproof vest led us to choose an option where I had to crawl underneath the boathouse; it's raised up on pillars, of course. We waited as long as we dared, and because it was possible that he was listening to us, we pretended that I was going to sleep. The last thing I did was disable the security camera covering the jetty. I disconnected it from the computer, because if William had discovered we had a camera there, he would have realised we had some sort of plan.'

'We worked out more or less where he would be standing to enjoy watching me die,' Berger said. 'Then we had to wait until he was within firing range.'

'And you can get a good idea how people are moving above you,' Blom said, 'through the tiniest cracks in the floor. But we only wanted to hit his feet. He wasn't supposed to die, under any circumstances.'

'And yet he did,' Allan Gudmundsson said.

Blom merely looked at him. Time passed.

In the end Allan closed the bundle of documents. 'The most important thing is that the monster has been rendered harmless. The shooting in the boathouse has already been classified as self-defence. As a police operation, your efforts were outstanding. There's every reason to believe that you saved the lives of these six girls. For that you have our unanimous gratitude and admiration.'

Berger caught Blom's eye. That wasn't really a conclusion.

Eventually Allan continued: 'But your future is now in the hands of the Security Service.'

41

Friday 30 October, 19.37

The mountaineers were clambering laboriously up the snow-covered mountain. Their dark silhouettes stood out in the distance against the extraordinary multicoloured sunset. But there it stopped. If the mountaineers had carried on a few metres they would have tumbled into a void. And, to their not inconsiderable surprise, would have landed flat on the wooden floor of a boathouse by the waters of Edsviken in Sollentuna, just outside Stockholm, Sweden.

Sam Berger and Molly Blom looked at the half-glued photograph. Then they screwed the lids back on the tubes of glue and looked at the remnants of the board, which lay strewn across the floor like the pieces of a puzzle.

They couldn't do any more. Not right now.

'You didn't say anything about the ammunition,' Berger said.

'And you didn't say anything about William's last words,' Blom said.

Their eyes met.

'William's dead,' Berger said. 'Six out of seven girls have been rescued. Everything except my conscience ought to be under control. And everything is under control, isn't it?'

'We're going to lose our jobs,' Blom said.

'You know that's not what I mean.'

'I know.'

They looked once again at the sad, half-repaired picture, which incorporated a now entirely empty whiteboard. Everything had been removed from it.

'There's a lot in what Allan says,' Berger said. 'William kidnapped Aisha Pachachi two years ago. You interviewed her parents. Then, when he needed a third hideout, it was logical to return there, to his childhood home. He got rid of the parents, who were now on their own there, bought the flat next door, and when the Pachachis' son came back from IS a heroin addict, he got rid of him, together with a junkie friend who was also a mass murderer. And Aisha had been in William's captivity the longest. Her body eventually buckled under the effect of those banned drugs, and she died while they were being moved between Märsta, Bålsta and Helenelund. End of story.'

'Are we happy with that?' Blom asked.

'Our aim was to rescue the girls and catch William,' Berger said. 'We've done that. We need sleep.'

'But are we happy?' Blom persisted. 'Is everything clear? Is the picture complete?'

'Stop it. You need sleep as much as I do.'

'I doubt it,' Blom said. 'But you feel that something's not right too.'

'But can I really be bothered with it?'

'You don't care where Aisha Pachachi is? There's one girl still missing, a whole family, in fact. William didn't hide his victims. Anton Bergmark was in a wheelchair, Simon Lundberg in the cave, the IS guys at the kitchen table, Aunt Alicia Anger in her rocking chair.'

Blom pushed a printout towards Berger. He looked at the grotesque picture of the old woman in the rocking chair, her face drained of all colour, a black sock sticking out of her mouth.

Berger pushed the photograph away with distaste. He'd seen enough for a while.

'The nursing staff and the police were sure it was an accident,' he said. 'Alicia Anger was confused enough to eat a sock by mistake and choke on it. You saw her, Molly, she wasn't exactly in full command of her faculties.'

'We've got the recording from your phone. Everything William said in and outside the boathouse,' Blom went on.

'But we don't need to play it,' Berger said. 'Because you remember it all anyway.'

She pushed the photograph back towards Berger and said: ' "Aunt Alice. She was kind. I didn't even know she was alive." '

Berger closed his eyes. 'I know,' he said. 'He didn't kill her.'

'So who did?'

'Explain about the ammunition again,' Berger said. 'Slowly this time.'

Blom breathed in slowly. 'When I go undercover there may be occasions when I'm forced to shoot people I shouldn't be shooting. Then it's important that they don't die by mistake. So I use fully jacketed ammunition, which passes straight through the body, and avoid the standard-issue police ammunition, Speer Gold Dot, which has a hollow point and expands on impact, causes much more damage. But my usual ammunition had been swapped for hollow-point bullets.'

'Dum-dum bullets,' Berger said.

'They sometimes get called that,' Blom said. 'But that's not really correct.'

'When would that have happened?'

'They're in my cases; they're always in the van.'

'So it must have happened just before you broke me out of Security Service custody and we took off?'

'Yes,' Blom said. 'I don't think William would have died if I'd had my usual ammunition. But it still feels pretty far-fetched.'

'Same as the conclusions about what William said when he was dying,' Berger said. 'I bet you can quote that too.'

'"I watched over them. I was the connection. It took its toll. I thought Anton would get rid of it, but that wasn't enough. My knuckle marks were in the door."'

'Yes,' Berger said, 'that was it. And what does that mean? It could be nonsense like most of what he said. He watched over the girls; he was the link between them. He thought his assault on Anton Bergmark with the hammers, the change of roles, would get rid of whatever was taking its toll, but it wasn't enough. So he moved on to the girls. And then the link to me, the knuckle marks in the door of his childhood bedroom in Helenelund.'

'But what if that wasn't meant as a link to you?' Blom said. 'That came later, after all: "It's not a house, Sam. It's the start of everything. Where I got my only friend." That's when he tells you that the third house is the Pachachis' flat.'

'I don't really follow, Molly.'

'Nor do I. Not really. But William was definitely trying to tell us something. He *watched over* someone. He was *the connection* between others. Maybe not the girls. Maybe he was watching over the people who lived where his *knuckle marks were in the door*?'

'The Pachachi family? Why on earth would he be doing that?'

'On behalf of someone,' Blom said. 'He was *the connection*. But he was weighed down by something, something unpredictable, a childhood trauma. In the end assaulting Anton wasn't enough, because his *knuckle marks* were in the door of one of the people he was supposed to be *watching over*.'

'Aisha Pachachi?'

'She lived in his old room,' Blom said. 'A fifteen-year-old girl, like the ones who had bullied and ridiculed him, had occupied the room where he got his only friend, Sam. And that only friend was you.'

'It's a bit thin,' Berger said. 'I don't really buy it. It's too vague. He was there, in his old bedroom? He *watched over* the people living in his childhood home? Watched over how?'

'On someone's behalf,' Blom said. 'He was *the connection* between Pachachi and someone. And it drove him mad, *it took its toll*. He tried to drown it out by systematically torturing his old tormentor Anton Bergmark, but that *wasn't enough*, because every time he was in the flat he saw the marks of his *knuckles* in the door to one of the rooms. And there was someone who reminded him of one of the fifteen-year-old girls who had humiliated him as a teenager. In the end he felt obliged to snatch her, and it all started.'

'He was watching over the Pachachi family on someone's behalf?' Berger said. 'Whose?'

Molly Blom rubbed her face.

'Who brought him to Sweden?' she said. 'Who gave him a job? A highly qualified technical job?'

'Wiborg,' Berger said. 'Wiborg Supplies Ltd.'

'And by extension?'

Berger heard himself groan. This wasn't where he wanted to go. Anywhere, but not here. 'By extension?' he said.

'Yes,' she said.

'Fuck,' Berger said. 'The Security Service.'

Blom grabbed his wrist and turned his watch towards her.

Condensation had begun to gather on the glass again, but the hands said eight o'clock exactly.

'She's the embodiment of punctuality,' Berger said, retracting his arm.

Sure enough, there was a knock on the door.

Blom drew her pistol and lowered it behind the carpentry bench. Berger went over to the door and looked out cautiously.

She was standing there with her thin, mousy hair glued to her head, as if she'd emerged from a week-long downpour.

'Syl,' Berger said. 'Come in.'

And Sylvia Andersson, known by very few people as Syl, walked into the boathouse and looked around.

'Charming,' she said, her eyes on the half-repaired photograph of mountaineers etched on the side of a snow-covered peak.

'Have a seat,' Berger said, gesturing towards a free chair by the carpentry bench, next to Blom, who was tucking her pistol back in its holster.

Syl nodded at Blom and sat down. Berger met her gaze. There was something unmentionable lurking there. A primal terror. But, on the other hand, that had been there for a while now.

'Have you got any further?' Berger asked.

'I don't even know what I'm doing here,' Syl said, trying to adjust her style-free hairstyle. 'Remind me.'

'Helping me,' Berger said with a wry smile.

'Yes, that's done me a fat lot of good over the years,' Syl said.

'What have you found?'

'The anomalies,' Syl said. 'There's actually been quite a lot of digging about in the archive. All at the same time.'

'The Security Service archive?'

'That is what we're talking about, isn't it?' Syl said caustically.

'OK,' Berger said. 'And this happened at the turn of the year, or thereabouts?'

'No thereabouts,' Syl said. 'Exactly.'

'When someone knew that security would be weaker?'

'That seems likely, yes. A number of files have been erased, the activity can be reconstructed, but not the files. At least not yet. I'm working on it.'

'Is it possible to say when the erased files were first created?'

'Specific historical moments, yes. The earliest I've found was from 1976.'

Berger and Blom looked at each other.

'Seventy-six?' Blom said. 'April 1976 by any chance?'

Syl looked at her seriously for the first time.

'That's right,' Syl said, '28 April.'

'After Nils Gundersen had been in Sweden to recruit mercenaries,' Blom said. 'And when he got a young woman named Stina Larsson up the duff.'

'There was a Security Service report about that?' Berger said.

'It's not possible to say anything about the contents of the file,' Syl said. 'It's just noticeable by its absence.'

Berger nodded. 'That was the oldest document that was deleted from the archive?' he said. 'When were the next ones from?'

'They're fairly regular, but no more than one per year for the following fifteen years,' Syl said. 'I was able to uncover the size of the missing files, if nothing else, and these annual reports were much smaller than the one from 1976. That remained the largest up to March 1991. That one was also large. A bit larger, in fact.'

'OK . . . 1991,' Berger said to Blom. 'Two years before sixteen-year-old William Larsson vanished without a trace. Have we got anything for March '91?'

Blom shook her head. 'Gundersen was forty-three, had been active on Saddam Hussein's side in the first Gulf War. William was fourteen and being badly bullied in Stuvsta.'

Berger nodded and felt his brain getting closer to boiling point.

'Let me guess: the next large intervention in the database corresponds with a file in the summer of '93?' he said.

'Correct,' Syl said. 'July. Although before that there was more activity from March '91 and the following three or four months. Four documents missing. Then one larger one again in July '93.'

'When William had just left Sweden.' Blom nodded.

'This goes a long way to explaining why Nils Gundersen is completely absent from the Security Service archive but crops up in MISS's files,' Berger said. 'He's been purged from it.'

'MISS?' Syl exclaimed. 'The Military Intelligence and Security Service? What the hell have you dragged me into?'

'What about after '93?' Berger said instead of replying.

'Less activity,' Syl said, staring darkly at her former boss. 'Back to annual reports again. One small document is missing from each year, and soon even less than that. Every other year after the millennium, then nothing until towards the end of 2012. Then another large file disappears. The largest of them all: 11 November 2012.'

'Three months before Anton Bergmark was attacked,' Blom said. 'That must have been when William returned to Sweden. And the Security Service had a file about it. A big one.'

'We don't know that,' Berger said. 'We don't know for sure.'

'We don't know anything for sure,' Blom said. 'But the circumstantial evidence is piling up like shit in the Ganges.'

'The sacred river,' Berger said. 'Then what?'

'That's where it stops,' Syl said, getting to her feet. 'Along with my involvement. You'll have to manage on your own now.'

Berger looked at her. For the first time since Police Academy he managed to see behind Syl's everyday exterior and get a glimpse of the Sylvia Andersson who had never really interested him, the single mother with a five-year-old daughter, Moira, the spitting image of her mother.

And what he saw was sheer, unalloyed terror. Possibly more for Moira's sake than her own.

'What do you suspect?' Berger asked. 'What can you see that we can't?'

'Nothing,' Syl said through her teeth. 'See nothing, hear nothing, and above all, say nothing.'

'In one word? Off the top of your head?'

'I see close collaboration between the mercenary you call Nils Gundersen and the Security Service, and I don't want anything to do with it.'

'And yet you said you were "working on it"?' Blom said.

'I don't believe I said that,' Syl snapped.

'She can quote you verbatim,' Berger said with a nod towards Blom.

Blom flashed him a dark look and quoted: '"A number of files have been erased, the activity can be reconstructed, but not the files. At least not yet. I'm working on it."'

'So what is it you're working on, Syl?' Berger said.

'My name is Sylvia,' Syl said.

'What are you working on?'

'Nothing. I've stopped working on it.'

'Could there really be a way of reconstructing the erased files? That sounds unlikely. Doesn't it, Molly?'

'Totally improbable,' Blom said, picking up the prompt. 'I

don't see how anyone could pull that off. Maybe in the future. Seven or eight years from now.'

'It does seem completely impossible,' Berger said. 'How the hell would anyone go about it?'

'I know of a possible method,' Syl said hesitantly. 'It would require quite a lot of extra equipment.'

'That you can get hold of?'

'Not free of charge.'

'Send us an invoice.'

'Us? So what are you, then?'

'Private detectives,' Berger said.

42

Saturday 31 October, 15.19

They got no further than the security desk in reception before it became clear that everything had changed. First Berger tried his swipe card. Nothing happened; the guard behind the bulletproof glass didn't even look up from the game of solitaire he was playing on his iPad. But when Blom tried her card he stood up, pressed a button and his voice rang out metallically: 'Please wait a moment. Someone will come and get you.'

It didn't actually take more than a couple of seconds before two powerful silhouettes emerged from the fluorescent lighting of the nearest corridor of Police Headquarters on Kungsholmen in Stockholm. Berger let out a deep sigh.

During the long walk through increasingly demanding security measures neither Kent nor Roy said a single word. They didn't even answer when addressed directly. In the end Berger and Blom were deposited on a sofa in the corridor of the Security Service's Intelligence Unit. Above them a sign indicated that the head of the unit, Steen, had his office behind the nearest door.

Berger and Blom looked at each other. They didn't say a word.

The compulsory fifteen-minute wait had already begun to acquire its own fifteen-minute wait when the door next to the sign suddenly made a low humming sound. Blom stood up, followed by Berger.

August Steen was sitting behind his desk. Berger had never met him before, and the first thing that struck him was the straightness of his back. It looked like he'd been sitting to attention for more than sixty years. He had a sudden vision of a fifties baby seat containing a steel-grey infant with a ramrod-straight back. It made the conversation that followed a little more bearable.

'Sit down,' August Steen said, giving the barest of nods towards the two low chairs on their side of the desk.

They sat down. After a pause Steen said: 'Well, there's no denying that the pair of you have put a rocket under the country's police force during the past week. And the very fact that you rescued six girls and stopped the perpetrator means that we can allow ourselves to overlook the majority of your transgressions and actual law-breaking with an easy conscience. However, I and many others have a serious problem with the crime of disloyalty to your superiors.'

'It was never about that,' Blom said. 'Everything we've done has been for our superiors, in other words the police, in other words the general public. Justice – isn't that was all police work is about? Getting justice?'

'By all means,' August Steen said, his stony gaze firmly fixed on Blom. 'But justice is a complicated concept, and involves more than a levelling of the scores once a crime has been committed. From the perspective of law enforcement it becomes even more important to prevent crime, stop miscreants before they set to work. Justice becomes less clear-cut when the crime hasn't yet been committed.'

'I don't see how that applies to our pursuit of William Larsson,' Blom said.

'Olle Nilsson,' August Steen said. 'We haven't found any trace of a William Larsson in this case.'

'Olle Nilsson,' Berger said, 'who managed to pass the Security Service's notoriously thorough background check with flying colours when he was employed by Wiborg Supplies Ltd in November three years ago.'

'And the reason for that is, quite simply, that he *was* Olle Nilsson,' Steen said, fixing his gaze on Berger. It was the first time he had felt it, and he really felt it.

'There has to be some trace of Olle Nilsson's past as William Larsson on his computers,' Berger managed to say.

'Analysis of his computer equipment is ongoing,' Steen said. 'But there is nothing in your "unofficial" investigation that proves your missing and presumably long-dead childhood friend William Larsson had anything to do with this Olle Nilsson.'

'We found the kidnapper,' Berger said. 'We would never have done that without Molly's unofficial investigation.'

'You found the kidnapper because he refused to use state resources to provide an illegal service to someone whom he, from what he could tell, believed to be a private individual – Molly Blom,' Steen said calmly. 'So he installed a warning in that illegal device so that we would discover you when you were in the process of committing a serious crime. You, Molly Blom, infected the interview room's recording equipment with a virus, and now you have the gall to claim that this isn't disloyalty to your superiors.'

'So it was just a coincidence that the technician happened to be the serial killer and kidnapper we were looking for?' Berger said.

'It looks like it,' Steen said. 'But, like I said, the investigation is ongoing.'

'So we just got lucky?' Berger exclaimed.

'Not at the denouement. You acted effectively then, albeit with a serious excess of force. But we're even prepared to turn a blind eye to that, seeing as it led to the rescue of six girls.'

'An excess of force?' Berger said.

'I daresay that every police officer knows that a shot from a range of one metre, using hollow-point ammunition fired directly into the genitals, is going to cause the kind of blood loss that will rapidly lead to death.'

Berger bit his tongue and glanced at Blom. She was sitting perfectly still and met his gaze with a neutral expression. It helped him to keep his tongue in check.

Steen went on: 'Because you were able to extract information from the perpetrator about where his victims were before he died, we have approved the request of the Stockholm Police that the shooting be regarded as self-defence. Even if it's perfectly clear that it wasn't.'

'What was it, then?' Blom asked.

'Murder, of course,' Steen said, looking back towards Blom. 'Murder, as retribution for some imagined childhood injustice. And that isn't the only suspicious death in your vicinity during this so-called unofficial investigation. When we finally managed to reverse the GPS in the stolen Security Service vehicle, you were on your way to a care home for dementia sufferers in Vendelsö. My men caught up with you there and you managed to evade them. But you left a body behind you.'

'We did?' Berger exclaimed.

'You were the last people to see a patient named Alicia Anger alive. Even in that instance we were able to divert the police investigation in order to save your skins and get this very obvious murder written off as an accident. But I can't help wondering what you wanted with this woman, and what she revealed that required her permanent silence.'

'You know perfectly well that we didn't murder her,' Berger said as calmly as he could.

'How am I supposed to know that?'

Berger managed to detect the trap built into the question just as Blom cleared her throat loudly and began to speak, 'Alicia Anger was William Larsson's aunt. We believed that she had further information about William's disappearance.'

'And did she?'

'Not at all. She was completely senile. She claimed to be a Valkyrie called *the red girl*, living in the tenth century. It was impossible to get any sense out of her. And of course we didn't murder her.'

'Hmm,' August Steen said, regarding Blom sadly.

Berger looked over towards Blom. He could see the strength of resistance in her eyes and realised which of them ought to do the talking.

August Steen tapped his desktop lightly with his fingertips, playing an imaginary piano for ten seconds. Then he said: 'It's extremely important that you don't withhold any information from the Security Service. We need to have a clear picture of the whole case now that the investigation is entering such an acute phase. Are you quite sure you've told us everything you know?'

'Yes,' Blom said.

Steen watched his former acolyte intently.

'Hmm,' he said once more. 'I'm not entirely satisfied.'

'What more can we say?'

'That's what I'm asking you. Right now I'm not getting a good feeling about the two of you.'

'Feeling?' Berger blurted out, and regretted it immediately.

'I don't imagine I need to explain the importance of feelings to you, of all people, Sam Berger,' Steen said. 'You seem to work *entirely* on feelings. So you know how valuable they are. And right now, like I said, I'm not getting a good feeling about you.'

He paused. 'You're far too cocky considering that the entire Swedish police force was recently trying to track you down. A trace of humility would have been more becoming under the circumstances.'

'Becoming?' Blom said.

'Not only that. Also more effective. If you had shown even a trace of regret or awareness of your many mistakes, I would have been able to make you an offer. I actually had authorisation from the senior management of the Security Service to do precisely that.'

August Steen grimaced briefly and stared at the wall above their heads. 'While you were absent, Superintendent Allan Gudmundsson and I agreed that charges should be brought against you; you would be held to account in a regular criminal trial, and then sent to prison. That is no longer the case. Both the Security Service and the Police Authority have come to realise that you were driven by an excess of ambition as police officers, and nothing else. So we are dropping the case that we had been preparing. But we can't overlook numerous instances of misconduct and multiple criminal offences. You've broken so many laws, written and unwritten alike, that it would be very difficult to retain you in the force. You simply aren't police officers any more. And I regret that.'

Berger and Blom looked at each other. None of this came as any great surprise. The best option was to soak it up. Keep quiet. Look upset.

It was impossible. Berger said: 'And the offer?'

August Steen frowned. 'Senior management was so pleased

with your efforts that they wanted me to offer you positions as external resources for the Security Service. But they left the final decision up to me.'

'External resources would mean that we worked for the Security Service but without being police officers?' Berger said.

'As of this morning, you are no longer police officers,' Steen said. 'That's irrevocable.'

'I get a suspicion that's only slightly better than being a junior clerk in the police archive,' Berger said, unable to hold back a smile. He felt like laughing out loud.

'That's not the case,' Steen said. 'Our external resources are important assets.'

'Like hell!' Blom exclaimed.

'Good,' Steen said. 'I wasn't going to make that offer anyway. Like I said, I'm not happy. We could of course dismiss you in black and white, but that wouldn't look good for either party. It would be better for you both to resign voluntarily. We're prepared to offer six months' pay as compensation. What do you say?'

'A year,' Blom said.

Berger stared at her, but managed to stop himself from saying anything.

'How so?' August Steen snapped.

'Obviously we have to take the question of the media into account,' Blom said. 'The release of Ellen Savinger and the other girls is a huge story right now – good luck finding anything else in the newspapers and on television right now, blogs, Twitter, Facebook you name it – and so far you've been able to keep these more sensitive details out of the public eye. I assume it wouldn't look good if it emerged that two rogue cops succeeded where both the Security Service and National Crime had failed.'

August Steen regarded her with icy cool. After a pause of

thirty seconds, he said: 'Let me see if I've understood. For one year's pay, you guarantee that nothing will reach the media, whereas that can't be guaranteed if you only receive six months'?'

'A reasonable summary,' Molly Blom said.

'You may go now,' August Steen said.

They turned and walked towards the door. When they were on their way out, Steen said by way of conclusion: 'I want to stress that it's of the utmost importance that you don't withhold anything from the Security Service. It's of the utmost important *for everyone concerned* that we have all the information you have.'

Berger and Blom looked at each other once more.

Then they turned and walked away.

43

Sunday 1 November, 10.14

An enchanted sun was filtering its weak rays through the leafless branches of the aspen trees and the grimy windows, settling like a thin layer of fluorescent paint across the interior of the boathouse. Molly Blom was walking around the building. She put her hand on the pillars, felt the mooring rings in the wall, crouched down and inspected the six bullet holes in the floor. Then she crawled over to the corner of the boathouse and listened for the sound of barely audible breathing.

Death and life.

She looked up at Sam when he rushed in from the jetty door.

'The hedgehogs are fine anyway,' she said. 'Fast asleep.'

'Come with me,' he said, taking her hand.

They went out onto the jetty. Down on the strangely still surface of the water was William Larsson's rowing boat. It was scattered with flowers.

'You'll never get me down in that,' Molly said, looking at the flowers.

'Don't chicken out, now,' he said. 'Why don't we call it an Indian summer? The last proper sun of the year.'

She smiled in spite of herself and climbed down into the boat, pushing the flowers aside and making herself comfortable. He rowed off. It was like something from from the eighteenth century. All that was missing was the strumming of a lute and the trilling of a few graces.

When they were some way out Sam let go of the oars and pulled a bottle of champagne from his old rucksack. He found two glasses and asked Molly to hold them. The cork flew ten metres, and half the contents of the bottle bubbled out into the waters of Edsviken.

'Cheers, partner in crime,' he said, raising his glass.

'What are we toasting?' she said. 'Getting fired? The fact that after years of loyal service – crowned by a spectacular rescue – we're now unemployed ex-cops?'

'The fact that we managed to keep our mouths shut, for instance?'

'We did manage that, yes,' she said. 'They can't have any idea that we know.'

'No,' he said, lowering his glass. 'But obviously we can't work with them until we know exactly what this is about.'

'Never,' she said.

Sam suddenly seemed revived. He raised his glass again. 'No, a toast to all the new opportunities life is offering.'

Molly raised her glass with a grim smile. 'A toast to one year's pay, if nothing else.'

'Two,' Sam said, and took a sip.

Edsviken spread out like a mirror, lending peace and calm to everything around them. To the badlads. The sunshine was only fleeting of course, so they had to make the most of the short time on offer.

Carpe motherfucking diem.

Sam dug about in his rucksack and pulled out his watch box. He opened the gilded catch and looked at his watches. There were five there now. He took off his Rolex Oyster Perpetual Datejust and noted that the condensation was gone. He put it back in its place. Now there were six of them. All six watches in their places. He picked up the Patek Philippe 2508 Calatrava and put it on his wrist.

'I change my watch every Sunday,' he said. 'And at this precise moment, one week has passed since we broke into the house in Märsta.'

'And what a week it's been,' Molly said.

They sat in silence for a while, watching the sparkle of the sun, enjoying the beauty of life, a beauty that always came back, no matter what.

'Time to look for a new job,' Molly said after a while, sipping her champagne. 'It almost feels a bit sad to leave this place. And I hardly think I can go back to life as an actor now that I'm pushing forty. But you can become a philosopher. They always need old men. You can be a professional cultural commentator.'

'That's what I meant when I said "two",' Sam said. 'We've got two years' wages to work with. If we want to stay.'

'Stay? Why the fuck would we want to stay?'

'I don't think I've heard you swear before.'

Silence spread out around them. At the northern end of Edsviken they could see for the first time the soft yellow facade of Edsberg Castle, with its parkland and its paths edging the water. It was incredibly beautiful.

Sam lay back and stared up at the blue sky. It was a ridiculously long time since the sky had last been blue.

He closed his eyes. 'I checked with a solicitor today. The legal tussle arose because the boathouse is the only remaining part of the shoreline that can be built on. But the two companies are fed up with the stalemate. They're prepared to sell quickly for a reasonable offer and split the money. So can I suggest a quick and relatively reasonable offer?'

'You think you and I should buy the building where a crazy murderer tortured me and where I killed him quarter of a century later?'

'You took the words right out of my mouth,' Sam said.

They laughed. At the same time. Neither of them was sure if that had happened before.

'You and me together?' Molly said. 'As freelance cops? With a shared business? A detective agency?'

'I'd rather call it a . . . hmm . . . professional investigative service available for private and public commissions . . . '

'That won't do,' Molly said. 'A . . . hmm . . . ultramodern investigative service for . . . oh, activities in the badlands.'

The boat drifted freely across Edsviken. Berger took out his old mobile. The SIM card was back inside. He brought up the pole star, the fixed point, the still point of the turning world. Marcus and Oscar in the ditch full of coltsfoot, eight years old.

It was time to call Paris.

The boat drifted on. Perhaps they fell asleep. Perhaps Sam never heard Molly say: 'Six girls rescued.'

And perhaps Sam never replied: 'That's what it was all about. The rest was bullshit.'

Either way, they were woken by the first raindrops. So far it was just gentle rain, almost mist. They both sat up in the boat as if risen from the dead.

'From now on, we never talk about this case,' Sam said.

'You mean like some sort of oath?' Molly said. 'We swear never to talk about this case again?'

'Yes, why not? An oath is good.'

They exchanged glances, from prow to stern and back again.

Neither of them was really sure if they saw the power of genuine conviction in the other's eyes.

'We caught William,' Sam said in the end. 'It's just that William wasn't quite who we thought he was. Sure, he was mad, but he didn't come here as a madman. He came here as a professional, employed by the Security Service to act as liaison with the Pachachi family, about whom we still don't really know anything.'

'Except that there's a big hole in the Security Service archive for 1991,' Molly said. 'That's the only gap we can't account for.'

Sam nodded and said: 'That's when the Pachachi family arrives in Sweden from war-torn Iraq. Gundersen, who had been fighting in Iraq, says something about the family that gets the Security Service interested. And some sort of link is established between them and the Pachachis.'

'A link that leads to them taking over the flat in Helenelund from William's mother.'

'That link between the Security Service and the Pachachi family is the key to all of this, I swear,' Sam said. 'I really hope Syl manages to uncover it.'

At that moment Edsviken was shaken by a powerful explosion. The sky had contracted to a heavy, greyish-black blanket of cloud, and not too far in the distance sparks of lightning shot back and forth across the sky.

They sat still. Waited for the downpour.

Then Sam said: 'Was *that* the last thing we're going to say about this case?'

'Oath?' Molly said.

'Oath,' Sam nodded, then laughed.

While Sam rowed back as fast as he could, the gently increasing rain seemed to be preparing for more grand deeds.

They threw themselves up the steps and stopped beneath the

roof extending over the jetty. They looked out across the water. The yellow facade of Edsberg Castle was starting to disappear into the distance with its parkland and paths.

Sam turned round and glanced down at his Patek Philippe. He couldn't quite see what time it was; gentle condensation was covering half the face.

He opened the door and looked up from his wrist.

There was a figure sitting with its back to them at one of the carpentry benches. Its hair was medium-length, thin and mousy, and it was perfectly dry.

'Syl!' Sam exclaimed. 'Great. What have you found out?'

As he went towards the bench and walked round it he glanced back at Molly. She looked oddly pale.

Then he met Syl's gaze.

It was broken; there was no one there. And out of her mouth hung a black sock, like a blackened tongue.

Then the heavens opened.